THE
EXTINCTION
CLUB

THE EXTINCTION CLUB

JEFFREY MOORE

ARCADE PUBLISHING • NEW YORK

A translation of foreign words and phrases that
appear in the text can be found after the Author's
Note at the end of the book.

PART ONE

PRE-CHRISTMAS

Brightly shone the moon that night
Though the frost was cruel …

⤷ **I** ⤶

It was dark—north-country dark—by the time I arrived but this had to be it: the Church of St. Davnet-des-Monts. Two sodden, grime-streaked signs, barely visible in the circle of my flashlight, were nailed to its front door. The first, its black medieval characters weeping freely, was a dispossession notice signed by the archdeacon:

> In sorrow we revoke the sentence of consecration,
> and release this building and its site for other use,
> with prayers that the purposes of God and the well-
> being of the community may continue to be served ...

The second, on a panel like the inside of a cereal box, was a jumble of red capitals, as if written wrong-handedly:

ELDERLY VOLUNTEERS WANTED
TO WORK IN MERCHANDISING
NEITHER AGE NOR MENTAL HEALTH A FACTOR

I moved my beam in dancing ovals to the top of the spire, then back down, side to side, the light playing over the rough gray walls, like the hide of some ancient pachyderm. Pocked with tiny holes, as if from automatic rifle fire.

Was this the right church? In the photograph it looked so much more ... well, churchly. Instead of stained glass I saw shutterboard, instead of florid tracery, graffiti. And where was the FOR SALE sign? I aimed my flashlight to the side, illuminating a corroded gate off its hinges, a meandering gullet wriggling its way through rocks and rubble, and a headstone cross sprayed with red swastikas.

A church bell began to ring, dully, from a distance. At midnight on the nail, on the last stroke of November, cold rain came down: fat splattering drops that turned thick as glycerine, coating everything they touched. My flashlight fizzled, then dimmed and died. I could have—should have?— waited till morning.

Some hundred yards away, beyond the church lane, came a rumbling and a single pin of light. A motorcycle ... No, it was larger than that, with something flickering on its roof. A gumball?

I bolted in the direction of my van, hidden on the other side of the church, but instinctively took the wrong fork in the path, which led to the graveyard. Two marauding animals, cats or racoons, scurried across the flagstones and I slid madly to avoid them, my city shoes as effective as bedroom slippers. I grabbed on to a large headstone—a stone carving of some unknown angel by some unknown artist—and crouched behind it. Pulled out a nightscope from my knapsack, waited until the car came within range.

The landscape glowed with the colors of things otherworldly, outside of nature: the tree line was neon yellow, the road nicotine orange, the car the eerie green of horror movies. I moved the wheel and sharpened the milky images. Something was flickering all right, but it wasn't a police flasher. It was something more sinister: a large furry animal with its paws ... dripping? Cut off? The light came from its mouth, which was propped open with what appeared to be a light bulb.

The car, which wasn't a car but a pickup with a raised chassis, rooflights and bulldog grille, came barrelling toward the church, heading for its front door. At the last second it swerved onto a narrow path that curved around the church, away from me, to the other side of the cemetery. It braked suddenly and spun ass to front, its engine stalled or killed. A silence of four or five seconds, then a *thwack*, a snapping sound like breaking glass.

As soon as I heard that sound I knew that I always would. The truck fired up again, its oversize tires churning on black ice, spitting out stones and dirt. It exploded back down the lane, into the roiling cloudlets of chill fog, and was gone.

I stood motionless, confused, wondering how I fit into all this. Whatever they dumped is none of my business. I returned the monocular to its case while picking my way to my VW van, a stolen rust-bucket that was tricky to start. It rumbled to life first time. I drove lights-out to the end of the church lane.

For at least a minute I sat there, hands clutched on the steering wheel, watching the wipers, listening to the sound of metal grating on glass. The rain syruped down the windshield and hardened. I slid the defroster to high. Stared at the back of my hands, which seemed to belong to someone else. From beneath the seat I extracted a bottle of Talisker 16 and drank its dregs. Another fall from grace and the wagon.

I hung a U, scraping the underbody as I hit the lane at a bad angle, back toward the cemetery. At the whirling skid marks I flicked on my brights: on one side, a dozen cattails rising out of vapor like giant hot dogs on spikes; on the other, a dozen tombstones, lopsided and rotting like a row of bad teeth. Every black root and tendril around them was rimmed with silver. I backed the van up, turned the wheel sharply. There.

Something embedded in the snowy ditch: a pale brown lump. I got out for a closer look.

It was wrapped in what looked like burlap and bound crosswise with red cord, like a Christmas present. A drug drop? Cash drop? I had no intention of untying the knots to find out more—until I heard something, a sigh or whispered moan. Animal or human, hard to tell.

I clambered down the bank, head afire and heart working double-time. Under the snow was a crust of ice, as solid as a soda biscuit, and I plunged through it up to my knees. It wasn't a ditch—it was a bog. But I felt only the slightest tingling as my shoes filled with freezing water. I yanked them out of the black muck and lumbered forward, punching through the ice, releasing the pungent smells of decay—of peat slime, swamp grass, animal dung. I was surprised at the weight of the mud, the effort it took to lift each limb, like walking with ball and chain. I hadn't tramped in mud since kindergarten.

When I reached the red cord I pulled one-handedly with all the strength I could muster, which was not a lot; I was off-balance and the sack barely budged. It was disappearing, it seemed, into the marshmallowy marsh, into the reeds and rot, and I along with it. It felt like a hand was tugging at my shoes. With one foot planted on a petrified log, like a crocodile forced up by saurian times, I pulled with both arms and felt the bag move. Inch by inch I hauled it across the crackling membranes and up onto higher, drier ground.

I stretched and pulled at the cord like a backward child, like someone unfamiliar with the concept of knots. I even bit into them, like trying to cut steel with scissors. Cold rain dripped down my face, mingling with sweat, burning my eyes. There had to be an easier way ... With blurred vision I saw a pink form protruding from a small slash in the bag. A thumb?

Elbow? I tore at the burlap from all sides, shredding it blindly from toe to crown.

After wiping my eyes with a frozen fist, I saw something that sucked the breath out of me, that most of us will never see. For three or four heartbeats time stopped; I was suspended in a force field of fright that calcified my bones, atrophied my muscles.

Some mysterious natural chemical, something defibrillating, suddenly surged within me. I picked up the bag as if it were a pillow and carried it from road to van, the frozen pebbles grinding harshly under my heels. The high beams illuminated the cloth with a chill fluorescent glow that made its red stains look shiny and black. Drops made puffs of steam as they hit the snow.

A shadow moved in front of me, made me freeze. It advanced dream slowly, in the direction of the swamp. On four legs. Then stopped and stared into the light—not my light but a full moon's—with eyes like sparkling emeralds. It swung its head from side to side, gave out a low moan, then loped soundlessly on, arching its long tail. I closed my eyes. The fallout—was it starting again? I opened my eyes and the creature and moon were gone.

With my pulse quickening and brain slowing, I fumbled with the back doors of the van and laid the wet bag down. *Don't get blood on the upholstery, you're in enough shit as it is.* I turned on the dome light, my fingers staining everything they touched, including a sleeping bag I hadn't yet slept in.

Okay, so where's the police station?

The police? What would I tell them? That I'd found a blood-soaked child—and by the way, officer, I'm in this country illegally, fleeing a charge of child abduction. Among other things. And yes, that's alcohol on my breath. They'll want a statement, a name, an address. Fishing in a Quebec swamp—where did that idea come from? *From long practice in doing the wrong thing:* my father's words. How about a hospital? I heard another muffled moan.

"Everything's going to be fine," I lied. "Just hold on ..." My voice had a quaver, I could hear it myself. "I'm taking you ..." Through snarled hair I glimpsed the child's face—as white and wet as milk, with a look of terror I'd never seen before except in dreams.

The freezing rain clung like shrink wrap, acres of it, and my bald tires could barely pull me up the first hill. And balked entirely at the second, despite two charges in first gear and one in reverse. Aslant in the middle of the road, I flicked on my four-ways, pointlessly, as there was no one within miles. To the count of ten I watched the lights turn a twisted green sign off and on. HÔPITAL 8 KM, it said, its arrow pointing upward, to the heavens.

Back down the grade I snaked, in reverse, stopping at a gravel crossroad with another sign: CHEMIN SAISONNIER. I swung right and drove recklessly for three, maybe four miles—over railway tracks that hadn't held a train since World War II, over a humpbacked wooden bridge that said UTILISEZ À VOS RISQUES ET PÉRILS—toward my rented cabin. My wipers scraped across my view, a blinding rime of ice covered my back and side windows, my tires spun. The hood, held down by bungee cord, bounced up and down with every pothole.

The lights were off inside the cabin, as were those of a cottage some fifty yards on. I cut the ignition and the engine went on coughing and sputtering for half a minute. Left my brights on, trained on the front steps.

I was carrying the child in, his head lolling like a marionette's, when it occurred to me I should have unlocked the door first. Propping the body awkwardly against the wall, I jammed the key in, shook the lock around and kicked the door inward. Stumbled in the dark toward my broken-bellied bed, knowing this was unwise, knowing my only bedsheets would be drenched red. Put the body down hard, nearly dropping it on the floor. *If he isn't dead already, he is now.*

I ran my bloodied fingers over the NO ANIMAL SKINNING sign above the headboard, fumbling for the bar light. Felt the white peg and pushed. Then stood and gawked in harsh fluorescence, blinking, panting, sweating. I felt the child's neck artery. Nothing. Got down on my knees, leaned forward and felt a faint breath mingle with mine.

Into a wood-burning stove whose embers were still flickering, I tossed two more logs. *Long practice in doing the wrong thing* ... Should I put him back where I found him? Take him to the hospital? How, dogsled? Even if I could climb that hill, we'd never make it in time. Might as well deliver him to the morgue. I watched the flames grow higher.

Stop the bleeding at least. Can you do that? Rack your brains, try to remember ... I searched my memory, but it was like groping for an object that had slipped through a pocket, into the lining.

I pulled at a wooden drawer that resisted my first pull and that my second yanked free of its moorings. It fell from my hand, its contents scattering over the floor. I took the Lord's name with a volume that surprised me, that reverberated inside the cabin and seemed to rattle the walls, that I swore could be heard miles away. Scrambled to find, on hands and knees, some makeshift instruments. A curved carving knife, like a pirate's dagger, caught my eye, along with a tube of Krazy Glue and some orange dollar-store scissors ...

I swallowed hard before unwrapping the body from its

burlap cocoon, scissoring the sticky patches that cleaved to the flesh. The body was doubled up like a jackknife, with red twine tied around the neck and under the knees. Not as tight, thank Christ, as it could've been. The hands were bound behind the back with white plastic cuffs. I fiddled blindly with the catch, fumbled in my shirt and coat pockets for reading glasses, then sawed through it with the dagger. And sliced the twine at nape and knees.

Now for the clothes. Jeans rolled down to the thighs, boxer shorts steeped in blood. I tugged at each pant leg, pulling them past each shoeless foot. A shirt and vest, each in tatters, were next. All that was left to remove was the boy's ...

Everything seemed to be happening at quarter speed, in another dimension. I was at the sink, robotically washing and wringing out a sponge, filling a saucepan with water. *It's a girl, you fool, not a boy.* I looked for something to cover the bed, eyeing first the living room drapes, then the quilted carpet. Neither would do. In the bathroom, I ripped off a clear plastic shower curtain speckled with a Milky Way of mildew, the metal hooks popping off one by one. Crammed it into the bathtub, hoping to find something under the sink to clean it with.

Amidst hardened rags was a can of clotted Ajax and a box of steel wool with a Bulldog logo discontinued in the eighties. I cranked the taps until the water rushed hot and loud. Looked down at my feet of mud and realized I couldn't feel them. Ripped off my shoes and socks, rolled up my pants, stepped into the tub. Began scrubbing with a manic intensity I hadn't felt in years, not since being locked away.

When the curtain was clean, I slipped it carefully beneath the young girl. She was short, stout, cherub-faced. Twelve, if I had to guess. Small tattoos of animals on each shoulder:

a cinnamon bear on her right, a butterscotch mountain lion on her left. A ring of red sores on her wrists—like chilblains, that Dickensian ailment—and every fingernail broken, filled with blackish blood.

I had barely finished sponging her down when I heard scratches on the front door, as if made by a dog that wanted in. I stopped what I was doing, listened. No, the scratches were coming from the very top of the door or the roof ... I was heading toward the sound when the door swung wide open. A shadowy shape stood on the threshold, stock-still. Haloed by a full moon. A Mountie in a fur coat? A bear on its hind legs? I moved closer.

Nothing there, nothing but the cursed ... fallout, afterglow. Alcoholic hallucinosis or Wernicke's disease or Korsakoff's syndrome or Jolliffe's encephalopathy. Or just plain old-fashioned madness. I shut my mind down. The trick, I'd learned long ago, was to reset, refocus, pick up where I left off. They couldn't catch you if you didn't stop. I hurled my body against the door, closing it against the rising wind. An antique-looking brass key was in the lock, which I turned.

There was not nearly enough light, so I moved one of the stand-up brass lamps, whose frayed extension cord buzzed and sparked before shorting out. I cursed again, thunderously, before going back to the kitchen for something to mend it, something I had glimpsed among the scattered items on the floor: a half-roll of green electrician's tape. I re-spliced and re-plugged, then tilted the lampshade to cast as much light as possible onto my operating table. Around the girl's face a ghostly blue after-image of the lamp floated like an aura.

On her abdomen, on the left side, was a gash just below the rib cage. Dark blood welled out, slowly but steadily. The other cut was in the inner right thigh, in the middle of the longest muscle of the body, the sartorius, which runs from the outside of the hip to the inside of the knee. There the blood was bright red, pumped directly from the heart, oozing out at each contraction.

Terrific. A bedful of blood and a corpse in my cabin. A *girl's* corpse. My ex and her lawyer are going to have a field day with this.

On weak knees I began to sway, and blood thunder pounded against my temples. Was I about to lose it? I shook my head violently, a dozen times, trying to regain some clarity. When that didn't work I banged my forehead against the door, not once, not twice, but three times. I opened the door, let the wind sting my face with sharp pellets so cold they felt hot. Then stepped out into snow.

From my glovebox, beside a plastic .38, I pulled out a pair of reading glasses and from under the passenger seat, my father's survival kit. I unsnapped it for the first time and peered in: a shake-to-charge flashlight, radio/lantern, first-aid kit, hand-cranked cellphone charger. But no cellphone. Toolbox, I'd need my toolbox. I rummaged under the passenger seat, but it wasn't there. Stolen? No, it was never under the passenger seat. It was by the inside hub of the back wheel. I grabbed that and my nylon sleeping bag.

Under the mended lamp I examined the contents of the first-aid kit. It was state-of-the-art, like everything my father owned. I pulled out two bandage compresses, unfolded them, and placed one over each wound, applying pressure with each hand. The bandages were soon saturated, so I opened up packets of gauze and placed them layer upon layer over top.

The bleeding wouldn't stop. *Think, try to remember, scrape the bottom of what's left of your brain.* There are twenty-six pressure points on the body, thirteen on either side. But where, and which ones should be pressed? I placed the heel of my hand directly on the crease in the groin area, mid-bikini line, praying this was the right spot, and applied pressure. The idea was to close the femoral artery, but it wasn't working ... I put my knuckles to my lips, nearing the panic point, smelling and tasting her warm coppery blood.

A paste of cayenne pepper, it came to me, can stop the bleeding in seconds. According to old wives, at least. But I couldn't remember seeing any spices at all, either here or at my neighbor's.

With the flat surface of my fingertips, I pressed directly over the artery and applied additional pressure with the heel of my other hand. Counted to sixty, to ninety. Okay, slightly better ... To one twenty, one eighty ... much better. I let out a breath that felt like it had been held for the full three minutes.

Now what? Elevate the wounds, above the level of the heart. Slow the flow, speed the clotting. I looked around. From the sofa I grabbed a cushion to slip underneath her but quickly changed my mind. *Errore molto grande* if she has fractures. So I dropped it on the floor, hefted up one end of the bed, kicked the cushion underneath. Then got the other cushion and did the same on the other side.

In the kitchen I turned on the tap full blast onto a spoon lying in the sink, which deflected the water up into my face. I wiped my eyes with my fist, filled a large metal cauldron with water and put it on the stove. I did the same with an old tea kettle, a heavy cast-iron affair, flushing out an alarmed spider. I struck a match and turned two switches. Propane. How long would that last?

From an inside pocket of my duffle bag I pulled out a Best Western sewing kit, with a needle and cardboard spool of black thread. I tossed them into the pot of water. From the toolbox I took out a pair of tweezers and needle-nose pliers. Clamps, I'd need clamps ...

On hands and knees on the kitchen floor, I pawed through the mishmash of gear. Nothing. I returned to the bed and stared at the gash in the groin, which was releasing streamlets of red. The numbers 9-1-1 began to bounce inside my head like lottery balls. *How can you possibly save her? Someone as spectacularly screwed up as you. You can't even save yourself.* There was no phone in my cabin, but there might be one in my neighbor's ...

I'd forgotten, already, how dark it can get in the north country. I looked up at the sky and wondered whether my eyes were closed. A blanketing coffin jet, wind out of the northwest pushing black clouds across a black sky. In the faint light of the flashlight I could make out only the outlines of brush and conifers, of huge lumps of rock like fairybook beasts.

> The snow is full of ghosts tonight, that tap and sigh
> Upon the glass and listen for reply ...

"Oh Christ, don't start that again," I advised myself. Turning sounds and shapes into other sounds and shapes, into aural and visual mirages. A throwback, I've been told, to the bicameral mind of prehistoric times.

The van wouldn't start so I put it in neutral, got out and pushed against the door frame. On a slight decline, it rolled a dozen feet. I clicked on the highs, lighting up silvery pinwheels of flakes and pellets, and in the distance, faintly, my neighbor's front stoop. I'd need a miner's helmet and pick to get to it. Feet sliding, arms flailing, I followed the paling bands of light.

On both the front and back doors were staple-and-hasp affairs with brass padlocks, so I snatched a cedar log from a cord of firewood on the porch and began bashing at the front windowpane, repeatedly, in overkill mode, insanity mode. The sounds, like the cursing and crash in the kitchen, thundered inside my skull. I dislodged shards of glass with my bare hands, then fumbled my way through the frame. I felt a tug of resistance on my arm and back, heard the sound of snagged fabric ripping. In pitch-darkness, the bits of glass crackled under my shoes as I groped along the wall for a light switch. Click. Power on! But the only phone I could find was a black rotary in the kitchen, whose cord had been ripped out of the wall.

What now? Send a pigeon? While staring at the torn strands of wire, I smelled something repellent, the scent of Javex, reminding me of a tight white coat I was once forced to wear.

I yanked open drawers and cupboards—all, strangely, filled to the bursting point. Cans of everything imaginable stacked up as if the owner was expecting a siege: soup, corn, peas, carrots, stew, salmon, tuna, condensed milk, maple syrup, hot chocolate ... At least twenty pounds of rice. Box after box of pasta, crackers, powdered milk, oatmeal, pancake mix, baking soda, canning salt ... But no coffee beans, only jars of instant dust, and no alcohol.

In a bathroom drawer, of all places, was a set of clamps, but large orange plastic ones, much too big for this job. There was also an under-the-sink disaster kit with bandages, witch hazel, gauze, rubber gloves, adhesive tape, steri-strips, butterfly tape, gauze pads, tweezers, Betadine ointment, baby shampoo ... *Baby shampoo?* In the mirror above the sink I saw that my arm and back had been slashed, and that my face and hands were laced with tiny cuts. I plucked out bits of glass then splashed freezing, rust-colored water onto my face.

With two green garbage bags I made a makeshift seal of the smashed window. Then stuffed as many food and medical supplies as I could into a third bag. I was heading out the door when I realized I'd forgotten something. A TAG Heuer watch with a blue face I'd spotted on the bed table. Break and enter, destruction of property and grand theft would now be added to my burgeoning file.

Into my iron cauldron, whose water was on the boil, I dumped a wad of unused J Cloths. And then a pair of scissors. I lowered the flame and put a lid on the pot. With steaming water from the tea kettle I rinsed out a glass pitcher and filled it with tap water. Tossed in three spoonfuls of my neighbor's canning salt and one of baking soda. Now to stir it ... I opened the cutlery drawer and took out a bread knife. *Stir with a knife, bring on strife:* my mother's words. I set the knife down. Took out a plastic salad fork. *Stir with a fork, bring on the stork.* I set the fork down. Took out a salad spoon, rinsed it with boiling water, and stirred. The cauldron lid began to rattle.

With the same spoon I fished out the hotel-kit. The thread was soft and creamy, disintegrating. In drawer after drawer, cupboard after cupboard, I searched for something to replace it. Nothing.

In the rafters I spied something promising, something trailing from a beam ... I stood on a kitchen chair and pulled at it: a tangle of waxed whipping twine. Already knotted on one end was a needle, a sail needle. But the twine was too thick and the needle too large. So what now? Forget the stitches. I'd use electrician's tape. Or Krazy Glue.

I glanced at my blue-faced watch, then scoured a metal cookie sheet with steel wool and Ajax for exactly three minutes. Rinsed it in the bathtub with hot water, then returned to the kitchen for the kettle and my neighbor's rubber gloves. Poured the scalding water over the metal sheet, then the rubber gloves.

From the boiling cauldron I spooned out the pliers, tweezers, scissors and J Cloths and set them on the cookie sheet. I cut the cloths into small squares. Then folded a dishtowel in half and placed it over my mouth and nose like a bank robber. I tried to tie it at the back but it was too short, so I secured it with an elastic band. Put my reading glasses on over top. *If she opens her eyes she'll die laughing.*

I pulled on the rubber gloves and set the metal sheet down on a kitchen chair, along with the saline solution and Betadine ointment, and carried it over to the bed. I knelt down, holding my rubber hands up, prayerfully.

With the pliers I dunked a half-dozen cloth squares in the saline solution until they were soaked through. After mopping out both wounds, I placed a square on either side.

Biting my tongue, I pulled the edges of the higher cut together and placed a butterfly bandage across it. I squeezed out globs of Betadine over the adhesive strip, and for good measure secured everything with overlapping wraps of roller gauze.

I wiped my forehead with one forearm, then the other, before turning my attention to the other gash, the one on the thigh. This one would be trickier. It was deeper, for starters— I could see layers of subcutaneous tissue along the sides. A bandage would be harder to keep in place, would loosen if my patient moved, and do little if edema kicked in. Stitches, I'd have to use stitches ...

I closed my eyes in concentration. I have a needle but no thread. What would serve instead? Strands of her hair? *Think.* My neighbor. He must have something. Should I go back, take a closer look? I looked at the wound, which was releasing blood in regular gouts. *You're running out of time ...*

Yes. I can see it now, in his medicine chest! Coiled in a white plastic box. I ran—masked, coatless, bootless—to get it.

Using tweezers and pliers, I threaded the needle with the Johnson & Johnson dental floss. Then paused to think. *There are three kinds of stitches: lock-stitch, interrupted stitch, and ... what's the third? Continuous? Doesn't matter, because I remember only the second.* At the midpoint I made a stitch and drew the edges of the wound closely together. I knotted the waxed floss with a square knot and cut it. The sewing was easier than I thought it would be. The needle pierced the skin, the line pulled through, my patient didn't budge. It reminded me of skewering a Christmas turkey.

Five stitches, spaced a quarter-inch apart. The knotting was the difficult part: I had to make sure the floss would pull the edges of the wound together without cutting into the flesh, the way it cuts into gums and makes them bleed.

I sat on the floor to rest, my arms afire with tension, my eyes watering. I inhaled deeply, held my breath, watched. Blood rose to the surface, filled the cloth squares. But gradually, without gushing. I mopped the blood and pressed out a line of Betadine along the laceration. Not sure if this was necessary, but did it anyway. Then opened a packet of adhesive gauze and, careful not to touch the portion that would touch the wound, stretched it over the skin.

Although both repairs looked shoddy, amateurish, like a child's repair of a stuffed animal, I thought they'd do the job. Not that it would make much difference. My patient's condition was unchanged: somewhere between intensive care and the crematorium.

In the living room, my back against the window, I stared at an end table on which the previous tenant had set up a chess problem I couldn't solve ("# in 3," said a finger in dust). With a sweep of the hand I sent the pieces scattering across the room. I then turned toward the window, not registering a thing, anesthetized against time and distance, feeling everything grow faraway and dim.

Under closed lids, lurid images assaulted me on a short loop of memory. From my makeshift bed of twisted sheets I couldn't blot out a single scene from the night before; the horror of it reached through me and made me shake. I saw every instant, every stitch, with merciless clarity, as though magnified a thousand power under a microscope. Over and over I tried to get up that hill, to the hospital—a mere eight kilometers away!—but my tires spun on pavement that wasn't pavement but an oozing tide of black-brown blood that was rising fast, that would engulf the van, sweep us away like a child's plastic boat ...

And that sound, that *thwack* of the body being dropped, woke me again and again, knocking inside my brain with the intervals of a church bell. An absurd association, but it reminded me of the thwack of the *Star-Ledger* on the stoop, a newspaper I delivered as a child.

In milky 6:00 a.m. light I arose from the sofa to inspect my guest, my princess of the bogs and rushes. Saint Lazarus's younger sister. Still breathing by luck or miracle. I began to wash. Everything. The rooms, myself, her. As the sun bladed through the front window, I wiped the shower curtain with a medicated cloth, shifting her body gently, painstakingly. I washed her from sole to crown, going back for hot water, then towelling down her nylon sleeping bag. For the first time I wondered why neither slash went deeper, why neither went for a major organ. A slow death seemed to be the intent—a bloodletting. Why?

Her matted hair was pasted with dried blood and gooey muck, to which there clung the faint tang of urine, so I wedged a cushion beneath her shoulders and eased her head into a basin of water. With my neighbor's baby shampoo I washed her hair. It was tar black and cut to shoulder length, straight across the bottom, like Joan of Arc's.

As I was drying it, I began to cough, unstoppably. I fell to my knees, burrowing my head into the floor, trying to return to yesterday through the squares in the carpet. Years of food and filth had been walked into the weave and I retched on it like a dog. I stumbled to my feet, braced myself against the window. Pulled the thick brown curtain to one side, trying not to gag from the dust unleashed, and peered out. The van looked iced, like a confection, and its headlights were jaundiced, near-dead, no brighter than Christmas tree bulbs.

🕊 🕊 🕊

Over the next several hours I checked for signs of infection: inflammation, heat, pus. If I found any of these, I'd have to remove the sutures and drain the infected site. I didn't. Things seemed to be progressing. Still, every time I saw her on the bed with her eyes closed I wondered if she were asleep or dead.

At my neighbor's house, in a locked closet whose key was hanging on the wall beside it, I found a microwave still in its box, with a happy-face Walmart tag. I lugged it back to the cabin and cooked up a storm in dingy Tupperware: beef consommé, tomato soup, cream of mushroom, cream of vegetable, hot apple sauce, hot chocolate. I avoided all solids, guessing she'd only choke on them.

My patient didn't touch any of this. She lay there, asleep, her arm dangling over the edge of the bed. Once she sighed, and once appeared to open her eyes, but I couldn't be sure. On her throat was a bruise, an expanding map of blue and gray and purple lines.

When I checked to see if there was any bleeding, the plastic sheet was drenched. But not with blood. Good Christ, how could I forget about that? In the kitchen I rummaged around for something to serve as a bedpan.

On the second day she would neither eat nor drink, and her temperature was off the scale. Starve a fever, as they say, but not here: malnutrition would slow clotting. She needed an I.V., but I'd have to settle for an older type of force-feeding. I prised her lips apart as if examining a horse. Her teeth were stained and crooked, like the cemetery stones. I tilted her head back and with an eye-dropper squeezed as much water as I could down her throat. I thought she'd cough it back up, but she didn't. I then tried some milk. It went down too, drop by drop. I stopped when she began spewing it back up, along with some greenish slime that dribbled down her chin.

I wasn't eating either, mind you, though I was drinking non-stop: black-sludged coffee that wired me twenty-four hours, cup after cup till my hands shook. I had slept two hours, tops, since finding the body. And maybe two more on my feet, like a horse. My mind, however, was surprisingly clear. It was a novel feeling being clean, a song of innocence, a return to the sweet long ago.

Around midnight I heard faint gurgling sounds, like those made by an infant. I stood over her and saw her lips tremble, her lids gradually open. She had no eyes! No, they were just dark red. I gaped at her, as though she were in a freak show or zoo, and she looked vacantly back. Her lips began to move, or was it my imagination? Ever so slowly, into the form of an "o."

De l'eau? Was that what she meant? I ran to the kitchen and returned with a full glass of water. I placed its rim next to her lips, but she didn't raise her head. She didn't have the strength! With my free hand, I gently lifted her head from behind. Then tipped the glass. Too abruptly—water ran down her neck. I tried again. This time I felt the straining of her neck muscles and heard a suction sound, an intake of air. She was drinking on her own! And swallowing, again and again, like a parched desert nomad. She then looked up at me, as if to say "enough." I eased her head back onto the pillow. She closed her eyes and fell asleep.

She slept most of the time, drinking only occasionally— water, vegetable juice, orange juice—but never eating. I tried to interest her in some beef consommé, but she just sniffed at it, her mouth firmly closed. A new plan was needed, so I crumbled some bread into a glass of milk and woke her every two hours, forcing her to eat a spoonful or two.

When I changed her dressings or washed her or took away the bedpan, she lay stone-still, watching my face with her tiger eyes, frighteningly bright and anxious, eyes filled with viridescent depths, with exotic ancestral blood—ancient Macedonian perhaps, or some lost Indian tribe.

« *As-tu mal?* » I asked. I studied the empurpled patches of ecchymosis that racooned her eyes and tattooed her throat. « *Est-ce que tu souffres?* »

Less alive than dead, she shook her head, although "shook" is hardly the word to describe that painfully slow movement. It was our first real mental contact, save for those bloodied green eyes boring in on me. I've seen green eyes before, but nothing quite like this: these eyes were from another age, another world.

*   *   *

It snowed for the next two days. A thick fall burdened the branches of the trees, whitened and concealed the river. There was a brief let-up on the third day, with brilliant sun shooting through clouds, but the fourth day was worse: walls of silver dust driven by howling northern winds. The trees, groaning under the weight of the snow, shook and swayed until heavy branches cracked and fell, vanishing into the soft white vaults below.

Gray bone-cold days followed, with black starless nights and blizzards one after the other. There seemed to be no pattern in the way the winds were blowing; they came from all points of the compass and at ever-changing speeds. I had picked a record year for snowfall, I found out later, the most since '71. I was not unnerved by these convulsions of nature; I found them bracing, a welcome distraction from my personal convulsions. Nor was I worried about starving or freezing to death—there was lots of food, and firewood everywhere you looked. What I was worried about was running out of medication. Her dressings had to be changed daily and she'd need more antiseptics, painkillers, anti-clotting agents. But how to get them? The van's DieHard was dead, but even with a live battery the road was impassable. It was a *chemin saisonnier*, to make matters worse, which meant that it wasn't plowed in winter.

One early morning, after a long dervish dance with insomnia, my regular nocturnal visitor, I returned to my neighbor's to look for snowshoes. Sweeps of high-drifted snow covered the porch steps and pressed against the door. With a small blue shovel, one better suited for the sandbox, I carved out a path.

Inside, despite the creaking baseboard heaters, things were starting to freeze, so I fired up the wood-burning stove. And nailed a wool blanket over the broken window. While doing so I spotted something out front, half-coffined in snow. A Sno-Cat.

This could solve all our problems, I thought exclamatorily, even though I'd never driven one of these before and had no keys. I wouldn't need any, as it turned out, for after unburying the Cat I saw that she was wounded, fatally, with snipped tubes and severed arteries and an instrument panel that looked to have been staved in with an axe. I say this because an axe was stuck in the glass. A decal on the chassis said RIDE SAFE, RIDE SOBER. I trudged back inside, and with little else to do as my patient slept and the snow piled, I began to root around.

Despite the deer head over the mantel, a trio of oil paintings of alpine grandeur, and a large calendar with a moose fending off wolves under a full moon, the place was more like a general store or survivalist refuge than a hunting cabin. A locked pantry, whose padlock I easily picked, contained a gas stove and canister, a survival blanket, Second Skin, bandages, compresses, a bivouac sack and liner, a GPS locator, a portable red flasher with cigarette-lighter adapter, and, best of all, a morphine shot. Inside a knapsack I found cashews, Jersey Milk chocolate, water, Advil, tea bags, and a hunk of moldy cheese.

But the most intriguing item was a large metal trunk, like one of those road cases that rock bands haul their equipment in. It had a high-tech digital lock on its clasp that was impossible to pick so I unscrewed the hinges, which took over an hour. I counted slowly to three before lifting the lid.

Green plastic garbage bags, each of them knotted, enclosed other green plastic bags, in the manner of a Russian doll. The third and final one held a Christmas cache of treasures: a fleece pullover, thick wool socks, camouflage jacket, Gore-Tex snowboots, Frontiersman Bear Spray. I would have left it at that, but noticed that the floor of the box was a tad high, and not metal but wood. A double-bottomed box? I prised out the sheet of plywood and discovered a large black parka underneath, unwrapped. On its breast pocket was a blue and yellow crest: a rainbow trout and Canada goose in the middle, U.S. DEPARTMENT OF THE INTERIOR along the bottom, FISH & WILDLIFE along the top. From the parka's bulging side pockets I pulled out a stun gun and service revolver. Inside the zipped-up coat was a Kevlar vest and a scabbard case, and inside the scabbard case was a .300 Winchester Magnum.

cs III ca

That was the kind of roll I was on. I'd broken into the
home of a law enforcer. But why was he living here, and
why American, and where was he now? Where was his car
or truck or whatever forest rangers drive? I'd heard about
cars caught in whiteouts and not found until spring, when
the coffin of snow had thawed. I'd heard about wardens shot
by poachers and reported as hunting accidents or left in the
forest to rot. Should I report this? How?

I was debating these questions while clearing my driveway
with my plastic shovel. It was backbreaking and rewardless
work, like rolling snowballs up a mountain. I was about to
call it a day when I heard a faint creaking, scraping sound,
which got louder and louder. An airplane? An airplane with
engine trouble?

Some hundred yards away an odd-looking machine
appeared on the horizon like a mirage. It rounded the bend,
slowed on the downhill stretch, and passed in front of me,
creating a higher bank of snow at the end of my drive than the
one I'd just removed. It was a snowplow, either customized or
from another era. It had a Plexiglas dome out front, attached
to the cab window like a gunner's turret.

I raised my toy blue shovel at the driver. He stopped
and shut off his engine. Then gawked, mouth ajar, tongue
protruding.

« Didn't expect to see you out here! » I shouted in French.

He didn't roll down his window because both were already

down. Frost clung to his eyelids and nostrils and his black beard was crawling with white snakes. He looked me over carefully before speaking. « Chief said there's a new uniform out here. Animal cop or warden or shit. That you? »

He spoke in a hayseed Québécois that took some effort to crack. « No, » I replied.

« What you doin' out here if you don't mind me askin'? Huntin'? Trappin'? » The words shot out of his mouth like bullets, leaving puffs of smoke.

« Something like that. »

He spun in his seat, climbed out of the cab. He was a pylonic man, two and a half yards high, but with a fleshy middle: an ectomorph with a paunch. Clad in an army-green parka, camouflage snowmobile pants and Montreal Canadiens tuque—all strained, all undersized. On his feet were furry snowboots that looked like two raccoons.

« You with that lumber outfit out by Hawkshead? » He wiped his beard and nose with a grease-covered snowmobile glove. A nose made for the nasalities of joual, sticking out of his face like a cork.

I was about to flap my hand at the stench in the air, the smell of clothes worn two weeks or more, but thought better of it. I shook my head.

« That your shootin' shack? » He nodded toward the cabin while grinning with an array of cement-colored teeth. « A bit o' pump action on the side? »

Seconds passed before I realized what the man was asking, realized that this was not hunting jargon. « You mean am I cheating on my wife? »

He continued to grin.

« No, I'm ... just, you know, a hermit. On vacation. »

The snowplower stared at me through watery pale blue eyes

that suggested ill health or imbecility or both. His arms hung with the palms facing backward, cavemanishly. « Alone? »

Hermits are generally alone, yes. I nodded.

« You don't get lonesome livin' way out here? Way off in hell-and-gone? »

It makes up for years of pointless companionship. « Not really, no. »

« Just enjoyin' the rare beauties of our woodlands, that it? »

Was that what I was doing? What did the rare beauties of woodlands mean to me? The absence of people. A system that ran perfectly well without humans. « You might say that. »

« You one of *them*? Tree-hugger? Leaf-eater? Bambi-lover? » Eyes fully open, mouth half open, he seemed to be waiting for the joke to be confirmed so he could erupt.

« Not exactly, no. Listen, I need to get to a hospital. My shoulder, I think I dislocated it while shovelling snow— »

« I got my rounds, eh? »

« I'm not asking for a lift, I'm asking for a boost. My battery's dead and I ... » I took out my wallet. « I'll pay you for your time. »

« Everything's out, eh? Wires down every which way. Hospital's on emergency power. Surprised you still got juice out here ... » He paused to examine footprints in the snow leading to and from my neighbor's. Then took off his tuque and scratched his head. Bald as a stone. Ears twisted and rubbery, as if they'd been boiled. He squinted up at the cabin, shifting his head one way, then the other.

I turned to see what he was looking at. In the front window a shadow, then the dark curtain falling back into place.

« I thought you said ... » The snowplower winked. « Put your goddamn wallet away. You got cables? Okay, gimme three of them twenties. Where's your car at anyway? Can't see duck turds on a plate out here. »

⤳ ⤳ ⤳

I padlocked the storm shutters, pulled the curtains shut. On my sleeping patient's bed table, as a hedge against dangerous times, I placed my neighbor's canister of bear repellent, stun gun and Sig Sauer handgun, hoping she had the knowledge and strength to use at least one of them. Left a bilingual note, grabbed a hefty wad of bills, double bolted the door.

In the recharged van I spun out of the driveway, which the snowplower had more or less cleared, and headed back toward the church in the wake of his plow. The road was like a tunnel, with overarching branches and lofty white banks on either side. I approached the old bridge carefully, lining up the truck's wheels on the twin wooden planks. Didn't get out of first gear until hitting the highway. The snowplower went one way, I the other.

This time I was able to get up the hill, which had been salted with cinnamon-colored dirt, and soon reached a green sign declaring the town limits:

BIENVENUE À SAINTE-MADELEINE
POP. 4 200, ÉLÉV. 810 m
(JUMELÉE À GEEL, BELGIQUE)

It bore what appeared to be bullet holes through all the zeros.

The snowplower was right about the storm. Broken tree branches and power lines had fallen onto the road, and all the buildings on the north side were dark. I passed a great structure of granite four stories high, surrounded by a wall of masonry twenty feet high: the hospital, I assumed. There was no traffic so I paused in front, watching a tall crane move spasmodically behind one of the buildings like a prehistoric forager. I looked around for the name of the place and found it in on a gate between two stone pillars with ball crowns:

L'INSTITUT PSYCHOGÉRIATRIQUE DE STE-MADELEINE
POUR LES CRIMINELS ALIÉNÉS
ST. MADELEINE PSYCHOGERIATRIC INSTITUTE
FOR THE CRIMINALLY INSANE

I continued on, down a commercial strip with Christmas decorations hanging off lampposts, through a snag of car dealerships, fast-food shacks, motels with snow-filled swimming pools, to a spanking new Walmart. Its parking lot was being plowed and salted as I entered.

Two competing banners were strung between old-growth fir trees, as tall as the Christmas trees in the Vatican or Trafalgar Square I saw as a child. One demanded unionization, the other proclaimed:

OUI NOUS AVONS DU COURANT! DES DINDES AUSSI!
WE GOT POWER! TURKEY TOO!

All bilingual signs in this province, I was beginning to notice, contained French three times the size of the English, as if all francophones were near-sighted.

The rock salt crackled under my feet as I walked toward the entrance, reminding me of the gravel path I had taken in the fall, following my father's body in the funeral procession.

And with the sound came flashes—of the coffin swaying on canvas belts, being lowered over chromed rollers onto green felt, shovelfuls of earth falling with thuds ...

Music intruded from outdoor speakers. Christmas music. I'd been so deep in my thoughts that I'd forgotten where I was and when.

> Later on we'll conspire
> As we dream by the fire
> To face unafraid
> The plans that we've made
> Walking in a winter wonderland ...

Inside, an old gaillard with a Santa Claus beard, real I think, greeted me jovially while pulling out a red cart. It had a wonky wheel but I pushed it anyway toward the Comptoir Santé. From the first-aid shelves I grabbed tape, gauze, swabs, ointment, forceps and a thermometer. I asked the pharmacist—Emad Azouz, according to his nametag—where I could find a bedpan. Aisle 7. And a bed tray table, you know the kind with little legs? Aisle 13. I then requisitioned sleeping pills, acetaminophen with codeine, syringes and a quart of Betadine, each of which he smilingly retrieved from behind the counter. But frowned when I asked for other things, like cloxacillin and morphine and lidocaine. And Cymbalta, antidepressants that I had left behind, stupidly, in my father's car. Along with my Risperdal (for hallucinosis), Antabuse and Baclofen (wagon straps), each of which my father had prescribed. Generation R_x: I was part of it, its poster boy.

> When it snows, ain't it thrilling
> Though your nose gets a chilling

We'll frolic and play
The Eskimo way
Walking in a winter wonderland ...

Onward, to the food section, where I began stuffing my cart with instant junk: violently processed microwave dinners, violently sugared cereal, violently salted snacks ... all the things little Brooklyn used to love. For myself, I grabbed six middling merlots (from the French for "blackbird") and arranged them gently in the cart. With shaking hands I then put two bottles back, rolled my cart a few feet, then put back the other four.

I left the cart where it was and went to get another. Pushed it to the children's clothes department and tossed in flannel pyjamas, little wool socks (doll socks!), cotton underwear, cotton T-shirts with reinforced necks, three for $10, made in Bangladesh. I knew all the sizes because my little-girl-lost was only a hair taller than Brooklyn. Albeit more than a hair broader. On my way back to the pharmacy I impulsively threw in items: a 17-inch flat screen and shocking-pink DVD player of Chinese manufacture, a half-dozen DVDs, a half-dozen CDs, including Arcade Fire's *The Suburbs* and The Stills' *Oceans Will Rise*, a stuffed bear that I changed my mind about, and a thousand-piece jigsaw of a snowy owl in a snowstorm for which only a convalescent would have the patience.

Back toward my other cart, then a U-turn to sporting goods to see if I could find a two-way hand-held radio. Known in the vernacular as a walkie-talkie. Known in French as a *talkie-walkie*. A middle-aged clerk with a Beatle cut, distracting me with the thickest glasses I have ever seen, led me to one. A good one, he assured me, static-free, on sale. With a distress button. Range: 8 to 10 miles.

« How about a cellphone? » I suggested. « That'd probably be better, right? More practical? »

He looked at me over the top of his heavy black plastic glasses, like the ones American soldiers get for free. « In the mountains? More practical? With all the dead spots around here, smoke signals might be more practical. »

Back toward the pharmacy with my *talkie-walkie*, mouthing the words of a carol, then to the hardware department for one last item. Propane.

> ... though the frost was cruel,
> When a poor man came in sight,
> Gathering winter fuel ...

« *Ça va bien?* » the cashier asked when I arrived with my two-cart convoy. She had pigtails and looked almost as young as my patient. Perhaps a classmate.

« As good as can be expected under the circumstances, » I replied in French, « which could be better and could be worse. » Answering idle questions, making small talk, has always been beyond me. I don't think she heard me, in any case, because the jigsaw's barcode wouldn't beep. This flustered her to no end. Red-faced, she looked around for help before entering the numbers manually.

« Those things would fit you, right? » I pointed to the stack of clothes she was now scanning. She went a deeper red, and I wondered why. Did she think I was offering them to her?

« *Je ... je pense que oui.* »

I paid from a sheaf of American twenties bigger than a wad of socks and she didn't bat an eye. « *Bonne fin de journée,* » she said, handing me some Canadian bills, purple and green and blue, along with a handful of colorful coins.

« *Pareillement,* » I replied while examining the bronze birds, nickel beavers, silver mooseheads. « *Et joyeux Noël.* » I handed her a mint American twenty, which she scrutinized as if it were fake. Which, in a way, it was.

On my way out, the old man who looked like Santa asked me if I'd bought a turkey. Before I could answer he said that when he was young he could kill, pluck, cook and eat a turkey in twenty-two minutes. Which was a record in these parts.

I loaded my cargo into the van, rolled back the two carts and looked around for a payphone. There was one inside the adjoining McDonalds. (Mikes, Moores, Wendys, Tim Hortons—were apostrophes banned in this province?) The dangling directory, in a black vinyl case, had chunks of yellow pages ripped out, but not the *V*'s. *Véhicules, Vêtements ...Vétérinaires.* I inserted two quarters and punched in the number of the Hôpital vétérinaire de l'Avant-Mont. As it rang I watched a startlingly fat woman in the parking lot hit a golden retriever, once, twice, three times, with a snowbrush. What is *wrong* with this world?

"Thanks, I'll be right there," I said after repeating then memorizing the directions. I ran back to the parking lot, but the woman and dog were pulling away in a silver Saab. I could make out only the last three letters of the license plate: RND. I fired up the van, which took a couple of minutes, enough time for her to make a clean getaway.

On the highway I fiddled with the chrome knob on the old radio, watching the red line scan the frequencies, stopping at Jean Leloup's "Le grand héron" at 96.9, then a French version of "Angels We Have Heard on High" at 99.5, then "Bye Bye Bye" by Plants and Animals at 99.9. What a signal, all the way from Vermont! You can't beat German radios, you can't beat a Blaupunkt!

Candy canes dangled from lampposts, and green bulbs winked at me from nests of pine boughs and tinsel. While admiring them I drove at a geriatric pace, trying my best to keep to the speed limit every inch of the way. And trying my best not to jam on my breaks for the benefit of the car behind, a tailgating yellow Hummer. The concept of keeping your distance, it would seem, is as foreign to drivers here as it is in France. I slowed to a crawl and flicked on my four-ways. The driver flashed his brights, three, four times, before passing me on the shoulder, displaying his longest finger.

I reached for the .38 in the glovebox but thought better of it. Pushed on the accelerator, primed for a chase, but thought better of that too. Instead, I wrote down the license plate (666 HLL) and flicked back to 99.5, a Montreal station. Classical music, my father's lawyer once told me, is good for anger management. Vaughan Williams's *Lark Ascending* was playing, which was perfect, but I couldn't focus. Questions were crowding my mind. From the police if I got pulled over: *Are you aware, sir, that the vehicle's registration expired two years ago and has not been renewed? Are you aware that this vehicle was involved in a serious crime? Are you aware that you are wanted in the state of New Jersey, and that a all-points bulletin is out for your arrest?*

The streets were all biblical: Matthieu, Marc, Luc, Jean. I turned right on Mathieu, left on Marc. Past a disused arena announcing a Pumas-Lynx hockey game from the previous year, past a schoolyard with a swing set, climbing bars and a slide in the shape of a dinosaur tongue. But where were the children? I hadn't seen a single one, anywhere. Why weren't they out tobogganing or skating or making snowmen? Or whipping snowballs at cars and windows? Where were they? Was this a retirement village?

Right on Luc, past the flash and trash of new condos littering the mountainside, to a veterinary clinic atop a small hill. The cars were parked in front at a steep angle, presumably with their emergency brakes on. Mine didn't work so I parked at the bottom and made my way up the slick staircase like a chimp on skates. At the top of the hill I looked down on a glaciated valley strewn with black boulders, at a line of birches and poplars that marked the course of a river whose wild waters defied the frost. I must have a suicide complex because I wanted to jump. It all looked so beautiful, pristine. And sad too, as if I were seeing the end of the old world.

A quaint habit of mine: trying to visualize landscapes from before Columbus landed—towering trees fifteen stories high, titanic fish leaping out of crystalline waters, ferocious mountain lions, bobcats and wolves skulking through lush boreal jungle ... Or trying to see in the other direction: toward post-human landscapes. It took ten thousand years to ravage Mother Earth, but after we're gone it will take only two hundred years for her to have her revenge. To turn the concrete jungles into the real thing. To bring every skyscraper down, like one 9/11 after another. To sweep away all the dams. To turn cities back into swamps (Paris was once a marsh, and so was London). To save most animals from extinction ...

I blinked, wiped the images from my head, gazed up at the sky. Among the clouds was a leaping dolphin, its body a graceful *S*, flanked by a leaping lion, its forelegs fully splayed. Hamlet, my doctor told me, saw camels and weasels and whales in the clouds before *he* went mad.

On the door of the clinic was a bilingual sign, whose 8-point English font said ANIMALS MUST BE HELD OR LEECHED.

The air inside had a slightly sour tang—the smell of medicine, of animal fear—and muffled whines and whimpers drifted in from the back.

I was in no mood to see a beautiful human but was now in the presence of one. A woman in a white frock with long wavy Pre-Raphaelite hair who stood by a bay window, tall and straight and queenly, with unfeasibly long legs. I was distracted not only by her, but by the male receptionist, who had bleached white teeth and skin bronzed with a chemical tanning agent.

I asked for syringes, cephalexin and pethidine, armed with a cock-and-bull story about a near-fatal injury to my cat, caught in a hunter's steel trap. To my surprise, the receptionist gave me what I wanted after getting a curt nod from the doctor. I thanked her but a swinging door was already closing behind her.

As my bill was being rung up, I wondered if I should talk to the vet about my patient's wounds. Or even bring her in for an examination. A medical doctor would be required by law to notify authorities; a veterinarian had no such obligation. At least in the States ...

« With the tax, that'll be $114.44, » said the receptionist. « For an extra ten bucks, I'll give you a tick bath. »

I laughed. Then asked, in a low voice, « You wouldn't have any diazepam, would you? Or something like that? » This was a tranquilizer, for me, because it seemed like I'd forgotten how to sleep.

« Yes, we do. But you'll need a doctor's— »

« Can you toss some in? » I gave him what I hoped would pass for a seductive wink and camp little moue. « Just, you know, like a sample? »

The receptionist bit his lip, looked both ways. Then spun in his chair and opened a metal cabinet. « On the house, » he said in a stage whisper, handing me an aluminum blister pack.

Zieline, it was called. Two would knock out a thousand-pound horse. « Uh, I don't want to sound fussy or anything but ... you wouldn't have anything milder, would you? For humans? »

« Oh my God! Wrong pack. » He spun around again and rooted through the cabinet. « How about these? »

"Perfect, thanks." I counted out six American twenties. Left a seventh on the counter, worth two tick baths. « *Joyeux Nöel.* »

On my way out, a poster on the door caught my eye: a missing-girl flyer. A dead girl, most likely. I looked closer. A fourteen-year-old with short dark hair and glasses, last seen at the Maison d'Hébergement Jeunesse in Ste-Madeleine: CÉLESTE JONQUÈRES.

$$\text{ℒ}\qquad\text{ℒ}\qquad\text{ℒ}$$

She was still sleeping when I got back, struggling and muttering like a dreaming dog. I put away my purchases noiselessly, placed the DVD player and crossword puzzle on the chair beside the bed, set up the TV on a kitchen chair at the foot of the bed. Punched it on, fiddled with its wire antenna until finding one semi-clear channel among twelve of snow. Then went back out, to my neighbor's, for my daily theft of wood.

When I returned, my foundling was bathed in the vampiric light of the TV, her teeth gritted and tears making glossy tracks on her face. I made some comforting noises—the kind made for pets and babies, the kind I used to make for Brooklyn—and patted her cheeks with a Kleenex. She responded with a series of groans and spastic movements that both perplexed and troubled me. Was she mentally retarded?

« Are you … in pain? » I asked in both languages, sitting on the edge of the bed.

She shook her head in a preoccupied way, then moved her lips as in a silent film. With her pointer finger she touched her mouth, tapping it two or three times.

« *Ma pauvre. T'as faim!* » I rose to get some food, but she clutched weakly at my wrist with her hand. Again she put her finger to her mouth, but this time made an "x" over her lips.

« Oh, I see! You can't speak! »

She nodded weakly, closing her eyes. Or perhaps rolling them at my stupidity.

I gazed at her for several seconds. A deaf mute. Well, obviously not deaf. A baritone on the box intruded: three Quebec soldiers, one of them from here in the Laurentians, had been killed by a suicide bomber in Afghanistan. I turned off the TV. Tried to refocus.

The sole words in my sign-language repertoire—"Hello," "How are you?," "I love you"—were met with a frown. She made frail little writing gestures in the air. Why didn't I think of that? I pulled a pencil from my breast pocket, along with some folded real estate notes.

On the back of one of them she wrote English words that I had to put on my glasses to read: *I'm dying, aren't I.*

I shook my head violently, but wasn't sure she noticed. She continued to write: *No police.*

I nodded. At least we agreed on that.

I don't want to be found.

There was a time, around her age, when I didn't want to be found either. She fell back on the bed, her head dangling over the side of the mattress. Her eyes remain fixed on the ceiling, unblinkingly.

"What's your name?"

She reached for her pencil, flat on her back. Wrote something and scratched it out. Then wrote again and held up the page. *Église de Ste-Davnet, you know it?*

"The church? Yes, that's where I found you. In fact, I may even be ..." I left the sentence dangling as she continued to write, or rather print. Not in a slow scrawl, as you might expect, but quickly, neatly.

Ring of keys in bird feeder. Backyard, rectory. Big key opens back door. I need my glasses. And sketchbook.

For a last will and testament?

Upstairs, first room on the left. Bed table. Smallest key.

"Okay. But how did you—"

And can you feed my 6 cats? And get me some smokes?

"Yes of course, but—"

BE CAREFUL.

"I will, but how did you—"

I used to live there. With Grand-maman.

"You did? And where's your grandmother now?"

In the cemetery.

IV

It's the glove I remember. An orange rubber glove, like the kind used to wash dishes. I was sleeping in my bed. I heard the creak of a floorboard — the creak that Grand-maman always makes. I heard the click of the bed light being switched on, the thump of footsteps from bed to closet, from closet to dresser — a routine that always ended with her leaning over & whispering "Asleep?" & my small groan that said Yes, I'm asleep but I'm glad you're here & that we're going to have breakfast together.

I heard the creaking sound but for some reason she wasn't going through the routine & that's what woke me. I waited sleepily for the light to go on, for the footsteps to move between bed & closet. Somehow the thought became a snake crawling down my spine, winding tight around my chest. Poor thing, it said to me, this isn't your grandmother at all. How could it be? She's dead.

I opened my eyes & a gloved hand slammed over my mouth. I saw a long shadow & heard heavy breathing & smelled beer. I bit down on the hand that gagged me, my teeth sinking into the rubber glove, grinding it as hard as I could. But there were two hands of course & the other, in an orange fist, slammed into my throat. I gagged & gasped & then blackness came.

When I came to I was tied up, with gooey muck in my face and hair.

★ ★ ★

I'm wrapped in bandages like a mummy. Dopey with painkillers & nauseous too. Just the thought of eating — or even smoking! — makes me want to hurl.

Without my glasses I can barely see. And with a broken windpipe I can barely breathe. At least it feels like it's broken. I feel like I swallowed a sleeping bird that woke up then panicked & is now thrashing its wings inside me. When I try to talk nothing comes out. But even if I get better, which is not likely, I'm never going to speak to anyone again.

★ ★ ★

I can't stop crying & the crying has a muffled, drowning sound. I feel like a duck trapped under the ice, its eyes frozen open, begging whoever walks above it to free it. Now. Please. I'm nearly 15 but I feel like I got mileage on for 115. I don't plan on making it to 16. I'm going out in my grandmother's Exit Bag. Before Christmas.

The family tree
Ends with me.

★ ★ ★

I'm feeling a bit better. And slowly starting to "get my bearings." I'm in a cabin in the middle of nowhere — from the tiny glimpse I get out the window it may be on that strip of land by the river with hunting cabins that crazy man Brioche built but can never rent because the land's flooded half the time & the roads aren't cleared in winter. Plus I've lost my voice. Which I might've mentioned already. I'm here with this strange American dude who seems to be a doctor who's got a night telescope or whatever it's called, black tar in a jar, a stamp collection & generally jumpy behaviour. He chain-drinks coffee from morning to night & paces up & down like an expectant father. Before going to sleep he writes in a small notebook or reads a paperback novel with no covers called Broken Wind. I asked him why it has no covers & he said that it's probably the result of it being flung across the room many times.

Every day I think up a new back-story for him. A heart surgeon who lost his nerve in the middle of an operation. A doctor on the run, fleeing a malpractice suit. A jailbreaker convicted of practising with forged medical credentials. An escaped mental patient who thinks he's a physician. But he might not even be a doctor. For all I know he could be President of the Jeffrey Dahmer Fan Club.

I don't know what he expects from me when I get better — if I get better. He obviously took my clothes off & God knows what else he did. But if he saved my life, I should be grateful, I guess, because it might allow me to do two major things before I die. More later, he's back with more firewood ...

★ ★ ★

With fuzzy vision I'm looking at water stains on the ceiling & one of them seems to be turning into the man with the orange gloves, but with his face upside down, mouth on top, eyes below.

★ ★ ★

Still trying to figure out who exactly I'm rooming with. I know he's an American from his accent (he says "HOWse" and "badderies" and "huh" instead of "eh" and "zee" instead of "zed" and "Eye-rack" instead of "Iraq"), but he also speaks Parisian French with machine-gun speed, especially when he swears.

I fed him a line about a girl gang sticking me because I was a fat stuck-up know-it-all science geek who prefers reading to iPhones & texting & cloneclothes. And he swallowed it. If he finds out what really happened he'll only screw things up, he'll end up blabbing it all over the place & getting us both killed.

It's not that he's stupid or anything but he seems, I don't know, like a fish out of water or a rabbit in New York City. Like a baby could take candy from him. He's certainly no match for Alcide Bazinet ...

He thinks I'm a poor little mute girl & I'll let him go on thinking that. I'll be like one of those Benedictine nuns in their refectories. Besides, I'm so painkilled I couldn't speak if I wanted to. If he only knew what a little chatterbox I am.

If I can get out of bed, I'll root around next time he's gone, try to find out more about him. He won't even tell me where he's from. Keeps saying he's from Neptune.

V

Céleste was snoring softly as I awoke in the pre-dawn dark. Nightmares had raided my sleep, caveman dreams in which I was rubbing two sticks together, nose flaring, eyes roaming and ears straining for hidden danger, my short furry legs ready to outrun the wind. Dozily, eyes half-closed, I looked out the living room window at a scene dim and vague with flowing mists and mastodonic shapes with tusks and horns. The trees were ghostly and bent, the ice burdening or breaking their limbs. I could feel myself out on one of them, saw in hand.

Birds began to sing, reminding me that not all birds fly south. Nothing familiar to me, like the ovenbird's *teacher teacher teacher*, or the catbird's *meow*, or the towhee's *drink-your-tea*. Just a few pigeon-like sounds, two repeated syllables, *doo-doo*, like the dodo is said to have made.

While listening to them I made a decision, a snap decision: to bolt, to go back to where I came from and face the music. I'd failed as a tourist, failed as a hermit; it was the end of my nature experiment, end of my doctoring. I'd stretched myself as far as I could and had no more stretch. Chalk it up to a bad month to be buried with the memory of other bad months.

Besides, how could I even *think* of living with a teenage girl after the charges I was running from? A teenage girl with *serious* enemies. A depressing foreign film is what I was in, complete with subtitles, handwritten ones. I was losing it, wobbling out of orbit. A pharmaceutical backlog—teenage acid, college weed, adulthood coke and alcohol, in unwise conjunction, joining forces in a time-release attack on my brain cells. Turning my gray matter into shaving cream. Why else would I come to these alien pines, this gutted church surrounded by homicidal bog men? Heavenly callings? Delusions of sainthood?

I would go to the police, turn myself in, report what I'd seen. And get her a doctor. A real one. Céleste would give me no explanation of what had happened to her that night, nothing credible at least, but she'd have to tell the cops. And they'd protect her.

But first I'd go to the rectory for her, as promised. Or rather second. First I'd make breakfast. I leapt out of bed, glanced at my patient, then yanked open the fridge door. *It's not giving up, it's growing up,* an inner voice reassured me.

While listening to the bacon and eggs in the skillet, to the pig and chicks cursing and spitting in anger and anguish, it dawned on me why Céleste wouldn't eat my breakfasts, or much of anything else. So I put the kettle on.

"You're a vegetarian, right?" I asked when she opened one eye. I had deliberately dropped her plate with a clatter onto her tray table.

She nodded slowly.

"I made porridge for you."

No response.

"You must be a rarity around here. Any vegetarian restaurants in these parts?"

Unsteady, dazed, she sat up and reached for a pencil and paper on the bed table. *As many as there are gay bars.*

I smiled. Wondered why she would make that comparison. "Are *you* gay?"

Céleste paused, wrote a few letters, scratched them out. Then simply nodded.

Can one be gay at fourteen? "That's ... you know, fine with me."

Glad you approve.

"How do you feel?"

Like I've been crumpled up in a ball for the last year.

"And mentally?"

I have a sense of impending doom.

Join the club. "No, I mean physically mentally, if you know what I mean."

Like I'm underwater.

I paused. "Why can't you ... speak?"

She wrote something, scratched it out, wrote again. *Tried to hang myself, damaged my voice box.*

This, I was almost a hundred percent sure, was false. "Would you like to tell me about it?"

About what?

"About who dumped you in the swamp. And why."

You writing a book? Make that chapter a mystery. She set her pencil down and turned away from me to face the wall.

"And don't tell me it was a gang at school because I don't believe you." I walked around to the other side of the bed. I know that girls this age love to keep their secrets, but this is ridiculous. "It's time, Céleste. Tell me everything."

She stared right through me, stared at nothing. Her eyes were open but they appeared sightless. And then I lost her, her blood-red eyes sliding away from me in a sullen glaze.

Once again I placed the stun gun, bear spray and revolver on her bed table. But this time, in case of emergency, she also had a walkie-talkie. She couldn't talk into it, of course, but she could send me a mayday (from the French *m'aidez*) with the push of a button. Or an all-clear. Provided she was paying attention when I showed her how. Provided I stayed within eight to ten miles. Provided it worked in the mountains. For good measure, I leaned the rifle against the foot of the bed. She's a country lass, she'll know how to use it. I padlocked the shutters, pulled the curtains shut, double-locked the door.

🕊️ 🕊️ 🕊️

Through my Vanagon window came the clean chill air, the smell of resin, of woodsmoke. The ship of sunrise burning, from ninety-three million miles away, turned the snow into a sea of diamonds almost painful to look at. Like all beauties.

At the top of the cedar-lined church lane I stopped in a kind of suspended time, or rather outside time, on the rim of the universe: the church cross and mullioned windows of the house were shimmering, mirage-like, in a sky of white and gold. A choir of angels sang inside my head. Angels we have heard while high.

Ding dong! verily the sky
Is riv'n with angel singing ...

The tension inside me, the sad feeling that churches have, the danger I felt all around me, the horrors of the bog— everything was softened by the dawn light, the wilderness air, the smell of wood and rock and snow. Again, I felt that mysterious natural chemical enter my system, immeasurably stronger than antidepressants. *You're here. You've been headed here all your life.* I gazed at the soft peaks and swells of the Laurentian Highlands, the dappled sunlight on pines, the black and ancient pond beyond the cemetery, the valley with the half-frozen stream rambling through it. I closed my eyes and listened to the sounds—the cascading water, the carolling of birds. It all stretched out before me, the very essence of ... what? Possibility? Redemption?

A faraway sound—a rifle blast from a distant ridge—triggered another sound inside my head: the *thwack* of Céleste's body hitting the half-frozen mud. I closed my eyes and clasped my hands over my ears. It was like I'd been hypnotized to react to that deafening sound. But how was I to react?

When the rifle refired, I knew. Knew why I'd come here, what I had to do. Everything became clear as the wide blue sky. I had not come north to make a new beginning, to escape the city, to find peace and happiness in nature. It was not my destiny to be happy; I had not been programmed for it. I had not come north to save anybody either—although that was part of it, a big part. No, I had come here to kill somebody. And be killed. *A vacation to die for.* Buying this church was not a beginning but an end.

🕊 🕊 🕊

The two-story Edwardian rectory was made of yellowish-brown stone, like the wicked witch's gingerbread house, and its severely pitched roof, built to ward off heavy winter snows, was a crazy quilt of gray and green bandages. Thick icicles shot with turquoise hung from the eaves. The doors were dark chocolate, as were the shutters on the small windows. Out front was an ice-coated wrought-iron fence, and a rusting gate that ground its teeth to let me pass.

Around the back, on a hemp mat by the door, was a pair of large army boots covered in dried mud, and inside each were orange rubber gloves. A sign tacked to the door bore handwriting I recognized: *BEWARE OF CATS.* I turned around.

In the middle of the backyard was a pole with a bird feeder, its wooden ledges strewn with millet seed. Was the sign a warning to the birds? On tiptoe, I felt inside the box and pulled out a ring of keys embedded in frozen bird droppings.

The first room I entered was the kitchen. Red-brick walls and wide-planked pine floors. A great black stove, a big round table. Items scattered willy-nilly, scarily, on the floor, including bottles and plates and knives, but on closer inspection they seemed less the work of a vandal than someone preparing to clean.

The first cupboard I opened contained rows of hardcover books. The second cupboard I opened contained rows of hardcover books. The third cupboard ... If I opened the fridge or stove, I had little doubt I'd see even more books stuffed inside, perhaps paperbacks. The fourth cupboard contained food, most of which was cereal, children's cereal: Frosted Flakes, Froot Loops, Fruity Pebbles, Cocoa Krispies, Cocoa Puffs, Reese's Puffs, Cap'n Crunch, Corn Pops, Count Chocula, Honeycomb, Honey Smacks, Lucky Charms ... The genre is full of "k" sounds, I noticed, like swear words. On the bottom shelf were metal bowls with embossed paws and rubber trim, and stacked tins of Fancy Feast Turkey & Cheese, Chicken & Salmon, Grilled Tuna. The cats, evidently, were not vegetarians.

I began emptying tuna into six bowls set a foot apart. "Here, kitty kitty kitty ..." I yelled out the door, several times. No response. But why *would* they respond to my voice? They need a good scent. I stacked the six bowls on top of each other, three in each hand, and carried them outside. Standing on the hemp mat, next to the size-12 army boots, I called again.

Two cats emerged from a toolshed and were soon purring at my feet, rubbing their shoulders against my ankles. One white, one black, both half-starved. Two or three others were feral and raced away, while another lay on its back, crying mournfully. I set the bowls down.

Back inside, not wanting to cramp their style, I watched them through the kitchen's bay window, whose sill was covered with dried mud footprints. Five cats ate ravenously, while the last one, a wary calico, crouched slowly from the shed, belly to the ground, toward the sixth and last bowl.

On the kitchen table was a pile of mail, which I nosily pawed through. Bills, for the most part, which I stuffed into my two coat pockets, and flyers, including one from the SAQ, the only place you can get liquor in this province. Instead of the regular price of $19.99, they were selling a Californian Pinot Noir for $19.49. Could I get there, I wondered, before the stampede?

There was a doggy door in the kitchen but no dogs in sight. I wouldn't have minded seeing one or two. I'd always been a dog man. Not because I was scratched in the eye by a kitten when I was five, or because I saw a cat eat a chipmunk when I was seven, or because an Abyssinian killed my grandfather when I was nine, walking between his legs and sending him headfirst onto a Chippendale lowboy. No, it was because of their notorious aloofness, their refusal to come when you called, to show their glee when you arrived home. A virtue, according to many poets, including Swinburne:

> Dogs may fawn on all and some
> As we come;
> You, a friend of loftier mind,
> Answer friends alone in kind.
> Just your foot upon my hand
> Softly bids it understand.

After the food was devoured I went back out with bowls of water. While they drank, or at least while two of them did, I went for a quick stroll through the cemetery rows. The most sociable of the beasts, a fluffy white cat with a red collar, followed me. She made little runs and darts across my path, as if trying to trip me. I was mystified at first, but then wondered if this were a ruse to get herself lifted from the frozen ground and carried. It was. The cat not only let me pick her up, but seemed to demand it. She rode back to the rectory on my shoulder.

🕊 🕊 🕊

The room at the top of the stairs, obviously the grandmother's study, was designed in a more-is-definitely-more style. It contained two leather chairs and a wall-length, floor-to-ceiling bookcase crammed with century- or half-century-old books on diverse subjects: William Beebe's *The Bird, Its Form and Function*, Albert Camus's *The Myth of Sisyphus and Other Essays*, Rilke's *Das Buch der Bilder*, Voltaire's *Candide*, *The Book of Common Prayer*, *The Atheist's Bible*, *Bring Up Genius!*, *L'Enfant prodige* ... Many were dusty or discolored by sunlight, while others, including E.M. Forster's *Where Angels Fear to Tread*, *The Complete Poems of Hart Crane* and *The Life of P.T. Barnum, Written by Himself*, were library books with white Dewey decimals and Due Date cards from the forties.

Shrivelled houseplants and crumbs of soil were scattered over a red and white Persian carpet. A cat or some other animal had clawed the plants out of their pots. From behind a Salvation Army armchair, its arms savaged by cat claws, gleamed two pairs of masked eyes. Raccoons. When I approached them they ran out the door with that humpbacked lope of theirs, claws clicking in the hallway. I listened as they scurried down the stairs and into the kitchen. Must lock that doggy door ...

On the other wall, across from the bookcase, was a stone fireplace with an atlas cradled in mahogany where the grate should have been, and an Anglican Church of Canada flag above it: the red cross of St. George on a white background with four green maple leaves in the quarters. Next to this was a large wooden desk covered with papers and books and diverse objects, including ivory chessmen on an inlaid board, a Telefunken short-wave, very nearly Edison era, and a manual typewriter, a Smith Corona primed with paper and carbon. Before making typewriters, my grandfather told me, L. C. Smith was known for his shotguns.

On the discordantly papered wall above the desk, which cracked and curled at the cornices, was a local newspaper article about Céleste, about a college entrance exam she passed at the age of twelve. There was also a photograph of her and a woman with long gray hair sitting in a small aircraft, with Céleste at the throttle. The plane, which had metal plates on its wheels, was parked on a frozen lake. I looked closer at the older person, the grandmother presumably. Her face was craggy but finely boned. Both of them were beaming. I'd never seen Céleste smile like that, never seen her smile at all.

Down the hall, after opening two closet doors, I reached Céleste's bedroom, which was an odd L-shape, a chess knight move. There were unaccountable cold spots in the room, as in a spring-fed lake, and its pine floor was filthy, covered with large mud footprints and traces of cloth swipes.

Like the rest of the rectory, the room contained more books than furniture. The house was a library. On the top shelf of a long bookcase, a homemade affair made of bricks and particle board, were miniature animals in plaster or pewter. At least thirty of them, many of which I could identify: Tyrannosaur, Brontosaur, Titanosaur, Stegosaur, Hadrosaur, Albertosaur, Pterodactyl, Eohippus, Triceratops, Megalodon, Mastodon, Smilodon ... We had something in common, Céleste and I.

On the sagging shelves below was an overflowing ashtray atop a stack of magazines, not those normally read by teenage girls—*The Philosophical Review, The New Atheist, Wildlife Forensics*—together with such books as *The God Delusion, Animal Farm, Dominion, The Ethical Assassin* ...

On a high gray desk, whose top looked like a mortuary slab, was an opened copy of *North American Wildlife* with an ad circled in red:

BECOME A WILDLIFE DETECTIVE
Don't be chained to a desk, computer or McCounter.
This easy home-study plan prepares you for an
exciting career in conservation and ecology!
Wildlife detectives find endangered species,
parachute from planes to help marooned animals,
catch poachers red-handed.
Live the outdoor life. Sleep under pines and stars.
Live and look like a million!

Live like a million? What would that mean? I continued to snoop around. On the wall beside the desk was a note that said "World's Most Dangerous Creature," with an arrow pointing down, toward a full-length mirror. Next to this was a cartoon: in frame one, a hunter is aiming his rifle at a bear as it peacefully laps water from a pond; in frame two, the stuffed bear is in the guy's living room, ferociously baring fang and claw.

Thumb-tacked onto a bulletin board was a map of Paris, much used, along with overlapping newspaper clippings, at least a dozen of them, including this one from the *St. Madeleine Star*, December 1958. It was yellow with age and encased in plastic:

LOCAL HERO

A mountain lion, rare in these parts, was shot last week by two local hunters out on Ravenwood Pond. The animal was chased out onto the ice by six hunting dogs. "My first shot slowed him down good, took the starch right out of him," hunter Moss Bazinet, 44, explained. "When we reached him the dogs were snapping and barking and the way he looked at me it looked like he was pleading for his life. I shot him in the face from ten feet. Got him right in the eye." The locals are calling him a hero, but Moss shrugs it off. "I do my best every day," he said modestly, "with the Lord's help."

And this more recent one on the same subject:

OTTAWA (CP)—The mysterious Eastern Cougar—missing and presumed extinct since 1958—may be prowling in the Laurentian region of Quebec.

A clue lies in the DNA molecules of a strand of hair in Dr. Marie Sabin's microbiology lab at Laval University in Quebec City. Tawny fur was caught this autumn in a hair trap in the rugged mountains.

"When we started this project two years ago, we laughed about this being the Loch Ness monster of the East. But now we have some really hard evidence of something more tangible. It's all very exciting."

Once widespread across North America, cougars were hunted during European colonization and driven into three last strongholds: the Rocky Mountains, the Olympic Peninsula in Washington State, and the Florida Everglades. The last known Eastern Cougar was shot in Quebec's Laurentian Mountains in 1958. Since then, thousands of cougar sightings have tantalized Ontario, Quebec, the Maritimes, and New England, but hard evidence of the cats has remained elusive.

To attract the cats, Dr. Sabin set up poles scented with cougar urine throughout Quebec's forest regions. The poles were covered with Velcro to catch the animals' hairs. The breakthrough came in December, when a hair sample collected by Dr. Sabin in the Laurentians came up positive. It was a cougar.

Where did the Laurentian cougar come from? There are only three possible explanations. The first is that it escaped from a zoo or from an owner who kept it as an exotic pet. The second is that cougars from elsewhere in North America are returning to colonize their old habitat in the East. The third explanation is that the secretive Eastern Cougar never really died out.

With the smallest of the three keys I opened the bottom drawer of Céleste's dresser, and promptly got a shock. A face looked back at me, from a ripped and blurred photograph of ... the veterinarian. It was unmistakably her. I set this aside, thoughts whirling, and sifted through various sculpting implements—modelling tools, chisels, wire-loops, rods, dowels, netting—until finding a pair of glasses, the utopian communard model with small round lenses and frames of the thinnest wire. No doubt a spare, judging by their scratched lenses. Underneath all this was a blue sketchbook with tiny black letters on the cover. I had to put on Céleste's glasses to read what they said: NOT TO BE READ UNTIL I'M DEAD.

꒤ ꒤ ꒤

There was no phone in any of the upstairs rooms, but in the kitchen was a black wall phone. I didn't expect it to have a dial tone and it didn't: it had a stutter-tone. I punched in the long-distance number of Brook's cellphone, in violation of a court order, and left a message so long it was cut off. I then called J. Leon Volpe, my attorney.

"Do you realize, Nightingale, you are in *serious* shit?" was his greeting. He was my father's attorney, to be precise, a chronically exasperated man with expletive-salted sentences and Italian suits who disliked everyone, especially me. He had a throaty, interrogatory voice that sounded less lawyerly than gangsterly.

"Yes."

In the background I could hear his favorite radio station, an AM channel trapped in the fifties, which he never turned off. "For the love of Christ, Nile, I've been trying to reach you for the last three weeks. Do you ever retrieve your goddamn messages? Does anyone even *send* you messages?"

He disliked me, in part, for my lawyer jokes. "What did you want?"

"What did I *want*? What the hell do you think I wanted? I wanted to know why I'm in the middle of a *shit parade*. Affidavits, warrants, restraining orders, complaints for damages. Phone calls and e-mails from Katz, Carp & Ferret. I'm drowning in this stuff. Am I representing you?"

How do you stop a lawyer from drowning? Answer one: shoot him before he hits the water. Answer two: take your foot off his head. "If you agree."

A loud theatrical sigh. "Can I just say, at this preliminary point, that I wish you had done me the courtesy of *consulting me beforehand*? And that I find your actions *grossly irresponsible*?"

His job, for the most part, seemed to consist of putting people in their place. "Yes, feel free."

Count to five. "And where are you now, your Highness?"

This was a reference to my drug use. Former drug use. "In a cemetery."

"Where? Colombia? Afghanistan?"

Through a frost-covered window at the end of the hall, I glimpsed what looked like a snowplow. It was heading toward the church, which was odd because the lane had already been cleared. It stopped halfway.

"Just tell me one thing, off the record, no bullshit. Did you, or did you not, abduct and assault Brooklyn Jessica Martin?"

I took the phone up the hall, stretching its gnarled black coil until it was no longer a coil, but before I could get a better look the plow had backed up and roared off.

"Is this a dialogue we're having, Nile? Or an interior fucking monologue?"

An interior monologue, pretend you're Hamlet. "I'm listening."

"Did you, or did you not, abduct and assault Brooklyn Jennifer Martin?"

He was said to be brilliant, although I never once heard him say a brilliant thing; my father, on the other hand, said brilliant things all the time. "Her middle name is not Jennifer."

"Nile, for Christ's sake—"

"Of course I didn't."

"Then what the *hell* were you doing with her?"

"I took her to a zoo. As requested."

"As *who* requested? *Which* zoo?"

"Brook. Cape May."

"Without your ex-wife's permission."

"She's not my ex-wife."

"But you lived together."

In the background I could hear the faint strains of "Earth Angel" by the Penguins. Along with keyboard clicks, as if he were double-tasking. Even when you spoke to him face to face, you got the impression he was double-tasking.

"Yes," I replied.

"At the funeral you guys seemed like such a great couple. And your father just loved her—and was ecstatic about having a grandchild. What killed it, Nile? You and your ... problems?"

I'm getting an abortion so get used it: my ex's words. "No, it was just ... you know, one of those things."

"Your *Wehmut* or *Weltschmerz* or whatever the Germans call it?"

"No."

"You still hearing things, seeing things? Prehistoric beasts, fairy-tale monsters, that kind of stuff? What's it called again?"

My father, who could no more keep his mouth shut than a catfish, must have told him about this, about my visit with a neuropsychologist in Frankfurt. "Pareidolia," was Doktor Neefe's conclusion. "A condition," he explained in accented English, "in which the brain interprets random patterns as recognizable images. We all have it to some extent, *ja*? When we see faces or animal shapes in clouds or flames, or the Virgin Mary's face in a piece of bratwurst, or a sex organ in a fig. Or *Steckrübe* ... turnip. Or a rat in toilet bowl stool. Or when we hear hidden messages on a Beatles record played backwards. Many artists have had it—Bosch, Blake, Munch and Magritte come to mind. Munch painted *The Cry* after watching a sunset whose clouds looked to him like 'coagulated blood.' Hamlet and Scrooge had it. Lewis Carroll. Many scientists too, especially Hermann Rorschach. But you, Herr Nightingale, you have a rather interesting form of it. A psychotomimetic form. Your visions would seem to be neurological reverbs, after-sensations, from the barrage of psychedelic chemicals you've been subjecting your brain to." A bit like pro football players, I thought at the time, the shocks and hits that come back to haunt them, debilitate them, years after they've retired.

"Hello? Nile? You still there?"

"Meine Halluzinationen betreffen Sie nicht."

"Whoa. Slow down. What?"

"My visions are neither here nor there."

"So you took the child a hundred miles away from home without the mother's permission."

"Brook phoned me, said she missed me, said her mom gave

us the green light, Girl Scout's honor. She was waiting for me at the end of the driveway." With a pink plastic suitcase.

"But you never made it to the zoo."

"No."

"But you made it to a motel."

"Was it my fault the car broke down?"

"No, it wasn't. An antique like that is bound to break down. But it was your fault you ended up in Atlantic City. Which isn't exactly the closest town to Cape May now, is it."

How does one say no to a young girl who's crying? I've never been able to. "Brook asked me—pleaded with me—to take her there. Said she'd never been, said she wanted to go on the world's biggest roller coaster."

"Don't say that in court."

"Because ..."

"Because it's not in Atlantic City."

"So we found out."

"And so you took her to a casino instead."

"Are you serious? How would she get in? She's got braces, for Christ's sake."

"Your ex-wife claims that you applied makeup to her and entered a casino, where she won ... let me see. Eighty-nine dollars and fifty cents. She found it in her ... pink suitcase."

"Nonsense. A pathetic lie. About the makeup, I mean. She did win some money."

"And where did she win the money?"

"At the motel."

"There was a casino at the motel?"

"No. I taught her how to play poker. After six riveting games of Fish."

"In your room."

"Correct."

"Strip poker?"

Sigh. "No, not strip poker."

"You were drunk, I presume? Or high?"

"Ish."

"And was she?"

"High? Yes. Rushing on four Fudgsicles and a mountain of M&Ms."

"And where did you play poker? On the bed?"

"Yes. A heart-shaped bed, in fact. With a pink chiffon bedspread."

"Where she won eighty-nine dollars from you."

"And fifty cents."

"Be right back, got to piss like a heart attack ..."

When Volpe put you on hold, his radio automatically kicked in, loud and clear. He was gone for the duration of "Chapel of Love" by the Dixie Cups. I set the receiver down and paged Céleste on the walkie-talkie, not expecting it to work, not expecting her to be awake. But she replied almost immediately with an all-clear. Smart kid.

"Nile? Nile? There's another item here ... Your wife's lawyer mentions some morbid act, some sort of satanic ritual that went on. Something involving a dead man's hand?"

Here I had to laugh. Her lawyer must have minored in comedy writing at law school.

"Glad you think it's amusing, Nile. But how would you respond to that in a court of law?"

With a wail of laughter. "In our last game I held an Ace of Spades, Ace of Clubs, eight of Spades, eight of Clubs, Jack of Diamonds. It's called the deadman's hand."

"Never heard of it."

"There are lots of things you've never heard of," I almost said, but I almost say things much more often than I say them.

"When Wild Bill Hickcock was shot in the back of the head, those were the cards that fell to the floor."

Silence. "Did anything happen between you two? After the game of poker, on the heart-shaped bed?"

"No."

"But you slept together."

"In the literal sense, yes."

"You got a room with one bed?"

"Two. But Brooklyn ended up on mine. As she often did with me and her mom. Whenever she had nightmares, or couldn't sleep." She couldn't sleep unless the place was lit up like Christmas.

"And when you went into the Jacuzzi with her the next morning, what were each of you wearing?"

"Objection. Leading the witness. It has not been established that Mr. Nightingale ever went into the Jacuzzi with Miss Martin."

"I'm just preparing you for the hell-roasting you're going to get from the prosecutor."

Volpe should know, he used to be one himself. After Fordham Law he began as a defense attorney, but crossed the aisle because he didn't want to spend the rest of his life being lied to on a daily basis. He then worked for the FBI, according to my father, which had become something of a haven for lawyers trying to avoid military service. Now he's a corporate lawyer, writing up steel-trap contracts for hedge fund firms owned by New Jersey crime families. So why was I asking him to defend me? A man who hasn't won a defense case since disco? Because he's the closest I have to blood: he was my father's best, most loyal friend since kindergarten. He visited us in Europe, even China. Although he hated everyone else, the lawyer loved the doctor. "Brooklyn used the Jacuzzi, not me. As far as I can recall, she wore a bathing suit. I was in the shower at the time."

"Naked?"

I paused. Was this a real question? "Yes. A nutty quirk, I admit."

"Don't you think it would've been wiser had you gotten two rooms?"

"In hindsight, yes. But Brooklyn didn't want to stay in a room by herself. She was afraid, she said. She was *ten* at the time—I would've been afraid at that age too."

"Why didn't you phone her mother?"

"I did, left two messages. Even though Brook said not to bother, that her mom was spending the weekend with her 'smiley new boyfriend.'"

"And what about the charge of road rage on the way back?"

"What about it?"

"The police report says that you had a drunken argument with another driver on I-9, that you screamed out threats and profanities, cut him off repeatedly, and waved a gun at him through the window."

Sometimes, after drink, I am prone to spontaneity. "He cut me off first, grinning at me with a sorry-ass mustache. After riding my bumper for twenty miles."

"But the rest is true? You were a drunk and disorderly rageaholic?"

Alcohol is one of my tripwires, oversensitizing me to the bad behavior of strangers.

"And exceeding the speed limit," Volpe continued, "by over forty miles an hour?"

Velocity is the ultimate drug and rockets run on alcohol. "Possibly."

"And the pistol?"

"Brooklyn's."

"Brooklyn carries a piece?"

"A Walther .38. The brand favored by James Bond."

"You've *got* to be kidding."

"An anatomically correct plastic version."

"The kind that can pass through metal detectors ... Oh, for Christ's sake, Nile, a water pistol? I wonder who gave her that."

"She asked for one for her birthday. I got her top-of-the-line."

"Did you know that killers get their early training with water pistols?"

"Oh, please. I must have had a dozen when I was a kid. Didn't you?" I couldn't imagine Volpe having a childhood.

"Did you ever *once* think of the repercussions? On an innocent, impressionable young girl who may never fully recover from this incident? Ever think of that?"

"She was in hysterics the entire time. Egging me on. Not just to catch the guy, to force him over, but to shoot him in the face. Which I did. When the cops pulled me over, she couldn't answer their questions because of a laughing cramp. And when we arrived at her mother's, she told me—and I quote—'That was the best weekend of my whole life, Uncle Nile, can we do it again next weekend?' Did she mention that to her mother? Perhaps her mother forgot that detail."

Volpe heaved another sigh, long and loud. "Do they have Internet up there? Up in ... central Quebec?"

"How'd you know ..." I stopped because I knew. "No, they don't have Internet up here, not yet. Or color TV."

"They don't?"

Who was putting on who? "No, it's prehistoric up here. You've never been? *The Flintstones* was shot up here."

"What are you doing there anyway, smart-ass?"

Three things—nervousness, alcohol and Volpe—could turn me into a smart-ass. "Not a lot."

"Why does that not surprise me? Why does that not surprise me one iota? You remember, Count Slackoff, what your father used to say about you?"

Let's see, what would the old man have said about me? That I was an arrested adolescent who'd end up arrested? That all my classmates had passed through the gates of adulthood except me? "No. Refresh my memory."

"'He wants to have his bread and loaf too.'"

"Very amusing, that. Thanks for reminding me."

"And that 'childlessness will condemn you to—'"

"'Childishness.'"

"Exactly. God, what a wit that man had. I could never keep up with him. Must have been lots of fun being around him."

I nodded. "A riotocracy of merriment."

"He had the energy of six men."

And I the energy of a sloth.

"And you the energy of a sloth."

"Once again, Mr. Volpe, thanks for reminding me."

"One of the seven deadly sins, that."

"So I've heard."

"Did you ever forgive him?"

"For ...?"

"For what he did to you in Paris."

"Yes, of course."

Awkward silence as we both listened to his AM radio: "Trouble in Paradise" by the Crests. "Did you get your shots before you left?"

"For ...?"

"I don't know, whatever they have up there. Mad cow? Hoof and mouth? Swine flu?"

"They don't breed animals up here. They're cannibals."

"Always the wiseass. Listen, whatever you do, don't speed, don't drink, don't get stopped by the cops. You get stopped, you're in a shitpot of trouble. There's an all-points out."

"Which means ..."

"Which means that if you're stopped for a DUI or traffic violation and the uniform radios in the information, the bulletin sends up a flag."

"Does this ... extend to Quebec?"

"Does a bear shit in the woods?"

"I believe so."

"Does a wooden horse have a hickory dick? Yes, nimrod, it extends to Quebec."

"I won't get stopped." I've been getting stopped all my life, I thought as the words left my lips.

"You've been getting stopped all your life."

"So I've heard. Listen, has the story, you know, made any of the papers?"

"Yeah, it's made all the papers. Headlines in *The New York Times:* 'Stamp Collector on the Lam.' Of course it hasn't made the goddamn papers." I could see him frowning, like one of my high-school principals. "I'll see what I can do, Nile, for the sake of your father. But I'll be straight with you—you could end up sleeping on a stainless-steel shelf attached to a wall."

VI

After several misfires starting up the van, I sat silently behind the wheel, thinking of questions I should have asked my lawyer: *How much does my ex want? What portion of my father's estate would help her maintain the chemical life to which she's grown accustomed?* And fielding questions from my father's ghost: *Have you learned anything from this, Nile? It's never a loss if you've learned something. Have you?* Yes, father, I have. After living with a beautiful woman, I learned the irrelevance of beauty.

The ignition finally caught and I was halfway down the lane when I saw her. The white cat with the red collar. By the side of the road, calm as can be, as if waiting for her limo. I hit the brakes, opened the door and she leapt in like a dog, up onto my lap. And then onto the passenger seat, staring straight ahead, like a dowager being driven to the opera.

But we weren't heading for the opera, unfortunately; we were heading for a kind of hall of mirrors, a gallery of characters of increasing bentness who took me back in time, to my institutional days. Unless they were all ghosts, the coinage of my brain.

The RE/MAX in Ste-Madeleine, the agency that handled my cabin rental, was open but empty. I could hear myself nervously whistling, which is not something I do often or well. « *Il y a quelqu'un?* » I inquired.

A toilet flushed, a door latch clicked, and a gaunt woman with thick gray hair and a cigarette butt emerged from a door marked Femmes. I stated my business and she pointed with her cigarette. « *Jusqu'au bout, à gauche.* »

I followed her instructions, pausing at the threshold of a surprisingly dim office. The agent's face looked ghoulish in the glow of his computer screen, his tongue protruding as he frowned in concentration. I cleared my throat to pull his attention away from what turned out not to be real estate files or the Internet but a video game.

« You're interested in *that* property? » the agent asked in French, his eyes still trained on his screen. He had yellowish hair like unravelled shredded wheat that hung over his forehead and eyes, and his face was pocked with acne. He looked less like a realtor than a bag boy at the supermarket. « That mudhole? » Like a child protecting a test paper from a cheating neighbor, he put his left arm around a manila folder beside his laptop. He looked coked to the gills. And I should know. « There's talk, eh? »

« Talk? »

« Of rituals and shit. Weird shit. Bad things that happened way back when. You'd be better off with a condo. Or even one of them flooded trailers from New Orleans. »

With his right hand he punched in numbers on a cell, turning his head away and speaking in a low voice. He folded up his phone and began tapping his index finger between the bottom and top rows of his teeth. It was not a sound I needed to hear.

« Okay, let's go, » he said after slipping his folder in a desk drawer and standing. He seemed to rise indefinitely; like the snowplower, he was tall, very tall, practically a furlong.

Something in the water up here? « To the bank. We can jeep it or walk it. » He inserted earphones into his ears before I could express a preference, and fiddled with his iPod.

« Jeep? I thought we'd take your skateboard. »

He pulled out his right bud. « Come again? »

« We'll take my van. »

The Banque Laurentienne, the agent explained as we drove four and a half blocks, owned the church. « The bank impounded it and shit, eh? »

« Foreclosed. »

« What I said. »

I looked in my rearview, trying to locate the cat. Put my hand under the seat and felt fur.

« Never been in one of these before, » said the agent, looking up, down, around. « Pretty beat up, eh? »

I nodded. Like its owner, falling apart and hard to start. « It runs. »

« A shag wagon from the eighties, am I right? »

« You are. So the foreclosure— »

« You wouldn't want to a move up a notch, would you? Or two. I can sell you a Ford Bronco, full-size, mint, ten thousand klicks, ten thousand bucks. »

« No thanks. »

He looked at me through the overhanging hairs of the brow, as do some breeds of dog. « But ... I mean, if you can afford the church, why are you drivin' this shitheap? »

A good question, that. Which might need Freud to answer it. Sentimental reasons was the short answer. I went out on my first date in a van like this. But I'd driven wrecks my entire life, maybe because I felt sorry for them, maybe to confuse and confound my father. « So the foreclosure was one of those subprime loans? »

« Nah. The guy who bought it ended up in Ste-Anne-des-Plaines. »

I turned, gave my passenger a quizzical look.

« Penitentiary, » he explained.

We passed by an Esso sign, which I hadn't seen in the States for thirty years. And two Catholic churches, both boarded up. « Lots of boarded-up churches in this province, » I remarked as we drove into the bank parking lot.

« You been to Montreal? It's worse there, eh? »

A chance to display my knowledge of Quebec, a morsel gained from the Internet. « Mark Twain said Montreal was the first city he'd been to where you couldn't throw a brick without hitting a church window. »

The agent paused, scratched his head. « You couldn't take a dump without hitting a church window? »

Something lost in translation. Before I could clarify, the agent was shouting a greeting to someone outside the bank: a panhandling punkette sitting on the pavement with a geriatric dog shivering in a blanket at her feet. As we approached I saw that she wasn't a panhandler; she was a native Indian vendor whose wares were spread out on one side of the entrance. On the other side was a male, her companion presumably, asleep in a coffin of cardboard.

"The Quebec government is illegitimate," she said softly to me in English as I examined the items for sale. "As long as there are whites living on Native lands."

"Which lands would those be?" I asked.

« Don't bother with— » the agent began.

"The whole province," she replied. "I studied law. I'm going to enter the system and ruin it from the inside. Plant a time bomb under Western capitalism."

As I examined a turquoise necklace that I thought Céleste

might like, turning it over in my hands, the agent whispered into my ear, « I wouldn't go north of a hundred large on that property. In fact, if I was you I wouldn't go there at all. It ain't worth the back taxes. »

Unusual advice from a real estate agent. I gave the woman what she asked for, along with a twenty-dollar tip.

A look of disbelief, of befuddlement, warped the agent's features. « What the hell did you just— »

« Why isn't it worth the back taxes? »

« Did you *tip* her, for God's sake? Are you from the bozo farm? »

« It's freezing out here, » I said by way of explanation. « So why wouldn't you buy the church? »

The agent, still shaking his head, opened the bank door and walked in. I followed. We paused under the fluorescence of the vestibule, next to two cash machines. One of them had a smashed-in screen with an *Hors Service* banner draped over it. Beside the other, taped to the wall, was a missing-girl flyer I'd seen before.

« Because it's an Anglican church," the agent explained in a low voice, "and it's gonna get torched one of these days. Or its bone zone is gonna get bulldozed. »

The question was hanging there, so I asked it.

« Why? » repeated the agent. « 'Cause people blame it for the lack of investment up here, at least in Ste-Davnet. Nobody wants to sink money into a town that's haunted. With squarehead ghosts. »

« Squarehead? »

« Anglo. »

« Right. »

After the agent spoke briefly to the receptionist, we sat down on a bench and waited. For some reason, drops of perspiration began to trickle down the side of his face.

« But why are there swastikas on the crosses? » I asked. « Are there Jews buried with the Protestants? »

« I don't know, I don't think so. But ... it kinda makes sense. They both speak English, eh? »

Is there a toxic chemical up here, I wondered, making people taller but shrinking their brains?

« Plus—you're not going to believe this—they used to hold same-sex marriages there, eh? »

I looked suitably aghast.

« Plus they bury animals there, eh? » He snorted horsily. « They bury their goddamn pets! »

« Yeah, I saw some of the inscriptions— »

« And Indians too. Plus the Bogs is bad country, eh? Stinkin' black mud—with evil vapors, so they say. Something real bad is going to happen in the Bogs. A pond like that with no bottom. Marsh like a sinkhole. Hunters lose their dogs in there. A team of horses went down, way back when, dragging the driver with them. »

So that's why they dumped Céleste there. "What would a team of horses be doing in a cemetery? »

« The dead rich Anglos used to be carried in by horse-drawn carriages. After dark. With mourners carrying torches. »

« And hunters lose their dogs? What would hunters be doing in a cemetery? »

« Chasing lions. »

« I'm sorry? »

« Mountain lions. Cougars. »

« Eastern cougars? But ... aren't they extinct? »

« There's been sightings, eh? Maybe one a year for the past fifty years. Plus there's this ... local legend or myth or whatever you want to call it. Total crock, but some people claim there's a kind of monster in that swamp. A *diable des marais*. Cross between a Jersey devil and a mountain lion. »

« So the holes in the facade of the church? That's from ... »

« Nah, nothin' to do with people chasin' cougars or bog devils. I wouldn't worry about that. Just hunters havin' some fun. Tryin' to ring the bell. »

The bank manager, in a grass-green suit and wide flowered tie, leapt out of his chair to greet us. His hair was as short and neat as synthetic turf and seemed to have been glued on. When we shook hands I was distracted by his tan belt, which was about six inches too long, with the end curling out limp from the buckle.

He had an elongated name, Pierre-François O'Hanrahan-Latulippe, as if to compensate for his height, which was leprechaunic. *So they're not all giants up here ...* His office was also small—I could have broad-jumped from one side to the other without straining myself—with dark gray walls that made it seem even smaller. Even a Trappist might have found it a tad claustrophobic. On the wall above the manager's desk was a poster of a bearded man with a long tunic, cap and winged boots, identified as "Hermes, the Greek God of Commerce." What it didn't mention was that he was also the god of cunning, eloquence, fraud, perjury and theft.

« *Assoyez-vous, assoyez-vous,* » said the manager more than once, even after all of us were sitting down. He swivelled once, twice in his chair, then shot balletically to his feet with a lightness made possible by the scant claims of gravity on his five-foot frame. In an incongruous radio announcer's voice, rich and resonant, he described the property in impeccable French.

« I won't detain you with its historical details, but there's a book in the local library on it if you're interested. Just ask the librarian. She might even let you take it out if you mention my name. She's my wife! » Here he let out a brief, slightly scary laugh. He took out his handkerchief and wiped his brow before continuing. « The church, which was built over a hundred years ago, in 1906 to be precise, is yet another victim of two seemingly unstoppable forces in this province: the decline of mainstream Christianity and the decline of the English-speaking population north of Montreal ... »

Here the agent's flip phone went off, trilling out Iron Maiden's "The Number of the Beast." The agent unflipped and the manager yelled, « *Farme ton crisse de téléphone!* »

He then continued his history lesson, composedly, but not where he had left off. « Under a law passed in 1824, all church property in Quebec belongs to a corporate entity called a *fabrique*—not to the diocese. No one can force a church to close unless the *fabrique*'s governing board of wardens agrees. »

« And they agreed in this case, » I said after a long pause, because it seemed he had lost the thread. He was gazing out the window at something.

« For the usual reasons, yes. Declining attendance—non-existent, in this case, unless you count the half-dozen old-timers bussed in from the asylum. An aging clergy—deceased in this case—as well as the prohibitive cost of maintaining and heating two edifices. And yet despite all this, the church might have been saved if it had received a grant from the Religious Heritage Foundation. »

Again I waited for a time that seemed it might extend, without straining itself, to the following morning. « But it didn't, » I prompted. The manager remained silent, while the agent didn't appear to be listening. With a pout, he was eyeing a number on the face of his vibrating cell.

« No, it did not, » the manager replied. « Which means that it can be converted into a living space. That was your intention, I take it? »

I nodded.

« The property abuts provincial lands, » the manager continued, « in case you weren't aware, so there will be no ... development, at least not in the foreseeable future. If that was your intention, Mr. Nightingale. The Weskarini tribe, who were thought to have been wiped out by the Iroquois in the eighteenth century, have laid claim to nearly two thousand acres adjoining it, and the litigation, which involves both the federal and provincial governments, could well stretch into the middle of this century. »

I assured him that I was not a developer and had no intention of buying up the surrounding land. I wanted him to get to the point. « What's the asking price? »

The manager cleared his throat. « For the rectory or the church? »

« Both. »

« For the rectory, which is ... in need of renovation, plus the church, which is ... empty, plus four point two acres, which are ... wet, two ninety-nine. »

Thoreau paid twenty-eight dollars for his peace on Walden Pond. « I'll take it. »

The manager cocked an eyebrow. « Note that this price does not include the cemetery. Not that you'd want it anyway. »

I would actually. « Will someone ... you know, come and look after it? »

« The cemetery? No. Its days are numbered. According to the Non-Catholic Cemeteries Act, a cemetery may be condemned by the Ministry of Health if it is deemed 'dangerous to the public health.' »

« What do you mean, 'condemned'? »

« Bulldozed, I already told you, » said the agent.

Yes, but your information is about as reliable as Wikipedia's. « But ... why is it dangerous to the public health? » I asked the manager.

« The sinkholes, for one," said the agent. « Gangs, for another. »

« It's an orphaned graveyard, » said the manager. « Its volunteer trustees have grown too old and feeble to clear the brush or even mow the lawn. Its fences are in ruins and its headstones are crumbling, sinking into oblivion. It's become a target for vandals. »

« But didn't you yourself say it had historical significance? »

« I ... I was referring to the church. »

« But what if I buy the land the cemetery is on? »

« And then what? You repair the headstones, replace the fence, stop the vandalism? »

« Well ... yes. »

« The cemetery's not part of this sale, » said the agent.

« Maybe I could buy it from the owner. Who does it belong to? »

« For the moment, » said the agent, « the new owner wishes to remain anonymous. »

I'd had just about enough of the agent. He was coming very close to being slapped.

« Does this change anything, Mr. Nightingale? » asked the manager. « Are you still interested in buying the property? »

Not as much. « Yes, of course. Does it include the pond? »

« It includes right of access, » said the agent. « But I wouldn't go near it, if I was you. »

If I was you, I'd jump off the nearest high bridge. « And why is that? »

« I already told you. It's haunted and it's got no bottom and everybody calls it L'Étang des Noyés. »

« *Allons donc,* » said the manager. « Local superstitions, nothing more. »

« People've drowned in there. Schoolchildren gone through in their ice-skates. Bodies never found. »

« That's was over a half-century year ago, » said the manager. « In the winter of '58, to be precise. Skating's not allowed there anymore, although everyone knows it's perfectly safe. Especially the snowmobilers. »

The agent was now fidgeting in his seat like a schoolchild. I looked down and saw a drop of blood on his shoe; I looked up at a red nostril. The exploding vessels, the burned-out septum. A snowbird: I've been there.

« For the rectory, you'll want to hire an inspector, I presume? » said the manager. He adjusted the wide flowered tie covering his entire torso, which might have worked on a bigger man but on him looked like he was in the midst of the Amazon. « Before making an offer? »

« An inspector? Not necessary, I know it's a ... »

I stumbled here: other words from other languages came, but not the French or English. Years of addiction had dissolved certain words and phrases—like books you leave boxed in the basement whose pages are crumbling or stuck together when you look for them years later.

"A fixer-upper?" said the manager in unaccented English.

"A handyman's dream?" said the agent in accented English.

I filled out forms at triple-speed before changing my mind, before some other fool put in a higher bid. When the grinning manager and sniffling agent mentioned a credit check and bank approval, I wrote a Central Jersey Bank cheque for the full amount. I also handed them the business cards of my father's banker in Neptune and lawyer in Newark. This seemed to satisfy them, though they stressed that approval could take up to ten working days.

« You'll be able to spend Christmas there, » said the manager, « if all works out. How nice, how fitting! »

I thought of Céleste. « Indeed. »

"Do you have a number in Quebec where you can be reached, Mr. Nightingale?" This he said in English, almost as if he were testing me.

"No, I ... my lawyer's the best one to contact."

At that, the manager gave his knees a quick smack with two flat palms and jumped to his feet. He smiled and extended his hand, but then quickly withdrew it. Sat back down. « There's one other matter to discuss, Mr. Nightingale, I almost forgot. I hope I'm not prying, but do you have a lot of furniture, or are you planning on buying everything new? The reason I ask is that the previous occupants' belongings have not been cleared out yet, and ... well, it looks like they won't be. But don't worry about that. The price includes all the furnishings, so you can keep them or dispose of them as you see fit. Once this sale is finalized, everything will be yours. So you see, you're getting quite a deal. »

« I don't mind returning everything. Who do the things belong to? »

« A fat old hag, » said the agent. « Who died. » He now had toilet paper cigarettes stuffed in each nostril. « And her geek granddaughter. The whale and the baby hippo. »

« They were *exceptional* individuals, those two, » said the manager, displeasured brow crinkled. « No-nonsense types,

spitfires, full of piss and vinegar. Smart, talented, creative—
Renaissance women, both. We didn't deserve them and we
won't see their likes again, not around here, you can be sure
of that. »

« Thank God. »

« Dr. Jonquères had more degrees than … than this whole
town put together. In psychology, theology, mathematics. My
wife loved her to pieces—she went to the library almost every
day. She was the only one who read around here … And her
granddaughter, Céleste, she's a prodigy, a wunderkind. There
was an article about her in the paper. An absolute genius,
that girl. »

The agent stared at the manager with his mouth open.

"She's gone missing, poor thing," the manager continued.
"But she'll turn up, wait and see. Cély can outwit anyone.
Mind like a steel trap. »

The agent closed his mouth. « What was it they wanted to
turn the church into? What'd they'd call it? »

« An animal rehab sanctuary, » said the manager.

« And you're gonna laugh, » said the agent, « when you
hear what kind of animal they wanted to rehab. »

I asked what kind. Humans?

« Bears! » He burst out laughing.

I was puzzled. Why would bears need rehabbing?

« Céleste's actually the one who— »

« Everything belongs to the bank, » the manager interrupted.

This was a non sequitur, but it silenced the agent. And
left me thoroughly confused, and unsure of which subject to
pursue: the left furniture, the bears in rehab, or the bank's
ownership of the church. I turned to the agent. « Didn't you
say the church's previous owner was in jail? »

« Oh, that gentleman," said the manager, « never officially owned the property. He did make an offer, and it would have been accepted if it weren't for ... well, you know the rest. »

« I don't, actually. What's happened. What's he in for? »

« Illegal trading, mostly. Animal parts. Surprising for a religious man, for one educated at one of Quebec's oldest seminaries. He used to be a *diacre*, believe it or not, at the Église St-François in Ste-Madeleine. As I understand it, he wanted to turn the church—the Anglican church, that is—into a ... now what did he call it? »

« Field and stream emporium, » said the agent.

« Ah yes, a field and stream emporium. In fact, you might have noticed his Help Wanted sign on the front door ... »

« I did, yeah. Looks like he was trying to recruit from the local asylum. »

« That's because no one else would be caught dead in there, » said the agent. « I already told you—the place is haunted. »

A thought came, like the slash of a knife. « Does he own a big black 4 x 4, by any chance? With a busted headlight? And big grille out front? »

The bantam banker and beanpole realtor exchanged glances. « Not that I know of, » said the manager. The agent shrugged.

« What's a field and stream emporium? » I asked.

« It's a kind of animal ... joint," said the agent. « A one-stop, all-under-one-roof kind of thing. Sell 'em, buy 'em, stuff 'em, mount 'em, eat 'em, learn to kill 'em. And when the bishop gets out of prison, there's going to be trouble. I warned you. When he gets out you might think about movin' to China. »

The *bishop*?

« Now now, » said the agent, smiling the dim sort of smile seen on freshly killed corpses. « Don't mind him, Mr. Nightingale. Everything will be fine. Always is in this town. »

I shook the agent's big hand, which was as bony as a chicken claw, and the manager's small hand, shaped like a dove, no bigger than Céleste's. They each gave me their card. The agent then wagged his haircut toward the door. He opened it carefully and peered out, as if snipers awaited us. After motioning me out, he remained with the manager, closing the door slowly behind him. I stood there, listening to the babble of muffled voices inside.

Outside, through the window, I could see their shadows on the wall, as in a puppet show. They appeared to be bent over. With laughter.

ᥫ VII ᥫ

Inside the van I felt under the driver's seat, then the passenger seat, and scratched a furry little head. Pulled the two business cards out of my left breast pocket, my reading glasses out of my right. The manager and agent, I remarked, had the same last name. The pygmoid strain in the blood had evidently skipped a generation.

I thought of buzzing Céleste again but decided not to bother her. She can always buzz me ... I jumped out of the van and crossed the street, trying to ignore the little tingles on the back of my neck that made me feel I was being watched. To a store called Earls, a wood-framed building that looked fragile and temporary, as if abstracted from a low-budget western. Earl's apostrophe had been covered with white hockey tape and the "General Store" lettering bleached with solvent.

When I entered Earl was drinking pink Pepto-Bismol from the bottle. He was a man much advanced in years, with fluffy white hair like the seed sphere of a dandelion. His cheeks were absolutely purple. He wore a wool-knit sweater, perhaps white when first knitted but now caramel, with a '50s hockey player skating on his back.

I walked up and down the congested aisles before pulling out a Montreal *Gazette* and two packs of Pounce cat treats, which I found misplaced on a shelf of dusty art supplies. On the counter, by the cash register, was a basket of bananas one step away from compost and a bag of rolls with a sticker that said REDUCED BECAUSE THEY'RE STALE.

"You need anything else with that?" Earl asked in English. "Matches?" He held up a box of Redbird Strike Anywhere Matches.

For the newspaper or the cat treats? "Okay," I said. Business looked bad so I tossed in a bag of old-fashioned Australian licorice for Céleste and a bottle of Quebec wine called Harfang des Neiges ("Snowy Owl"). It was mixed in with a row of blue Gatorade, which reminded me of barbershop comb disinfectant. "How's business these days? How are the separatists treating you?"

He flexed his fingers and made the joints pop. "Break-in last week. First I thought nothin' was took. But a day or so later I see the Maalox are all out. You know, for the brown nasties? Imagine that. I think I know who done it too. A friend of mine, Bobby Adams, who's older than I am. Here's some advice for you—never trust anybody over ninety. And there was a flood too. Foot deep in the store."

"Last week, you mean, during the storm?"

"No, back in the eighties. Anything else? How about this?" He held up a New Year's Eve noisemaker, a ratchet device that he swung around feebly. "Or these?" He picked up a twin pack of playing cards, a scantily clad blonde on one deck, a scantily clad brunette on the other.

Cards wouldn't be a bad idea. "Um, well, okay, but are these the only ones you have? I need some for a teenage girl." I closed my eyes, wished I hadn't spoken that last phrase.

Earl took the cards from my hand and put them in the bag. "Teenage girls like these cards. They like smokes too." He winked at me before pulling back a burlap curtain, revealing shelves of cigarettes in cartons and bags with names like Native, Montcalm, Broncos, DKs. Fifteen bucks for a bag of two hundred.

"I'll take these," I said, grabbing some Popeye candy cigarettes from the counter and setting the pack atop the playing cards.

I paid in American bills and he handed me back, with fingers as brown and tough as dog paws, big Canadian coins. The dollar coins, I would learn later, are called "loonies" (having a loon on one side) and the two-dollar coins "toonies" (instead of, say, loons and doubloons). It's stuff like this you want to point to when Canadians say they don't understand why Americans make fun of them.

"Did you know that a man living in the States can't be buried in Canada?" he said, holding up one of the bills to the light.

This gave me a bit of a start. "I ... why is that?"

"Because he's still alive."

I let out a sigh. "Good one."

"My friend Bobby Adams told me that joke. Only one he knows, tells it over and over till you just want to clobber him. You heard it before?"

"No, that's ... the first time. I'll have to remember it. Listen, this Bobby Adams, he wouldn't know *the bishop*, would he?"

"The bishop? Who's the bishop? Joey Bishop? Bishop Tutu?"

I tried another tack. "He doesn't drive a black 4WD with *a broken headlight*, does he?"

"What's a 4WD?"

"It's all right, never mind."

"No, tell me."

"A four-wheel-drive truck. This particular one had a big grille and a rack of lights. And oversize tires."

The man seemed to be thinking it over. "Bobby Adams. He used to go around the neighborhood sharpening scissors. He always did good work."

Beside the door, in a spotless white plastic stand, was an incongruous array of ... I wasn't sure what. "Microgreens" it said on top, in professional lettering. Everything was labelled. Exotic stuff I'd never heard of, like red brassica and cilantro and perilla and tatsoi and mizuna and mache. Some of it was familiar: pea shoots, chives, watercress, arugula, red cabbage, fennel, French sorrel, Chinese edible chrysanthemum ... There were also some hairy and mucilaginous pods of okra, which I tossed into the bag.

"That's not a microgreen," Earl informed me.

"I'll still take it."

"My grandson's doing," said Earl, nodding at the stand. "He grows all this shit in his hothouse. Out Hawkshead way. He's queer as a French horn but he's a good boy. A crime against nature, the wife used to say. But she's dead now. And the stuff sells, eh? City people buy this crap. Cross-country skiers and snowshoers with their fancy getup."

I smiled because he was smiling. "This is for the okra." I rolled a double sawbuck into the shape of a cylinder and pushed it into Earl's sweater pocket. It seemed like a gesture the old man would appreciate.

Inside the van I coaxed the cat out from under the seat with a handful of Pounce, which I hand-fed her as she wobbled on my lap. She sniffed at the okra in my other hand, but let it be. Then returned to the passenger seat, sitting upright, staring calmly straight ahead. Home, James.

While struggling with the ignition, I glimpsed a snowplow at the top of the lane, blade up, coming at me at a fair clip. As it rumbled closer and closer I realized it wasn't going to stop.

Surely it would stop ... The cat jumped down, but I grabbed her before she could wriggle under the seat. I put her inside my coat, hurled the door open and leapt out.

The snowplow stopped, its blade an inch or two from my windshield. The driver leaned out the window, cackling. It was the same black-bearded man. « We meet again, *mon ami!* »

Yeah, long time no smell. I got back to my feet and set down the terrified cat onto the driver's seat. I closed the door as the driver turned off his engine.

« Had you goin', eh? Thought I was going to ram you? » His voice was even more nasal than before, to the extent that a clothes peg seemed to have been clipped onto his nose.

After wiping snow from my mouth, I conceded that ramming had crossed my mind.

« Now *that* was funny. Shoulda seen your face, eh? Wait'll I tell the guys back at the garage. I'm famous for that kind of stuff round here. You'll see. »

I told him it was one of the cleverest practical jokes ever played on me, and that I looked forward to seeing further examples of his work.

The snowplower blew out another high-pitched witch's cackle but stopped on a dime. He glared, breathing through enlarged nostrils, like an annoyed bull. «You messin' with me? You mess with me I'll take your teeth out with a wrench. »

I retorted in an unworded way.

He scratched at his beard with gloved fingers. « Time to scrap that shitheap, eh? Looks like it's been painted by a five-year-old. Then rolled down a mountainside. »

« It runs. »

« It wouldn't outrun a fatman. »

« It'd outrun your plow. »

The driver spat in the direction of a snowbank, without quite reaching it. By my foot was a viscous ball of speckled matter resembling toad spawn.

« You don't know who I am, do you? »

I waited to find out.

« Champion two years running of the Truck Rodeo, that's who. Over in Notre-Dame-du-Nord? Don't tell me you haven't heard of that. » He looked me hard in the face, defying me to tell him that.

I closed my eyes and pressed a finger upon my forehead. « I did hear about that, yeah. You were on *Oprah*, right? You and your truck? »

The driver considered the question briefly, his head at a quizzical-dog angle. « You messin' with me again? Like some wiseacre city fuck? You mess with me I'll make you cry. I coulda squashed you like a ladybug in your little Kraut van. Still can. »

I glanced over at the snowplow. While nodding in agreement I noticed something about its municipality markings. The letters had not been painted by a professional with a straight edge and steady hand. Or by someone who knew how to spell.

« I can do a 12.7, 12.8 quarter-mile in a semi, eh? »

I think you have me confused with somebody who gives a shit. « Very impressive. »

« You bet your ass it's impressive. » He belched. The cabbagey rot of his molars, mixed with whatever homebrew he'd been drinking—juniper berry and brake fluid—drifted toward me. « When you gonna get that coil fixed? »

« Coil? »

« Ignition. »

We'd had trouble with it the day he gave me a boost. I shrugged.

« And your exhaust. Sounds bad, eh? Cam and headers and God knows what else. »

I tend to procrastinate when it comes to repairs, when it comes to doctors or dentists or lawyers or mechanics. I treat my car the way I treat my life.

« Why don't you just hot-wire the sonofabitch? » he said.

Hot-wire the sonofabitch? I couldn't hot-wire a toaster.

« I'll do it, » he offered with the confidence of one who'd helped make Quebec the car-theft epicenter of Canada. « Simple as pissing in an ashtray. »

A literal translation. « No, it'll kick in. »

« Done it just about everywhere. All over this country, stateside too. I've been in just about every goddamn place and done just about every goddamn thing. Except one. Wanna take a guess at what that is? The one thing I never done? Go on, take a guess. »

"Uh, let me see ... used a toothbrush?" is not what I said. I was still picturing the van being squashed like a ladybug. I simply shrugged.

« I never went down on a dwarf. » His head went back and a series of loud guffaws exploded from his mouth.

At this flash of wit we both laughed, until his gasps and chokes subsided. « The bank manager turn you down? » I asked.

His wide grin vanished, quick as a wink, again turning into that confused-dog look. « What's that supposed to mean? You messin' with me again, city boy? You mess with me I'll lay you out flat and stomp on your head. Goodbye nose, goodbye teeth. »

This was his second threat involving teeth. Perhaps instead of snowplowing he should've gone into dentistry. From his higher vantage he began to stare at something on the passenger seat of the van. The cat? « I seen your van back there, eh? » He nodded south, in the direction of the real estate office. « Plannin' on buyin' somethin' in this lovely neck of the woods? »

« Maybe. »

« The Anglo church? »

How did he know that? I shrugged.

He climbed down from his rig. « I got you pegged for the new warden, workin' undercover like. Am I right?" He gave me an assessing squint while sticking a cigarette into the wiry scrub of his beard. « And that there's your showcar. »

« My what? »

« Showcar. For buys. Stings. »

I nodded. Did he mean for drugs? « Drugs? »

« No, nimrod, not drugs. Bear galls, paws, eagle feathers, that kind of thing. But I guess you wouldn't tell me if you was now, would you. »

This was the second time in one day that I had been called a nimrod. It means hunter. The "mighty hunter before the Lord" in Genesis. « No, I suppose not. »

« Got yourself a good disguise in any case. The hair, clothes, hat. You were smart, you fooled me. »

That wouldn't make me smart.

« Get yourself a mask and you can go trick-or-treatin' as Zorro. » He snorted porcinely before taking a long haul on his cigarette, halving it. « And that's why you've been splashin' them U.S. dollars around. Like you're a dealer, am I right? »

Was I being tailed? Where did he get this information?

He picked a fleck of tobacco from his lower lip. « So I guess you heard what happened a few months back to one of your ... comrades. Ranger or warden or animal-lover or whatever you want to call him. »

I shrugged.

« Now that surprises me, that surprises me a lot. It was a big story up in these parts. Where are you from, anyway? France? »

Despite the cold, the driver's coat was unzippered and shirt unbuttoned, displaying the hairiest chest I'd seen outside a zoo. « Yes. »

He shook out an unfiltered cigarette and offered the pack to me. « 'The French they are a funny race, they fight with their feet and fuck with their face.' My uncle used to say that. 'Cause you guys invented sixty-nine, eh? »

I was no longer much of a smoker but took what was offered—a brand called Hawks—and the driver tossed me a book of matches. On its cover was a platinum blonde with a seemingly inflatable bust, the same image as on Earl's playing cards. The French *invented* sixty-nine? « So what happened to the game warden? »

« Shot. Hunting accident. Funny thing was, he was wearing a bulletproof vest. Hit with a .500 Nitro. »

I had no idea what that was but mimed surprise. « The bullet went through the vest? »

« With one of those babies you can blast a hole in a wall big enough for a dog to jump through. But no, it didn't go through the vest. »

I waited as the driver drew another chestful of smoke from his reservation cigarette.

« The bullet hit him below the belt, if you get my drift. Bled out in three minutes flat, said one of the paramedics. Thing's like a fire hydrant the way it spurts out. »

He glared at me, his eyes shifting from my face to my groin, suggesting perhaps that if I was the new ranger the same would happen to me. He turned his head aside, seized his nose between thumb and forefinger and blew twin strings of mucus onto the snow. « You like girls? » He wiped his fingers on the inside of his army jacket's breast pocket, originally designed to carry grenades.

I pulled a match from the cartoon blonde, fired up the Hawk. « Yeah, sure. Or are you asking— »

« I ain't askin' if you're queer, no, I'm askin' if you like girls. Me, I seen too much muff. You heard of the Cave out on 117? That's my uncle's place. »

I blew out heavy blue smoke, dizzily. Glanced down at the address on the matchbook. « I've passed by. »

« Now guns—I like guns. Maybe you and me we go up in the mountains some time, kill some birds. »

Right. When cows learn to synchronize swim. « I'm not a hunter. »

« That's right, I almost forgot. You're one on them *enviros*, am I right? One of them *antis*. »

I had nothing against hunters—my Uncle Vince was one and he was a good man. Plus I had stopped weighing things on my scale of ethics, not because I didn't have one, but because it had been skewed for years. « Not really, no. »

« I know you ain't, I seen your rifle. »

Oh shit. « I ... I don't own a rifle. »

« I seen her too, eh? »

« Seen who? »

"Céleste Jonquères. I'd stay away from her if I was you. »

I answered with unhinged mouth and words that neither of us could make out. My brain was disconnected from my vocal cords.

« Half-breed hellcat. Just like her mother's tribe, all fighters and hotheads and generally all-around bad ones, ask anyone. Plus after what happened, she's just damaged goods, eh? Never be the same after what happened. Nope, never the same ... »

« But ... what happened? »

« She killed her grandmother, a 'mercy killing' she called it. She put the bag over her head 'cause she pleaded, 'cause she couldn't stand to see her suffer. A half-breed swamp slut, just like her mother. Shot out of a cannon. I'd steer clear of her if I was you. She's killed before and won't think twice about killin' you. »

I coughed out more words, questions, but the driver had already switched on his flasher and back-up beeper and was reversing out of the parking lot.

VIII

I'm now going to tell you what I know about my host, which is not a lot. His first name is Nile (his parents honeymooned in Egypt) & last name Nightingale (no relation to Florence). I've never felt comfortable with men, to tell you the truth — men & school, those are my kryptonite — but Nile might be an exception. He seems OK. He's distant & quiet, at least when he's not muttering to himself. I can spend time with him without him breaking into my thoughts. And he's smart enough too, for an American, for someone who believes in angels & the afterlife. "There was a herebefore and there will be a hereafter," he said to me. "Nothing in the universe, including the universe itself, can terminate entirely."

He talks malarkey like this, the gloomy little saint, but at least he doesn't use an adult tone or weird voice as if I'm a baby or puppy. He has a quiet voice & a grace & gentleness too, like a swan or some grallatorial bird. But one that's not from this area — an "accidental," one that's tired from flying so far off-course.

As far as looks go, he's what my grandmother called a Monet. Handsome as hell from a distance but not as much up close. His hair grows wild in thick clusters like it hasn't seen a brush in his lifetime & it seems to prefer standing up to lying down. He has dark-tinted reading glasses & dresses all in black with a purplish-red scarf like a retired pirate or rockstar roué.

He looks dead-tired, like a soldier coming back from a war or something, and his eyes are dog-sad, a bit like Jesus's in the east window of the Church. For some people, according to Grand-maman, there are things that happen in their lives that they just can't live with. Things that "take the shine off the universe." For Nile, it might have been his mom's death. Or maybe his dad beat him or something. Or maybe he suffered from "possession overload," what my grandmother called "affluenza," which is a kind of virus that makes people want more & more things but makes them less & less happy. "For everything you get, you lose an equal amount," she used to say.

Nile's mom was from a rich family & so was his dad, who was a doctor, even though he didn't have to work for a living. Nile was a "chip off the old block" because he got into med school when he was a teenager. To celebrate this, his parents gave him a car he always wanted: a Delage, an extinct French sports car from the 30s that he drove all over Paris & then had shipped over to the States. He showed me a picture. It's a wreck, just like the van he drives.

Nile grew up in Europe and Asia with cooks, cleaning ladies, chauffeurs & native-speaking nannies. Which explains how he speaks 5 languages (!?) & knows Chinese fairy tales. When he went back to the States & lived on his own he worked as a translator & still does from time to time. He said he saw one of his books at Walmart. When I asked him if he'd give it to me for Christmas, he said no, I wouldn't like it.

Nile also collects stamps. I'd never have guessed in a million leap years he'd have a hobby like that. I mean, is there anything nerdier? People call me a nerd for being interested in science &

reading all the time but I think he's topped me. But he says that Edgar Allan Poe & Sherlock Holmes & Julian Barnes were stamp collectors & so were Freddie Mercury, Kurt Cobain, Thom Yorke & the bass player of Arcade Fire.

Nile listens to classical music a lot. "Its audiences are going gray & will soon die," he told me one night. He also writes a lot in a journal — a black one with a silver lock & silver pen, which was a gift from his mom. Sometimes he copies stuff from my grandmother's books & reads them to me at night. Like José Saramago's line about not knowing whether the tree you plant will end up being the tree you hang yourself from. Is Nile thinking of killing himself too? Has he been reading my journal?

Not everything is good about Nile (it never is about anyone). There's something haywire about him. Tilted off centre. A spring-loaded kind of thing. Like he has a wickedly hot temper or fits of madness. I'll give you an example. After dinner last night (some kind of okra mash, which was totally gross), he drank some Scotch & his personality changed, a Jekyll & Hyde switch. He got funnier, more confident — and then a killer-on-the-loose look in his eyes. I thought things were really going to go sour — until I saw him pour the rest of the bottle down the sink. "A touch of brain fever, that's all," he said. "Happens from time to time." He turned on the tap & the water hit a spoon & bounced back up into his face & I didn't dare laugh.

★ ★ ★

Nile also sees things that aren't there. Everywhere he looks. Like Osama bin Laden in an icicled cliff, or a wolf biting a deer in a stain in the ceiling, or a brontosaur in the frosted front window ... I mean, I see them too, sort of, but only after he goes to great pains to point them out. Is Nile on something?

★ ★ ★

I'm starting to feel a bit better, to eat more, and now have an URGENT need for a cigarette. For a carton. Must put in another request.

★ ★ ★

Nile asked me today how I knew the "vet" from Ste-Mad & I said what makes him think I know her & he said that when he was getting me my sketchbook & glasses he saw a picture of her. I hemmed & hawed (I'm not a very good actress), then simply said it was none of his business.

★ ★ ★

I've been snooping around a lot (I'm a terrible snoop, my worst fault, according to my grandmother) & I should stop before Nile catches me in the act & strangles me or something.

★ ★ ★

I just found some things in Nile's duffle bag. As in criminal things. VERY scary ...

More later, I hear some noises out front. Like Gervais' plow. That's it for now & maybe forever.

ᎧᏇ IX ᏇᎧ

I fired up the engine first shot and flew back to the cabin, the speedometer needle juddering to the right of the circle, to a figure well past the limit for paved highways and double the maximum for winding dirt lanes in winter. My cargo shifted about as I pulled some hard G's on the curves. I used the hazard lane to pass cars, swerved to miss a fatality marker while buzzing Céleste on the two-way. Once, twice, three times, but no answer ...

With the cabin in view I reached under the seat, pulled out a bottle. The cat was now leaning into the windshield with her paws on the dashboard, balancing against the pitching of the terrain. I stopped the van, opened the door and she jumped out. I took a quick belt of Talisker, then another. Rolled down the fogged-up window.

Black cobras of smoke curled out of the cabin's chimney, and the light from inside made milky blue patches on the snow. The living room windows, their frames jagged with frost, looked like giant postage stamps. The door was narrowly ajar, its padlock hanging open.

I pushed it squeaking the rest of the way and looked into the small, dark, perfect circle of the barrel of a high-powered rifle. Céleste was holding it, her finger on the trigger.

A humming sound began inside my head—the sound of fear? sleep deprivation?—and a voice that seemed to come from a great distance, like the sound of faraway geese. I put my hands above my head, as they do in movies.

"Why'd you do it?" said Céleste in a small, dry eggshell voice. She was on the bed, sitting up, back against the wall.

I looked at her in perplexity, as if a dog or cat had just spoken. "But ... I thought you—"

"Yeah, it's a miracle, I can talk. They'll make you a saint one day."

"But how—"

"Get down on the floor, face down. Or I'll blow your head off."

Her voice sounded like a stroked balloon, like a young Marge Simpson. I lowered my hands but remained standing. "Why?"

"Because you tipped him off."

"Tipped who off?"

"Gervais."

"Gervais?"

"The snowplower."

"Shit. So he came back?"

"Take a look at the door, Sherlock."

Around the handle were splinters of wood, and the lock was scraped and bent. The only thing I had in common with Sherlock Holmes was dope fiendom. "What'd he want?"

"To make sure it was me. That's it. Because he didn't have a gun on him. And I did. He stayed like, thirty seconds."

I put my hands down. "I didn't tip him off."

"Get down on the floor," she said. "Or else."

"Else," I said. "I'm not getting down on the floor. I didn't tip him off."

"You already said that."

"So he'll be back?"

"No," she replied calmly, after a long stare. "But others will. Not today, probably not tomorrow. He's got to let his cousin know first. His cousin makes the decisions. Gervais' dumb as a horseshoe."

I could easily rush her, take the gun away. "And who ... where's his cousin?"

"In jail."

She's half my size, a third my age, and weak from injuries. Plus I'm fortified with drink. "When's he get out?"

"Soon."

With the rifle barrel she pointed to some gilt-tooled letters on my father's attaché. "These your initials, B.C.N.?"

"No."

Holding the rifle in one arm, she flipped the catches on the case, raised the lid. "You a drug runner?"

"No."

"Then why are there stacks of American cash in here?"

"Mad money."

"Next to a gun."

"You take a look at it?"

"The cash?"

"The gun."

"Why would I?"

"Because it's a water pistol."

"It ... whatever. How about this? She pulled out a slip of yellow paper from an inside sleeve of the case. "You're on the run, right?"

You can't run away—whatever you're running from, you just bring it with you: my father's unoriginal words. "Right."

"Because you're a perv? A pedophile?"

I closed my eyes. "Yeah. I'm the Humbert Humbert of the North."

"I want an explanation."

"I think I liked it better when you couldn't talk."

"I want to know who you are and what you're doing here."

"I could say the same."

"You escape from the pen or something?"

"No, I was pardoned by the governor. I was strapped in the chair when the power went off. Ice storm. Act of God."

Céleste stared at me, unamused. "Is the law hunting you?"

"Everyone's hunting me."

"What for?

"Picking up fourteen-year-olds and burying them in the woods."

"Because you're a criminal. On the run."

"I'm on the run."

"It's okay, I don't mind. It's all right if you were that way once—as long as you aren't that way now. I know lots of criminals. And ex-criminals. I'm one myself."

I thought of what the snowplower had said, that she was a murderer. "Interesting. I didn't know that about you. What crime did you commit?"

"There are many interesting things you don't know about me. I may tell you about those things later and I may not. It all depends. I haven't decided yet. Whether to confide in a *child molester*."

"Was it murder?"

A faint look of surprise. "I'm asking the questions. Are you a draft dodger?"

"There's no draft where I come from."

"Where do you come from?"

"Neptune."

She rolled her eyes. "What do you do for a living?"

"Tennis linesman."

She re-rolled her eyes. "Why did you bring your stamp albums? And all the other ... stuff."

"None of your business."

"Is that how you make your money?"

"Once upon a time."

"Are you an addict?"

My legs and arms still jerked involuntarily now and again, especially in bed, hypnagogic and hypnopompic lurches. She must have noticed. "Recovered."

"Cocaine? Heroin?"

Crack, crank, X, special K, LSD, you name it. I drew the line only at bleach, Sterno, gasoline, formaldehyde, glue and cleaning products. "Mostly alcohol."

"And you quit?"

A friend of mine quit for two years, then out of curiosity or nostalgia did one single binge and died of an overdose. I knew the same could happen to me. I stared at Céleste in silence.

"Talk. Pretend I'm an adult."

She had a point. "Eleven years, maybe not all that time but most of it, I've been trying to quit. It's a high ladder." The twelve-step ritual, the curriculum of deprivation and pain. Struggling to not give in, to keep everything in balance, to see pleasure not as an end but an accident. "After my father dies? I stop on a dime. No AA, no NA."

Céleste put down the rifle, deftly removed the cartridge. She began talking about symbols and Freud, but I wasn't following; my thoughts were miles to the southeast. If I wanted symbolism I'd go watch early Bergman. The next thing I knew she was flicking out a thumb and four fingers.

"I have ... three, four, five more questions," she said. "All right?"

"If I get five."

"One. What's this?" She held up a photocopy of a legal document, a complaint for damages served by my ex's lawyer.

"An extortion attempt. By someone more screwed up than I am."

"Your wife?"

"Ex-girlfriend." In all fairness, my ex's lawyer is probably more screwed up than she is.

With her hand Céleste made a gun, aiming it at the attaché. "Where'd all the money come from?"

"From a bank."

"As in bank robbery?"

"Sort of. It used to be in my father's account." I sighed, wondering how much I should add to this. "I didn't feel like leaving an AmEx trail a mile wide, okay?"

"Who's trailing you?"

"My ex's lawyer, for one."

"What does he want?"

"She. The money in the bank. Or as much of it as she can get."

"And you're not going to give it to her."

"No." The hardest part was losing Brooklyn. She wasn't mine, I wasn't married to her mother, I had no legal rights. "But I might give some to her daughter."

"Brooklyn Jessica Martin? The girl you abducted and molested?"

Sex charges have become a hackneyed form of revenge, yet they're still effective, always believed—you can destroy anyone that way. Once that poison gets into the air, it never really goes away. "Allegedly."

She snapped the attaché lid down, the reports of the catches like distant gunshot. "So you're going to pay her off?"

Not that's it provable, not that it has any weight in a court of law, but if you asked Brooklyn who she loved more, who she really wanted to be with, she'd have said me. "No, she'll tell the truth eventually." I flashed to the first time she took my hand as we walked on the boards, by the sea, the way she tugged on my coat to get my attention. Young girls are like old cats: if they don't like you, nothing on God's green earth will make them pretend they do.

I could see in Céleste's eyes that she still believed I was a perverted swine who'd bear watching. "That's more than five questions, isn't it?" I said.

"One last one?"

"If I get five."

"Why weren't you afraid? I was pointing a *rifle* at you. I scared seven shades of shit out of Gervais."

What could I say? That I didn't care about living? That with every day of life more and more is being subtracted from less and less? Minus this second. Minus this second. That I was tired of collecting the millions of minutes, killing the idle thousands of hours? That the end years, awaiting AD or the big C, would not be golden but tin?

"I've led a long pointless life," I said finally, "with more behind me than in front. So what's to be afraid of?"

To my surprise, Céleste's eyes began to moisten. This wasn't my aim. She turned her head so I wouldn't see. "You're old," she said, "but you're not *that* old."

I had the weariness of the old. *A struggling spentwing drifting through the universe:* my father's words. Death had been a faint dirge inside me since my teens; it was now a loudening song, like the one sung only once by a dying swan. I was 44—the Chinese double digit for death—and knew I wouldn't see 45.

"I *feel* old. Felt that way most of my life. You wouldn't understand, Céleste, not at your age."

She continued to avert her gaze, staring hard at the floor. "I do understand," she said, almost inaudibly. I moved closer to hear her and saw tears popping in the corner of her eyes like glass beads. "Really I do. I've already gone through it. What Grand-maman called *le réveil mortel*."

Réveil mortel. The wake-up call to death, to the reality of death. The recognition, the acceptance, of your own mortality that marks the end of childhood. My mother used the same phrase ... I must *pretend* to be alive, I thought to myself, to have hope, spirit, for the sake of Céleste, so that she won't give up. She's *fourteen*, for Christ's sake. I considered and dismissed four or five things to say, then did something that surprised us both: I put my arm around her. Gently at first, but when she threw her arms around me and sobbed against my chest I held her as tight as I'd held anyone. I then lowered her head onto the pillow and watched her curl up, fetally, with a clump of sheet in her mouth. I pulled the wool blanket up to her chin and sat in an armchair beside her until she drifted off.

I picked up the coverless novel I had found next door, which one critic called "pure poetry." A half-hour later, a half-page in, Céleste turned to face me, palming her blotched eyes. She was awake and ready to talk, she said, ready to answer what she knew would be my questions. Her voice was little more than a whisper but I hung on her every word.

X

Let's be clear about something. I'm not writing this to attract attention to myself or tell you every last detail about my stupid private life — it's not like a blog or something. My grandmother said that kids today have no sense of shame, no sense of privacy, that they're showoffs, fame whores who post their diaries, cell numbers, stupid poetry & nude photos online. Who talk in illiterate instant messages. I'm not like that. My grandmother wouldn't let me be like that. She wouldn't even let me watch TV. Which may be why I have no friends & no one talks to me.

No, I'm writing this journal so that others will know the truth after I'm gone. I hope that even useless, powerless people like me can leave something useful & powerful behind. I want to feel that my life has amounted to more than just taking up space, breathing in oxygen, consuming products & generating garbage.

★ ★ ★

It all started with a total accident. I was walking in the forest in the fall with my binoculars & motion-sensitive camera (both gifts from Gran), trying to spot a wolverine or lynx — two of my favourite animals because they're very rare & very beautiful. Gran said she'd seen both animals in the northeast woods around this time last year. Two women hunters shot a lynx in this area, she said, because they thought it would make a good rug. I'd like to make a good rug out of them. Anyway, on my way home, after not seeing a trace of either a lynx or a wolverine (no footprints, no scat), I took a shortcut that I hardly ever take because it's rough & dangerous. Hunters & bikers hang out along this path.

They'd probably kill me on the spot if they caught me doing the things I do. For example, not too long ago I found the body of a cottontail rabbit & when I went to bury the poor thing I saw a tube buried in the ground beside it. It's called an M-44 cartridge & it's illegal. It's a spring-loaded device & comes with smelly bait. When an animal tugs on the bait, the spring shoots a pellet of sodium cyanide into its mouth. When cyanide mixes with moisture, it turns into a deadly gas. I showed it to my grandmother & we took it to Inspecteur Déry, who's a wildlife officer, and he said he'd look after it but he didn't seem to care & he didn't do a thing about it. More on him later.

I was following what looked like cougar tracks (?!), which look a bit like a dog's but are bigger. Obviously. Here's how to tell the difference:

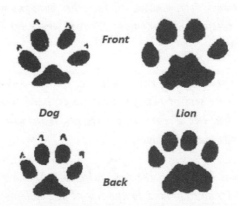

Front

Dog   Lion

Back

Nobody has seen a cougar in these parts for years, so I was probably wrong. Along the way, though, I found two things, a leg-hold trap, which I smashed with a rock, and then some "dirty bait" under a birch tree, with a wooden platform nailed to the branches above it. The bait was made of anise seed, gummy bears & chocolate-covered raisins. I buried everything in a dried-up creek bed, scared out of my mind that someone would see me but no one did.

I continued along the path, and sometimes off the path whenever I saw a beer can or a strip of cloth tied to a tree, which are both used as bait pile markers. I found a Vienna sausage tin, an orange Cheezie bag & two rotting wedges of pizza, all-dressed. Plus scat, which was human, a huge pile flagged by a banner of toilet paper. Treats for the forest creatures.

It was near dusk when I passed the old drive-in, where you can still see some of the posts where the speakers used to be, and the old bowling alley, which has been closed for years too. I was surprised to see a light coming from inside. Along with smoke or vapor coming from a vent. I was going to keep walking, but since I'm a total snoop I walked over to see if I could see anything through the back door window. All the other windows were boarded up, except a high one near the roof where the light was coming from.

I couldn't see anything but I could hear things. And what I heard was these sort of high popping sounds, hard to describe really, and then two or three loud screeches. They were not the kind of sounds made by humans.

I was about to bang on the door but changed my mind at the last second. I walked around to the side of the building & looked up, at the high window. If I could somehow get up on the roof, which was flat, I might be able to lie on my stomach, swing my head over & look through the top of the window. But I'd need a long ladder to get up on the roof & there weren't any ladders around. (And if I had one, I wouldn't need to get to the roof, just to the window!) I didn't like the idea of going all the way home & back for a ladder, especially since it would be dark by then, so I tried to think of something else.

I walked around to the front entrance. On the crumbling parking lot overgrown with weeds was a black SUV with dark-tinted windows. And next to the SUV was a red maple, which stretched above the roof. Young maples are not the best climbing trees, and even if I managed to climb it, there was a big gap between the roof & the nearest branch — one strong enough to hold me without snapping in two. Assuming I could climb the tree, I would have at least a two-metre jump. And then how would I get down?

I climbed the tree. I won't describe the perils of the climb, or how agile I was despite being overweight or how I walked right to the end of the branch like a chimpanzee, risking life & limb. Because that would be bragging. There was something about those sounds coming from inside that got my adrenalin going, that pushed me on.

Upside down with my binoculars, a camera dangling from my neck, feeling blood rushing to my head & mountain sickness, I leaned over the edge of the building & peeked through the window.

Here's what I saw: small metal cages, about twenty of them, on two of the old wooden bowling lanes. There was shadowy movement in some of them, but from my angle I couldn't tell what kind of animals were inside. And if I leaned out any farther, I'd fall right off the roof!

So I made my way back to the maple. I didn't like the look of the jump, so I tried to find another solution. There was a small mound of earth not far from the tree, by the north side of the building, covered with couch grass & laurel shrubs. If I hung from the roof by my fingertips & let myself drop, I might land safely.

It was a surprisingly soft landing. I survived it with only a few scratches on both arms & both legs. I knew I shouldn't have worn shorts! Now, I thought, I would go around & bang on that door.

But I didn't have to. Before I got there I heard the creaking sound of the door being opened. When I reached the corner I peeked out & saw a man bend over & stick a piece of wood in the door frame. As a door jamb. Then he lit a cigarette, cupping his hands around it the way gangsters do in old movies. He was short with greased black hair. An Oriental man.

I picked up a rock, stood back from the side of the building & threw it up toward the roof with all my strength. I could hear it bounce off the roof & land in the bushes on the other side.

I went back & snuck another quick look from behind the wall. The man was still standing there, smoking. Was he deaf? I thought of going around to the other side, to the bushes, and shouting out something. But what would that do? I couldn't think of anything else, so I did the same thing — picked up another rock, a bigger one, and heaved it toward the roof.

This time I heard him shout out something. I watched him walk toward the sound, toward the bushes, his back to me. I tiptoed over to the door, removed the door jamb & closed the door. With me on the other side of it.

What have I done now? I asked myself as my eyes adjusted to the light. "Hello?" I said softly, my voice cracking. "Hello?" I shouted. No answer.

★ ★ ★

I walked down a small flight of stairs to another door, which I thought would be locked. I pulled on it hard with both hands & it scraped open like it was on a chalkboard. What a smell!! A gross mix of things. So powerful I nearly gagged.

I sidled along a rough concrete wall till I reached what used to be the side lane of the bowling alley. Directly in front of me is where the automatic pinsetter would have been. But now there was just a hole. "Hello?" I called again.

Along two of the middle bowling lanes, which used to be wood but were now mostly cement, I could now see the dim outlines of cages. There were bare light bulbs here & there dangling from the ceiling, but they didn't give much light. As I walked to the cage nearest to me, after stumbling in one of the gutters, I heard some pounding on the back door.

At first I didn't understand what I was seeing inside the cage & then it made me sick to my stomach. A bear, a large Black Bear, was trapped inside a cage so small he couldn't move. There were metal bars all around it & the floor was made of bars too

— he had nothing solid to stand or sit on. He moaned & reached a paw out of his cage. I grabbed the paw & held it, which was not the smartest thing to do. It was then that I saw a metal tube sticking out of a hole in its belly.

There were over a dozen cages, set up over a metal trough that water flowed through into a drain. It smelled awful. There was also a strange contraption that looked like a shower stall with strips of dangling plastic for a curtain. On the floor beside it was a huge silver boom box.

I moved on, quickly. In one of the cages were two cubs, who were making that popping & screeching sound I heard earlier. From the other cages, I began to hear low, deep growls.

I closed my eyes & took a long breath. Then grabbed my camera. I snapped away blindly, at the cages, inside the cages, at the stall, anywhere & everywhere until I heard sounds coming from the front of the building. A door slamming, then footsteps on cement.

I ran toward the back door, along the wall & up the steps. At the door, I paused, afraid there was someone waiting for me on the other side. Should I ditch my camera?

As I was looking around for a place to hide it, I heard clicking noises, like someone was running down one of the bowling lanes with baseball spikes or golf shoes. And then some shouted words that I didn't understand, neither French nor English. I pushed the door open.

Nobody waiting, no ambush. I sprinted toward the path, the dangerous path that my grandmother said never to take, which I could now barely see in the half-light. I ran & tripped & got up & ran some more, sobbing for breath, on & on, pushing through the trees. Every time a bird chirped or branch snapped I thought it was some bad guy come to tackle me. I ran with a painful "stitch" in my side, until my lungs nearly exploded, until I thought I was going to die. After a while I could barely make out the path & began to run into branches & bushes & briars. But when I saw a steeple through the branches I knew I was almost there, back home, back with Grand-maman. With a story that was too awful to believe, that I barely had the breath to tell.

★ ★ ★

Bears are classified into 8 species. The largest is the Brown Bear (Grizzly & Siberian), followed by the Polar Bear, American Black Bear, Asiatic Black Bear, Sloth Bear, Panda, Spectacled Bear, Sun Bear. The Koala is the smallest of all, but it's not really a bear. All of these species are endangered.

They are hunted for many reasons: trophy hunting (especially North America, Europe), pest control & nuisance bears (Japan,

USA), food & body fat (Canada, Turkey), and medicinal purposes
(worldwide). Wild bears caught as cubs are also used for
entertainment purposes, either as dancing bears (India, Pakistan,
Bulgaria & formerly Greece & Turkey) or in bear-baiting
(Pakistan & formerly throughout Europe), where dogs attack a
bear chained to a stake.

For obvious reasons, I would like to talk about the medicinal
reasons for capturing or killing bears. China was the first
country to use bear bile & gallbladder in traditional medicine, over
5 centuries ago. It's now used for just about everything: burns,
inflammations, sprains, fractures, haemorrhoids, hepatitis,
jaundice, convulsions, diarrhoea, and so on. It's put in wines, tea,
eye drops, suppositories & shampoos.

It was the Chinese Crude Drugs Company that came up with
the idea of "bear farming," of extracting bile from bears raised in
captivity. Which they called "milking." Hundreds of small farms
were set up where individuals or families could keep bears in
cages in their houses. "Superfarms" came next, which today hold
thousands of bears.

Bears (most often Black Bears) are caught in the wild or
born on the farm & through a surgical procedure have a metal
or rubber catheter inserted into their bile duct or gallbladder.
The bear's bile fluids are then "tapped" from a tube coming
out of its belly. In some cases, the bile leaks into a plastic sack
continuously. In other cases, the tube is opened & drained out up
to four times a day. To prevent the bears from scratching at the
bile sack or catheter, they are often fitted with a metal jacket
or "corset." Or their necks are snared with wire.

To make milking easier, the bears are sometimes declawed & their teeth cut out or filed back. Many of the farm workers who collect bile wear crash helmets. Why? Because during milking bears may gnash their teeth, kick, bite, or hit their heads against the bars. After it's over, the bears are more peaceful — they curl up in their cages, trembling, holding their paws to their stomach.

The animals are lured into these "milking cages" or "squeeze cages" or "coffin cages" with water containing sugar or honey. The bears have no free access to water at other times, so they will be very eager to drink. For the pleasure they pay a high price.

To restrict their movement, the cages are small, measuring around 1 metre by 1 metre by 2 metres. Pressure bars hold the bears down. The animals, which can weigh up to 260 pounds, can barely sit up or turn around. The bars pressing against their bodies leave scars, some over a metre long. Because the cage floors are made of widely spaced metal bars, the bears can never rest their feet on flat ground. So they end up with bleeding lesions.

Most bears have broken & worn teeth from biting the bars — if their teeth haven't been pulled out beforehand. They also have injuries to their heads, paws & backs from repeated rubbing & banging against the cage bars.

At some farms, where cage bars are more closely spaced, bears are forced to lie in their own feces, which may be several centimetres deep. In these cases, the animals try to create latrines in their small spaces.

In the winter the bears are not allowed to hibernate, despite temperatures that can drop to minus 30. It should be remembered that these are naturally solitary animals. They are wild animals with wild instincts. They are inquisitive & range over a large territory. The claustrophobia they must feel — it's beyond imagining.

The mortality rates are high, with 60-80% of bears dying during or shortly after their bile operation. The average life span of bears with catheters is under 10 years. The life span of Black Bears in the wild is 25 to 30 years.

The captive bears live their lives in permanent pain. This is the only case I've heard of where an animal wants to die, mutilates itself & tries to commit suicide.

★ ★ ★

The cubs that are born on farms are taken away from their mother when they are 2 to 3 months old, whereas in the wild the cubs would stay with their mothers for 2 to 3 years. They are taught circus tricks — standing on their hind legs, handstands, carrying chairs, walking a tightrope, throwing a ball, riding a bicycle, boxing & so on — to attract visitors to the farms, to help market the bile products. Being photographed with the cubs is part of the fun.

The performing life of a bear is short — it may last only for a year or two. Once a bear reaches two and a half, they will be put in the cages & milked. When they stop producing bile, they are no longer fed. They are either left to die or killed for their paws & gallbladder. In most bear farms, the bears' paws can be cut off *if a customer requests it. Fresh bear paw costs around $250 & in 4-star hotels a bear paw dish sells for around $500.*

★ ★ ★

When bear populations in Asia began to drop because of overhunting, wildlife traders looked for bear gallbladders in other countries. North American Black Bears, Grizzlies, Polar Bears & even South American Spectacled Bears have been found slaughtered in the wild with just the gallbladder removed. Smugglers have been caught with whole gallbladders dipped in chocolate, trying to pass them off as chocolate figs, or packed in coffee to hide the smell. The growing trade is driving some species, such as the Sun Bear, toward extinction. In Canada alone, the illegal trade in bear parts is estimated to be worth $100 million a year.

In the 1950s Japanese scientists chemically synthesized UDCA, the active ingredient in bear bile. It's widely available & cheap. There are also over 50 herbal alternatives to bear bile, including Chinese ivy stem, Madagascar periwinkle, dandelion, Japanese thistle & chrysanthemum. Still, people want the "real thing." As my grandmother used to say, old myths & magic potions, like religions, die hard.

To be continued ...

XI

Céleste was telling me all about "bear farming," things that boggle the mind, chill the spine, when she suddenly stopped and said, "To be continued." She then closed her eyes, curled up next to a purring Moon, and fell instantly asleep.

"I have to leave you alone again," I explained to her sleeping body and again in a note, "but this will be the last time." I took my customary precautions, placing her weapons and two-way within easy reach, bolting the windows, closing the curtains. You couldn't trust a teenager these days to look after a hamster, but I trusted Céleste to look after the shack, don't ask me why.

As I opened the door I got a surprise, not from outside from inside. Moon leapt off the bed and shot through my legs, out onto the snow. She waited for me by the van, calmly biting ice from her claws.

The real estate agent was not in his office and the bank manager was on vacation, but there was a padded envelope of documents waiting for me at the bank's reception desk. Along with a small, gift-wrapped box with a green Post-it on top. Normally, I would've ripped them open on the spot, but my mind was elsewhere. I couldn't get those bears out of my head. I sat down on a chair in the lobby and stared gloomily at the burnt-orange carpet. What was the end of the story? What happened to them?

I eventually rose from the chair and stood in line to pay off a sheaf of overdue oil, electricity and phone bills from the rectory. When that was done, I sat back down and listlessly opened the envelope.

The sale had been approved, the manager wrote in his impeccable French in one letter and the agent in his peccable French in another, although there remained certain formalities to go through with a notary in Ste-Madeleine in January. Nevertheless, I could move into the rectory for Christmas, on or after the 22nd, if I wished, and enter it for inspections or repairs anytime before then. I looked at my watch: it was the 19th. I was dumbstruck, expecting thickets of red tape and a mountain of back taxes or fines to settle. Or an outright rejection. I ripped open the gift box and pulled out a brown-and-green leather key wallet. Inside it were six brass keys and a silver crucifix. *Joyeux Noël!* was written on the Post-it, in two different handwritings. Bless them.

Except now I was having second thoughts—third and fourth and upward—about the move. Was this the right place for Céleste? How harrowing, re-horrifying, would that be? Not only was she dumped in church mud, but her grandmother was boxed in it. And she'd be a prisoner there—she'd never be able to step outside. I should find another hideout, where no one knows her. In Alaska, say, or New Jersey ...

On my way out I passed the two Native vendors, who were setting up shop. The man was clearing away snow with a wooden board, preparing his bed of cardboard, while the other was unfurling a blanket with the colored pattern of a jaguar, in whose coat the Mayas saw a map of the starry heaven. A placard lying on the ground said DEMOCRACY WILL NEVER WORK. THERE AREN'T ENOUGH SMART PEOPLE TO ELECT SMART PEOPLE. As an American, I felt she had put her finger on something. I smiled at her, but she didn't smile back. I continued on.

"Want a swan?" she asked in English.

I stopped, thinking I'd misheard. "A what?"

From a cloth bag with a drawstring, she pulled out a pearlescent figurine and handed it to me. It wasn't a swan, it was two swans, with their bills and breast feathers conjoined. A fine piece. Nicely proportioned, intricate detail. Although I know nothing of these things.

"How much?" I said, reaching a hand into my pocket. The bird was a favorite of Céleste's. No other waterfowl, she said, was as fast in the water or air.

"A gift," she said.

I pulled out a thick slab of twenties, hesitated, then put it back. "It's a beautiful piece," I said. "Did you make it?"

She pointed toward her friend. "He's the artist. I'm the anarchist."

I looked over at the artist. "Thank you," I said, but he didn't look up from whatever it was he was doing. "That's very kind of you ... both." I'm a fool for things like this, these unexpected acts of kindness, so I got out of there fast, before I started bawling or something.

The van was a little balky, the way only a thirty-two-year-old vehicle can be, but I hung in there until the engine kicked to life. Headed toward the church, now my church, bearing a ring of golden keys. "What treasures will these unlock?" I asked Moon, shaking the keys in front of her. She swiped at them, once, twice, with her right paw. I was adrenalized—she and I both—but kept to the speed limit, or a hair above. An impatient motorcyclist rode my bumper for a while, which I couldn't figure out. It was a two-lane highway. What did he expect me to do? Speed up? Pull over to the shoulder? When I did neither he passed me on a solid line, while tapping his finger against the side of his head. He had the biggest, blackest, loudest Harley ever made. On the back of his leather jacket were letters stencilled in white:

> IF YOU CAN
> READ THIS
> THE BITCH
> FELL OFF

As I neared the church the sun moved behind a mountain and everything went gray, as if a giant bird had just spread its wings. At this latitude, at this time of year, the sun sets before five. No wonder they drink as much as I do. Did.

In the failing light, at the front door of the rectory, I misinserted three of the keys while clutching Moon to my chest. Before trying the fourth I noticed the door had a metal clapper, a splendid winged-cat gargoyle that I was surprised wasn't stolen. It made me think of Scrooge's pareidolia, his perception of Marley's face in the door knocker ... The cat began to scramble so I tried the fourth key, which fit. The door resisted at first, then opened with a luscious crunch. I set Moon down and she scampered down the hall, toward the kitchen.

I should have been dancing on air—pride of ownership, symbolic passage and all that—but all I could think of was the death that occurred upstairs. And that the place wasn't really mine. I was about to move on, to the church, when I remembered something more pressing. Leaving wet boot tracks, I made my way down the wood-floor hallway to the kitchen. Only five of the six cats answered the dinner bell.

Mercury, Venus, Jupiter, Pluto and Comet. Moon seemed to have disappeared.

On my way to the church I couldn't resist taking a long-cut through the ruined graveyard, which looked like something out of Poe in the crepuscular mists and eerie polar half-light. From a pine or spruce came the threnody of a sparrow, a white-throated sparrow known as the Canada bird, according to Céleste, because of the song the males sing: Oh-sweet-Canada-Canada-Canada. A trio of crows began to drown it out, cawing as they hopped from stone to stone, chortling at my wingless body. I followed them to a tall white pine, under whose skirt of branches I glimpsed three tiny headstones. One had a smashed, forgotten wreath. The others were defaced with felt-tip capitals: FLQ! on one; BETTER DEAD THAN GAY on the other. Must ask Céleste what FLQ stands for. And what solvent best dissolves Magic Marker.

Beyond the tree was the section reserved for animals, which the real estate agent had found so preposterous. I paused to examine the modest stones. The epitaphs—poignant, sad—often contrasted humans with beasts. There was this tribute, for instance, the oldest one I could find, to an Irish setter named Bailey, died December 31, 1906:

> Approach, vain man! and bid thy pride be mute;
> Start not—this monument records a brute.
> In sculptured shrine may sleep some human hog—
> This stone is faithful to a faithful dog.

And this one to a husky named Grey, died April 5, 1942:

> Here rests the relics of a friend below,
> Blessed with more sense than half the folks I know;

Fond of his ease and to no parties prone,
He damned no sect, but calmly kept to his own;
Performed his functions well in every way,
Blush, Christians, if you can, and copy Grey.

As I was mulling these words over I heard a series of sounds, seconds apart, from two different directions. First the noise of a revving engine from the church lane. Then a louder sound, a growl from directly behind me. I turned round. All the hairs on my body prickled up, and my face felt like it was on fire. A large cat, like a sabre-toothed tiger, was crouching in front of me, with a head and body tinged with gold, and a tail at least three feet long. I yelled out, not from fright, not to scare it away, but because I felt its claws, or conceivably teeth, sinking into my right leg. I closed my eyes in pain before kicking out furiously with both feet, thrashing the air with both arms. The sequel was dead silence. I opened my eyes and the cat was gone. I looked down: no tattered clothes, no teeth or claw marks ...

Another *ignis fatuus*, another sign of an unsound mind, nothing more. As I shook my head in disgust, another sound, this time very faint, came from the same direction. A little white cat—Moon—was scratching at the snow and mud between two crooked, crumbling stones, where other cats were buried and where, soon enough, she would be buried too. Her effect on me was strangely tranquilizing, exactly what I needed after being scared half to death. When she saw me she headed my way with finical steps, but after a few feet gave up and cried after me in her narrow voice. I walked toward her, she walked toward me, we met halfway. I picked her up and she rode back to the rectory on my shoulder.

🕊 🕊 🕊

Someone had parked a red sports car out front, as close to the front door as possible without driving it into the living room. Its driver, whose foot rested on the back bumper as he fiddled with some hand-held device, looked vaguely familiar. An actor?

I set Moon down and opened the front door for her. Then walked toward the visitor. « *Je peux vous aider, Monsieur?* »

He didn't answer me right away, or even look up from his device, so I had some time to look him over. Around my height, a hair over six feet, but built like a tractor. One of those thin beards that trace the line of the jaw and a mustache just as thin, each of them brindled, the color of used kitty litter. Fluorescent orange hat, heavy rubber waders, and a game vest with a rubber packet in the back where the bleeding birds would lie. Everything top of the line and brand new, as if he'd just snipped the plastic price loops.

He slipped his BlackBerry or iPhone into a breast pocket, squinted at me, held out his hand. « François Darche. »

Right, of course. He was a hockey player, an "enforcer" with the Minnesota Wild, recently retired or fired or suspended. I was prepared to be maimed by the handshake, but it proved to be rather spongy. As we traded wary smiles, I wondered what a *hockeyeur* could possibly want with me.

What he wanted, he quickly explained, was an "easement" through church lands to the luxury home he was building six miles away. A shortcut, in other words.

« But it's a cemetery, » I informed him. « And wetlands. »

« The cemetery part I already took care of. As for your swamp, we just fill it in, put in a gravel road. Like a causeway or whatever it's called. »

« A causeway? It's a biome, for God's sake. »

« What's that mean? »

I wasn't sure. « It's a ... an ecosystem. » I was trying to remember what Céleste had told me. « It's got a heronry and swannery and ... lots of other ... ry's." Froggery, duckery? « Do you know how many creatures you'd displace—kill—doing that? »

Not for the first time, Darche shot a quick glance at his Ferrari, as if worried some delinquent brave or bear would drive off with it. A powerful-looking bow sat on the passenger seat, the razor points of its arrows glinting in the dying sun.

« What's a few turtles and toads? I'm offering you twenty grand, Reverend. »

The area was thick with these types, according to Céleste. Bankers and lawyers and hockey players who carted their friends and business partners through the Laurentians in decked-out Land Rovers and ATVs, shooting and hooking all moving feather, fur and fin.

« It's probably a giant mosquito hatchery, » said Darche. « And the rot—it must stink to high heaven around here. Think about it. Twenty big bills. »

I shook my head.

« Twenty-five. »

I paused, as if considering it. « How much you make last season? » You could ask athletes questions like that these days, since it's part of their stats.

He smiled. « Two point four. »

« Mill? »

« Right. »

« That's my price. Take it or leave it. »

He left. After some angry revving and a window-rattling blast of Metallica, Darche put his car in gear and the back end lifted from the power surge. He sped down the church lane, in reverse, and veered onto the highway without slowing down. Then forward, squealing like a cat in rut, unspooling clouds of rubbersmoke. I was hoping that would be the last I'd see of Monsieur Darche; it would not be.

The phone in the kitchen began to ring. Repeatedly, in a way you don't hear anymore in the age of answering devices. I picked it up on what could have been the fiftieth ring.

"Nile." A muscle-bound voice had me by the lapels.

"How'd you get this number?" The answer was obvious. I should think more before asking Volpe questions like that.

"You should think more," said Volpe, "before asking me questions like that."

In the background I could hear "Teen Angel" by Mark Dinning. "Earth Angel," "My Special Angel," "Johnny Angel," "The Angels Listened In"—a most spiritual times, the '50s. "What's new?"

"Another lawsuit. Some author and publisher in France. I had to hire an interpreter to shovel through the shitpile they unloaded on me."

I'd almost forgotten about that.

"You trying to set a Guinness record for litigation? What the hell is this all about, Nile?"

"I improved his book."

"You improved his book. The suit says you, quote, 'distorted an original work of art, mistranslated it wilfully and wantonly, with malice aforethought.' Did you?"

A work of art? "I made the odd change, yes."

"What kind of changes?"

"Little things. I tightened up the plot, spiced up some tedious dialogue, killed off an obnoxious character and added a chapter of sex."

"The artist and publisher claim you rewrote it from cover to cover. They're asking for $100,000 in damages. Compensatory, punitive and exemplary."

The "artist" had broken the transition problem wide open, beginning each paragraph with *And then*. The "publisher" had the book printed with the pagination backwards. "The author spoke his book into a dictaphone and the publisher operates out of a phone booth."

"Irrelevant, immaterial, non-germane."

Why do lawyers speak in synonyms? "Yes, but is it extraneous, inapposite or inconsequent?"

"It's a question of intellectual property, Nile. Not to mention artistic integrity. You can't mess with that."

"Artistic integrity? The book's a *mystery*, for Christ's sake, the kind left behind in airports and hotel rooms. Or hurled out of windows."

"It says here he received a writer's bursary for it from the French Ministry of Culture."

"Governments should give these writers money on condition they write no more."

"How's the book selling in France?"

"Like whatever the opposite of hotcakes is."

Another long sigh into the receiver.

"I forgot to mention something," I said. "Which may or may not be relevant. Or ... pertinent. The publisher didn't pay me for my services."

"They didn't pay you."

"No. In lieu of payment, I accepted a percentage of the sales."

"You translated a book for *nothing*? Where did that idea come from? I know where, because your father told me. 'From long practice in ...'"

"'... doing the wrong thing.'"

"*Exactamente*. So how am I supposed to clean up this mess, Nile? What do you expect me to do?"

I expect you to do what you always do: obfuscate and delay, wear people down with lawyer fees. "I don't know. Hire O.J.'s jury consultant? The first one?"

After buzzing Céleste, and getting the right response, I went for a quick look at the church. I'd seen pictures of the interior and caught glimpses of it through the windows but never actually stepped inside. Céleste had warned me that it was empty, that everything of value had been carted out by thieves. Everything not of value as well.

I tried the back door first, because it was closest, but the first five keys I tried didn't fit. I would've tried the sixth, but I was distracted by a faint whistling, human whistling, coming from the front entrance. Darche?

As I walked around to investigate, the sound stopped, replaced by three hefty knocks. And then a fine tenor voice: *"On the first day of Christmas, my true love gave to me ..."*

I peeked around the corner, distinguishing nothing but a strange-looking foot. I took a bold step forward.

"... a partridge in a pear tree. On the second day ..."

"Can I help you?" I interrupted, because the song went to twelve.

"Oh, hello there," said an elderly man with a long silver beard. And Druidical aspect. "Happy Christmas."

"To you as well."

A bare light bulb between us caused him to squint, ramifying the lines on his face. "I've come regarding the vacancy." His beard sparkled like a moonlit brook.

"The vacancy?"

He pointed to the rain-wrinkled poster on the church door. "In your firm, the position advertised. 'Elderly volunteers wanted to work in merchandising ...'"

"'Neither age nor mental health a factor.'"

"Very crafty, that."

"What is?"

"Hiring former asylumites." He had a Welsh accent, or something close to that.

"Oh, but it's not me who—"

"You declare them as employees, as tax write-offs, you get the government subsidies for hiring them. But you don't have to pay them because they think they're volunteers."

"Oh, I see. But it's not me who—"

"*Au fond*, they don't even have to exist. A bit like Gogol's *Dead Souls*, if you follow me."

I stood there, not following him, but nodding as if I were. I must read more.

The man winked at me. "Don't worry, my lips are sealed, my mouth as tight as a choirboy's arse."

Did I mishear that last bit? I examined the man under the light of the naked bulb. He had the avuncular look of the man on the Quaker Oats cereal box, except that he was wearing dentures that didn't fit him, a reddish tweed coat that looked like a dusty carpet, and galoshes over shoes fastened with duct tape.

"What type of merchandising are we looking at exactly?" he asked, coughing. A deep-lunged hack, so deep I thought it might disgorge blood or bile or part of his esophagus.

"We are not looking at any type of merchandising. I did not put up that sign." To prove it I tore it down, or what was left of it. "But I am looking for help. A cleaner or restorer, so if you know anyone around here who—"

"Destiny is a door that hangs on the hinges of chance."

"I'm sorry?"

"I'm an antiquarian by trade, Mister ..."

"Nightingale."

"I once ran a shop in Wales, Mr. Nightingale. As my grandfather did before me. I was born there, in fact, delivered in a carton marked 'This Side Up.'"

I smiled politely. "Right ... But, you see, what I'm really looking for is someone to ... well, restore the interior, seal and retile the roof."

"My specialty was toys, antique toys. Lead soldiers, rocking horses, miniature musical instruments, that sort of thing. Wind-up monkeys who comb their hair in a mirror, who bang cymbals and dance jigs. I bought them, repaired them, sold them. Is there an organ in the church? I could tune it for you."

"Uh, no, I think the organ was ... removed. Are you from ..." I almost said "the Institute" but changed my mind. "Ste-Madeleine?"

"For the time being, until I can get back to my *atelier* by the lake. Lac St-Nicolas. You can't miss it—it's the little cottage with the red-and-white stripes. Like a candy cane."

We stared at each other without blinking, like frogs. I wasn't sure what to say next. "You wouldn't happen to know anyone who drives a big black pickup with a broken headlight, would you?"

"I know everyone around here, and everything they own."

I decided not to pursue this. "Listen, is there anyone around here who does church renovation? I've asked around, but it seems that no one—"

"You might as well try turning water into wine. They'll accept you up to the fence, the villagers, but they'll never let you open the gate."

What the locals resented, I soon learned, was that I was trying to restore a symbol that was abhorrent to them; rationally or not, they viewed the church and its grounds as a dark sinkhole of death, a haunt of fiends and swamp devils.

"I shall work like a carthorse, Mr. Nightingale. Scour the place from top to bottom, renovate from stem to stern. I am in tip-top shape, a born athlete. Don't let this pear shape fool you. I bloom at this time of year like a poinsettia. Leave things to me. I'm a lucksmith, you'll see. Gray power is what's required here. I shall wash the pews with Murphy's Oil Soap and the floors with Heinz vinegar." He extended his hand. "Myles Llewellyn at your service."

I extended mine, which he squeezed several times in quick succession. Like a bulb horn or turkey baster.

"I can start tomorrow if you like. Or this very moment. Work does not deter me. It does not *faze* me. I am not one to hit the snooze button. Shall we get started, then? Hop to it?"

The old man was about as able to hop as he was to fly. I smiled and he smiled back, crinkling the corners of his eyes. The stamp UNEMPLOYABLE seemed to burn on his brow. How could I tell him, gently, that his services were not required, not now, not ever? How could I tell him this a week before Christmas?

"Mr. Llewellyn ..." Adopting a mien of authority not unlike my father's, I paused to clear my throat. In a maelstrom of indecision I closed my eyes, and on the back of my lids my father's face leered at me. *Just do it!* he hissed. *Tell him, for the love of Christ!* "Mr. Llewellyn, you are ... just the man I need. You're hired."

🕊 🕊 🕊

I drove my new employee back to Ste-Madeleine, wondering how he got to the church in the first place. He was vague about this. And how did he know about the sign on the church door? "A little birdie told me," was all he said.

For part of the way I followed a big cement truck with its tilted ovoid vat turning slowly. When it made a slow left onto the asylum road I was expecting Mr. Llewellyn to say, "Follow that truck." But he didn't. He asked me to drop him off at Les Trois Rennes, a brasserie about two miles on.

In the empty parking lot I was going to write down the phone number of the rectory, but then realized I didn't know it.

"I'll ring you at the rectory, Mr. Nightingale. Would St. Stephen's Day suit?"

This is what the Irish call Boxing Day. "Fine. Here, take this." I peeled off three twenties. "An advance."

He squinted at the bills. He had a tired eyelid that drooped a little over one eye. "You're the American forest ranger, am I right?"

How does this sort of thing get around? At bushfire speed, even to the asylum? "Where'd you hear that?"

"I won't let the cat out of the bag, don't worry. We need men like you up here. There's all kinds of scoundrels and scamps on the loose—and I'm not talking about pot farmers or meth cooks. I'm talking about poaching rings with radios, assault rifles, spotter planes. Teenage motorcycle gangsters running animal parts. That's your modern world for you."

"What else did you hear?"

"That you and your partner are buying the church as a headquarters, a place to store your evidence. Freezers full of illegal wildlife, animal parts, that sort of thing."

"My partner?"

"Céleste Jonquères. A real clever-boots, that one. Smart as a firecracker. There was an article about her in the paper."

This gave me a start. "Céleste who? I'm afraid I don't ..."

"I also heard you're trying to nab Bazinet and Cude, the worst scoundrels of the lot. A pair of black hearts, those two. They're cousins, you know."

"Yes, I ... I'm aware of that."

"Well, here's something you may not be aware of. I'm the one who put Gervais Cude's army boots on the mat. I found them in a ditch near the old bridge. With rubber gloves inside."

Blessed are the cracked, for they shall let in the light.

He opened the door and stepped out of the van. "You take care of the cousins, I'll take care of the Dérys."

"The *dairies*? What do you mean?"

"You'll find out." With that he made his way swiftly, spryly, to the entrance of Les Trois Rennes.

Céleste was unsurprised at the rumors going around, given my run-ins with Gervais. And Earl. And throwing around American twenties left right and center.

"What's that got to do with it?" I asked.

"Because most of the buyers deal in American twenties. They think you're trying to set up a cover. For stings."

Gervais had already explained this to me. I told her what Myles Llewellyn had said about the army boots.

"Mr. Llewellyn? He put them there?" Her brain seemed to be turning. "How'd you meet him?"

"Just ... ran into him. You know him?"

"Yeah, he's a ... senior delinquent. Used to be a hunter. He went a bit nuts after his wife left him and started buying bigger and bigger guns—I'm talking elephant rifles. But instead of using them on animals he used them to scare away poachers. Night hunters with jacklights and spikehorns. He ended up shooting a ranger. Accidentally. Or maybe not, since the ranger was on the poachers' payroll. Anyway, they put him in the Saint Mad Institute. He escapes from time to time, as you ... well, found out. But where'd you meet him?"

"At the church."

"The church? What was he doing there? What were *you* doing there?"

"Just, you know, checking it out. Llewellyn seemed to think I was the new owner. He was looking for a job."

"Did he tell you he was one of Santa's elves and five hundred years old?"

"No, he ... forgot to mention that."

"Did he have a British accent?"

"Yeah. Said he ran an antique shop in Wales."

"He's never been out of Quebec. According to my grandmother, at least."

I paused to think about this, about the mysterious Mr. Llewellyn. And his promise to "take care of the dairies." "Oh, I almost forgot, he said something about—"

"What I don't understand," said Céleste, "is why he would think you're trying to buy the church."

I shrugged. "Well, maybe because ... I don't really know.

But now that I think of it, that might not be a bad idea. If we went there. You and I. Temporarily. We can't stay here any longer, that's for sure." I hesitated to say the words I'd always dreaded hearing from my father: *We're moving.*

"But we can't go there, it's not mine anymore, I was kicked out. There's probably a new owner by now."

"There is, actually."

"Even though I keep ripping down the For Sale signs ... There is? Already? I'm going to fight this, Nile, I'm going to get a lawyer, a pro bono lawyer, and take this right to the Supreme Court. It's not right and it's not legal, the house belonged to my grandmother—"

"Did she pay all the taxes?"

Céleste glared at me as if I were the enemy. "She might've been a bit behind near the end when she was running out of money because of repairs and vandalism and because the town kept raising the taxes because they were out to get her when they found out she was an atheist and spotting cougars and tracking poachers. But she did her best, she really did, she even sold her Piper Cub."

"What's a Piper Cub?"

"To someone she hated! Inspecteur Déry! I'm going to get a lawyer and I'm going to sue ... It's an airplane."

"Who's Inspecteur Déry?"

"Just ... someone."

"Who are you going to sue?"

"Who do you think? Whoever bought it. Illegally."

"Do you know who the new owner is?"

"Yes, I do."

"Who?"

"Alcide Bazinet. If it's any of your business."

"The guy in jail? The bishop?"

Her eyes focused sharply on mine, as if she could see into my skull and was surprised at what was there. "Who told you that? Mr. Llewelyn? Earl? Good for you. First you find a little thread. The thread leads you to a string. The string leads you to a rope that ..."

"That what?"

"That you'll be hog-tied with and dumped in the bog if you keep poking around. So just ... stop asking questions, please, you're making a fire burn in my head."

"Alcide Bazinet doesn't own the property."

"You don't know a thing about this. You haven't got a clue. And I'd keep it that way. Stop digging around or you'll get yourself killed, I'm serious. Maybe you should go back home, back to wherever you came from. The planet Neptune."

"I'll be leaving soon. But you don't have to sue anybody to get your house back."

Céleste put her hand on her forehead and grimaced, as if she had a massive migraine. "And why is that?"

"Because I bought it."

She didn't speak for several seconds, but her eyes ran over me like a truck. "Good for you. Life must be hard on a trust fund. Hope you enjoy it, like all the other American tourists. Send me a postcard."

"And that's where we're going to live. Soon. In three days."

Céleste continued to stare, but with a different expression, as if she were dealing with one of Llewellyn's fellow inmates.

"At least until I figure out what to do with you," I added. "Until you're well enough to travel. And go to school."

"I'm not going to school, ever. And ... and then what happens? You flip it?"

"Do whatever you want with it."

Céleste sat there, not moving, not looking at me. "Am I on glue or did you just say I can do whatever I want with the house?"

"That's what I said."

"Are you crazy?"

Always a trickier question than it looks.

"Is this some kind of sick joke?"

I shook my head.

She took one of the buttons of her top between a finger and thumb and twisted it back and forth like the dial of a safe. "What do you want from me?"

I didn't quite know myself, to be honest. An excuse to stay clean, a wagon trail back to sanity? She and the church seemed to quell my vague anger, my flair for violent outbursts. "If you don't want to live there, if it's too hard, I'll understand. Go somewhere else."

"No, I want to stay there. For the rest of my life. I don't want to go anywhere else."

"Then stay there."

"With you?"

"For a time."

"With my six cats?"

"Of course."

"Off the grid? As anchorite and anchoress?"

I gave her a complicitous smile. We were both hermits at heart, though with this difference: I stayed away from people to stop them from finding out how little I knew about anything; she stayed away from people to stop them from finding out how much she knew. "If you like."

She bit her lip, first the top one then the bottom. "Okay, but I'm warning you, I'm impossible to live with. I'm no saint. I've got a wicked temper, you'll just have to get used to it. I can be quite mutinous. And just because I'm a girl doesn't mean I'm doing your cooking or cleaning. Or anything else, if you know what I mean ... And I'm not going to school. I'd rather drown myself in the Pond than go there. And I'll pay for my room and board. And for all your help. Plus expenses."

"You have to pay me back in another way."

"I knew there was a catch."

"You have to tell me everything. The truth this time. I want to know all about Alcide Bazinet."

The name, once again, made her flinch.

"I want to know if he's the one who dumped you in the swamp. And put those bears in the bowling alley."

"I'll tell you everything, I will, I promise. But you can't ... you know, leave me after I tell you. They'll make me a ward of the province, for God's sake."

"Don't worry, I—"

"Don't leave me alone, Nile, please. I won't last long on my own. I'm still pretty young, you know."

With the back of my hand, I brushed one of her cheeks. Affectionately, not checking for tears.

"If you're checking for tears, there aren't any. I never cry. Or almost never. And I don't want you to do that again."

"Okay."

"And get that gooey look off your face."

I tried to.

"All right, I'm going to cry now," she said, "and I don't want to hear a word from you. Not one goddamn word, okay?"

I nodded.

"And don't you dare put your arms around me or stroke my hair and tell me everything's going to be all right because you're not a fortune teller and you're not a crisis goalie. And don't give me any of that wise fatherly crap like a guidance counsellor because you're not my father and you're not a guidance counsellor."

Again I agreed, but I don't think she heard me. She began to gasp and cough and choke, unstoppably, her teeth chattering, her eyes blinded by tears, like a young girl who'd lost her only parent, like a young girl who'd been attacked by grown-ups and left for dead, like a young girl who'd just got her home back.

XII

"Over 90% of murderers are male, and the number one motive given for killing is 'love.' Over 90% of hunters are male, and the number one motive given for killing is 'love': love of animals, of the wilderness, of conservation, of God."

— Dr. Dorothée Jonquères

Nile asked me today about Alcide Bazinet & I told him. Told him that he's like a rabid pit bull running down the road & nobody knows but you because he looks so dozy & harmless. Told him that he's the scariest, loosest cannon in the Laurentians, in the province, maybe the whole country. That he's a one-man forest fire, a one-man flood, a one-man plague. Worse than Jim Roszko, the pot farmer out west who killed four Mounties. His eyes have seen things I hope mine never do.

Young boys, as everybody knows, like to torture & kill things. Maybe some young girls too. But they usually outgrow it. Bazinet never did. He was filled with hate then & now & nobody knows why. He started with insects, pulling off their legs & wings & burning holes in them with a magnifying glass. He kept frogs in a jar, closed, to see them open their mouths wider & wider as if they were singing. But they weren't singing, they were suffocating. When he was 6 or 7, according to Earl, he trapped a robin, tried to electrocute it on a cattle fence, then cut off its head with pinking shears. When his father told him to get rid of a litter of puppies, he buried them in little holes in the backyard up to their necks. Then ran a lawn mower over them, decapitating them.

It seemed that every animal Bazinet saw lived under a death sentence. I don't know what he has against them, or why he thinks they're his ticket. Because they're vulnerable, because he can outsmart them, because they'll cower, grovel & cry? Which gives him a feeling of power, makes up for all his deficiencies & weaknesses? Like bikers, really, or little runts with guns, like Phil Spector, Ted Nugent, Sarah Palin, the Safari Club, the NRA ...

He told my grandmother that when he was young he'd look at himself in the mirror and tell himself he'd become the most powerful and dangerous man in the Laurentian forests. "Lord of the wild beasts." After an "illegitimate" daughter got him kicked out of the seminary, Baz set up a puppy mill in the old red-brick bungalow next to Lavigueur's video store. The idea was to breed dogs & train them to sniff out dope & explosives at airports. The way to get rich, he said, was on government contracts. But that didn't work out because the dogs were sickly & starving & he didn't know how to train them. So he got rid of them, no one knows how. Then he decided to breed golden retrievers. Not for pet shops but for Chinese businessmen who come to Mont Tremblant to ski or hunt — obviously a cover — & leave with crates of dogs. Air Canada, Montreal-Shanghai. A friend of my grandmother's, who everyone thinks is a vet but is really something else, lent us a video shot by the Humane Society, which shows what happens when these dogs arrive. They're tied down while being skinned alive, whimpering for mercy, actually licking the hand of the skinner! Like an apology. Their fur is then made into expensive coats and the dead dogs are sold to restaurants. The video also shows cats stuffed into tiny cages, huddling in terror as one after the other is strangled to death — noosed and hung inside the cage so they don't bleed on their fur.

Baz saw others making money at this sort of thing, lots of it, and he wanted in. "Dogs and cats will never become extinct," he told me one time, after I accused him of firing at one of my cats. "Why should they be any different than seals or minks? Why shouldn't they too provide fur? The Asians have the right idea about cats and dogs — food & clothes."

After a year or so Bazinet's kennels were knee-deep in waste & rotting corpses. He got a livestock vet who owed him money to cut out the dogs' vocal cords to stop them from yapping. He was charged under the Criminal Code with cruelty to animals & skated away with a $500 fine. Not enough, obviously, to stop him from doing it again. Which he did for a while before selling the business to his cousin Gervais, who was just as savage & way stupider. Gervais bred beagles for animal testing, shipped them to Europe, Air Canada Montreal–Paris, as many breeders do. If you fly this route often enough, banker Latulippe told me, you can hear the dogs howling from the hold.

Gervais was shut down last year & the red-brick bungalow was demolished as a biohazard. He's now a snowplower. In the off-season he fences more stolen goods than eBay.

Bazinet, meanwhile, went on to bigger game. He learned that in the woods and villages every hunter is a big shot. Noticed, respected, feared. Which is why he'd come back with bleeding moose or elk or deer strapped to his hood, or bears on a steel platform, usually with their paws cut off. He wanted to be seen. He was sending out a message.

Baz's life seems to be divided into 3 basic activities: talking about the last hunt, hunting, and planning the next hunt. He hunts in & out of season, with illegal blinds, bait & traps, almost always over the bag limit. Only once did he get caught — for hunting moose at night. Here's how he "hunted." On the back roads after dark he'd go out in his customized truck with raised chassis, reinforced bumper & protective grille. When he saw a moose he'd pull the string on one of those Klieg lights & the animal would freeze, blinking in the brightness. Then he'd ram it, breaking its legs. He hired two native Indians to ride with him in case he got caught. In court, the Indians testified that they were invoking their constitutional right to hunt at night. He walked.

Bazinet made money, tons of it, enough to buy old man Beauchamp's bowling alley. And hire a full-time bear farmer from China. I didn't have to catch him red-handed or videotape what he was up to there. He shot himself, so to speak. He made his own videos, promotional videos, and distributed them to The Cave & buyers around the world, including businessmen from China & Vietnam & both Koreas, the same suits that bought his golden retrievers. And to other twisted toons & bent pennies.

His worst video, the one that got him sent to jail, was also given to Gran by the "vet" from St-Mad. It wasn't a promotional video, it was something else entirely. The vet wouldn't say how she got it. She suggested that we take it, along with my photographs, to the police in Montreal, outside of Baz's sphere of bribery. She'd do it herself, she said, but she "feared for her daughter." She'd explain some other time. Make copies, she warned. And hide them.

★ ★ ★

"La Soupe," which is the name of the video, is set in a restaurant north of Mont Tremblant, inside a Vietnamese restaurant named Chez Bao Dai. According to the time on the tape, it's just after midnight. The restaurant has Christmas decorations here & there & it seems to be empty except for the 2 cousins and their 4 amigos — Darche, Déry & his 2 sons. They're sitting at a long table, but all on the same side, not across from each other. En banc. On the other side of the table, on the floor, is a large metal basin filled with a yellowish liquid. Underneath the tray you can see blue flames. The camera pans to a saloon door & we see Bao Dai pushing it open. He announces that the moment they've all been waiting for has arrived. "Time to prepare special soup," he says. "One thousand dollars back in my country. For one bowl. For millionaires only!" He smiles & the others laugh. He then claps his hands & there is silence. The lights dim & the camera tilts up toward the ceiling. It's too dark to see anything at first, but you can hear scraping noises & some laughing & hooting. Then you see it. A crush cage, like the kind I saw in the bowling alley. It's being lowered, slowly, on ropes. Bit by bit you see black paws on the metal bars, moving, changing position. A live black bear is inside. As the cage descends, the hoots & laughter get louder. It keeps coming down until you hear a sharp sizzling sound, then a high-pitched cry that lasts for minutes & stops all the laughter. The cage is now at ground level & the bear remains in the boiling oil until his feet are cooked. The video ends with a voice-over from Alcide Bazinet, who explains that the therapeutic effects of the flesh are magnified by the bear's fear.

★ ★ ★

Baz was convicted of unlawful possession of dead wildlife, trafficking dead wildlife, hunting wildlife during the closed season, unlawful export of endangered species & cruelty to animals.

Here's the transcript, at least the tail end of it (J is Judge Johanne Lebrun and B is Alcide Bazinet):

J: And do you have any children, Mr. Bazinet?

B: I have a teenage daughter, born out of wedlock. Which is why I was forced to leave the church. Quite rightly. "God wants you to be holy, so you should keep clear of all sexual sin." Thessalonians IV, 3-4. Which is why I wear this purity ring, and why I urge sexual abstinence among young people.

J: Does your daughter share your views on animals? Have you raised her that way?

B: I do not see the relevance of these questions, your Honour. But I'll answer them. I have taught her that we have dominion over the animals. That it is written in the Bible, Genesis I, 24-26: "And God said, Let us make man in our image, after our likeness; and let them have dominion over the fish of the sea, and over the fowl of the air, and over the cattle, and over all the earth, and over every creeping thing that creepeth upon the earth."

J: Does the Bible say we are allowed to let them suffer? Is there not a biblical law, in fact, that says, "It is forbidden to cause any suffering to any living creature"?

B: Where does it say that?

J: In the Talmud.

B: The Talmud? That's not the Bible. Are you Jewish? The Bible says that we may lawfully use them for our needs, even if that causes pain. God commanded animals to be sacrificed. Presumably, that hurts.

J: Do you not think, Mr. Bazinet, that we have evolved from those distant times? Modern environmentalism and the animal rights movement —

B: Animals don't have rights. Because they don't have reason —

J: I will ask you once again, Mr. Bazinet, not to interrupt. Modern environmentalism and the animal rights movement propose that we open our hearts to our fellow creatures. That we have sympathy for them, that we attempt to share their being, feel their being. Whether they have so-called "reason" or not. We don't know what they're feeling. All they have is life — and people like you, Mr. Bazinet, have no qualms about taking that away.

B: Animals feel hungry and they feel ruttish. And when they eat and when they mate, they feel pleasure. But that's not the same as being human, is it, your Honour?

J: I've not finished. Most of us are able to imagine ourselves as someone else, whether animal or human. Able to imagine ourselves on the receiving end, as a victim, but there are some who clearly cannot. In extreme cases, we call these people psychopaths. Would you say, Mr. Bazinet, that you have a sympathetic imagination?

B: The animal rights movement, deep ecology, eco-feminism, the worship of Gaia, Mother Earth, the Endangered Species Act

— all of these have the stench of pagan nature-worship. Or Far
Eastern mysticism. They are alien to our Christian moral outlook.
To our Western traditions. Wild creatures are placed there by
the Almighty for man to study, follow, hunt, kill, cook and eat.
The eco-loonies want to take man from the pinnacle of creation
and make him a simple cog in the system. This is not what the
Almighty intended.

J: And what did the Almighty intend?

B: Death and killing are part of life, a part of the universe that
the Lord created. It's a natural thing, a natural dynamic. We
kill animals for food, food that I'm guessing you yourself eat, we
kill them by the millions every day in slaughterhouses. And some
animals kill — it's what they do, part of what defines them. And
humans? We're animals too, so why shouldn't some of us kill?
Why shouldn't that be part of what we do, what defines us?
There's something called the hunter's high, an irresistible feeling
of pleasure. What some hunters call being "stoked." Which God
gave to us as a gift. And to animals too. Don't you think many of
them, like lions and bears, want to kill us? The big eat the small.
Some animals, in fact — like rabbits or antelope — live their
entire lives in a state of fear.

J. Animals are not cruel. They don't torture beings for pleasure,
for the hell of it.

B. A cat ...

J. Which brings us back to my earlier point about compassion,
about a sympathetic imagination. The last charge against
you pertains to the notion of cruelty. Wanton cruelty toward

animals, inflicting unnecessary pain. Upon our fellow creatures
— God's creatures, to use terminology you seem comfortable with.

B: A cat has to kill and torture a mouse. That's his nature.
A man has to kill and torture animals. That's his. You're an
educated woman, your Honour, so allow me to quote Nietzsche, who
said that life is essentially "appropriation, injury, overpowering
what is alien and weaker, suppression, hardness, imposition of
one's own force ... and exploitation."

J: Might is right, and hunters with guns can do what they please
to those without guns?

B: Yes. The weak are meat the strong eat. Listen, the
government itself says that weaker animals in the wild will only
die miserable deaths by starvation and exposure without hunters
to control their population.

J: But it's the bigger, stronger animals they're killing and
maiming — the very opposite of natural selection.

B: I have no time for Darwin. I prefer Sartre, who said that
"when one loves animals and children too much, one loves them
against human beings."

   Bazinet smiled after the judge sentenced him. He said
everything he did was legal in the court of God. And in the courts
of many other countries.

   "When you are released from prison," said the judge, "I suggest
you go and live in one of them."

As Bazinet was led out of the courtroom he looked like ... I don't know what. His face looked like it was made of rubber & his hair of plastic. Everybody knows it's not his real hair. It's a wig made of muskox and baboon hair mixed with synthetic fibres. At least that's what he tells everybody.

On his way by us, in clunking boots with a heel that got him up to five-ten, Baz turned to me & Grand-maman. "You caused me to lose face," he said, calm as can be, his smoky gray eyes not looking at either of us but somewhere just above us. "No Bazinet loses face. No Bazinet goes to jail. No Bazinet forgets." I didn't know how to respond to that, so I flipped him off.

"You are dead meat," he told me from the doorway, still not raising his voice. "You will be cut open like a fish." His threats always seemed to involve animals. "Bled like a deer."

XIII

These were more than threats, as it turned out, and my grandmother was included in them. But no one, including the police, would believe me. So now, once and for all, I'm going to set the record straight, because so many lies have been told about her. That she was a witch, a demon, the anti-Christ, etc.

After my mother died, Grand-maman came up here to get me, to take care of me. She was working at a church in Montreal, but she decided not to go back. She got herself transferred up here, where there was a position open at the Église Ste-Davnet. It had been open for years, not just because there was practically no congregation left, but because there was no salary for the job, just room & board.

Gran had lost her faith by that time & was much more interested in her first love, mathematics. She believed in measurement, not God. From time to time, every third Sunday or so, she would give sermons at the church about the misery that religion has caused in the world. Not that anyone understood what she was talking about — there were only six members in the congregation by that time, one over seventy, four over eighty, one over ninety & none sane enough to follow what she was saying. Except maybe Mr. Llewellyn.

What she was saying basically is that religion & the afterlife & all that is childish nonsense that we should have outgrown ages ago. That people have been afraid of death from time immemorial, afraid of nothingness, so they invented God & religion.

Here's a poem (or maybe part of a play) that she gave me to read when I asked about heaven and hell. It's by Seneca, circa 55 AD, translated by the Earl of Rochester (who was not only a poet but Ranger of Woodstock Forest):

After death nothing is, and nothing, death:
The utmost limit of a gasp of breath.
Let the ambitious zealot lay aside
His hopes of heaven, whose faith is but his pride;
Let slavish souls lay by their fear,
Nor be concerned which way nor where
After this life we shall be hurled.
Dead, we become the lumber of the world,
And to that mass of matter shall be swept
Where things destroyed with things unborn are kept.
Devouring time swallows us whole;
Impartial death confounds body and soul.
For Hell and the foul fiend that rules
God's everlasting fiery jails
(Devised by rogues, dreaded by fools),
With his grim, grisly dog that keeps the door,
Are senseless stories, idle tales,
Dreams, whimseys, and no more.

The archdeacon ended up firing my grandmother, defrocking her, and putting the church up for sale.

★ ★ ★

Gran did not kill herself, as most people think. "No animal," she once told me, "commits suicide, or kills others while committing suicide. And I won't either." (She was wrong about animals committing suicide, but that's another story, one I've already told.) It's true that Gran was dying of cancer, but it's not true that she ended her life because of that. She was murdered.

It happened on the day before Hallowe'en, just before dinner. When I came back from town on my bike there was an ambulance out front, its spinning light making bonfires in the trees. The driver told me they found my grandmother in a chair in her office upstairs. With a plastic bag over her head. This bag is called an "Exit Bag" or sometimes an "Aussie Bag." It has a Velcro collar that fits snug around the neck & a hose that carries helium from a tank to displace the air inside. It causes a person to die from lack of oxygen. It's a method approved by the Right to Die Network of Canada, which my grandmother belonged to. Which is why they ruled it a suicide. But you need someone to help you use the bag & as I say, I wasn't there. So who "helped" her? The person who made the nine-one-one in a little girl's voice and said it was me. Play the tape, I said, and you'll see it wasn't me but they said there is no tape.

The Exit Bag was forced on her. And I know who did it. A man with big army boots (thank you, Mr. Llewellyn) and a gut hanging over his underpants like a bag of wet cement. Who I'm going to exterminate.

～⃝ XIV ⃝～

Céleste did not make a sound as I removed, with nail scissors and tweezers, her dental floss stitches. An act of bravery? No, I had given her a power-dose of pethidine. It worked so well that she asked if I could get her a year's supply. I looked for signs of infection around the two knife wounds but couldn't find any: no pus, no redness, no swelling, no heat. If lucky, I might just avoid a malpractice suit.

"What do I owe you, doc?" she said, comfortably asprawl on the bed.

The purplish-blue lines on her throat were fainter and the ring of red sores on her wrists and ankles—rope burns—were almost gone. But there were still marks beneath her eyes like bruises under the skin of an apple.

"Just a few more details."

Céleste adjusted her pillow, folding it in two to make it higher. "About ...?"

"Bazinet."

She groaned. "Don't do this," she entreated, her bloodshot eyes begging me to leave her alone. "It's not the right day. How about tomorrow?"

"How about today, how about this very second? It'll be like climbing a ladder. We'll go up one rung at a time." I had adopted a tone not unlike my attorney's.

"All right, Mr. District Attorney. But before we go up this ladder of yours I just want to thank you, you know, for pushing the point, for digging into me and stirring up all this shit."

"I'm sure there were things that happened—forces—that warped Bazinet as a child. His parents must have had a role in turning him into ... well, whatever he turned into."

"There's no excuse for Bazinet. His parents were good people—and his brother and sister turned out just fine."

"But this kind of thing—the cruelty and brutality you told me about—it just doesn't come out of nowhere. He's a sick man and he obviously needs a good doctor. But I was wondering if—"

"Oh, really? And what's the good doctor going to do? Cure him? Don't make me laugh. What Baz needs is a good hangman."

"But I was wondering if this cruel streak has ever been ... you know, directed at humans." I nodded at her scars, at the slow death that seemed to have been the aim.

"He was in jail at the time."

"But he ordered it?"

"I'm going to go out on a limb here and say that yes, he's the one who ordered it."

"He's a bully and a coward, am I right? Call his bluff and you defang him, neutralize him?"

"No."

So much for that hoary theory. "Was his cousin in on it? Gervais? Was he the one who knifed you?"

"Don't know."

"Was he the one who punched you in the neck?"

"Don't know."

"Was he in the truck that dumped you?"

"Don't know."

"Why did they dump you there?"

"They dump lots of things there. Sofas, fridges, grocery carts, dead animals. It's a giant sinkhole."

"You're lucky it was partially frozen."

"No, *you* were lucky."

"The truck, the black pickup, had only one headlight. Does that mean anything to you?"

"No."

"It also had a big grille and some sort of platform welded on the bed, with an animal on top. And a light bulb stuck in its mouth."

Céleste frowned, but said nothing.

"And its paws were cut off," I added.

"When they take a gall, they usually take a paw too. To prove freshness."

"So he sells them, the bear galls, in Quebec?"

"Quebec, Canada, the States, anywhere there's a big Asian market. But most of them end up in China. Where there's a backlog of orders that Bazinet and Company are doing their best to fill."

"So it was his truck, the black one I saw?"

"Wouldn't be surprised."

"When does Bazinet get out of jail exactly?"

"Month after next. Fourteenth."

"Saint Valentine's Day?" Instead of red hearts, I saw a red decapitated head. The only thing I knew about Saint Valentine was that he was beheaded on this day.

"Or maybe sooner."

"Is there anywhere you can stay? Temporarily, in February? Some place far away, until I think of some way of beheading him?"

"*Beheading* him?"

"I mean dealing with him."

Céleste tilted her head, gave me the kind of look my therapists used to give me. "We'll be in the house when he gets out and I'm not leaving it. I'll barricade myself in. Just get me a gun. The bigger the better. A cannon."

"So you know about guns?"

"There's not a whole lot to know. You just point at what you want to hit and blast away. They're pretty much idiot-proof."

"So he'll be looking for you when he gets out?"

"Duh."

"How about a friend's place? Or relative's. In Montreal or something."

"I already told you. I don't have any friends or relatives."

"What about your father? Where's he?"

"Missing in action. Never laid eyes on the man or heard his voice or even saw a photograph."

"And your mother?"

"So strung out on crack that Child Services took me from her. After I ran away."

I went back in my mind till I was about Céleste's height, when I had done the same.

"Cue the uplifting music," she said with a sigh.

"You were a runaway?"

"More like a throwaway."

"Do you ever see her, your mom? What happened to her?"

"She walked into Ravenwood Pond. On acid. Quite a trip."

God, I thought I had it bad. "Suicide?"

Céleste shrugged. "I don't feel like talking about it. Now or any other time, okay?"

"What about ... your grandfather?"

"Dead."

"Did he live with you guys up here?"

"No, when Gran got the gig at the church, he refused to come with her. He was making good money with the Gaming

Commission. At Kahnawake. He was part Indian, enough to get him on the reserve at least."

"So you're like ... half Indian?"

"More like a sixteenth. Along with French, Greek and a shot of Scotch, way back."

"So is your Indian blood part of your ... I mean are you, like, proud of your heritage or—"

"All Indians are screwed up. Almost as much as the whites. The hunters especially. Asking for the animal's forgiveness for killing it—*pulease*. And rubbing a boy's face in blood when he kills his first deer—*hello*? I've seen tribes put hawks in cages. Everyone knows that a hawk won't eat inside a cage. All it'll do is die. Plus they've destroyed, or helped destroy, lots of species."

"But did they know the animals were endangered?"

"They know bald eagles and golden eagles are endangered but they still shoot them, still poison them, still sell their feathers on the black market, still use dancing sticks with eagle heads. They know that trumpeter swans are endangered but they still kill them. Why? Because they're worth a thousand bucks a piece. They know the woodland caribou is almost extinct but a few weeks ago the Quebec Innu killed forty of them, out of the hundred or so left. They know the wolverine is endangered in Quebec, or 'extirpated,' but they're not interested in saving them, in bringing them back to their forests—even though they're supposed to be a link with the spirit world. Why? Because they're rare and protected and therefore not a 'fur-bearer resource.'"

"Are you talking about *all* Natives, or just a few louts, a few bad apples?"

"They know the peregrine falcon is endangered but they

still rob the nests. Rappel down cliffs, wearing hard hats to protect themselves from the females."

"Why do ... what do the females do?"

"They peck them in the head when they get too close. Wish I could do that, come to think of it."

"But why? I mean, why go to all that trouble?"

"The peregrine's the fastest bird in the world. People want a piece of that. Sheikhs come over here, pay two grand per bird. And the price is getting higher as the birds ... disappear."

"But every race, every nationality, has its share of thieves and thugs and poachers. Why single out Indians?"

"They know the whales in Ungava and Hudson Bay are endangered, but when the Department of Fisheries cut their seasonal quota—by twenty-seven whales—they called it 'genocide' and 'terrorism,' a 'threat to our way of life,' a 'denial of our human rights.'"

"But it's an age-old tradition. By people who were here long before us."

"Just because it's a tradition doesn't means it's good. Traditions can be changed, replaced with other ways of doing things, better ways. Which become traditions themselves."

"But if their livelihood, their main source of food—"

"They know that polar bears are threatened, yet they continue to slaughter them."

"But don't they eat them? And use their fur and hide to survive?"

"Continue to hire themselves out as guides to well-fed American trophy hunters."

"All trophy hunters are American?"

"European, Asian, whatever."

"No Canadians?"

"And they chase wolves on Ski-Doos till they drop. Now

they're trying to get them off the endangered list. So they can be wiped out all over again."

"I thought that was in Alaska. Where they shoot them from planes."

"Whatever."

"So is it all Indians you dislike? Or just Indian hunters."

"Mankind."

From what she'd seen of it in her short, nearly foreshortened life, who could blame her? I groped for something to say. "What kind of Indian blood do you have?"

"Laurentian."

I nodded, though I'd never heard of the tribe. "Can you speak the language?"

"No, it's extinct. And the last speakers left only a few words behind. Well, really only one word."

"Which one?"

"Canada."

"You're kidding. Which means?"

"Village. When Cartier first landed he asked the Laurentians what they called their homeland, pointing all around. 'Canada,' they replied."

I tried to steer things back to Bazinet, to some sort of defense strategy, but on this subject Céleste's conversation tended to tread water. She said we had until February to worry about all that.

"For now," she said tartly, "we have other things to discuss."

It had been building for a while now, like an overblown balloon—I could see it in her eyes, the color of her cheeks.

A burst, an explosion, was coming. Something to do with the church, with my buying the church? Or with hunters and poachers and collusive rangers? "Such as?"

"Cigarettes. And why you're not getting me any. After I've asked you a gazillion times."

"I got you some."

"Very funny. Those were *candy* cigarettes. You think I'm five years old or something? I'm an adult. Practically."

"You're not an adult. And you're not having any cigarettes. They're not good for you."

"They're not? Gee, thanks for the scoop, Mr. Drug Addict. How dare you tell me what I can and can't have."

"I'm your doctor."

"You are not my doctor. You're my ... my *bourreau.*"

This means torturer. "You're not smoking in here. Not while you're recovering. And barely eating. Not just for health reasons either—this place is a firetrap."

"So I got to wait till we move to the house?"

"No, you're not smoking there either."

"Oh really? I'll smoke wherever and whenever I want. Don't tell me what to do, you big bully. I'm going to the store right now."

"I'll tell you what. You can have a licorice pipe."

Her eyes, large and clear, were circles of wrath. "You can go to hell!" She stumbled out of bed and grabbed my winter coat from the back of a kitchen chair. After digging in the pockets for car keys, she wore the coat like a cape while hobbling to the door. But I beat her to it, and stretched my arm across the frame.

"Get out of my way, you junkie."

"Please go back to bed, Céleste. You're not well enough to go out."

A brief pause, as if she were listening to reason. She let the coat fall to the floor. "All right," she said, but when I lowered my arm she lunged at the door handle. I grabbed her hand.

"Let go of me, you big bully, don't you dare touch me!"

The minute I let go of her hand she turned and began to hit me, pounding her fists on my arms and back.

I pretended to cower under the assault, which was more like a Japanese massage. She caught my eye and didn't like what she saw. "Don't you dare laugh at me, you ... deviant. You American terrorist. I'm never speaking to you again as long as I live. You are not my father. Or even a friend. You are a ... passing acquaintance. Who I'll forget like a chewed piece of gum."

I held my tongue.

She clenched her teeth. "I'm staying at the house alone. I can paddle my own canoe, is that clear?"

I nodded.

"Remind me," she said between quick shallow breaths, "why I tolerate you."

"Because I'm your lord and master?"

"You ... are such a little ... I hope you go to hell forever. Wait'll I tell ..."

"Tell who?"

"Never mind."

"I thought you didn't believe in hell. Or heaven."

"Cigarettes keep my weight down," she pleaded. "Please."

"No. This is a perfect time to quit. You'll thank me in a few years."

"A few *years*? Don't make me laugh. I don't plan on living for years. I plan on living for *days*. So give me a bloody cigarette. Now."

"You're planning on killing yourself?"

She glared at me with cold reptilian eyes. "This is *so* wrong, on *so* many levels."

"If you're going to kill yourself, why worry about your weight?"

Unused to logical ambush, I'm guessing, she stared wordlessly at me for several seconds while gnawing at her lip. So forcefully I thought she was going to draw blood. Her entire mouth began to quiver. "You ... it's none of your effing business. Who says I'm going to kill myself? Did I ever say that? Did I ever once say that? Where did you get this information? From dialing 411? From reading my journal? You did, didn't you. You're nothing but a goddamn snoop—"

"I didn't read your journal. But is it true?"

"Yes, it's true! Now just shut up about it, all right?"

"So why are you on a diet?"

"I just told you to shut up about it. Some things aren't logical, okay? And there are some things that you'll never understand. That aren't in your *range*. Because you don't think straight, you think curved. So please don't talk anymore. I'm burned out talking to you."

XV

Nile put me in a bad mood so now I'm going to get on my "pulpit," my "soapbox," which Grand-maman said is my second-biggest fault. She said that pulpits & soapboxes are not for 13-year-olds, that you have to be older, you have to have earned it. But now I'm 14 going on 15 & I've earned it.

Here's my argument "in a nutshell": that the Wildlife Ministry in this province is not interested in fighting poachers. To do this, they'd have to hire more agents & make the laws tighter. But they won't, because they don't want to make the hunters mad, the people they really work for. As Inspecteur Déry told me, "We serve hunters like welfare departments serve welfare bums." Ask any ranger in this province & he'll say the same thing. The Ministry makes money from selling permits & the tourist industry makes money from the killing of animals, legal or illegal — outfitters, guides, lodges, hotels, airlines. They just don't want to mess with that.

In Quebec there's not a lot of enforcement looking over your shoulder. It's pretty much open season. In the past 5 years, one out of 3 rangers has been fired. And it's the good ones they let go! Most of the ones they keep, who've got seniority, have spare tires from sitting behind desks, filling out tables & charts. We should put radio collars on them instead of animals to see how far their butts get from their chairs.

Some of them — surprise, surprise — have been investigated for taking bribes from poachers or gangs fronting as hunting guides. There are 2 agents in Ste-Mad who've been on the take for almost 30 years. They pick up their monthly pay packet or drug sack on some back road & agree to stay out of X areas for X number of days. Everyone knows who they are: the Déry detectives, père & fils. So why doesn't somebody blow the whistle? Because Dery's other son is a biker. The last guy who blew a whistle got his hands placed in the door jamb of a Ford Bronco. Others end up in hunting accidents or drowning accidents or snow burials inside running cars.

★ ★ ★

I've calmed down now, so I'll talk about something else. About some mischief I got into last night.

I had this major nicotine fit and really gave it to Nile because he won't let me smoke. I lost control, totally — I went berserk, I even hit him! I couldn't sleep because of this so I decided to get up in the middle of the night and apologize. Plus I was afraid, I have to admit, that he'd change his mind about taking me with him to the rectory.

I crawled over to Nile's bed on my hands & knees. I put my hand on his stomach & it went up & down & he didn't even wake up! Then I leaned over & bit the top part of his ear & he still didn't wake up! Then I ran my finger along his cheek, which had spines & prickles like a cactus, or porcupine. This made him open his eyes, but he didn't even act surprised, he just asked if I was all right, if I needed anything. "A cigarette," said I. When he frowned I yelled, "I'm kidding!" And I was. I didn't really want to

smoke — it'd probably just make me throw up. Anyway, I started
to say I was sorry for "blowing a gasket," but Nile interrupted
me right away.

"You want to hear a story?" said he, wiping his eyes and
yawning. "A true story. Set in Paris. I was just dreaming about
it."

I nodded. I did want to hear a true story, especially if it was
about Nile in Paris.

"Do you want the light on or off?" said he.

"Off," said I.

"Do you want to go back to your bed to hear it? Or stay
here?"

"Stay here," said I.

It was near Christmas, he recounted, and his father had
promised to take him to a stamp exhibition at the Grand Palais.
Nile was like, 7 or 8. On the way his father stopped at a hospital
to get something & said he'd be back in 2 seconds. He parked
at the back of the hospital & left Nile alone in the car, with
the keys in the ignition. He wasn't gone for 2 seconds, he was
gone for 2 hours. Nile couldn't get out of the car & into the
hospital to look for his dad because 4 teenage boys appeared
out of nowhere & surrounded the car. First they wrenched the
Jaguar ornament off the hood & then started banging on the
windows when they saw Nile crouching in the front seat. They
all pushed their flattened noses against the glass & made faces

at him. One of them then stood on the hood & urinated all over the windshield. And then another stood on the trunk & urinated on the back window. Nile was petrified. He didn't know how to drive a car, but he tried to. But all he managed to do was to put the car in reverse & bang it against the hospital wall. With four boys on top of the car, laughing & shouting in French & Arabic. So he then pushed on the horn until they got angry & one of them smashed in the passenger window with a rock. A hospital guard, meanwhile, had come to investigate the banging sound of the car hitting the hospital wall. The boys took off. The guard wanted to call the police, not to report the gang but to report the father. He wanted the father charged with negligence. And he would have been if he hadn't been such a bigwig doctor.

So what happened? When Nile's father arrived there was an emergency, a man hit by a car, and because it was Christmas time the hospital was short-staffed. Nile's father attended to the man immediately. And forgot his son was in the car.

"Did you ever forgive him?" said I.

"Of course. But my mother didn't."

"Did he save the man's life?" That would've been the perfect ending to the story.

"No, he died."

★ ★ ★

After we each had a bowl of porridge, Nile gave me a gift. A pair of snow-white swans. Some sort of gypsum, I think. Satin spar or alabaster. SO beautiful. I tried to jump out of bed & hug him or maybe even kiss him, but I got a huge spasm in my leg & knocked over my tray table & fell on the floor. Nile picked me up in his arms like I was a feather.

I asked him why he was so nice to me, apart from the smoking ban, and why he was helping me. "Delusions of sainthood, I guess," said he. I asked why he gave me things like this, hoping he'd say he'd fallen madly in love with me, but he said the swans were given to him by an Indian anarchist (I think I know who he means — is he having an affair with her?) & that thinking about me helps him stop thinking about other things. But he didn't say what those other things were.

I asked if he'd ever suffered from mental illness & he said he was born with a nervous breakdown.

"No, seriously," said I.

"You really want to know?" said he.

"Yes," said I.

"I spent 3 years in an institution."

This surprised me & even scared me & I didn't know what to say.

"And another 2 as an outpatient. In a halfway home for the half-crazy."

"Why? I mean, what's wrong with you, Nile?"

"It's never really been ... fully diagnosed."

"Schizophrenia?"

"In that family, a poor cousin maybe. If you throw in depression. It has to do with a bicameral mind, which you've probably heard of. No? It's what cavemen used to have, where one part of the brain seems to be speaking & a second part that listens & obeys. Which is why man invented gods — to explain the voices. But that, as they say, is another story. My problem is ... let's just say it's an exciting challenge to medical science."

"What was it like there, being in the ..."

"In the nuthatch, the cracker factory? The whole thing's a big gap in my life. A big gray gap. Two years of tranqs & TV & plastic utensils. And seeing the institution's motto in my dreams: 'Gib mir deine Hand,' which I think is from the Beatles. Two years with analysts as nuts as I was, going nowhere together. And 'safety-coated' whenever I became ... oversensitive, shall we say, to the misbehaviour of strangers."

"A straitjacket, you mean?"

"Every time I smell chlorine I'm reminded of it."

"This was in ... Paris?"

"Frankfurt. In Paris I was in rehab."

Good God, I thought I had it bad. "And what was it like ... I mean, with the other patients ..."

"I had a private room, thank God. Or rather thanks to my dad. So I could usually avoid Dieter the Drooler, Manfred the Masturbator, and Ursula the Urinatress. And an octogenarian who thought he was one of the psychotherapists, who wiped his snot on every available surface."

"Oh my God! This reminds of when I went to school."

"Me too, come to think of it."

"And your being there ... Did it have anything to do with ... you know, your father?"

"My father? When he left me in the car in Paris, you mean? Hell no, I got over that in two days. My haywireness is nobody's fault. Not my father's, not my mother's. I was born with a tangled electrical mess in my head, that's all — which D & A made worse. So if it's anyone's fault, it's my own."

I didn't know what to say. "You were born in Paris, right?"

"No, Neptune."

This was a joke, a "running gag" I think, even though his face was serious. "So that's why they locked you away? Because you're an extraterrestrial?"

"Well done. You finally guessed my secret."

Céleste thought I was messing with her but I wasn't. Neptune is a town in New Jersey—Jack Nicholson was born there. And Danny DeVito. The third most-celebrated Neptunian is my father, Dr. Bertram Christian Nightingale, a military surgeon, pancreaticist and international medical administrator who appears in the last two editions of *Who's Who*. Here's the entry:

> **DR. BERTRAM CHRISTIAN NIGHTINGALE** (b. 1932 Neptune, NJ; d. 2008 Paris, Fr.). PhD (John Hopkins), MSc (Harvard). Military physician with American Armed Forces (1947–1965); pancreatic surgeon and researcher at the Centre National de la Recherche Scientifique (1965–1971); co-founder in 1971 of Médecins Sans Frontières International (MSFI), a non-profit humanitarian organization offering assistance to victims of disasters or armed conflict. From 1984 to 2000, Dr. Nightingale supervised the training of local medical staff for MSFI and established the "Group of 9" research and recruiting centers throughout the world (Paris, London, Lisbon, Madrid, Athens, Frankfurt, Milan, Shanghai, New York). Up until his death in 2008, Dr. Nightingale was engaged in a variety of philanthropic activities, including fundraising for pediatric oncology institutions.

We traveled extensively, needless to say. For me, it meant five schools in seven years, which in theory should have made me sophisticated and worldly-wise, given me an array of experiences of life and culture. My father thought he was doing me a favor with all this traveling, giving me an exotic gift I'd remember for the rest of my life, something that would make me a fuller, more interesting being. "The only way to get the feel of the country is to become part of it," he advised. "Learn the language, interact, expand. Bloom where you're planted." But I did not expand or bloom; I shrank and shrivelled, withdrawing into myself. With the help of five nannies I learned five languages, not to socialize or learn local customs, but because I liked breaking codes. I collected and remembered phrases the way I collected and remembered stamps.

In Europe for six years and Asia for one we wandered, my father penetrating into the real life of nations, me skimming over it, shut up in boarding schools or the pages of stamp albums. I withdrew from people like someone backing out of a swamp he had stumbled into accidentally. I was beginning to feel that I was suited to solitude, that the presence of others blurred me in some way, that a monk's cell or the desert would be ideal for me.

My father didn't encourage me to follow in his footsteps, but when I expressed an interest in medicine he got me into the Broussais-Hôtel-Dieu in Paris. After a year and a half there I'd come to the conclusion that I wasn't meant to be a physician, and I had reason to think that my instructors had come to the same conclusion. You need a predisposition that begins at birth that I didn't have. You need a sympathy toward your fellow creatures—a belief they are worth saving—that I didn't have either.

So I changed directions, checking myself into the Hôpital Marmottan, a drying-out facility on rue d'Armaillé in the 17th. My father was more relieved than upset, saying that I was "error-prone, accident-prone and addiction-prone," that I was "not the sort of man who was good in an emergency or particularly endowed with courage." It was not the first or last time he would say this.

Here's my entry:

NILE CHRISTIAN NIGHTINGALE (b. 1964 Neptune, NJ; d. ?, St. Davnet, QC). No degrees or diplomas of any importance. A dilettantish translator and philato-drudge who frittered his time away on earth, engaged in a game of one-downmanship as to who can lead the worst life; a flounderer and failurist who jumped from job to job in a vaporish daze, squandering his family contacts, working his way from high-level to entry-level positions; a man who, especially when compared with his illustrious father (**see Dr. Bertram Christian Nightingale**), silently slid through the world, making no impact on anyone or anything, leaving not a trace behind. The Nightingales, like the whooping crane, have now vanished from New Jersey.

Drugs allow us the illusion that it's better to be alive than dead, said a voice inside me at an ATM near the Prudential Center in Newark. It was a warm Hallowe'en night, well past the trick-or-treating hour, and my mind was spitting out overs: overpopulation, overproduction, overmarketing, overconsumption, overexpansion, overagression, overmedication ... And overspending, I added to the list after failing to draw money from a sub-zero account.

The machine in the wall was next to a club called Homo Erectus, which had a stainless-steel door secured with great looping chains and huge flat padlocks shaped like hearts. I sat down on a sticky curb out front, head bent, and removed my father's fedora. Emptied my life savings into it. Three crumpled fives, four ones and ... one two three four five six cents.

You're living on borrowed time. You owe more money than the government of Gabon. If you don't end up in the slam, you'll be eating dog food till you die. A quirk of mine was to speak softly but audibly to myself in the second person.

I was interrupted by a shuffling passer-by, a barefoot man in a buttonless coat with flies buzzing close. My doppelgänger, my future come calling?

"How's it hangin'?" he asked. Boston accent. From beneath his coat he produced a short wooden stick, like a policeman's truncheon.

Madmen have always been attracted to me, come bounding up to me, shouting out nonsense, wrapping their arms around me or grabbing me by the throat. And I've always been attracted to them, to their blazing minds. Birds of a feather and all that. "Straight down the middle," I replied, which didn't appear to be the right answer because the man began tapping the bar against the palm of his hand. I now got a closer look at it. It was a miniature baseball bat, the kind used by Little Leaguers. The kind I used on a team sponsored by the Philatelic Institute of New Jersey. "A hard yard," I tried, which caused the man to grin, drop the bat onto the sidewalk and root around in several pockets. He dropped a quarter, a dime and penny into my hat before shuffling on. Nineteen dollars and ... forty-two cents.

In terms of strungoutedness, this might've been the moment I hit rock-bottom. It was either then or a few hours before, when I tried to go to a Rangers-Devils game and paid a guy two hundred bucks for a Newark bus transfer.

A chemical reagent began to form in my brain, helping me to see how the pieces of my life fit together. Although it had forever been murky and mystifying, surrounded by icebergs and dense fog, my entire life now acquired perfect clarity, made perfect sense. And the sense it made was that it was totally, unreservedly pointless. Pointless desperation followed by pointless hope followed by pointless recollections. *You might as well have hibernated in a cave your entire life. Or been shrink-wrapped and stored in a freezer.*

I lurched down the sidewalk, then the gutter, then the middle of the street, straining to make it appear that I was sauntering. Drivers blasted their horns and cursed at me as I wove my way to the other sidewalk. In behind two cool Japanese dudes with pompadours and pointed shoes, to a panhandler sitting on a curb. His head was bent and he was wearing a black Borsalino fedora—as I was earlier, uncannily. The hat appeared to be mine, stolen from me, which was impossible because I could feel mine on my head. Next to him was a piece of cardboard with scrawled words on it. As I approached, he looked up at me. It was the man with the mini-bat who gave me thirty-six cents. The smell of fermented pee now steamed off of him. His sign said:

NEED MONEY FOR BEER, DRUGS, HOOKER.
HEY, AT LEAST I'M NOT SHITTIN' YOU.

He took off his fedora and I dropped various items into it: three fives, four ones, six pennies. And a stray button. I kept the money he'd given me, the quarter, dime and cent, because it would've been rude to give it back.

After an unknown period of time, minutes or hours, I stumbled upon my car. Strange, because I wasn't looking for it. It was double parked with the keys in the ignition. There was a piece of paper on the windshield, not a traffic ticket, containing one word: DUMBASS. I remember scratching my head at this, thinking it should have been two words, or at least hyphenated. Otherwise, you pronounce the "b."

I drove back to Neptune whacked, wasted, past two state troopers who did not give chase. Inside my apartment— or "oubliette," as my father called it since it was a sunless hole—I locked all the doors and windows and spiraled into the deepest and darkest dysphoria of my life. Which is saying something. Concentric circles expanding above my head, the black dragon with its scaly skin and spiked tail hovering over me, making me afraid of ... well, everything. Fire and flood and earthquake and God knows what to come.

And things did come, in a cluster bomb that hit me from the blindside in the span of a month: my father died of deep-vein thrombosis; the New Jersey State Police charged me with road rage and impaired driving; my ex accused me of child abduction; a French writer was suing me for ... I can't remember the term. One of these alone would have sent me into a weeklong bender, but together they put me in a state of motor and mental stupor. I did not leave my apartment for weeks, not for alcohol, not for tobacco, not for drugs, steeping in my withdrawal like a festering tea bag. Living on credit pizza and Chinese, the stinking boxes piling up beside my bed like ... like stinking boxes. Mail piling up outside, neighbors ringing to see if I was still alive.

I began to have trouble telling time, or rather understanding what clock times actually signified. I had trouble telling the difference between five minutes and five days. I had a peculiar feeling that every day was neither weekend nor weekday, but some eighth day of the week.

The smallest tasks—filling a glass with water, brushing my teeth—took an enormous amount of gearing up. Clothing, no matter how much I put on, would not keep me warm. Cold sweats made me think my waterbed was leaking. But I didn't have a waterbed. Bathing was near impossible: even warm water shocked my skin and even the softest towel felt like steel wool. I was abrim with filth and my hair stood up boy-band style, not with gel but with grime. I was constantly dropping things, as if my hands had been exchanged for paws. I did not walk so much as waddle, as if my feet were webbed. I did not recognize myself in the mirror. Was I turning into another species? Something non-human? With the exception of elephants, apes and dolphins, non-human animals do not recognize themselves in the mirror. Was it now official? Was I certifiable? Or rather, recertifiable?

In a panic I increased my intake of antidepressants, tossing them back like M&Ms. They seemed to be working, putting me to sleep for 23/24ths of the day. And the only side effects, in the hour I was awake, were blurred vision, vertigo, itchy feet, thickened tongue, nosebleed, breathlessness, and cloudy urine.

One drizzly morning I heard a voice inside my head— someone else's—that summoned me back to the real world. It sounded a bit like my mother when she had a cold. Never one to spring out of bed, I did so on this occasion. Threw a heavy winter coat over my long johns and bathrobe, and baseball shoes over wool socks (all my other shoes seemed to be missing the left or right). From the floor of my hall closet, which was so shallow that the coat hangers hung at a slant, I scooped up sheaves of legal documents. Stuffed nearly all of them into two large padded envelopes, addressed them to someone who would know what to do with them. Got into my Delage Lynx, which was bleeding from the gut and nearly dead, and crawled painfully to the post office on Neptune Avenue. From there down to Woodland Avenue, to the family manse in Avon. Or Avon-by-the-Sea, as it's officially called. About fifty miles south of Newark-by-the-Smell.

I parked in the garage beside my father's car and removed one thing from the glovebox: Brooklyn's plastic .38. Ascended the sixteen steps as quietly as possible, lest any sounds draw the neighbors on either side. Not easy in spiked shoes. Leaned my head against the door's cool plane, listening. For what? Ghosts? Turned the key, a thick Medeco I hadn't used in so long I wasn't sure it would fit the hole. The lock's tumbling sounded like a gunshot.

To stop the squawking alarm I punched in 1906—my grandfather's year of birth—then entered the sunken dining room. It had been repainted in Chinese red, but not reappointed: it still looked like a reception room in an embassy, with furniture one mustn't sit on, either frail from age or upholstered in silk or velvet that a hand or foot could easily mar. The maid had obviously been in, while Dad was dying in a French hospital, because it was as ruthlessly clean as ever. It smelled of Lemon Pledge and Brasso. I walked through it, seeing childhood images of glass plates with melting brie, pungent bleu de Bresse, Roquefort veined like marble, halves of browning pears ... Past a stretch of tall plants and a conservatory through which sound could not penetrate, to the winding white staircase that led to my room.

It too was frozen in time, a reminder for my father of an era when his scion was a good obedient boy from a good loving family, before he went "off the rails." The room had pneumatic furniture and a waterbed, along with several posters of French actresses. My old baseball trophies and plaques were also on display—a shock because I hadn't seen them in decades. My father must have hauled them down from the attic, along with a framed picture of me wearing a cap from my Little League team, the Rhinos. I looked from photo to mirror and shook my head at the sad gulf.

At least put some clothes on. I riffled through closets and drawers, ending up with black narrow-legged pants (*pantalon cigarette*), a black leather belt with studs, and pointed black boots with a complex crosshatch of straps and buckles. All acquired at Camden Lock. I had no problem with the fit: bucking the American trend, I had grown thinner with age. *Black. You were happy when you wore black. You shall wear black from now on.*

How could I *not* be happy, coming back to America for two years of high school with an English accent at the crest of the British New Wave? The girls mistook me for a rockstar.

I switched on my Dual turntable and set the needle onto an EP which, unless my father or the maid had been listening to it, had been sitting there for years.

My intent was to start tossing things out, but my heart wasn't in it. I pulled a folded green garbage bag from its pack, but that's as far as I got. How could one throw out vintage music and apparel from the '80s? Or movie posters torn from walls on Boulevard St-Michel in the '70s, one of Isabelle Adjani in *Possession*, the other of Catherine Deneuve in *Repulsion*? The magnetism of mad women: it drew me early.

"Love Will Tear Us Apart" ended so I put it on again. From a tottering mound of sleeveless records I plucked a Psychedelic Furs EP ("Heaven") that wouldn't play because it was covered with candle wax. Don't remember that night. "In a Big Country" was next, then "Don't Fear the Reaper." The 45! Which I cranked. It wasn't until the next day, in the big country of Canada, that I made the connection. Three songs: two singer suicides and a suicide anthem.

I looked for *Abbey Road* and *The White Album* to test out the aural pareidolia Dr. Neefe had mentioned—*I buried Paul* and *Turn me on, dead man*—but couldn't find either. So I moved on, down the long hallway to my father's office. On one side it looked over a garden, with its pillared porch and gazebo and widow's walk; the other side looked over the ocean. The room was surprisingly congested for a chronic minimalist: a long row of filing cabinets containing a half-century's worth of tax junk; a massive desk from Thessaloníki that I'd always coveted; an antique jade box from Carcassonne containing items I'd always scorned, like diamond cufflinks, gold tie clips and Cartier pens; and a large wooden chest from Inverness with souvenirs from around the world. I opened the latter's lid and found three things that belonged to me: a *Stanley Gibbons Improved Postage Stamp Album*, a leather-bound *1001 Poems*, and an empty black book with a silver lock and pen entitled *Mon journal intime*—all lost gifts from my mother. Why do I love the things Mom gave me, I wondered, and feel indifferent to the things I give myself? I sat down on a sage-green chair I'd never seen before, and turned each item over in my hands.

Paris and London in the eighties: my real home was in the past, I'd always thought, but I was forced to live in the present. But now I backed off from this view. It was not the lands of lost content that I yearned to revisit. My homesickness, I came to realize, was for no place in particular but for some universal place I had never known. I examined my image—intently, as one examines a stranger—in a full-length mirror from Barcelona. My father was a great one for mirrors. I was with him when he bought it, bickering with a salesman on Las Ramblas. "I won't haggle like a whore," he said in Spanish, pretending to walk away. His angry eyes lay across mine like a mask.

In the blurred background was a daybed covered with a green and white early-American quilt, homespun by a weaver in New Hampshire. My mother was a great one for quilts. I could see her reclining on it, gazing sadly into a hand mirror. In just over a year, I paused to calculate, I would see changes in my face that she had not lived to see in hers.

I closed my eyes. *A vacation, you need a vacation. About twenty years would do you. Not to the past—you've tried that before and failed—but to somewhere new, in the future. A vacation to end all vacations, a vacation to die for.* My head began filling like a suitcase.

Maybe not a vacation exactly—you can't take a vacation from doing nothing—so much as a permanent relocation, to an impossible-to-find place where life was quieter, slower. I would leave the confusion and clamor of the city, the oxygen-poor air poisoned by industry and cars, for the calming, anchoring bedrock of nature. Where older, more natural processes were at work. Like Euripides, who moved to a cave by the sea because cities had become insufferable. Or Saint Anthony, a wealthy Egyptian who did the same after giving all his money away.

"Death is dwelling in the past," my father said inside me. "Or in any one place too long." Northward I would go, then, toward some old dream, some new darkness. Melt into a Canadian backwater not found in any atlas, restart my life where no one knew me, live as an anchorite on some lake isle.

*I will arise and go now to Canada
And a small cabin build there, of clay and wattles made ...*

I left Jersey, as the expression goes, under a cloud. I packed not a scrap of food or much in the way of clothing or essentials. I packed several unessentials, though, including my philatelic gear: albums, tongs, magnifying glass, perforation gauge, stock books, glassine envelopes, mounts, hinges, drying book, watermark fluid and tray. Jammed them into my uncle's canvas AWOL bag, along with my leather-bound anthology of poems.

And I shall have some peace there ...

I drove my dad's BMW a block and a half before hanging a U, back to the house for his survival kit and leather valise. And knapsack, into which I placed three bottles of his finest Scotch from Skye. I couldn't help it, I really couldn't.

Then on to the Central Jersey Bank, the West Sylvania branch, where I cleaned out, with the manager's assistance, one of my father's lesser accounts. I ranged the packets of twenties in his Halliburton valise, durable and waterproof, the kind favored by criminals to haul cash.

Along Ocean Avenue, weaving in and out of traffic, engine thrumming, in a very powerful car. North on I-87 as darkness fell. I shut my eyes against the winding chain of taillights ahead and opened them again. The inside of the car glowed with precise, confident signal lights—including a radar detector—telling me everything was running optimally. With my teeth I opened a bottle of Talisker, took a quick slug. Wiped my mouth with the back of my hand with a drunkard's gesture that I caught in the rear-view. Along with something else: a semi, the tyrannosaurus of the freeway, an eighteen-wheeler, which honked fiercely as it passed. I honked back. Then pressed the down button on the window, the passenger side by mistake, and unfastened my watch. It was heavy and gold, a Nightingale family relic. I tossed it out the window and watched it in the mirror as it slid across the hazard lane.

Repeated the procedure with the car's cellphone. Discarding
the technology, I'd read somewhere, sharpens the senses,
leads to deeper awareness. From my front pocket I pulled
out four folded sheets of paper and spread them over the
steering wheel. Turned on the dome light.

The top three contained Quebec real estate information,
downloaded from my father's computer: hunting cabins for
rent; "renovatable" churches for sale; and a travel piece
that described the Québécois people as "proud," which in
the lingo of these things usually means "suspicious, with a
persecution complex." I set these aside and focused on the
last sheet, directions from my Uncle Vince.

Vince Flamand was my mother's half-brother, a six-foot-
six southpaw who was a first-round pick of the Detroit Tigers
in 1967. At seventeen he could throw a tailing fastball that
hit 96 on the gun, and despite his records for hit batsmen
in every league he played, he went from high school ball to
Triple A Toledo in just over a year. So why did he end up in
Canada? Because, he explained, he didn't want to fuck up his
arm in Vietnam.

For about six months, once or twice a month, Uncle Vince
would send me postcards or first-day covers from towns in
Quebec, New Brunswick and Nova Scotia. With lines like:

> *Hey Nile buddy,*
> *Thought you might like this stamp of a grizzly … Just*
> *had a tryout with a club in Halifax, Nova Scotia. A nut-*
> *freezing twilight doubleheader. Threw two innings of*
> *shutout middle relief in the first game and saved the*
> *other—struck out the side in the 9th on 9 pitches. 8 heaters*
> *and a change. The ball's not great up here, but it's not great*
> *in Nam either.*

Vince ended up playing not in Nova Scotia but in New Brunswick (as did Matt Stairs), pitching and hitting clean-up for the Marysville Royals. You can look up his stats on the Net. After feeling some soreness in his shoulder, he returned to the States, thinking he could con the draft board into a four-F. A few months later he was captured by the Viet Cong and spent several years in a bamboo cage.

He came back from the war with two shattered heels and an asocial gloom so severe that he moved into a shack in the Adirondacks the size of an outhouse, eating his meals from plates of bark, using whittled sticks as cutlery. When his weight dropped below a hundred, my father got him into a VA hospital in Lyons, some sixty miles from Neptune, which he's been in and out of ever since. If he'd been only one inch taller, my mother told me, he would never have been drafted.

Before leaving Neptune, I e-mailed him for advice and got this reply:

Hey Nile buddy, I was just thinking about you, about the last time we took in a ball game. You remember, you smuggled in a bottle of Jim Beam and the Mets beat the Yanks at Shea? Or maybe the other way round. Or maybe it wasn't with you. I was tanked, what do I know? You still playing ball? I remember you were one bad-ass third baseman. Bad-ass means good, right? Or was it second base? You could've been a pro if it wasn't for that upper-cut swing. OK, here's what you need: penlight (not a flashlight), compass, black clothes, tar, wirecutters. North on I-87 for about 150 miles, to RT-3. Turn left on Blake then right on 190, then left on 11, right on 189, left on Frontier Road. Number 524 on right. That's where Lightning lives. You remember Lightning? Don't talk to him and don't leave your car in his drive, ditch it some place in the woods. Put the tar on your face, and walk back to his place. In one corner of the backyard is a big STOP sign and a small

stone pillar with USA on one side and CANADA on the
other. Don't go anywhere near there. That's where they put
the sensors and cameras. Go to a spot directly in line with
his back door. There used to be a dog house there. If the
Feds have put a fence in since the last time I was there,
that's why you brought the cutters ...

"Lightning" Leitner (I forget his first name), whose
nickname derived from his slowness of foot, was one of
Vince's old catchers, a fellow draft dodger. He's still up there,
true, but six feet under. In any case, it worked. It worked in
Uncle Vince's time and it works now, post-9/11.

The night I crossed, as I was trying to find the STOP sign
and obelisk, I heard sounds from behind me, from a tangled
growth of bushes and stunted trees. Sounds not unlike human
whispering. I turned off my penlight and froze.

A quivering beam of light was directed my way, which got
closer and closer. And the whispering became louder and
louder. I recognized the language.

"*Nǐ hǎo,*" I said. "*Bing jia ná dà.*"

I turned on my light and saw the scared faces of two
women, one old, one young. I'm not sure what scared them
more: the tar smeared like warpaint on my face or hearing
words in their own tongue.

"*Nǐ shì shéi?*" said one of them. (Who are you?)

"*Wǒ jiào Nile.*"

"*Jǐng chá?*" (Police?)

"*Péng.*" (Friend.)

Silence, then a quivery voice. "*Hěn gāo xǐng rèn shí nǐ.*"
(Nice to meet you.)

"*Rèn shí nǐ wǒ yě hěn gāo xǐng.*" (Ditto.)

"We follow?" asked the older one in English. "You know
place?"

"I think so." I pointed my flashlight toward a high chain-link fence with barbed wire strung along the top. There was no dog house in front of it, but the spot was roughly in line with the back door.

"We take bicycles?"

"I wouldn't if I were you."

They took their bicycles. I cut the hole and the three of us bent the wires back and jammed the bikes through. A dog barked in the distance, but the house remained quiet and dark.

On the other side of the fence was an evergreen jungle and an uphill slope that made for tough zigzag slogging, especially with bicycles that had to be dragged or carried, but we soon hit a well-worn path. A Canadian path. "Where are you two coming from?" I asked as we made our way slowly along it, three flashlights lighting the way.

They were smuggled into the U.S., the older one explained, aboard a freighter that docked in Seattle. How did they end up here, on the other side of the continent? She didn't seem to know, or didn't wish to tell.

You have been to China, sir? whispered the younger one in Mandarin. She was quickly reproached by the other.

Yes, I lived there for a year or so. In Shanghai.

We come from nearby! said the older one.

Did you like it, kind sir, in Shanghai? asked the younger one.

I hesitated. The city's a kiln, a steam-bath infused with oil and gas fumes, with methane and ammonium hydroxide, the way the world might have smelled when life was first being formed. It contains the prototype for the world's worst air terminal, Hongquia, and a bar where depressed people can go to cry, where you pay an hourly rate for Kleenex, sad music, and life-size dolls to throw around. *It was very nice.*

Did you go to the countryside? she asked.

Yes, I went hiking in the mountains. And didn't see a single bird. Or animal of any kind.

Yes, said the older one. *They have all been consumed.*

What are you going to do in Canada? I asked.

Xíong dǎn, said the younger one, which I didn't understand. Something to do with bears? The older one slapped her on the shoulder, hard, and nothing more was said.

We walked together in thoughtful silence, the three of us heading north into I knew not what. We reached a cyclable road near Franklin, Quebec, about a four-mile trek, as the sun came up. And then paused, wondering which way to turn. *Zài jiàn,* said one and *Zhù nǐ hǎoyùn,* said the other as they mounted their bikes and waved their Chinese maps at me. We parted in opposite directions.

While walking briskly, my duffle slung over my shoulder like Santa, I formulated a plan for breakfast: once inside the first town I came to I would stop at the first restaurant on the left and wait until it opened. Or perhaps at the first *boulangerie* or *charcuterie* on the right. But when I reached the first town there were none of these on either side. Wasn't this a French province? I paused in front of a discount carpet store. There was a bright red notice taped to the inside door pane with a phone number on it, which said to call P. Tremblay in case of emergency. *Hello, Tremblay? I hate to bother you at home like this, but I need a rug right away.*

On the outskirts of town, a short hike away, I reached a double-wide trailer posing as a diner, whose original name had been painted over with three black letters: TCG. A handwritten sign in the window said it opened at 07:00. When, back in the '90s? I peered in and saw a light about as bright as an oven bulb. I wiped the last of the tar off my face with a Kleenex, sat down on the steps and waited.

The blinds were eventually rolled up and an unsmiling strawberry-blonde opened the door for me. She was wearing a white apron printed with an anthropoid cat walking erect and the words TOM CAT GRILL. She said she'd be right with me and headed for the kitchen. I sat down in a room with wood panelling and white ceiling tiles with holes in them, as in a suburban basement. The place smelled of paint and mineral spirits, though neither the walls nor the ceiling appeared to have been painted. A defective fan clicked with each revolution. On the table, beside the napkin dispenser where the menu should have been, was a sticky brochure from the Parc Safari in Hemmingford, only a few miles, or rather kilometers, away. I pored over every word, enjoying the heat of the vent on my legs. Among other attractions, it announced the arrival of three White Lions, "rarities found only in the Timbavati region of South Africa, whose survival is threatened." Two females and a male were brought over to Quebec to help increase their numbers. What a strange destiny for these cats! Maybe I'd check them out one day with Brooklyn.

Some fifteen minutes later, when I could have recited the contents of the brochure by heart, I delved into my bag for more reading material. My Internet travel notes, written by an American from my home state, informed me that the Québécois are restless people. That their first thought is to get away from other Québécois. Here, there, Ontario, British Columbia, Maine, Mexico and Florida—"especially Florida." Impatient people, always jumping around. Nervous people, something in their DNA. "In all Québécois literature there is not a single novel with a followable plot."

When the waitress finally returned to my table, I was about to say "No big deal" to her apology, but no apology came. She said they had no menus yet and that breakfast was eggs, home-cured ham basted with cider, beans in maple syrup, and poutine. They had no cereal. When I asked what poutine was, she laughed. When I asked if there was a used-car dealership in town, she laughed again.

« *Non, mais t'es fou? Dans ce trou? Mais ... tu trouveras peut-être quelque chose au bout de ce chemin-là.* » She pointed out the window, her eyes twinkling with mischief. Was I being set up?

After eating her heavenly breakfast I loitered as long as possible, flipping through copies of *Boxing Roundup* and *World of Wheels* and a stack of hook and bullet magazines with articles like "10 Best Ways to Hammer Hot-Weather Bucks." The waitress refilled my bowl with robust café au lait and my plate with stacks of multigrain toast, on which I spooned a complicated homemade jam from a jar with a thick seal of paraffin on top. She had little else to do, apart from her crossword puzzle and filling Heinz bottles with liquidy generic ketchup, as there were only two other customers that morning, both take-outs. One of them, an old man as skinny as a parking meter, told me she was "*dans le jus*" (busy) at lunchtime. As he pulled away in his huge silver rig, the waitress wiped my table with a pink sponge that had a soggy half-Cheerio riding on the stern. I thought she said they had no cereal.

When I finished the plate of toast, at exactly nine o'clock according to a large institutional clock on the wall, she placed a glass jar on my table. It was a goldfish bowl, filled not with fish but with peanut-butter cookies with corrugations on top where a fork had been pressed onto them. I ate six. And asked for six to go. After paying the bill (only $28!), I folded a crisp twenty in four and slipped it under the bowl.

At the end of the road she had pointed to, a gravel cul-de-sac over a hundred yards long, I reached a vast driveway that dwarfed the solitary house it led to, a shabby clapboard box that wouldn't have passed for a garden shed in my part of New Jersey. The drive was crowded with run-down or wrecked snowmobiles, two identical turquoise doghouses, as if for twins, two frosty lawnmowers, a motorcycle of the menacing variety, and a mound of something covered by a tarpaulin. Next to the mound, one wheel on the tarp, was a heavily primered VW van with a sign on it: $500. Perfect. A Westphalia with a camper, late eighties. A Vanagon. My dad had one when we lived in Frankfurt.

The buzzer was mute so I pounded on the door's splintered surface, perhaps harder than necessary. Dogs began to bark. Twinned, echoing barks. I was on the verge of leaving when I heard a death rattle in the lock. The door opened and a man appeared in a leather vest with nothing underneath and steroidal biceps as big as bowling balls. On the left one was a tattoo, a snake with its mouth open, tongue and fangs extended; on the right was a single, unfinished fang, as if the tattoo-artist had been practicing. The man's cornrowed head was tilted to one side and his arms and feet set in a boxer's stance. Only when I pointed to the Westphalia did his vein-popping arms relax.

Without a word, he grabbed a ring of keys hanging from a nine-inch nail and strode past me, down the steps and onto the mud and slush of the driveway. In big furry slippers. He started up the Westy, not on the first or second or even third try, then told me to take her for a spin. Solo.

I threw my duffle onto the passenger side and paused to adjust the mirrors with hands that were trembling. *Why so nervous, Nile?* I backed up with a lurch and heard the crunching sound of tire on tarp, then a metallic clang as I hit what I think was a lawnmower handle.

I drove the van back down the road with clumsy violence, grinding its gears, bouncing through ruts and puddles. Screws on the dash were backing out of their holes and the glove compartment flew open. I stopped in front of the diner and waved through the window at the waitress, whose face looked startled under the unnatural neon glow. Did she think I'd come to get her? Was Fang her boyfriend? I sped off, in rubberly fashion, and opened her up on the highway. In kilometers: 100, 110, 120, 130. Runs like a cheetah. Sounds like an elephant.

I was feeling good, which speed often does to me, and found myself waving or grinning at everyone I saw. At oncoming motorists heading for work, at pedestrians bent on their errands, at a blue-and-white aircraft gliding low. *I am an American of good will in a German vehicle. I will try to observe your Québécois customs.*

Cars passing me threw a slushy spray up from the road. I turned on the wipers, which made things worse. Where was the lever for the spray? Couldn't find it.

Back on the owner's driveway, after a blurry ride home, I inspected the interior. Absolutely foul. Dark brown stains on the passenger seat, filters smashed into black smudges on the floor mats, McDonald's plastic filling both footwells. Red carpeting in the back like the sham upholstery put in coffins. And a battered wooden tool box with a nightscope sitting on top.

I jumped out and looked over the exterior: the hood

was held down by bungee cord, the side door dented, the front bumper wired in place. The body had been repainted, seemingly by a child, with wide brushstrokes. On the door were letters, faint ones, barely visible beneath the army-green latex paint: CLOUD 9 POTATO CHIPS.

I banged on the door again, and again had to wait. From my father's valise I pulled out a slab of twenties and counted out twenty-five. Then banged again.

Fang eventually opened it, but with his back to me. A strand of turquoise beads now circled his neck like a dog collar. And a Q-Ray bracelet, for energy and vitality, circled his wrist. Were these put on for my benefit? He was bent over, struggling with something adhering to the heel of his slipper.

« Do you want to keep this? » I asked in French, holding up the army-surplus nightscope. « Or the toolbox in the back? »

Without looking at what was being shown to him, he shook his head. He was more interested in what was clinging to his slipper. Something made of clear plastic. Or perhaps vinyl. He looked up only when I held out the roll of bills, which he accepted and then counted, lips moving, to *vingt-cinq*. He handed four back.

« Did I ... miscount? » I asked.

« Exchange rate. »

« Forget it. »

He nodded. « Tell you what. I'll throw in a plate, a good one, on the house. »

He crammed the wad into his tight hip pocket without another word. He spoke so few words, in fact—gravelly monosyllables for the most part—that I thought he might be laryngitic. Or perhaps a death metal singer. But after handing me a blue-and-white license plate with the province's motto

(*Je me souviens*), he began to form full sentences in a clear voice, explaining that he was a welder who ran with the Hells, Châteauguay chapter, and that a stoolie had been shot in the van's passenger seat.

PART TWO

CHRISTMAS

Bring me flesh and bring me wine
Bring me pine logs hither ...

∽ XVII ∾

On the 22nd of December, in pre-dawn darkness, I began loading up the potato chip van. Not only with things that belonged to Céleste and me, but with things that belonged to our neighbor. I put on his forest ranger parka, in case we ran into trouble along the way, slipping his badge into one pocket, his U.S. Fish & Wildlife business cards into the other. Wrapped in an elastic band, they had no name on them, just a blue, orange and yellow logo. I also took the ranger's portable red flasher and stashed it under the driver's seat.

"Are there any books I could read?" I called out to Céleste, who was putting on her own uniform in the bathroom. "Like *Forest Ranging for Dummies*? Or ... *The Bluffer's Guide to Wildlife Detection*?"

Her reply through the door was muffled. She opened the door and limped out, wearing a ski-mask and my black suede coat with the collar up. She was quite a sight, like she was Halloweening as a terrorist.

"I'll coach you," she said. "If we run into poachers we'll use the walkie-talkie. You just follow my instructions, like Christian in *Cyrano de Bergerac*."

I nodded, still eyeing her outfit.

"You've read that, right?"

"Well, I ... saw the Steve Martin movie."

"I thought you went to the best schools in Europe. What did you do there anyway?"

"Drugs, mainly."

"Give me the badge."

"What?"

"Give me the badge."

I plucked it out of my pocket and handed it to her.

"Put your hand on your heart."

I looked ceilingward but obeyed.

"Do you promise to faithfully execute your duties to the best of your abilities, to protect the wildlife and natural resources of the province of Quebec, and to tell the truth at all times?"

"I do."

"Do you swear on the bones of your ancestors?"

"I do."

She pinned the badge onto the left breast pocket of the parka. "By the powers invested in me, you are now a wildlife detective. You have the authority to arrest villains and killers and evildoers. And anyone at all, for that matter."

Despite her valiant attempts, it was too painful for Céleste to climb into the back of the van, so I had to lift her. I flashed to the first time I'd lifted her in, in her coarse, wet, unwieldy sack—so different from the soft and dry and malleable form I now had in my arms! I set her down on the same sleeping bag and covered her with a wool blanket, though by this time the Westphalia was warm.

From behind the wheel I looked up at an iron sky: gray on gray, swift clouds threatening snow. I flipped on the wipers, which groaned as they crossed the glass, in counter-rhythm with a song on CBC:

Over the river and through the woods
To grandmother's house we go
The horse knows the way to carry the sleigh
Through white and drifted snow ...

"How are you doing back there?" I shouted as we bumped along the perilous *chemin saisonnier*. The pot-holes and ruts gave off a silvery blue sheen, and the white plumes of low branches glided overhead. It was so cold that the snow creaked as we drove over it. I turned the radio down and repeated my question.

"Not dead yet," she replied.

On the highway the street lamps were still on and the morning stars blinked faintly between the clouds. Silver beads of ice glazed the wires overhead. We were the only car on the road.

"I've got to be careful," I said, glimpsing my passenger in the rear-view. She had discarded the blanket and was drawing triangular faces of cats on the back window fog. "I haven't a clue how fast I'm going!" I tapped on the dash. "Speedometer's dead!"

Céleste made her way to the front of the van, gingerly, through columns of packed boxes. I objected, but not strenuously, asking only that she keep her mask on. She looked over my shoulder at the instrument panel, then out the window while glancing at my watch.

"You're fine," she said after a few seconds. "You're going ... 79.6 kilometers an hour."

I looked down again at my speedometer, odometer, tachometer. All on the blink. "How do you know that?"

"Well, I know the telephone poles are sixty meters apart. The calculation's really quite simple."

She clambered into the passenger seat, wincing. Then reached over and thumped the dash, once, twice. Third time lucky. The speedometer needle, and all the other dials, became unstuck. I checked our speed: a hair under 80 kilometers.

"What's that in miles?" I asked.

"Forty-nine point four."

"And in ... knots?"

A slight pause. "One forty-seven point three."

"I was kidding."

"I know."

Not far from the church, a yellow vehicle appeared suddenly in my wing mirror, getting bigger and bigger. It pulled up beside us, in the oncoming lane. Cops? No siren, no flashing lights. Céleste, as alert as ever, slid down into the footwell.

The car, or rather tank, remained there, cruising abreast, matching my speed. When I looked over, its passenger window came down. A faintly familiar face, with a drunkard's grin and periscopically rising middle finger beside it. He sped up and veered into my lane, missing my bumper by a hair. Hummer, license 666 HLL. My second encounter with this idiot. I pressed on the accelerator, to the floor, until I felt something around my ankle. Céleste's hand.

"Don't," she said calmly.

"You know the guy?"

"No, but let him go."

I took my foot off the gas. She was right of course. But if ever there was a third encounter of the close kind, I vowed, I would give chase, not stopping until I shot him in the face with Brooklyn's Walther .38.

I didn't quite know what to expect from Céleste when we arrived. Joy? Horror? Relief? She felt none of these, as far as I could tell. As I prepared cranberry-bloodorange tea and a cat's breakfast for six, she sat motionless at the kitchen table, staring out the window, her mouth curved in a vague expression of resignation. Even the cats couldn't seem to cheer her up, although she had a kind word and a hug for each. I told her about the first time I fed them, about Moon following me through the cemetery rows, but she didn't respond. I told her about the two racoons I had seen in her grandmother's study, who had come and gone through the doggy door. It was as though she were deaf.

"How are you doing?" I asked.

Moon was on her lap, the only cat that wasn't eating. "I'm not bragging," she rasped. Her voice was sounding worse and worse, like she had lung cancer and was talking through a hole in her trachea.

"I'm going to bed," she said. She gave Moon a kiss and set her down in front of her dish. Declining my help, she then hobbled up the stairs, pausing at each step, head down, moving as if sleepwalking through a nightmare. She disappeared from view and I heard her bedroom door being shut and locked.

A churchly silence settled on the house, on its living and lately dead, and a sense of guilt began to dye my time there.

XVIII

I slept all day & all night which was a big surprise because
when we arrived I couldn't stop thinking about Grand-maman.
I walked to my bed with jelly legs and when I closed the door I
started shaking so hard that I couldn't stop myself. I pulled the
covers right over me & felt like a bird with a cloth draped over
its cage for the night. I started to panic. I was sure I'd hear
strange sounds all day long, like footsteps or windows being pried
open. Or that I'd pass out from lack of oxygen. But when I made
a little air hole & put my head on the pillow, I fell asleep almost
right away! Because I feel safe with Nile?

In a dream I saw Gran's face & she pointed her finger at me
& told me not to be sad, that her time had come, and that Nile
would take care of me. Did she mean that we would get married?
Anyway, it was just a dream.

Then I started thinking about other things. About bears, and
one bear in particular. And about Baz cutting me open like a fish &
bleeding me like a deer. I got out of bed & threw up in the toilet, with
the taps running full blast so that Nile wouldn't hear. I sat down &
started shaking again, so hard that the toilet seat began to rattle.

"I'll never get back to sleep," I thought. Then, without
warning, I was in another dream talking to Santa. I was sitting
on his knee, waiting for Mom to take my picture, when he
whispered in my ear: "Only good girls will make Santa's list this

year." I couldn't get the words out of my head so I forced the dream to end & got out of bed again. It was around lunchtime — the next day! I crept down the hall to see which room Nile had taken. He took the guest room, the second-smallest room in the house, just below the maid's old room in the attic. I told him he could take Gran's room but he didn't & I'm glad.

Nile served lunch, if that's the word, some plant fibre that reminded me of a braided door mat. Stewed weeds on the side, tomato sauce mixed with something white, perhaps toothpaste. After I secretly tossed it, Nile asked if I'd like to watch a movie. I said no, I had work to do (making gifts, though I didn't tell him that) but he talked me into it. He had a big Walmart bag full of DVDs that he spread out on the table. He doesn't rent them, he buys them! Some were comedies, to cheer me up I guess. I said that I appreciated the gesture, but that I would not watch any movie with a midget in it. And that includes Danny DeVito. Some were "stamp" movies: The Mandarin Mystery, Decalogue IX and Charade. I chose Charade, which was shot in Paris & stars Cary Grant & Audrey Hepburn. After the film Nile rewound and freeze-framed an image near the end, of the 3 valuable stamps everyone was after: the Swedish 4-Shilling of 1854, the Hawaiian Blue 3-cent of 1894, and the Gazette Moldave, supposedly the most valuable stamp in the world. In the movie they were worth $85,000, $65,000, and $100,000.

Nile said that it's really the Swedish 3-Shilling of 1855 that's valuable. There was a mistake in the colour — the printer made it yellow instead of green. Only one copy of this stamp has ever been found — by a young Swedish boy looking through his grandfather's collection. It sold in 1996 for $2.3 million. It's the most valuable stamp in the world.

As for the Hawaiian Blue 3-cent of 1894, Nile said that it's actually the 2-cent of 1851 that's valuable, worth about $750,000 if unused. In 1892 one of its owners was murdered for it by another collector. To be specific, Hector Giroux killed Gaston Leroux. I wrote all this down — my memory's good but not that good.

As for the "Gazette Moldave," Nile says it doesn't exist.

While I ate Lucky Charms out of the box, with Mercury on my lap & Comet on one side & Moon on the other, Nile told me some interesting things about the movie. About the casting. He said that Cary Grant was worried about the difference in their ages (over 25 years, more than me & Nile!) so he insisted that the Hepburn character pursue him, rather than vice versa. Which is cool because it cancels out the creepy factor. Why am I mentioning all this? Because it gave me an idea: I will pursue Nile, even though he's a bit off, and it will cancel out the creepy factor.

I'm not beautiful like Audrey Hepburn, so I'll be Jane Eyre instead. Jane was plain like me, and an orphan and runaway too. And Nile will be Rochester — old, rich, proud, sardonic, moody & morose. Naturally, his moroseness goes away after he meets me. He calls me his "elf," his "changeling." And Nile's ex is like Rochester's wife — mad — and he never goes back to her. Then we separate for a while & I dream that Nile is calling my name & when I finally find him he's blind. But he regains sight in one eye so that he can see his child when it's put into his arms ...

More later. Is that a snowplow I hear?

☙ XIX ❧

Céleste slept like the dead her first day back home but seemed to be awake for the next two. I could hear her pacing about in her room in the wee hours, or wandering the halls like Ophelia.

Although she never mentioned it, she must have heard the same things I heard during the night: a snowplow grinding up and down the church lane, snowmobiles roaring through the graveyard, a ringing black phone with ghosts on the other end ...

"Don't come in!" she would hiss each time I knocked on her door. A whispery voice that rasped like a file.

She was making ornaments for a Christmas tree, I soon discovered, for a tree she didn't want. At least not at first. "It's a stupid tradition," she said over a quick lunch I'd prepared, a blameless shiitake conchiglie with dark opal basil and white cilantro sauce, from a recipe Earl had given me. "It's stupid to take the life of a young tree, and plastic ones are just as stupid." Her mouth was encarmined with tomato sauce, which matched her bloodshot eyes. When I told her that I had found a red pine in the cemetery, one that had been felled and left to rot (two other taller ones had been poached), she thought that decorating it would be a nice memorial.

"Can you get some gifts for the cats before the stores close?" she asked. "Nothing for me, though. Promise? And some candles?" She then raced back to her room, or rather limped quickly.

For once I was ahead of her. While she was locked away upstairs the previous morning, I had slipped out, riskily, and purchased two dozen candles, six packs of Luv cat treats and as many catnipped fluffballs. Along with a Christmas log, microgreens, pink champagne, and three gifts for Céleste.

"And leave you alone?" I replied. "Sorry, can't do it."

Late on Christmas Eve, close to midnight, Céleste began trimming the tree with her handmade decorations: multi-colored clay figurines of deer, lynx, cougars, wolverines, bears (riding on the backs of cardinals) and swans, a pair of each, some of which she had just made, others from Christmases past. Added to these were some of her plaster and pewter dinosaurs, to which she attached red ribbons and loops. No angels, no star. After arranging and lighting the candles, two of them in corner nooks beside old brass snuff dishes, she put two wrapped boxes under the tree.

"You believe in God, right?" I asked.

"Yeah. God and the Easter Bunny and the Tooth Fairy."

"No, seriously."

"I'm an evangelical atheist. Like my grandmother."

"So why are we celebrating Christmas? You believe in Christ?"

"Do you?"

I didn't answer.

"I've never doubted," she said, "that a Jewish troublemaker was hauled away for disturbing the peace two thousand years ago. And in fact I've always had a bit of a soft spot for him. But as for his being the son of God? No."

"Because there's no God."

"Well, your friend God really took great care of my

grandmother. And my mother. And me. And all the animals around here killed for fun."

"So why are we celebrating?"

"Because this is a holiday from pagan times too. Candles, lights, even trees. It's not altogether Christian." She walked over to the foot of the stairs. "I'll be right back."

While she was in her bedroom I placed my own gifts under the tree. And hung two Christmas stockings lumpy with walnuts and tangerines. Should I deck the halls with balls of holly? I parted the curtains, wanting a white Christmas backdrop. Low in the sky, near the horizon, were vaporish waves of light, the blue-green streamers of an aurora. It's a wonderful world.

I was stoking the pine-log fire, and seeing goldfish and guppies and angelfish swimming through the flames, when Céleste made her grand entrance. Slowly down the stairs she came, sans spectacles, squinting, in a distressed black frock, black ankle boots with a crisscross of laces wound through button-hooks, and tights of billiard-table green. But for the black lipstick and mascara, she might have been a pubescent Victorian widow. As she paraded by me on her way to the tree, I told her she looked great.

She waggled her eyebrows. "Miss America on the runway, that's me."

We opened our presents at midnight on the nail, that being the Quebec tradition. Céleste put her glasses back on and lackadaisically pulled out my unwrapped offerings from three plastic bags: a stamp album (she'd asked for one); my album of prehistoric animal stamps (she'd admired them); a telescope (which she'd not asked for); and *The Best of Jimi Hendrix* (ditto). She said thank you, but I think I had disappointed her.

"Do you know who Jimi Hendrix is?" I asked.

"No."

A shocking gap in her home-schooling, that. "He was ..." I didn't quite know how to describe him in a sentence or two. "The greatest ... well, you'll see. He was part Indian like you."

I received two well-thumbed volumes from her private collection—Bertrand Russell's *Why I Am Not a Christian* and J.M. Coetzee's *The Lives of Animals*, both wrapped in white paper adorned with hand-drawn silver swans—along with something protected between two heavy pieces of cardboard. A drawing? Yes, a blue-pencil portrait. Of yours truly.

"Beautiful," I said, my eyes slowly taking in the subtle shadings and sure lines. "Now I know what I'd look like with successful plastic surgery." It was the first "normal" drawing of a human I'd seen of hers. Her figures were most often grotesque and distorted à la Bosch or Bacon or fitted with devil horns; her animals, on the other hand, were always true, always beautiful. "Thank you." I reached over and gave her an awkward hug.

"That one I just dashed off," she said, blushing. "Look under the tissue paper."

I did so and found another drawing, one that had taken much more time: a painting of Céleste and her grandmother in an airplane, after the photograph in the study. It was in the photorealist style, which I'd always thought was pointless non-art. Until now.

"Thank you, this is stunning, I ... I'll treasure it, I really will." I examined the faces, the detail of the blue-and-white plane, the little metal "skis" over the wheels, the colors of the frozen lake. "Thanks for ... you know, all this. The books and ... all the work you put into ... thanks."

"Yeah, sure. After all, not like you ever did anything for me."

I nodded, my eyes trained on the painting.

"I started that one a while ago," she admitted, "but just finished it last night."

I looked again at the farcically flattering portrait. Thought I'd better change the subject before ruining it with teardrops. "Can a plane take off on a frozen lake? Or would the wheels just spin all over the place? Or the skis just ... slide."

"When I was seven I asked my grandmother the same question."

Sounds about right. "I guess you were a bit backward at that age."

"Think about it."

I used to be fairly good at thinking, but over the years I seem to have weaned myself off the habit. "Do I get three guesses?"

"It's amazing, Nile, how many people don't understand the concept. The wheels have no friction, or practically none. They're on the plane to *reduce* friction. They don't drive the plane. They're only there to stop the plane from dragging its guts along the ground. Its fuselage. Other than that, they apply no real force on takeoff. The engines act on the air *above* the ice, pushing the plane forward, and since the plane can move forward, it can generate lift and take off. Once it reaches a certain speed, of course."

Of course. I was about to ask more questions, about her grandmother's piloting experience and plane, but Céleste hobbled off to the kitchen. As I unfoiled a bottle of Perrier Jouët Fleur de Champagne Rosé, a connoisseur's pink according to my father, she returned with yet another gift-wrapped present. "Open it," she said.

From the irregular shape and translucent paper I knew what it was, but of course didn't let on. "What could this be?" I said. "A tie clip?" I unravelled the red ribbon, tore off the white tissue paper.

"It was given to my grandmother, so I'm regifting. But I know she'd want you to have it."

It was something I'd stumbled upon in the basement while looking for Christmas-tree lights, in a kind of hidden alcove, like those secret caves in Europe where wines were kept from the enemy until peace was restored. The label on the box said Абсинт Кристмас ("Christmas Absinthe") and alluded to some chess tournament in Czechoslovakia. No date, but obviously Soviet era. It was a gift set, complete with glass, spoon and lighter. Just what a recovering alcoholic didn't need. "Thank you," I said, giving Céleste another hug. "Just what I always wanted. Amazing."

"You've never had it before?"

"No," I lied. "But I've always wanted to try it. Shall we have a drop?"

"No, but you can," she said. "I don't like the smell of that stuff. The anise—it reminds me of bear hunter's bait."

I didn't trust myself with *la fée verte*, afraid I'd drink the bottle in one sitting. Or falling. I used to be able to drink it till the cows came home. When I was amped on speed it didn't slur my speech or lame me. It just took the edge off my hot nerves. I stashed the bottle in a high kitchen cupboard, out of sight, out of mind.

In the living room, beginning to sweat and trying not to twitch, I popped and poured pink champagne into two unmatching flutes. This I could handle, this I didn't like enough to overdrink. Its liftoff was good but touchdown bad.

"I think that's the most beautiful bottle I've ever seen," Céleste enthused hoarsely, as if her vocal cords were numb from cocaine. She picked up the clear bottle, held it up to the light of the fire. "Art Nouveau, right? And these flowers are anemones?"

I shrugged, botanical dummy that I am.

"A toast," she said.

This champagne's too good for a toast—if you mix up emotions with stuff like this, you lose the taste: my father's words. Only since his death had his voice sung inside me, sometimes the accompanist, sometimes the soloist. "Good idea," I said. "Do you ... know any?"

"'Drink to me with thine eyes. And I will pledge with mine. Or leave a kiss but in the cup, And I'll not look for wine.'"

"That's ..." I was going to say "romantic" but thought better of it. "... Ben Jonson."

"It's the only toast I know," she shrugged. "You know any?"

"'To alcohol. The cause of—and solution to—all of life's problems.'"

"Who said that?"

"Homer Simpson." We clinked glasses. "Merry Christmas."

"Say Merry Christmas in every language you know."

I paused. "*Joyeux Noël, Feliz Navidad, Frohe Weihnachten, Buon Natale, Feliz Natal, Χαρούμενα Χριστούγεννα, Shèngdàn kuàilè.* That's it."

"Say ... 'The quick brown fox jumps over the lazy dog.' In ... Spanish."

I hesitated. "Do you mean literally, or an equivalent that uses all the letters of the alphabet?"

"Literally. No, the equivalent."

"*El veloz murciélago hindú comía feliz cardillo y kiwi.*"

This had some letters missing, but it's the only one I knew.

"Okay. In German. Literally."

"*Der flinke, braune Fuchs springt über den trägen Hund.*"

"Greek."

"*Ηγήγορη καψρετιά λ ϖόν ϖηδά ϖέρα ϖό το οκνηρό σκνλí.*"

"Italian."

"*La volpe marrone rapida salta sopra il cane pigro.*"

A smile. "All right, now say ... No, tell me about your childhood."

My memories of childhood were short-lived; they burned like newspapers. "I'll tell you when I've finished it."

"About Christmases in places you lived. Like ... Germany."

A holy trinity: booze, sentiment, gluttony. "I was confused as a kid. They seem to have a dozen Santa Clauses, each with a different name. The oldest one, the original one I guess, is Christkind, a child with blond hair and angel wings. Then there's Weinachtsmann, Aschenmann, Pelznickel, Boozenickel, Hans Trapp, Klaubauf, Krampus, Schmutzli ... depending on the region. Oh, and Ruprecht, who has bright red hair."

Céleste smiled. "How about ... France? Same as Quebec?"

"I don't know much about Christmas in Quebec. In fact, I know nothing at all. You guys have a Père Noël up here?"

She looked at the ceiling. "It's the same as in America."

"In France, it's close. Père Noël is like the American Santa except the French consider his reindeers as important as him. On Christmas Eve they leave hay and carrots out for them, in their shoes."

"Get out of town. You're making that up."

"I'm serious."

"Really? That is *so* wicked. I mean, to think of the animals like that. So then what happens?"

"Père Noël takes the reindeer food and leaves gifts in return. He comes twice, though. Once on December 5th, the Eve of St-Nicolas, and once on the 24th."

"I've always wanted to go to Paris," said Céleste.

"Maybe I'll take you there one day."

"I don't think that's in the cards. Somehow."

"What are you, a fortune teller?"

"Touché. Did you like living there?"

They were the best years of my life, and they weren't very good. "Yeah, it was great."

"What's it like?"

"Like the postcards."

"Come on."

"When I lived there? People carrying baguettes under their arms, old men wearing berets, women walking poodles, Art Nouveau entrances to the métro, bookstalls along the Seine and *bateaux mouches*, people reading newspapers in sidewalk cafés, lots of scooters, bad drivers, congestion, impossible squares and narrow lanes, dogshit and overweight tourists—"

"Okay, you can stop. That's kind of what I thought."

By and by, as the champagne kicked in, we began to sing two songs by the fire, simultaneously. Neither were Christmas songs. I started a round of "Row Row Row Your Boat," which Brooklyn loved, and Céleste jumped in with "Show Me the Way to Go Home," which her grandmother loved.

Céleste then asked me to sing Christmas songs I'd learned while living abroad. I thought for a moment before launching into "We Three Kings." First the standard variation, learned in an American school in Athens:

We three Kings of Orient are
Trying to smoke a rubber cigar.
It was loaded, we exploded,
Now we are traveling far ...

Then a version learned from a Floridian girl in France:

We three kings of Orient are
Trying to sell some cheap underwear
Superfantastic, no elastic
99 cents a pair ...

And this from a drunken headmaster in London:

We three kings of Leicester Square
Selling ladies underwear
Oh so drastic, no elastic
Only tuppence a pair ...

As I sang, Céleste stared at me with concern or perhaps fright in her eyes, as if I were becoming increasingly unglued. So I began a serious—and stirring—rendition of Lennon's "And So This Is Christmas," which I'd also heard for the first time in London. I went in and out of at least three keys and faltered on the words. Céleste prompted me in a flat monotone but did not join in; instead, she did something that shouldn't have surprised me, but did. Turning her head away, she began to cry. I asked if it was because of the song and she said no. I asked if she was thinking of Christmases past, pining for her grandmother, and she said no, she was thinking of Christmases to come. That there wouldn't be any.

I had a similar feeling—that there would be no future, that the door to the future had been closed and locked. "That's nonsense, complete nonsense. I mean, who knows what tomorrow may bring?"

She wiped her cheek with the back of her hand. "The arrival of wise men wouldn't hurt."

"Let me see that."

"See what?"

"Just hold out your hand, palm up."

She held it out, reluctantly, and I took it in mine. Her lifeline was short, truncated. I pointed. "See? I knew it. You'll live to be ninety."

"That's total bull."

"Okay, maybe not ninety. But at least eighty."

She moved her head slowly from side to side in a firm negative. Then wiped another teardrop, this time with her shoulder.

"You survived the first attack, didn't you? And together we'll survive the second. And the third too, if it comes to that."

Tears began to well up again, so I put my arm around her, falteringly, and it remained there in the quiet as the fire and candles flickered around us.

"Tell me a joke," she said suddenly, sitting bolt upright. "Make me laugh. Please."

I looked up to the ceiling, pensively, despairingly. One thing I had always been able to do: make Brooklyn laugh. One thing I had never been able to do: make Céleste laugh. My jokes during her month-long convalescence had left her stone-faced—the same ones that left Brooklyn tear-faced.

"You don't like my jokes. You said—and I quote—they're 'childish and stupid.'"

"No, I liked them. Really. I was fibbing. It's just ..."

"Just what?"

"Well, I was ... just, you know, jealous or something."

"Jealous?"

"Yeah, because I don't know any jokes, I've never told one. I don't have a sense of humor, ask anyone. My grandmother didn't either and I take after her. I've never said anything funny in my whole life."

This was one of the saddest things I'd ever heard. Every child has a sense of humor; every child wants to laugh and make others laugh. "But what about when you said, 'The arrival of wise men wouldn't hurt.' That was funny."

"It was?"

"Yes."

Céleste paused to consider this. "It didn't make you laugh."

"Well, that's because—"

"My grandmother was agelastic and so am I."

I paused, trying to figure out what that meant. *Gelos* is Greek for laughter; *α* means 'not.' "Do you mean ..."

"Unable to laugh. Or uninclined to. It's in my genes."

I stared at the floor, reflecting. She's a gifted child, a prodigy; maybe that's the price some of them have to pay. Newton, for example, was said to have laughed only once in his entire life (when asked what geometry could possibly be used for).

"Gran even thought of eating sardonia. You know what that is?"

I nodded. It's a Sardinian plant that causes convulsive laughter ending in death. Whence the word *sardonic*. Was her grandmother joking?

"Weren't you supposed to make me laugh?" said Céleste.

I strained, like the sad clown, to get on with the job, sifting through my clean-joke repertoire. "Can you cross your eyes?" I said.

She frowned skeptically, but crossed her eyes.

"Céleste, stop. You're not allowed to cross your *i*'s. You're supposed to dot your *i*'s and cross your *t*'s. Didn't they teach you anything at school?"

Not a ghost of a smile. No indication that a punch line had been reached. "I never went to school. Well, almost never."

"You didn't?"

"I already told you, I was home-schooled."

"Did your grandmother teach you phys. ed?"

"Sort of."

"Can you do a somersault?"

"Of course. Well, maybe not now."

"Do you know why it's called a somersault?"

"Yeah. It's from the Middle French *sombresault*, from the Latin *supra*—over—and *saltus*—leap."

Christ, was she ever home-schooled. And she's just ruined the joke. "That's ... not the reason," I improvised. "That's a common misconception."

Céleste looked at me warily. "Okay, so why's it called a somersault?"

"Because it starts with a spring and ends with a fall."

Céleste squinted at me, without even a sixteenth of a smile, as if analyzing the joke. Or preparing to smack me. "More."

I stopped to think. Maybe the trick was to tell something factual. "Okay. True story. Did your grandmother teach you anything by Hart Crane?"

"Of course. The poem about the Brooklyn Bridge."

I nodded. "As you probably know, he committed suicide ..."

"He jumped into the Caribbean and drowned."

How many jokes was she going to ruin? I paused. "His father invented LifeSavers."

"Really? That's ... a coincidence but there's nothing clever or instructional about it."

"Do you know who Dutch Schultz is?"

"The gangster?"

"He was gunned down in a restaurant in New Jersey, not far from where I used to live."

"And?"

"Before he died he babbled nonsense for a couple of hours, which was all taken down by a police stenographer. Guess what his last words were."

"How should I know?"

"'French-Canadian bean soup.'"

Céleste stared at me, her eyes peering over the top of her glasses. "Okay, thanks, Nile. That was ... hilarious. You're a real screamfest. I think I'll go to bed now."

Not exactly laugh therapy, not exactly a gelastic seizure, but at least she'd stopped crying. "Do you want me to read you a bedtime story?"

"I'm fifteen, for God's sake."

"I thought you were fourteen."

She grabbed my wrist and turned it. "Fifteen as of ... an hour and fifty-seven minutes ago."

"Are you serious? You were born the same day as Jesus?"

She nodded.

I looked at her in silence. For a child, possibly the worst day of the year to be born. "Okay, I owe you another gift."

"Don't bother. No one else ever did."

"Merry Christmas and Happy Birthday." I raised my glass.

"Where have I heard that before?"

We clinked glasses and drank the last drops of champagne. "Shall I open the absinthe?" I asked. She's only fourteen, I realize, or rather fifteen, but it was a doubly special occasion.

"No thanks."

"How about a bedtime poem?"

"Since when do I have a bedtime? Who says I have to go to bed, ever?"

"But ... you just said you were going to bed. So let's go." My voice sounded strangely like my father's. "Chop chop. Doctor's orders."

"Heil Hitler."

"I've spoken. It is my will."

She stuck her tongue out. "My grandmother let me go to bed whenever I wanted. She was a firm believer in letting children act on their stupidity until they learned better."

My mother's policy too, more or less. "But what if, like me, the child never learns any better?"

"Okay, read me a poem," she groaned. "But with someone in it like me, someone I can identify with."

While Céleste got ready for bed, I went to my room and dragged out my duffle from beneath the bed. I pulled out my book of poems and flipped through its pages. This might be difficult, might call for some ad-libbing. But I was used to that. Brooklyn wanted a bedtime story every night, but only ones involving cats or else she'd wail. So I had some adapting to do: *Cat and the Beanstalk; Snow White and the Seven Cats; The Cat and the Tortoise; The Pied Cat.*

Céleste was under the covers when I knocked on her open door. Her eyes were closed, but she was playing possum. "Find a character like me?" she asked in a pillow-muffled voice.

"That would be hard, Céleste, you're one in a million."

She rolled from her side to her back and pulled the blanket up to the bridge of her nose, Arab style. "So that means there's over six and a half thousand people like me in the world?"

I sat down at the foot of the bed. "How about this one?

She would joke with hyenas, returning their stare
With an impudent wag of the head:
And she once went a walk, paw-in-paw, with a bear,
'Just to keep up its spirits,' she said.

But he perceived that her spirits were low,
So he repeated in musical tone
Some jokes he had kept for a season of woe
But she would do nothing but groan.

She is known for her slowness in taking a jest.
Should you happen to venture on one,
She will sigh like a thing that is deeply distressed:
And always looks grave at a pun."

Céleste smiled, to my surprise. "Yup, that's me all right. You just make that up?"

"No, it's from *The Hunting of the Snark*. Lewis Carroll."

"Never read him."

How could any child not have read Lewis Carroll? "You haven't? Why not?"

"He was a pedophile. What's a snark?"

"It's a ... an imaginary animal."

She arrested a yawn. "Did you know that the hyena doesn't have a bone in its penis?"

I was in unfamiliar territory. With Brooklyn, the subject of penises had not been broached. "I ... didn't know that, no."

"Only three other mammals don't have one. Zebra, kangaroo and ... guess which one."

"I give up."

"You!"

I nodded.

"Human males!"

"Right. So how about another poem?"

"Is your face getting red, Nile?"

"Of course not, why would it be? Because of hyena penises? It's probably just a ... you know, a bit of an alcohol flush—"

"Yoko Ono said that if she had a penis she'd be laughing all the time."

"You get used to it."

"Did you know that Japanese restaurants charge $500 for seal penis?"

No, but I know that one billion Chinese dream of eating tiger penis. I paged through the book. "No, I didn't."

"Have you ever used a penis enlarger?"

"Céleste ..."

"No, I'm serious. They don't work, right? I mean ... that's what everyone says."

"I haven't a clue about penis enlargers. I would imagine they don't work. But how did this subject—"

"You a prude or something?"

"Me, a prude?"

"It's estimated that eighty percent of bikers and hunters—trophy hunters—have small penises. If it weren't for small penises, there'd hardly be any bikers or hunters. So it's worth it—for society—to invent an enlarger that really works."

This was airtight, logic-wise, but I didn't feel like pursuing the subject. Not only because I felt uncomfortable discussing penis enlargers with a teenage girl, but because sex in general was a subject I tried to avoid with anyone, of any age. I could never understand today's obsession with talking about sex. Once you do, especially if you use words like *rumpy-pumpy* or *wooshy-wooshy*, the magic and mystery are gone. No? I stared at the ground, at a nail that stuck up fascinatingly from the floorboards. Yeah, I suppose I was a prude.

"Okay, I'll stop," she said. "Read me one last poem. No, let me see that. I'll read you one."

Now this would be interesting—which one would she choose? D.H. Lawrence's "Snake"? She flipped through the book like a deck of cards, and I was reminded of an old TV show, *My Favorite Martian* or something, in which one of the characters could read books just by riffling through them. She handed the anthology back to me, gazed aloofly out the window, and recited the following lines:

At midnight in the churchyard
A tomcat comes to wail
And he chants the hate of a million years
As he swings his snaky tail ...

He twists and crouches and capers
And bares his curved sharp claws,
And he sings to the stars of the jungle nights
Ere cities were, or laws.

Beast from a world primeval,
He and his leaping clan,

When the blotched red moon leers over the roofs
Give voice to their scorn of man.

She let her head fall back onto the pillow. "Don Marquis," she said softly. Then entered the Land of Nod before I could count to ten or conceivably twenty.

A noise from outside, a faint rumbling, drew me to the window. I tried to peer through its thick frost, which was shaped like a map of Africa, but couldn't see a thing. I melted a peephole on the glass with my palms, then twisted the latch and pushed the window open. A loud snapping sound made me think I'd broken the glass, but it was only the ice breaking. I stuck my head out and saw a dim gray form with a horn-like protuberance. It was about twelve feet long and five feet wide and as my eyes grew accustomed to the dark it took on the *exact* form of a woolly rhino. It grumbled then roared, as if catching its first glimpse of a hairless, ape-like man.

By the time I made it downstairs with my nightscope, it had reached the main road, driven away perhaps by alien human odor. It paused, its ruby eyes shining from the back of its head, before lurching onto the highway. I adjusted the lens: it was a red sports car.

The next morning, Christmas morning, I burned something resembling a vegetarian breakfast. "No roast corpse on Christmas," Céleste had stipulated. "And no birthday cake either, if you don't mind." So I made scrambled tofu and grilled okra on granary toast, seasoned with Earl's microgreens: parsley, chia and fennel. Cranberry relish with orange rind on the side. And a sprig of holly for decoration, which Céleste said was really winterberry, or black alder.

Rubbing the sleep out of her eyes, she arrived in her grandmother's kimono—faded red silk, covered with clouds and birds and bamboo fronds—which dragged along the ground and smelled of rye and tobacco. She sat down and pushed her plate away after two bites. But gulped down my café crème, two large bowlfuls, after sugarizing it with six cubes.

"There's something I should probably tell you," she said.

"What's that?"

"I'm not really a vegetarian."

"But when I asked you—"

"My grandmother was, but I'm not. I just don't eat red meat. I know it's not consistent. Or right. And I really don't mind going all the way, if you like."

"You mean if I learn how to cook?"

"You'll get better with practice. I could be like the sous-chef. Can I have some cake now?"

Defying her orders, I had baked an angel food cake out of a box and stuck fifteen candles into it. But I'd hidden it inside an old wooden bread box that looked like it hadn't held bread since the forties. I'd also bought a *bûche de Noël*, a foot-long cylinder with chocolate icing stroked into the texture of tree bark. This I'd hidden inside a knotted plastic Walmart bag in the fridge. Which one had she ferreted out?

"Cake?" I said. "What are you talking about? What cake?"

"I'll blow out the candles, I'll even make a wish. But for God's sake, Nile, don't sing 'Happy Birthday.' Promise?"

While lighting the candles with a Redbird Strike Anywhere match, struck against the black denim of my thigh, I promised.

"You wouldn't have any cigarettes, would you Nile? For the occasion?"

"Nope. Gave them up when I was fifteen."

After a theatrical frown, Céleste halfheartedly blew out the fifteen candles, then carved out a massive wedge of cake with her fingers and coffee spoon. My father would have had a conniption.

"Has anyone ever told you, Céleste, you have terrible table manners?"

"It's come up."

"In case you didn't notice, I set out a knife and fork and—"

"Look at that!" she said with her mouth full and strawberry icing on both cheeks. She pointed to the end of the table, where a large ant was dragging something, perhaps a fallen comrade, perhaps a cake crumb. She swallowed. "I think that's the biggest ant I've ever seen. Look."

Had my ex been there, she would've crushed it by now. But was it really an ant? Don't they hibernate or something? "I've seen bigger in India," I said.

"You never told me you lived in India."

"I haven't told you a lot of things."

"Where'd you live?"

We continued to watch the ant's progress. "Around. Jaipur, New Delhi, Rawalpindi ... Islamabad," I said, rattling off whatever came into my head.

She turned to look at me. "Those last two aren't even *in* India."

"I know, I was ... referring to the general area. The ants there are bigger than horses."

"Don't be ridiculous."

"It's true. They put harnesses on them, and they haul logs and things. And saddle them up for tourist rides."

"You'll never get me to believe that, not in a million leap years. I'm not five years old." There was a long silence, disturbed only by the sound of the refrigerator motor kicking in, as we watched the insect crawl down the table leg. "Do you mean that ... they're related to the ant family, or evolved from them? What kind of ants are we talking about exactly?"

I let the moment stretch. "Elephants."

Instead of laughing, which was what Brooklyn did when I told the same tale, Céleste put her hands on her hips and sighed, eyes half-closed. Then smacked me on the shoulder with her coffee spoon, leaving a round trace of strawberry icing. Perhaps harder than she intended, perhaps not.

"Tell me about your ex," she said suddenly, with eyes that looked like they were cooking up trouble. She lifted up her bowl and, tilting her head back, slurped down the dregs, less coffee than wet sugar. "Is she a blonde?" With the sleeve of her kimono she wiped her mouth and cheek.

I wiped my shoulder. "Unnaturally, yes."

"Skinny?"

I nodded. She had reached that stage of addiction where food is an afterthought.

"Did you know right away you'd ... end up together?"

I knew she was arsenical yet willingly opened my mouth. Desired her the way a twice-poisoned dog eyes a third piece of meat. "Sort of."

"Beautiful?" Céleste asked.

Knockout beautiful past the genes of either parent, beauty thrown up out of manure. "She's a beautiful woman, yes. With a drug problem."

"Much better looking than me, I guess."

"Well I ... I wouldn't ... Two types of beauty, really ..."

"Oh shut up. Is that why you left her? Her drug habit?"

I was an expert in dying relationships, in black-sky unions, in the death march that drags on and on till someone makes a move. I stayed with her out of a kind of recklessness that was as vain as it was pigeon-hearted. She said I was morose and taciturn and dull when sober, but fun and electric and interesting when drunk. "No, I had some bad habits myself."

"So why'd you leave her?"

Because of an abortion that killed the fetus *and* me. "It was just ... you know, one of those things."

"How was the sex?"

Again, I did not feel like discussing this subject with a fourteen-year-old. Or fifteen-year-old. Or any-year-old. "You don't do drugs, do you?" I changed.

"How many times did you make love to your ex per week?"

The question, out of the blue like that, made me laugh. My ex and I were like gorillas, who when kept in cages too long begin to smack each other in the head instead of mating. "Per week? I'd need a decimal to answer that one."

Céleste paused, rewound. "Of course I do drugs."

"A kid your age, are you serious? You mean like ... the odd joint, sniff of gasoline, belt of cough syrup?"

"I'm not a kid, okay? Friends younger than me have had abortions."

"Christ. Have you?"

"Not exactly."

"What does that mean?"

"It means ... nothing. I haven't had an abortion."

"You don't do coke, do you?"

"That is so old school, so twentieth century."

"Don't ever start."

"I do crystal meth."

"You don't."

"All the girls up here do. It's the best way to keep your weight down. Riding the white horse, it's called. It's packaged like candy, like Pixy Stix."

Acid, I remembered, used to be moulded like Bart Simpson, and ecstasy decorated with dolphin stickers. I was a frequent flyer back in those days, I'd do anything. If it took five to kill you, I'd take four. "Jesus. You won't be doing any riding as long as I'm around. It's bad for you."

"Yes, Daddy."

"What's it cost?"

"Ten to fifteen."

"A gram? Much cheaper than coke."

"Have you done heroin?" she asked. "What do you guys call it in the States?"

H, horse, smack, dynamite, black tar, brown sugar, mud, scat, shit, jones ... "No, I've never done it," I said. I didn't feel like describing how cosmic it is. Assuming she didn't know already.

"They say it's like shaking hands with God."

I blinked. "I thought you didn't believe in God."

"I was speaking metaphorically. Do you know why it's called heroin?"

"Yeah, it's from the Greek 'ηρωίνη.' Hero, warrior."

"I know, but why?"

"Why is it derived from 'hero'? I think because ... I don't really know."

"Because of the delusions of heroism you get from using it."

"Really? I get those delusions from whisky."

"I know."

"You do?"

She nodded. "Dutch courage, it's called."

"Do you drink?"

"Of course."

"Whisky?"

"Of course."

"What kind of whisky do you like?"

"Scotch, Irish, rye and bourbon in no particular order."

"Single malt?"

"Single, blend, 'shine, who gives a shit after the first shot?"

I smiled. This sounded like her grandmother talking. She then went on about May-December romances for some reason. About Emma and Mr. Knightley, Jane Eyre and Rochester, Edgar Allan Poe and thirteen-year-old Virginia Clemm, Samuel de Champlain and twelve-year-old Hélène Boullé, Marlon Brando and Maria Schneider ...

"Marlon Brando and Maria Schneider? You mean in *Last Tango in Paris*? You haven't seen that, have you?"

"Twice."

Good Christ. Was she having an affair with an older man, was this where we were heading? "You're not having an affair with an older man, are you, Céleste?"

She shook her head, her little black mane sweeping back and forth.

"Have you ... you know ever ..."

"Had sex with an older man?"

I nodded.

"Of course. Well, maybe not as old as you. But a guy nearly as old jumped me one time when I was walking home—along this path in the woods that my grandmother told me to stay clear of. It was so weird, almost more weird than scary. The guy starts yelling at me—you know, for sabotaging traps and blinds?—and then he gets me in the crook of his arm and the first thing I feel is his front teeth smashing into mine—it's not really a kiss, it's all wet bone and tongue and tobacco and I can hear him laughing and snorting too. It's so gross when you hear saliva in a person's laugh. And his hands were gross too—oily white fingers like slugs and fingernails clogged with dirt. Anyway, he pulls down his zipper then starts ripping off the buttons of my shirt, one by one, real relaxed like, so I stabbed him in the neck with a 6H pencil. It must've gone in an inch! He just sat there dazed and confused in the middle of the path—with the thing sticking out of his neck! Like Frankenstein! I always keep a pencil handy, a hard and sharp one. You can kill a man by ramming one up his nose and into his brain."

Her words went through me like a spear, but I tried not to let it show. "So ... then what happened? What'd you do?"

"What do you think I did? I ran like a jackrabbit, I ran till my lungs almost exploded."

"Jesus. And you ... I mean, you were all right after? You got over it?"

"Well, I thought I did but my grandmother thought I didn't and she studied psychology. I felt okay and everything, but it was around that time that I sort of ... well, exploded. Became a stress eater. I don't think there's any connection, though, because it started before that. Whenever I got stressed out I lost control and ate tons of junk, especially cereal, right out of the box, that's all I felt like eating, twenty-four seven. I got Earl to order different kinds and I hid them from my grandmother. But it's not connected. I'm just telling you. In case you thought I had a gland problem or thyroid problem or something like that. I'm just a stress eater. And Déry stresses me out. And so do his sons, big time."

"Déry's the guy who jumped you?"

Céleste chewed a nail, didn't answer.

"*Tell me.*"

"It's a long story."

"Shorten it."

"What do you want to know?"

"Who Déry is."

"He's a wildlife officer, okay? Inspecteur Déry. A real bad-ass on the take. Both him and his son Jacques, Jr. His other son's a biker. You've met him—in the winter he scares the shit out of everyone in his yellow Hummer."

"That tailgaiting idiot? I thought you said you didn't know—"

"I'm scared of them, all three of them, I really am, they give me the creeps. But my grandmother wasn't scared at all and she marched into Inspecteur Déry's office and read him the riot act. I don't know what she said exactly, but the guy never went near me again. Or his sons either. He told me I was too fat and ugly to bother with, that my face was plain as margarine, that there were lots of other girls to take my place. He was right too."

"He wasn't right. Don't ever think that because it's not true."

"It's what everybody says around here. That I'm like a homely little librarian headed for spinsterhood. Well, maybe not little. More like the Dandurand sisters down the road. They're obese."

"You're not obese, far from it. Everybody around here is wrong, dead wrong. And anyway, librarians are cool. Very cool. And so are spinsters."

"I'm no oil painting, that's for sure. More like a grub hoping for some sort of metamorphosis."

"You're at that age, or close to it, when young women transform into beautiful swans."

"Have you been reading Hans Christian Andersen or something?"

"Your eyes, for one, are stunning. Unique."

"They're green, big deal. Hardly unique. Like Anne of Green Gables, Jane Eyre, Ichabod Crane and Pinocchio."

"But everything together ... you're a true original."

"What's that supposed to mean?"

"The beauty of an original is in the originality of its beauty."

Céleste rolled her emerald eyes. "Is that supposed to be deep or something?"

"It's from a car commercial. The point is you're not the garden-variety kind of girl. And you're not ... homely. Not by a long shot. Everyone around here is jealous of you, that's all. Because you're smarter than everyone else."

"I'd rather be beautiful than smart."

I stared at the floor, saddened by this. Beautiful women are for men with no imagination, I wanted to say, but it's not what she would've wanted to hear. "You're both," I said cheerily. "In equal proportions."

Céleste closed her eyes, let her head drop. "You think just 'cause I'm young I can't tell when a guy's lying? I'm a goddamn human polygraph."

White lies introduce others of a darker complexion: my father's words. "I'm not lying."

"You are. You're trying to snow me."

"No, I'm not."

"You totally are."

"I'm totally not."

"Why haven't you made a move on me then?"

"A *move* on you? You can't be serious. You ... you're young enough to be my daughter. Maybe even granddaughter ..." I faltered here, struggling with the math. "If I had a kid ..."

"If you had a kid at fifteen and the kid had one at fourteen."

"Exactly."

"I guess it's because you're used to *Parisian* women. Anorexic high-society women, rich divorcées who ... who'd meet you at sidewalk cafés and take Gitane cigarettes out of their alligator handbags or meet you on the Champs Élysées or some bookstall along the Seine or some famous bridge or ..."

I was determined not to smile, let alone laugh, which would make her stop the tour. "Or where?"

"Or in the Louvre or Luxembourg Gardens or at the Flore or the Dôme or the Récamier, wearing dashing capes or foulards with ..."

I waited.

"... *fancy logos.*"

I furrowed my brow, wanting her to know that I was giving this due and proper consideration.

"Don't you dare laugh at me," she warned.

"I'm not laughing."

"I want a cigarette, Nile. Now. You're torturing me. I want a carton of Gitane. Or Gauloise. Like your old girlfriends used to smoke."

"My girlfriends in Paris, or rather girlfriend singular, didn't smoke."

"Oh please. Don't make me laugh. Every woman in Paris smokes."

I let this pass.

Céleste let out a long sigh. "So it's because I'm ugly and overweight that you're not hitting on me? Because my teeth are all crooked and my eyes are all bloodshot and I've got more scars on me than a practice corpse?"

I began to pace back and forth, thoughts muddled, tongue-tied, a headache derailing my train. It is tact that is golden, not silence. "I repeat, you are not ugly. And your teeth are ... eccentric. Which is a good thing, it makes you different, interesting."

"*Eccentric? Interesting?*"

"Yes. And you are not overweight—"

"What am I? Pleasantly plump?"

"Not even. Not anymore." From a hundred and plenty, she'd gone to a hundred and a hair. And she was getting prettier and prettier as her bruises faded, her hair grew out, her skin regained its luster.

"You know what they used to call Gran and me? Ten-ton and two-ton. The whale and the baby hippo."

"What's wrong with whales and hippos? Fabulous animals, both."

"Oh, so I guess it was all meant as a compliment. Silly me."

"You've probably lost thirty pounds in the last month. Or more."

"Gee, maybe I'll write a book. *How to Lose 30 Pounds in 30 Days—I Did It and So Can You!*"

"You're going to have men crawling all over you, wait and see. You'll probably marry some future Nobelist. Or be one yourself. After getting your PhD, your second one, after finding the key to universal field theory or something. Or becoming a famous painter. Or sculptor. Or poet."

"No I won't."

"Yes you will."

"No I won't."

"Yes you will."

"No I won't."

And so on. Like the conversations I used to have with Brooklyn when she was eight.

"Why would I ever get married?" she said. "So I can have a car, get fatter and raise lazy surly kids?"

She had a point. "It's not always like that."

"Besides, I'm not interested in universal field theory."

"You're not? What're you interested in?"

"I'm not interested in anything. Not anymore. And I'm not that smart, okay? And I never was. It was an idea my grandmother had, that's all. To make me as smart as she was. Because I hated going to school, because I hated everybody there because nobody would go near me and I had no clue about what they were talking about and everybody was fatsophobic. So I got interested in animals instead and tried to save them and all it did was get Gran killed and me nearly killed and you next in line and now all I want to do is kill myself."

In the afternoon I took a long thoughtful shower, with a mind as clogged as the shower head. Instead of gushing, it trickled, and its proper mix of hot and cold was hard to compound. While brooding over Céleste, I saw a pair of hands washing themselves against a green medicinal cross with *Sauberkeit!* underneath, a word from the institution that used to braid its way through my open-eyed dreams. As I was drying myself, the sound of kitchen cupboard doors slamming distracted me, displacing the word and cross. I wrapped the towel around me, tiptoed down the hall and peeked around the door.

Céleste was sitting at the table in front of a bowl of soup, a plate of peas, and a family-size bottle of Diet Coke. She was holding up a box of Count Chocula, with its buck-toothed vampire on the front panel, and looking into the chrome mirror of a toaster. "Who do I see in here?" she said, with what I took to be a vampirish voice. "A girl who's pretty in a way. In a way that doesn't hit you over the head. She's probably had a rough life." She set the box down, picked up a soda biscuit and licked it absently, like an infant learning to eat. Then nibbled it with a rapid movement of her front teeth, like a squirrel.

I walked quickly past the door and was halfway up the stairs when she yelled out, with her mouth full, "Nile? Can I talk to you for a sec? Nile?"

Back down the stairs and into the kitchen. "What's up?"

She swallowed. "Still like me?"

The question caught me off guard. "Of course I do. Why do you ask?"

"No reason."

I nodded, not knowing what to say. "Okay. So I'll just ... let you finish your ... lunch." I took a step toward the stairs.

"You're not going to leave me, right?"

"No, of course not."

"You kidnapped me, I mean rescued me, so now you're stuck with me, right?"

"Right."

"I wasn't serious about ... you know. I mean, I was serious about not being smart and wanting to kill myself. But I wasn't serious about the other things. I've never ... you know."

"Never what?"

"I've never drank alcohol before."

"Never *drunk* alcohol before. But I thought you said ... I thought you said you liked whisky."

"My grandmother did, I can't stand the stuff. And I've never done crystal meth either—or any other drugs. I smoked grass once when I was like, ten, and got so paranoid I thought a tree was trying to strangle me. And I've never made love to an older man, or a younger man or ... well, anybody. I'm sorry for lying. It's my third-worst fault according to my grandmother."

"What are the first two?"

"And I'm sorry for asking why you haven't tried to hit on me. Did I say anything else? Stupid, I mean?"

"I think that just about covers it."

"We could just, like, delete the stupid stuff, right? Or rewind?"

"Okay."

"I don't necessarily agree with everything I say."

I nodded.

"Pals forgive pals, right?"

"Right."

"I was just sort of, you know, being like a duck."

"A duck?"

"A female duck. They always hit on the first male closest to them. You're the only half-decent male in my postal code. Which isn't saying a lot. No offense."

I stopped to think about this.

"It's just, you know, social pressure," she added. "Something called *l'hypersexualisation des jeunes*. You may have heard about the phenomenon."

I had seen it first-hand with Brooklyn, who was tossing her hair and wiggling her hips like Shania Twain at seven, plucking her eyebrows at nine, wearing kid-sized thong underwear at ten. When I made the daring suggestion that she spend some time reading good books or jumping rope instead of watching music videos, she asked what jumping rope was.

"You mean how advertisers are brainwashing young girls?" I said. "Sexualized marketing targeting younger and younger audiences?"

Instead of eating the peas on her plate, Céleste was rolling them around the racetrack of the rim. "It's all part of the shifting sexual tectonics."

The shifting sexual tectonics? "I see."

"But I've decided that men are a waste of time. And sex too."

"Good call."

"I understand how it's being packaged and sold, and it leaves me cold."

I nodded. Geniuses always have trouble in the sex department.

"Besides, as Aristotle said, copulation makes all animals sad."

How would he know that, I wondered. "You've read Aristotle?"

"And Spinoza associated desire with disconnected thinking."

I nodded again, knowingly.

"No, I've not read Aristotle, or Spinoza either. These are just things I've picked up and can rattle off. Like a parrot. Or trained seal."

Was this exaggeration, self-deprecation?

"But Nile, I am not your daughter, and don't ever think I am, okay?"

"Okay. Can I be like, a godfather?"

Céleste put her head on the table as if it were to be chopped off. "A fairy godfather, just what I always wanted."

"How about an uncle, then, an honorary uncle?"

She propped her head lazily up on an elbow. "No."

I was an only child and used to badger my mother about bringing a sister back from the hospital. "How about a brother then, a wayward orphan brother?"

She thought this over with a fresh saltine sticking out of her mouth, while absentmindedly flicking peas across the table like marbles. « *À la limite,* » she said grudgingly, crunching the words along with the cracker. She swallowed. "Oh, and one other thing before you go."

I braced myself. "What's that?"

"There's someone living in the church."

🐦 🐦 🐦

I was planning on going to the church anyway, it being Christmas and all, but I wasn't planning on taking a Sig Sauer with me. Loaded, seven in the magazine. The black steel frame and fluted grips felt cold and hard in my hand. Céleste had shown me how to work the slide and snap the safety off, how to press a button to pop the clip out of the bottom of the grip. All that was left, I suppose, was to pull the trigger.

Céleste was vague about who she had glimpsed through her telescope coming and going through the back door of the church. He was wearing a ski-mask, she said in her matter-of-fact way. And carrying a sleeping bag. How does she stay so calm? Did her grandmother keep a stash of Valium? Or Quaaludes?

With my back to the wall and gun raised beside my ear, as they do in the movies, I shot two glances through a side window of the church, one quick, one lingering. I saw nothing but blackness the first time, two faint orange lights the second. And then heard something just as faint: a whistling sound. I paused to follow the melody. "Good King Wenceslas." I shifted my gaze toward the rectory, and saw Céleste's head sticking out the attic window. *Courage, show courage. The non-Dutch kind.* I peered through the window again. The orange lights were now extinguished and the whistling had stopped.

I was heading for the back door, my ring of keys in one hand, my revolver in the other, when the squeak of wood against metal made me jump. The sound of a resistant door being pushed open. Then a man stepping through it, with a black balaclava over his face.

"Mr. Nightingale, how are you this lovely afternoon? Enjoying Boxing Day? A good time to relax, they say, after all the hurly-burly. Not for me, though. I must remain active, even during the holidays, or else I go stark raving mad." He slowly peeled off his mask.

I slipped the gun quickly into my parka's side pocket. It was Myles Llewellyn. Wearing the same outfit, more or less, as the last time we met at the church: reddish tweed coat, reddish jogging pants, black galoshes over laceless shoes fastened with duct tape. "I'm fine, Mr. Llewellyn but ..."

"Stop right there. Call me Myles."

"But ... today's not Boxing Day. Myles."

"No? There I go again. At my age all the days begin to blur, shuffle like decks in a card. I mean cards in a deck. Oh well, no damage done. I can come back tomorrow. Any day you like, in fact. Unless you've changed your mind—or perhaps forgotten—about our ... agreement?"

"No, I ... not at all."

He was walking back toward the door. "Come with me," he

said, crooking his finger and narrowing his eyes. "I'll explain my plan to you. My vision."

The church interior, I saw once my eyes adjusted to the light, was as stark and bleak as the first time I'd seen it. Not a single pew remained, let alone altar, crucifix or pulpit. Even the floor was bare, with only yellowing glue or rusty nails to suggest where the altar carpet and wide-slat pine flooring had been. There were partially frozen puddles here and there, fed from the holey roof. By the sacristy door were two space heaters and an unrolled sleeping bag. And on the pulpit steps was a large clock radio, which, I would soon find out, also housed a cassette player.

"I hope you don't mind," he said, following my gaze. "I'm setting up some sleeping quarters, à l'improviste. So I can get cracking first thing in the morning. Avoid the to and fro. I have to face facts: I'm getting old, I can no longer draw on reserves."

I hadn't noticed any vehicle outside. How did Llewellyn get here, with all this gear? And how did he get inside? With a skeleton key? "How did you get here, Mr. Llewellyn?"

He didn't answer. He simply smiled and pointed up. "Look at those lights. The last time I saw that color—peacock blue, I suppose you'd call it—was at Chartres. The most beautiful things in the world are the most useless: peacocks and lilies, for example. Ruskin said that, or something like that."

He was pointing at some unremarkable side windows, or "lights" as they are called, which had been broken by children's stones or bored hunters' bullets and half-heartedly mended with masking tape. One displayed the familiar image of the Good Shepherd holding a sheep in his arms, the other Saint Davnet herself with a sword in her hand and fettered devil at her feet. The blue light shone through her.

I pointed. "That's Saint Davnet, right?" I knew this because her name was inscribed along the bottom.

He nodded. "Better known as Saint Dymphna. Davnet's an Irish version of her name."

"And who was she ... exactly?"

"Patron saint of the insane." He paused as we both gazed up at her. "And incest victims, runaways, that kind of thing. It's over a hundred years old, that window—almost as old as I am. Robert McCausland is my guess."

"The artist?"

"The firm in Toronto. The oldest stained-glass company in North America."

I looked closer at the saint's sad face. "Was she—Dymphna—insane?"

"No. Her father was the insane one."

I waited for him to go on. "And ... who was her father?"

"An Irish king—seventh century, pagan. When his wife died he scoured the countryside—not just in Ireland but all over Europe—for someone to replace her. Someone just as beautiful. But he couldn't find anyone up to the mark so he, well ... 'turned his attentions,' as they say, to his beautiful daughter. Who was fourteen. She fled to Belgium, trying to get away from him. But the king tracked her down, in Geel, and when she refused to go back with him he went into a blind rage and decapitated her."

Good God, was any of this true? I was about to ask him more but was distracted by his arms, which he raised in a gesture that struck me as oddly papal.

"This project will immortalize my name in the annals of ecclesiastical architecture. How good is your imagination, Mr. Nightingale?"

"It's ... good. It's beyond good, it's out of control."

"Rectangular plan. Raised pulpit, projecting chancel and vestry. A transept suggested by gables on the north and south elevations. Gothic influences, you see. Gabled roof clad with ribbed copper sheeting, double-ridge ventilation. The chancel—similar roof, but at a lower height, with a small section of clerestory. The vestry—skillion roof. The western elevation will have twin stone entrance porches, three lancet windows and a stone cross at the top of the gable. Dressed stone work around the windows and to the top of the gable, and an inscription reading NUNC ET IN HORA MORTIS NOSTRAE. Three lancets, two quatrefoils and a rose window on the chancel gable, surmounted by a vesica. The eastern nave gable—surmounted by a carved stone bell-cote from which a new bell will be hung."

So far so good. But his words took a sharp turn, becoming harder and harder to follow. Links and linear logic fell by the wayside, and yet somehow, like an abstract painting or mosaic, it all made sense. And even had a certain beauty. His phrases, in any case, stayed with me for weeks, reverberating inside me like a ... bell.

"You disagree?" he said.

"No no, I ... it's not that, it's just that I'm no real expert in—"

"Do you remember the uproar over the Sistine Chapel? Or when they suggested the Earth was round? I am building you a dream emporium, Mr. Nightingale. I am meticulous—I believe in the absolute power of detail. A ladder-back chair and some kickshaws, that's all we need for now. And we shall adopt the Walmart model: no unions, no grievances ...

"This is not about handouts, about making money, this is about survival. This church is all I have left. Why? Because the love of my life left me after thirty-two years with a note of two lines. I will do this work *gratis* ...

"Stop right there. I do not know the word no. I do not grasp its meaning. It impinges on my retina, it races into my auditory canal, but to my brain it is gibberish. No, I will not brook refusals, Mr. Nightingale, I am quite deaf to them you know ...

"I showed myself, I thought, to be a man of oak and iron. I put my hand to the plow and did not look back. And yet ...

"'My name is Deborah,' she said to me, holding out her hand. She came onto *me*, you see. I was cool as Labrador. I'm thinking, place the tennis ball back in her court ...

"'What-ho, my dear. This is a dashed rummy place for you to be living, what?' I thought this sort of thing would impress her, you see. The accent. She was so young, so lovely. I thought it would charm her ...

"She threw me over! For a younger man! I'm past retirement age—who's going to look at me now?

"You're only saying that to make me feel better, Mr. Nightingale. Nobody wants me now, not at my age. I'm on the scrap heap ...

"It's all a bit of a hot stove. Best not touched. I'll be fine. It doesn't do us any good, does it, to wring our hands over the far-off things. What can't be cured must be endured. Look at that stained glass ...

"Sublimate, I must sublimate. I must keep active. I am one of those organisms that never want to go to bed and never want to get up ...

"Music, we must have music! Hang on ...

"Ah yes. *Yes*, listen ... Da duh-duh-duh da ... Inexplicable longings surge within me whenever I hear this. I base my life on its form, in fact, and I advise you to do the same. Allegro, Andante, Waltz, Allegro. I'm now in the Waltz, and shall end my days *allegro con vivace* ...

"I'm a bit of a dinosaur, I know. But the music is still good. It has not been surpassed by rock and roll or hip-hop ...

"People everywhere seem to want to live in the past, and when you stop and think about it, who can blame them?

"I'm willing to pay for my blunders, but in a single lump sum, not on the instalment plan ...

"I cut all ties with my family, you see. With blunt scissors. And now, now I cultivate the inner garden ...

"Listen to this bit ... Yes, I know, I'm too old to whistle, I haven't the breath for it. But you know, I don't *feel* old. Inside, I mean. I feel like I've got the youngest part of my life still ahead ...

"A little excess weight will help you live longer, according to the studies ...

"I asked the doctor how much time I had to live. 'Let me put it this way,' he said. 'Don't buy any green bananas.' A little joke of mine ...

"Most people go on living long after they ought to be dead, don't you think? We lounge around and then die. That's all the Earth is, really—a big extinction lounge, an extinction club, membership awarded posthumously ...

"There are too many of us, anyway. A tiger is worth ten thousand humans. Read Blake."

A long silence followed, broken only by the papery rustlings of mice, the scampering of cats, Llewellyn's sighs.

"Not faulting the company, Mr. Nightingale, but I'd best be alone now. Retire into the kingdom of my mind. I'll see you tomorrow, then?" He winked. "On St. Stephen's Day?"

I invited him to the rectory for Christmas dinner, even to sleep there, but he declined. He had a place on Lac St-Nicolas, he said. So I closed the door and left him there, to retire into the kingdom of his mind.

Neither Céleste nor I saw any lights on in the church that night, and we did not see Mr. Llewellyn the following day. Or the day, week or month after that. I never saw him again, in fact. But Céleste did.

XX

It's New Year's Eve & I'm looking out the window with my telescope at the ice-cream hills of the Laurentians, the oldest mountain range in the world. People from out west or Europe might not think they're very high, but as I say, they're older.

I wish there was such a thing as a time telescope, so I could see how they looked when the first Europeans arrived, when they were the home of Algonquin Indians. When the forest was 30 to 50 meters high, with some areas nearly 80 meters. In other words, between 12 & 15 storeys high & in some places as high as 25 storeys! The first settlers — the French, Irish, Scottish & American homesteaders — basically saw this forest as something to get rid of. They cut down the trees like weeds. Today it's 4 storeys high.

The Laurentians got their name from Saint Lawrence. This is because when Jacques Cartier arrived in the Gulf in 1534, it was on this saint's day, August 10th. But he only named one small bay after Saint Lawrence. The river was called the Saint Lawrence when Cartier's maps were translated into Spanish. Why did the translator change the name? Because the saint was born in Spain.

Lawrence was responsible for the church property in Rome & was promoted to Keeper of the Treasures in 258 after Emperor Valerian cut the heads off the rest of the officials. But Saint

Lawrence didn't exactly keep the treasures — he shared them.
When he was asked to come forward with the church's valuables,
he produced the blind, the crippled & the sick. "These are the
treasures of the church," he said. Probably in Latin. For this he
was roasted to death on a gridiron. As he was being grilled, he
asked to be turned over, saying he was underdone on the other
side. This is why he is the saint of laughter.

A few kilometers from where I live, south of the Bogs &
Ravenwood Pond, is the Rivière du Diable. It runs for about
70 kilometers through a valley formed by the Laurentide Ice
Sheet. This glacier was about 2,000 meters high, a gigantic wall
of ice that would dwarf a city like Montreal or even New York,
towering over their skyscrapers. A thousand years ago, if Nile & I
had stood on Mont Binoche, which is the high ground around here,
we would have looked WAY up to the icy mountains to the north,
higher than the Swiss Alps.

The first humans to pass through the Laurentians probably
saw the last of this glacier. The Weskarinis? The Montagnais?
If they did, they left us no record of what it was like. We
haven't found anything yet, at least.

★ ★ ★

I will now tell a story about St. Lawrence whales. In
1861, P.T. Barnum led an expedition to capture white whales
from Quebec for his circus aquarium in Manhattan. In his
autobiography he wrote: "On this whole enterprise, I confess I
was very proud that I had originated it and brought it to such
a successful conclusion. It was a very great sensation, and it
added thousands of dollars to my treasury. The whales, however,

soon died." So Barnum sent out his agents to capture two more whales. They soon died too.

In the Saguenay River, which flows into the St. Lawrence, there were once more than 5,000 beluga whales ("beluga" means "white" in Russian). When fishermen began complaining that these whales were eating their fish, the Canadian government put a bounty on their heads. Hunts were organized where sportsmen could shoot whales from boats. Like the way Americans used to shoot buffalo from trains. The population was reduced to about 500.

Today, when a St. Lawrence beluga whale dies naturally, its body is so contaminated that it's considered hazardous waste.

★ ★ ★

I asked Nile if he was happy staying here with me and he said he was "on cloud ten." Which made me smile and made me feel great. Especially after what happened. I'm not using it as an excuse, but I should never read novels, just science books. And never drink champagne.

★ ★ ★

Nile doesn't know it but I've been listening on my headphones to the CD he gave me for Christmas. My grandmother would've hated it because she hated rock music but I like it. A lot. There are 3 songs I play over & over & over: "Foxy Lady," "Purple Haze" & "All Along the Watchtower." I'm also reading Nile's book of poems because I kind of like Lewis Carroll, I have to admit, even though I'm 15. This poem was circled in pencil, probably because "The Mad Gardener" is SO much like Nile:

He thought he saw an Elephant,
  That practised on a fife:
He looked again, and found it was
  A letter from his wife ...

He thought he saw a Buffalo
  Upon the chimney-piece:
He looked again, and found it was
  His Sister's Husband's Niece ...

He thought he saw a Rattlesnake
  That questioned him in Greek:
He looked again, and found it was
  The Middle of Next Week ...

He thought he saw a Banker's Clerk
  Descending from the bus:
He looked again, and found it was
  A Hippopotamus ...

He thought he saw a Coach-and-Four
  That stood beside his bed:
He looked again, and found it was
  A Bear without a Head ...

He thought he saw an Albatross
  That fluttered round the lamp:
He looked again, and found it was
  A Penny-Postage Stamp ...

★ ★ ★

Poor Mr. Llewellyn, I can't stop thinking about him. I hope he's all right.

★ ★ ★

I've lost my voice again. But this time I have a feeling it's never coming back ...

More later. Guess who just popped in. Nile from Neptune. He's heading my way, balancing a bottle & two wineglasses on a chessboard, like a waiter ...

✿ XXI ✿

It was New Year's Eve, a time for merrymaking and madcappery, so I proposed a game of chess. Naturally, I intended to go easy on her. Start with a Sicilian, but make it elastic. Porous, if necessary. She's still in rough shape, still feeling bad about her drunken antics—wouldn't want to break her spirit, poor thing. Especially when she's lost her voice again, and is convinced she's never going to get it back.

She was lying in bed wearing one of my T-shirts, writing or drawing in her NOT TO BE READ UNTIL I'M DEAD sketchbook. She would invariably close it whenever I came too near, which is what she did now. To the title on the cover she had added, in smaller capitals, AND NEVER BY NILE NIGHTINGALE.

Céleste reopened the book when I asked if she played chess, and under a nice sketch of a horse head, wrote in blue pencil: *You any good?*

I set down my cut-glass goblets and Welsh grape juice and considered the question. Why be modest? "Well, let me put it this way—it takes a pretty heavy-duty computer program to beat me." As a child in Baden-Baden I played a game of fast chess called Blitz with my father, in a park with chessmen bigger than me, and won more often than not. "How about you?"

She made a *comme ci comme ça* roll with her hand.

"You play much?"

Now and then. With Grand-maman.

"Ever beat her?"

Near the end, when she wasn't ... She probably let me win.

"Maybe I can show you a few things. A few tricks."

Céleste reached for a vial of Voxangel, a voice-loss medicine whose label warned of such side effects as reduced alertness and impaired thinking. She took a swig from the bottle's neck. *No doubt.*

Her king's pawn opening followed by a move of the king itself might have sent a player less humane than I into wild, uncharitable laughter. Talk about unorthodox. An opening favored by kindergartners. "Well, okay, I'm not sure ... you know, whether that's the best strategy ..."

Let's play it through.

"Fine with me."

After a dozen moves with running commentary, as I was showing her how to bend a Sicilian defense into a variation of my own device, I was checkmated. Obviously a trap I'd fallen into while pedagogically preoccupied, something her grandmother had shown her.

You don't have to take a dive. I don't mind losing.

I stared at the board. Then set it up again, turning it around so that Céleste was black. I moved my king's pawn two squares. "Your move."

This time I lasted longer, my fingers drumming on the bed frame, my kneecaps pumping like pistons, taking forever between moves. No clocks, thank God.

Suddenly, in a reckless move, Céleste left her queen unprotected. "Careful of your queen," I warned, not wanting to win this way.

I watched her take another slug of medicine and then scribble *Your move.*

All right, if that's the way you want it. "*En garde.*" I moved my knight to fork her king and queen. "And check."

She moved her king out of the way. I hastily captured her queen with my knight, hitting it, sending it flying across the board. She took my knight with her bishop, putting me in check. I moved my king diagonally forward, and she took my rook with her bishop. How did I not see that? Oh well, keep up the attack. I moved my queen menacingly forward ...

She ignored this thrust, rashly I thought, and instead nudged an irrelevant pawn. In desperation? I countered with a pawn move of my own, preparing the way to slaughter. She moved another pawn forward, putting my king in exposed check from her other bishop. Three moves later I resigned.

We played six more games. Céleste made her moves quickly, unerringly, advancing without mercy to the inescapable conclusion—a bit like Garry Kasparov playing a chimpanzee. Not once did she queen a pawn; she always chose a horse, her favorite piece. Once she asked if she could leave the pawn there as a pawn, since she already had two horses. Between moves, she did not study the board; she doodled in her sketchbook.

I caught glimpses of things like this:

And this:

In a clear attempt to distract me, she ate pieces of black licorice, with her head thrown back in the way of a sword-swallower. She also whistled "Auld Lang Syne," her lips stained with grape juice, and asked irrelevant questions.

What beautiful bird has a horrid name?

"I don't know."

Peacock.

"I'm trying to concentrate."

In which movie does a couple fall in love while playing chess?

"I give up.

Hitchcock's The Lodger.

"Your move."

Did you know that Hitchcock didn't have a belly button?

I shook my head.

It was eliminated when he was sewn up after surgery.

"I'm trying to concentrate."

In which movie does a man play chess with the devil?

"Céleste ..."

Bergman's The Seventh Seal.

"I knew that."

How's that book you're reading?

"Which book?"

The one with no covers. Broken Wind.

"It stinks."

She moved her black-square bishop one square, in a fianchetto, then wrote *Mate in 2. Happy New Year.*

I refilled, dazedly, two glasses with juice. Then set up the board for another game. As I was carefully pondering a complex opening, a Nimzo-Indian variation, Céleste dozed off.

While pulling a wool blanket over her, I caught a glimpse of her sketchbook, opened at this half-page image:

Okay, I admit it. Fifteen-year-old Céleste Jonquères is smarter and quicker than forty-four-year-old Nile Nightingale. Smarter and quicker than any computer I've played. She could play against God, give him an extra bishop and win. Next time we'll play cards.

XXII

I'll let you in on a little secret, one that I haven't told anyone
(except Nile). It's this: I'm more parrot than owl. I'm not really
that smart. I just read smart people, and remember. Everything
else I know, or almost, came from my grandmother.

I should've told Nile last night that she represented Canada at
the Nice Olympiad in 1974. And in Prague in '76. She lost at both
places, but she was a grandmaster.

★ ★ ★

I'm thinking of becoming a stamp collector. After the
chess game Nile showed me an amazing set of chess stamps
from Afghanistan. Which I'd already seen because I'm such a
snoophound. When I told him how beautiful they were he said I
could have them. And that I could have his whole collection if I
wanted! I said no. But I was just being polite & I think he was
kidding anyway.

He said that his grandfather's collection (which is now his)
contains one valuable stamp from Canada, the 12-pence Black of
1851, and one valuable stamp from Australia, the Inverted Swan

of 1855. One is worth $125,000, the other $85,000. But that he doesn't plan on selling either one.

He also said that by 2040 there will be no more stamps in circulation. Or newspapers or books, for that matter. "I won't be around to see that," said he, "but you will." Wrong.

Speaking of stamps, we watched another "stamp" movie today, from a 10-DVD set by a Polish director named Kieslowski that I was very skeptical about because it's based on the 10 Commandments. Volume 9 is about two brothers who inherit their father's stamp collection. It's great, and it's not really based on the 9th Commandment, but the funny thing is that it uses the SAME plot device as Charade: a young boy naively trades 3 valuable stamps for a shitload of worthless ones ...

Again, Nile rewound the film to freeze-frame the stamps, but this time I wasn't listening. When I saw the images going backwards I thought it would be nice to have a reverse button in life. I imagined my body shooting back up from the Bogs, the Exit Bag coming off my grandmother's head, the bear going up not down on that ramp, Bazinet's bullets travelling back into his rifle, Déry unjumping me, his penis unpenetrating me.

I haven't mentioned that last part to anyone, not even my grandmother. Why? Because Déry said if I told anyone what happened before I stuck the pencil into his neck, he & his sons would come & kill Grand-maman. And gang-rape me.

"That's very interesting," I said to Nile, who knew I hadn't followed a single word he said.

★ ★ ★

Nile & I were talking about suicide today. He brought it up, I guess because I brought it up the other night. He said that a kind of suicide happens every day. That there are lots of collisions on the highway where nobody seems to have put on their brakes, as if the victims had somehow decided on death. And that there have been cases of people stopped on railway tracks with lots of time to get off, who simply sat there. Why was he telling me all this? Because it happened to his mother? He'd told me that she died in an accident, so I asked him if this is how she died, stopped on a railway track, waiting for the train to come. No, he said, she died from "internal decapitation," where the skull is detached from the spinal column. She was rammed by a tailgating truck. ●

✧ XXIII ✧

After the chess game, as Céleste slept, I leafed through two books I'd stumbled upon in the den, one on child geniuses, the other on how to raise a child genius. The latter, called *Bring Up Genius!*, was written by Dr. Laszlo Polgar, who claims he can turn any healthy baby into a genius. To prove it, he kept his daughters out of public schools, considering them factories for mediocrity, and instead home-schooled them in his apartment in Hungary. Now adults, all three are brilliant, and two are chess grandmasters, the top two women in the world.

The second book, *L'Enfant prodige*, was written by Dr. Dorothée Jonquères, Céleste's grandmother. Most prodigies, she points out, had at least one brilliant (or wacko) parent who was hell-bent on raising a brilliant child. They often become introverts, these children, either extremely shy or downright afraid of people. Or hateful. Leonardo da Vinci despised human beings from an early age, calling them "sacks for food," "fillers-up of privies." A young Nietzsche called them "the bungled and botched." Many child geniuses die young or become suicidal, but bear no resemblance to the near-sighted, forlorn and bookish creatures that populate so many stories about precocious children. And yet Céleste is near-sighted, forlorn and bookish, almost as if she's playing a part, including the bit about dying young.

Here are some historical examples cited by Dr. Jonquères:

Caravaggio, who painted his first masterpieces in his teens, didn't die young, but had some early problems fitting in. In 1600 he was accused of beating up a fellow painter, and in 1601 he wounded a soldier. In 1603 he was imprisoned for beating up another painter, and in 1604 he was accused of throwing a plate of artichokes in a waiter's face. The same year he was arrested for throwing stones at the Roman Guards. In 1605 he was seized for misuse of arms, and two months later he had to flee Rome because he had wounded a man in defense of his mistress. In 1606, during a brawl over a disputed score in a game of tennis, Caravaggio killed a man.

Thomas Chatterton began his career as a poet at age eleven and was famous by age twelve. On the night of August 24, 1770, the young genius poisoned himself with arsenic. Age seventeen.

Terence Judd made his debut as a classical pianist at twelve, playing with the London Philharmonic Orchestra. At twenty-two he threw himself off Beachy Head, just before Christmas 1979.

Ian Curtis led the seminal new wave band Joy Division while still in his teens. He hanged himself in his own kitchen on May 18, 1980. He was twenty-three.

Kurt Cobain, a singer, guitarist and songwriter of preternatural talent, blew his brains out on April 5, 1994. Age twenty-seven.

Early entrance into university, it appears, sends more phenoms into early burnout than Olympic gymnastics. Sufiah Salem fled Cambridge University in 2000, aged fourteen, after her third-year exams. When police found her after a huge hunt, she blamed her parents for too much pressure, never finished her courses, and became an administrative assistant for a plumbing firm in Hull. Rita Lafferty graduated from Oxford at the age of thirteen with a first-class mathematics degree in 1999. She now works as a prostitute in Amsterdam.

At the end of the book were figures from a study by Dr. Catherine Morris Cox, estimates of how sixteen famous men (no women), whose childhood was well documented, would score on a modern IQ test:

Drake: 130	Luther: 170
Washington: 140	Kant: 175
Napoleon: 140	Da Vinci: 180
Lincoln: 150	Descartes : 180
Rembrandt: 155	Galileo: 185
Franklin: 160	Voltaire : 190
Mozart: 165	Newton: 190
Johnson: 165	Goethe: 210

After Goethe, in a child's hand I recognized, was this female addition: *Dorothée Jonquères: 211.*

🕊   🕊   🕊

The next morning, the book still open in my arms, I awoke with a start, not because of an animal roar or caveman flight, but because I felt something beside me, touching me, wrapped in the sheet like a shroud. It wasn't Moon, because Moon was sleeping at my feet. I peeled back the sheet.

It was Céleste, sprawled on the bed on her stomach. She was in a fathomless sleep, making gentle rasping sounds. Around her neck was the turquoise Indian necklace I had bought her.

I looked up, toward light. The rising sun gilded the window frame before lazily entering through the glass, burning a new pattern on the frost. Almost like the outline of a face. No, wait. It *was* a face. With a woodpecker nose and drowned-rat beard. The snowplower! The curtains ... How could I forget to close the curtains? I leapt out of bed, looked out. Nothing.

Céleste's eyes opened, though she didn't move. For a heart-stopping second she looked dead.

"I couldn't sleep," she said softly and blinked her bright green eyes.

"Would you like to go back to your bed?"

"Not really."

"Come on." I eased my hand under her and by old habit perhaps, she reached for my neck. In an instant I had her in my arms, blanket and all, carrying her into her bedroom, where every light was on.

Since arriving at the rectory, I had left my door open in case she should call, in case she should wake in terror. I had suggested she sleep with her own door open, lights on. I had suggested she send me a mayday whenever she got scared, couldn't sleep, had nightmares.

"What keeps you awake at night? The pain?" I set her down on the bed, then sat beside her.

"No. The pethidine takes care of that. Can you get more?"

"Then why can't you sleep? Fear?"

"I can't sleep, that's all. My mind keeps jumping like a kangaroo."

"What do you think about?"

"Everything. And then when I finally drift off, nightmares wake me up. Then I start thinking again."

"Nightmares about ... being dumped in the swamp?"

She pawed sleepily at an itchy cheek and nose. "No. About other things."

"Such as?"

"What happened to my grandmother. The bears in those cages. That poor bear being lowered ... And then there's

Déry. And Gervais and his snowplow—which I saw from my window, I almost forgot. And a red sports car too."

I had seen them too, of course, creeping along the highway or down the church lane, lights off, but decided not to mention it.

"And about getting cut open like a fish and bled like a deer, which is what ... never mind."

Cut open like a fish? Bled like a deer? Her nightmares are as bad as mine. "Do you mean ... what happened to you that night? The knife wounds?"

She shook her head. "What kind of nightmares do you have?"

"Me? What makes you think I have nightmares?"

"You shout out things during the night."

"What kind of things?"

"Like ... grunting sounds."

"Caveman grunts, monosyllables?"

Céleste smiled. "Yeah."

"I'm talking to my caveman family." There are a handful of modern words, according to glottochronologists, that ancient hunter-gatherers would have understood 20,000 years ago. Seven altogether, which I seem to repeat over and over in my dreams: *I, who, we, thou, two, three* and *five.*

"Some were real words," said Céleste. "Repeated, like."

They make for fairly limited conversations. "I have two nightmares, with variations. In one scenario my wife and child and I are chased by animals—prehistoric usually, but sometimes mythical. The chase ends up inside a fenced-in space, a rectangle or square. And we always end up trapped, with no way out. And I know I'm going to die. Not my family, just me."

When I told my father about this, he said it was nothing to worry about. Just bad dreams, which everyone has. But when I told him I had similar visions when awake, he set up that appointment with Doktor Neefe (pronounced *nay-fuh*) in Frankfurt. "These animals that you see," the doctor explained, this time in German, "are echo-images or after-sensations. Neural traces left by the imprint of a visually fixated stimulus. The strength of the after-sensation or the speed of its disappearance varies greatly in individual cases. Persons who are field-dependent—who tend to observe a field in its totality—show weaker after-effect traces. Field-independent subjects—people like you, Herr Nightingale, who by selective attention are more likely to consider a specific stimulus apart from its context—show stronger perceptual after-effects. Which can be made even stronger by the use, past or present, of psychotropic drugs." The stamps I had pored over endlessly as a child—the prehistorical, mythological and cryptozoological beasts that constituted my specialty—had thus come back to haunt me. "Is it true, Doktor Neefe, that whatever has once been seen is in the mind forever?" The doctor steepled his fingers and smiled. "*Ja, in der Theorie.*"

"I get it," said Céleste. "I understand."

"I somehow doubt that."

"Caused by images from stamps, right? From when you were a kid? Kind of like flashbacks, maybe triggered by drugs?"

I thought I was used to this sort of thing by now, this preternatural precocity, but evidently not. I gaped at her for several seconds. "*Eine kluge Analyse, Doktor.*"

"I don't speak German, but I take it I'm right?"

"Did you figure that out because you have delusions too?"

"I don't have delusions."

"Yes, you do."

"No, I don't."

"You're in denial."

"No, I'm not."

"See what I mean?"

Sigh. "Okay, what kind of delusions do I have?"

"BDD. Body dysmorphic disorder. Commonly known as 'Imagined Ugliness Syndrome.'"

Céleste paused to think this over. "You're delusional. What's your second dream?"

"The second one's very short, very simple, but it's repeated over and over, on a loop. A large metal spoon is in a white sink. I turn on the tap, the jet of water hits the spoon and comes back up into my face."

Céleste smiled, came close to actual laughter. "But I've seen you do that in real life! Lots of times!"

"It's my destiny, I can't escape it."

This time she erupted. A real belly laugh. All right, I thought, I understand now. Forget the wordplay. It's slapstick that snaps agelastics, makes them gelastic.

"How did you end up choosing prehistoric animals?" she asked, hand over mouth. "I mean, as your stamp ... whatever, specialty." She began to cough, the way you do at school to conceal laughter, and motioned for the glass of water on her nightstand. "Sorry. Continue."

"It's the most popular theme for kids. By far. For boys, at least. It's amazing how—"

Another detonation. She laughed until water came out of her nose. "Sorry Nile, really, I just ... I don't usually ... Can you hand me that box?" She nodded toward some Kleenex on her desk. "Thanks. Continue."

"Where was I?"

She blew her nose. "It's amazing how ..."

"It's amazing how many countries put dinosaurs on their stamps."

"Because they know that kids, or their parents, are going to buy them?" She wiped a tear of laughter from her eye, struggled to control herself.

"Exactly. Then I went on to mythological animals, then extinct."

"Not endangered?"

"I'd need a big album for that. A mile wide."

"So that's the area you made your money in?"

"No. Those are stamps I bought, never sold."

"So how'd you make your money?"

"Forgeries, mostly."

"You were a counterfeiter? I *knew* you were a criminal."

"I didn't make them, I bought them—famous ones, usually at a laughably low price. And then sold them later—at a much higher price."

"You sold them as authentic, you mean?"

"No, as forgeries."

"Hold on. Time out. What?"

"I bought the stamps from sellers who advertised them as genuine. I told them I knew they were forgeries, but that I'd take them off their hands. And not report them. So I usually got them for next to nothing."

"I still don't get it. How can you—"

"Because fakes and forgeries have become a collecting area of their own. Some forgeries are more valuable than the originals. By masters like Jean de Sperati, who worked in Italy and France, or Raoul de Thuin in Mexico. I had a pretty good sampling from each. And rich collectors wanted them."

"How brilliant, how ... diabolical! What did your dad have to say about all this? Did he approve?"

"No, not at all. At least not at first. He changed his mind when his lawyer sent him an article from the *Star-Ledger*. And *The New York Times*. About one of the sales."

"You made *The New York Times*? God, I had no idea stamps were ... newsworthy. I thought it was more like a hobby for little nerds. Little male nerds. What was the story about?"

"It wasn't about me. It was about postage stamp mistakes, typographical errors, which is another thing I got into. I was mentioned because I sold an upside-down airplane to Bill Gates's cousin or cousin-in-law, I never got it straight. For six figures."

"What'd you pay for it?"

"Five figures."

"You crook, you capitalist crook!"

"That's what my mother said. That I was like her father."

"So she disapproved too ..."

"No, she was with me all the way. She's the one who got me started, gave me my first album. And when she saw I was serious about it, she gave me her father's collection. One of the finest French colony collections in the world."

"Is that what you brought with you in your duffle bag?"

"No no, that's ... in a safe. I brought the album my mother gave me."

Céleste nodded. "Why that one?"

Because it's a book of memories, because each stamp takes me back to a time when I was happy. "A whim."

"But why would you bring stamps up here if you don't ... I mean, what do stamps mean to you exactly?"

What do they *mean* to me? Cancelled trips. A record of a past moment, a past transaction, literally stuck in time. "I don't give them much thought. That's all in the past now."

"So why did you bring that one album?"

Collectors, I once read, acquired physical matter to substitute for what they lacked in the spiritual department. "You already asked me that."

"You avoided the question."

"I brought it to ... to try again."

"Try what again?"

Happiness. "Years ago my psychotherapist suggested I get a hobby—to help me stay dry, stay sane. That's why I brought it. To try again."

"So you're no longer a collector or dealer? You just ... stopped one day?"

"After my mom died, I stopped doing pretty much of everything." And have had a foot in the hereafter ever since. It's the mother, they say, who stands between the son and death.

"Except alcohol," she said.

I thought of stopping the interrogation, but the truth was I didn't mind it. Céleste was asking me questions that few had asked before. "Right."

"What was she like? Your mom. Was she American?"

She was a beautiful Frenchwoman who became an alcoholic to endure a workaholic. "No, French. She was ... well, beautiful. With a kind and loving heart. And a touch of madness." A family trait.

"And your girlfriend? What was she like? Like your mother?"

"Not in the least."

"What was she like?"

"French. Beautiful. With a touch of madness."

Céleste smiled. "But without the kind and loving heart."

"Correct."

"What was your father like? Was he a good man?"

I looked up at the ceiling, to see what might be written there about the kind of father I had. His mission, it seemed, was to heap distinction upon himself, and indistinction upon his son. Rightly so, in both cases. "He was a good man, yeah. Absolutely. His mission in life was ... well, lofty. He won all kinds of humanitarian awards."

"What'd he do when he retired? Did he keep busy?"

He became addicted, it seemed, to the pizzazz and foofaraw of auctions and black-tie balls. "Yeah, he was a workhorse, he never stopped. He raised money for pediatric oncology institutions, for sick kids in New Jersey, Manhattan, the outer boroughs, Long Island, Westchester. That kind of thing."

"Ped onc? All that does is keep babies alive so they can pass on their bad genes. It's Darwin in reverse."

Was this more ventriloquism, her grandmother speaking?

"And he treated you well?" she asked.

"Of course." Count to ten. "How about you? Did your grandmother treat you well?"

"Of course."

"She wasn't too strict, didn't push you too hard?"

"You can still love someone who pushes you hard. Venus and Serena Williams still love their father. I think."

Snow began to fall that evening as I sat serenely in the living room, in a large gray armchair whose springs had gone. Moon was sprawled across my lap, her motor running. My coverless paperback was open on top of her.

Céleste, along with two or three cats, was on the uppermost floor, under the mansard roof, in an attic refuge a squad of inspectors could never find. You had to go through a hall closet to get to it, ducking under clothes, to a small dry-wall door, then up a flight of dark stairs. She had renovated the space herself: white wall-to-wall carpet, hyacinth-and-hummingbird wallpaper, an antique wicker chair and a rocking horse with a mop for a mane and a marble for its one eye. Behind one of the walls, embedded in pink insulation, was a cache of documents: photographs, videos, DVDs and court documents, all relating to the Bazinet poaching ring. Along with Gervais' boots and rubber gloves. Céleste had pried open a nailed panel to show everything to me. Why? "In case something happens to me," she explained.

"You're not afraid of them burning the whole place down?"

"Yes, I am."

Despite the streams of frigid air, Céleste would stick her telescope out the attic window and peer through it for hours, drawing constellations in her sketchbook or trying to find Apophis, the next asteroid scheduled to collide with Earth.

I was feeling good in my new home, my castle over a bog. It was the holiday season and I wanted to sit back, feel the peace on earth and mercy mild. Or lie back, shut my eyes and wake up deep into next year. Forget that a war was raging inside my head, that time was running out, that the future loomed like a cliff. The police would soon be here, with questions about a missing girl or missing ranger or my impersonating a missing ranger. Child Care, or whatever it's called up here, would also come calling, as would a certain Alcide Bazinet ...

I gently placed my hand on Moon's flank, feeling the motion of her breathing, then heard a soft harrumph followed by a purr that sounded like a distant motorcycle. Cats have over a hundred vocal sounds, according to Céleste, while dogs have only ten.

From the Telefunken upstairs came a carol sung divinely by a boys' choir:

> *'Twas in the moon of wintertime when all the birds had fled*
> *That mighty Gitchi Manitou sent angel choirs instead;*
> *Before their light the stars grew dim*
> *And wandering hunters heard the hymn ...*

"The Huron Carol," which I hadn't heard since I was a boy, since ... I put my head back and listened. Images of a school in France, a brick prison six hundred kilometers from the Seine, circa '76 ...

"What a divine carol! Written by Jean de Brébeuf, the patron saint of Canada, as I'm sure you all know. What you may not know is that Brébeuf's bones are buried not far from Midland, Ontario, at the Martyrs' Shrine. He was tortured to death, I shudder to relate—stoning, slashing with knives, a collar of red-hot tomahawks, a baptism of scalding water, and finally burning at the stake. Because he was so brave and showed no signs of pain, his heart was eaten by the Iroquois. Okay. Our next song, our final carol of the evening, was requested by ..."

The radiohead's words unleashed a chain of images inside me—of red knives and tomahawks and hearts—so the next song didn't register until halfway in. It too was sung by a boys' choir, perhaps the same young angels, and it too took me back, this time to the Nine Lessons and Carols at King's College Chapel:

> *... But with the woes of sin and strife*
> *The world has suffered long;*
> *Beneath the angel strain have rolled*

Two thousands years of wrong;
And man, at war with man, hears not
The love song which they bring;
O hush the noise, ye men of strife,
And hear the angels sing ...

"It Came upon a Midnight Clear." Which the phone in the kitchen savagely interrupted. Moon lazily raised her head, her eyes like wet shiny pennies. I let it ring at least twenty times before displacing cat and book.

"Please accept without obligation, express or implied," said a thuggish baritone, "my best wishes for a socially responsible, non-addictive and environmentally safe celebration of the winter solstice holiday as practiced within the traditions of the religious persuasion of your choice, but with respect for the religious or secular persuasions and or traditions of others, or for their choice not to practice religious or secular traditions, and furthermore for a fiscally successful, personally fulfilling, and medically uneventful New Year, viz. the generally accepted calendar year, including, but not limited to, the Christian calendar, but not without due respect for the calendars of other cultures. The aforesaid wishes are extended without regard to the race, creed, color, age, physical ability, religious faith or sexual preference of the wishee."

This was law-school stuff, which Volpe reeled off annually in the cause of high wit. "Same to you."

"You freezing your ass up there? Do they have central heating in Quebec?"

I paused to listen to his radio, to "Jingle Bell Rock" by Bobby Helms.

"No, not yet," I replied. "It was so cold yesterday I saw a lawyer with his hands in his own pockets."

Count to five. "Does that sort of thing pass for wit up in Canada? That could be the lamest lawyer joke ever told."

"Yeah, it's ... my brain really isn't—"

"I bring you glad tidings."

"My ex is dropping all charges."

"Uh, well, no. Not that good. But still good. You ready?"

"I am."

"The French novelist and publisher have withdrawn their lawsuit."

As if I cared. "And why is that?"

"You really don't know?"

I had a pretty good idea. The book was bad enough, tawdry enough, to make it to the pharmacy racks. "I saw the book at Walmart."

"*A Vacation to Die For* is number six on *The New York Times* bestseller list! Doubleday has bought paperback rights. Doubleday! And one of the Coen brothers has asked about film rights. You say they owe you a percentage of sales?"

"Yeah."

"How much?"

"Fifteen percent stateside. Twenty world."

"Nile, you're a goddamn genius. Send me the contract. I'll make sure you get what's owed. Every last cent." His words were suddenly indistinct amid sudden whuffling sounds, as though he'd just clamped the receiver between jaw and shoulder.

"What'd you just say?" I asked.

"I'll make sure you get every last cent."

"No, before that."

"Send me the contract."

"Before that."

"I said you're a goddamn genius."

"Say it again."

"You're a goddamn genius. A chip off the old block. God, how your father bragged about you. God, how he loved you."

I stopped walking circles around the garbage can, paused for one, two, three heartbeats. "He what?"

"Got another call."

PART THREE

POST-CHRISTMAS

Fails my heart, I know not how,
I can go no longer ...

∽ XXIV ∾

The days after the twelve days of Christmas have always been a dreary and dismal time for me, so it was no surprise when some dreary and dismal things began to happen, here in the Quebec woods, on the thirteenth day of Christmas.

It came upon a midnight clear, with loud engine noises coming from the direction of the cemetery. I peered out the grandmother's window. A phalanx of high-powered snowmobiles had formed, five of them in a line, all shiny black, revving their engines. One by one, as in a military show, they peeled off the line and roared through the cemetery, tossing up snow and noise and diesel fumes, weaving single-file through the tombstones. The last one, with two riders and a provincial logo on the side, was dragging something white, hard to distinguish because of the snow, no bigger than a hat.

Two of the vehicles left the formation and zoomed around the perimeter of the pond, in opposite directions, on what looked like a collision course. No such luck. They slowed and stopped a few feet away from each other, then turned abruptly, accelerating across the pond, back toward their comrades. This surprised me. The marsh and pond were frozen, but how frozen? Would it hold all that weight? It did.

After a while the revellers abandoned their steeplechase and congregated in a five-star circle. My hope was that they were planning to go back wherever they came from, but they shut down their engines and dismounted. The brief silence was followed by music, if that's the right word: bottom-heavy Quebec goth. Do snowmobiles have sound systems? A bonfire soon lit up the sky.

With my surplus Russian nightscope I tried to see what they had been dragging. The first object I focused on was a silver blaster stuffed with D batteries, and the second a white-tuqued man twenty feet beyond. He pulled down his pants next to a gravestone, to the applause and laughter of his friends, and sprayed an angel with urine. The sound of a chainsaw was next. I didn't need night vision to see what the man was about to cut down: a rare white pine born before his grandparents.

"Céleste! Céleste!"

Her bedroom door opened. "I see them," she said calmly.

"Get in the attic. Now. And stay there. Take the pistol, take the Taser."

"Where are you going? What are you going to do?"

"I'm not sure."

"Don't, Nile. That's what they want you to do. They'll kill you if you go out there, say it was a hunting accident."

I flew down the stairway four steps a leap and picked up the phone. Dialed 122 then hung up. That was the emergency number in France. My mind was not working right. Dialed 911 but there was no dial tone. Wires snipped? I hurled myself back up the stairs, to my bedroom closet, grabbed a certain article from its hanger. Hesitated. Put it on. Should I take the rifle? I don't even know how to use it. I took the rifle. And a flashlight.

Back downstairs and into the kitchen, hyperventilating. I paused to compose myself, counted slowly to eleven. Took two stiff belts of Christmas absinthe.

⚡ ⚡ ⚡

"Turn the music off!" I shouted in English. Then in French, twice, three times. To no effect. « Now! » I pointed the Winchester at the boom-box guy. « I said turn the music off! » I shone my light in his eyes. He was Asian, perhaps Chinese, with a patchy spade beard, greased-back hair and a face like a potato that had been in the ground too long. 难看 came into my head: *nánkàn*, ill-favored, literally hard to look at. "*Guān bì yīn lè!*" I tried. He turned the music off.

With the rifle slung nuzzle-down from my shoulder, attempting to look rangerly, I strode toward the pine killer. As the others, with their helmets on, sniggered and yelped and pranced around the fire, I wondered if some base part of their brains was recalling ten-thousand-year-old rituals, if I was seeing the genetic wheel going backward.

I stepped through the powdery snow, my parka making small rustling noises like a battery-operated toy. From five or six feet away, I aimed my light at the woodcutter's head. All I could see was stainless steel and a white tuque. « Turn that off! Now! And lay it on the ground! »

The man waved the saw in the air, gunning it for good measure. He either didn't hear me or didn't feel like laying it down. I didn't ask which. I took my rifle by the barrel and swung it like a baseball bat, reflexively stepping into it, rotating my hips and shoulders, extending my arms and pulling the rifle through the strike zone. The way my uncle taught me.

He raised the roaring saw to protect himself and there were sparks as metal hit metal. The chainsaw kicked back on him and he howled, holding his forearm. I swung again, this time with an upper-cut swing, hitting him square under the jaw. His head snapped back and his tuque flew off, snagged in branches. His knees buckled and he staggered like a drunk before falling head-first into the trunk of the tree he was trying to cut down. The saw lay on the ground beside him, in snow, inert.

My hands were stinging, throbbing, as if thrust inside a hornet's nest, and blood was roaring in my ears. I was breathing not air but an inflammable gas: my head was on fire. I had to get away from this guy before I did something worse. Three strikes and you're out. In my mind I saw his eye dangling out of its socket on the grayish pink string of the optic nerve. I blinked hard, and blinked again, trying to chase the image. I slung the rifle back over my shoulder and headed back toward the others, my pulse pounding like a racehorse's. All I could think of to hold off this show of madness was to keep walking, keep moving. Let the voices and images die.

By the bonfire the three Stone Agers watched me, without retreating, without fear. Why should they be afraid? An attacking force, a history teacher once told me, should be three times the size of the defending force.

« Well I'll be dipped in shit, » said the tallest one. « If it ain't the Lone Ranger. »

I strained to see a billy-goat beard behind the tinted visor, but even after flashlighting it I couldn't be sure. But I recognized the nasal twang. And the smell of beer and sweat and animal blood trapped inside his clothes.

« The butt stuffer with the prissy Parisian accent who eats micro-veggies. I *knew* you were a leaf-eater, moment I laid eyes on you. » He let out a hoggish grunt.

The man beside him, who didn't join in the ensuing brays of laughter, said, « Gervais, you didn't say nothin' about no game warden. » He was staring at my parka. I shone my flashlight through his smoked visor. It was Darche, the hockey player with the Ferrari. Slung across his back was a bow and a quiver of arrows. « If this hits the papers ... »

I saw movement in my peripheral vision. The chainsawer was making his way toward me, zigzaggedly, clutching his wrist. I threw my beam in his face. Like Gervais, he had a currentless, flatlined look in his eyes. Eyes that were still in their sockets, thank Christ. His head was hairless, and his nose beaked sharply. A fierce overbite made him look like a snapping turtle.

He unleashed a phrase I didn't understand, what I'm guessing is the direst oath in the Québécois canon, followed by an arc of puke, luminous over the fire. He removed his snowmobile glove and wiped the blood and vomit from his mouth with his bare hand, flicking it into the flames. « Thanks for your help, Gervais, » he spluttered. « You yellow-bellied sapsucker. I'm outta here. I ain't goin' back to jail, and I ain't doin' no community service neither. I didn't know he was the goddamn law. »

« Don't be a hole, » said Gervais. « You crybaby whiny ass. You scared of a uniform? »

The man held his jaw, groaned. « I feel like fuck on fire. »

Gervais smiled, turned to me. « You ought a be wearin' orange, Mr. Forest Ranger. Mr. Ecoholic. Get yourself shot in that getup. »

« No one said anything about a ranger, » said hockey player Darche. « I thought he was some sort of churchman. A pushover, you said. Who we were just going to *intimidate*. But it doesn't look like we *succeeded*, does it. »

Oh yeah, you've succeeded, I thought. I'm intimidated—terrorized in fact. But the terror and danger fascinated me somehow, and I stepped back from it to get a better look.

« He ain't no ranger, skunk dump, » said Gervais. « How many times do I have to tell you? He's here to get the bishop. And protect that fat four-eyed mole. Dickless Tracy. I know who you are, squaw lover, and you're not from France. You're from the States, am I right? »

This is not what I wanted to hear. Where was he getting this information? From the four-eyed mole? From Earl? I said nothing. I shoved my hands deep in the pockets of my parka, to prevent him from seeing how much they were shaking.

« What's the matter, rifleman? » said Gervais, watching me closely. « Got the shakes? »

I stretched both hands out in front of him, angrily, relieved to see that although I seemed to feel them trembling there was no sign of it. Anger chases fear.

Gervais removed his helmet and wiped his sweating dome. « The feds send you, fuckweed, or you a goddamn bounty hunter? »

I waited for the words to unsilt themselves, strained to grasp Gervais' meaning. Had Bazinet run afoul of American law? Lines from the book I translated, *A Vacation to Die For*, came back to me. « All you need to know, pond slime, is that I'm takin' him back, dead or alive. As soon as he walks. And you know why. »

« That uniform don't fool me. 'Cause I know who it belongs to. Who you really workin' for? Yourself? »

I didn't know what to say. The Royal Canadian Mounted Police? I cleared my throat, took a deep breath. « Snowmobiles on private land, let me remind you— »

« This is public land. »

« Snowmobiles on public land, let me remind you, must be registered and display a decal. And snowmobilers riding on public roads must have a driver's license and ... possess a snowmobile safety certificate. »

Gervais brushed away this smoke with a laugh, but it seemed to impress the Chinaman, who began to apologize in Mandarin. The only law he was breaking, I told him, was a Chinese one: wearing more than three colors at once.

« Who you workin' for? » Gervais interrupted.

I glanced back at the rectory, toward the attic window, wishing Céleste were here to prompt me. It was a mistake, a rookie mistake. Gervais followed my gaze to the window, from which a nightscope protruded.

« I'm with the ... » I was about to say the Department of the Interior but he seemed to know that was untrue. « The World Justice Bureau, » I said. *The World Justice Bureau?*

« The *what*? »

I took another deep breath, steadied my voice. « Wildlife Detachment. Unit commander. »

« What the hell is— »

« So listen up, plowboy. I don't want to see you anywhere near this church again. Not in your plow, not on your Ski-Doo. If I catch you or any of your peckerwood pals within ten yards of Céleste Jonquères, I'll kill you. You've already had one crack at her. You won't get another. »

« The fuck're you talkin' about? I never laid a hand on her. Who said anything about harmin' the girl? If you think it was me who cut her, it wasn't. »

« Who said anything about cutting her? »

No reply, at least nothing intelligible. As he grunted and snorted I remembered other lines from the book.

« You go near her again, you can count your remaining minutes on one hand—and you'll still have some fingers left over when you're done. So get lost. Piss off. Now. » I unslung my bloodied rifle but didn't cock it or anything because I didn't know how.

For a few elongated seconds, Gervais stood stock-still. He said nothing until the Chinaman began talking to me, politely, something about a *wù jiě*, misunderstanding. « Shut your trap, rice rat! » said Gervais, spittle flying from his lips.

In a low murmur of grumbles, following Gervais' lead, everyone began packing up their things. They gunned their engines, one by one, before roaring off, leaving me finger salutes and foul exhaust. The last salute, which dripped blood, looked strangely familiar. Its owner had made the gesture twice before, I suddenly remembered, from a yellow Hummer.

Are these the homicidal inbreds, the freelance psychopaths, that slashed and dumped Céleste? But weren't there *five* sleds? Where was the fifth, the one with two riders?

I kicked snow on the fire before returning to the scene of the chainsaw massacre. The damage to the old pine was minimal. The moron was cutting not the trunk, but a large branch. A few feet away I spotted the long rope I had seen through the nightscope, which had been cut loose from the snowmobile. I followed it with my flashlight until discovering what was at the end of it. I closed my eyes. It was a small animal. With white fur and a red collar.

When I reached the rectory with Moon clutched to my chest the door was wide open. I walked in slowly, stepped through the kitchen, my boots crunching on glass. I set her down on a blanket on the kitchen table.

"Céleste! Are you all right? Céleste!"

No answer. How could there be? She couldn't speak ... I flew up the stairs and into her bedroom. "Céleste!" She wasn't there. Down the hallway to the very end, to an unpainted door that looked like the door of a linen closet. Through it to a half-flight of steps.

I heard the revving of an engine out front. Through the attic window I watched a snowmobile roar off. With two riders. Or was it three? Was that Céleste sandwiched between them?

Another sound, from the direction of the grandmother's study. My wet boots made squeaking sounds as I raced down the attic stairs and along the hall.

The room was severely agitated, in pain: chairs and filing cabinets capsized; books ousted from their beds, splayed, spines broken; shattered pictures and frames, smashed radio and typewriter and globe. Disorder on the scale of an airplane crash. Nothing breakable was unbroken, nothing slashable unslashed—including the flag of the Anglican Church of Canada and the photo of Céleste and her grandmother.

I found Céleste rolled into a ball on the floor, beside the stone ledge of the fireplace. Her eyes were wide open, but her expression was not one I had seen before. It conveyed no recognizable human emotion. Her face was filled with abject, bestial fear. Above her, on the mantelpiece wall, were words she said were written in animal blood: CHILD-FUCKING YANKEE GO HOME.

XXV

I tried to act like a grown-up in front of Nile. But I couldn't stop the tears, I just couldn't. It seems like I'm crying all the time these days. It's a very recent thing. I never used to cry, even when I was a baby.

Nile helped me write an epitaph — he came up with the best bits—and said he'd get it chiselled in stone.

MOON
2006-2010
Where are you now, my gallivanting
Girl, who so happily dwelt with us,
Played with us, fed with us, felt with us,
Years we grew fonder and fonder in?
You who just yesterday sprang to us,
Are we forever bereft of you?
And is this all that is left of you —
One little grave, and a pang to us?

How I wish we were in ancient Egypt, where they had the death penalty for anyone who killed a cat ...

Nile said he never knew a cat like Moon and felt very sad. After the burial the sadness turned to anger. He was torqued, totally. I could see it in his eyes. And he wasn't drunk either. Was the pin finally out of the grenade?

ᕙᘓ XXVI ᘓᕗ

We buried Moon the next morning. Céleste spent half the night crying, and the other half composing an epitaph. I spent the night maniacally cleaning up the study. And when that was done I cleaned up the kitchen. And when that was done I started on the bathroom, trying to ignore the blotched and bleary man in the mirror, the sound and stench of engines and chainsaws in my head. Neither one of us slept a second. Anger—or rather rage, red blindness—can do that to you. In my one hour in bed I counted diminished joys, counted sheep on their way to the slaughterhouse.

It's only a cat, I kept saying to myself, *it's only a goddamn cat* ... High-minded individuals, of whom I used to be one, feel that those who are cruel to animals are just ordinary human beings. They're not criminals; they're just sick. They don't need prison; they just need a doctor or drugs to straighten their bent neural pathways. But now I feel that those who commit these acts, like those who commit murder or rape, have cancelled their membership in the human herd. They must be culled.

Céleste didn't see the intruders. She was watching me from the attic when she heard the back door being bashed down. There were two of them, she said. Her voice had half-returned, badly rusted, a shade above a whisper.

"Who were they?" I asked.

"I didn't see them."

"But you heard their voices."

Céleste hesitated.

"*Tell me*," I said.

"The Dérys, *père et fils*."

"Shit. Did they ... What were they after?"

"Me. And when they couldn't find me, they went after other things."

"Such as?"

"Videos. My grandmother kept some in her office. Hidden, like."

"Did they get them?"

"Some of them, but I've got copies."

"In the attic?"

She nodded.

"That's it. The end of the line."

She stared at me, hard. "What do you mean? You bailing?"

I stared back, trying to form words. *Sometimes you've got to jump head-first into things:* my father's words. I opened my mouth, released a kind of sickly quack.

"Nile? Are you bailing?"

I've never jumped head-first into anything; I was a breech baby, born feet first. I was feeling light-headed, and the room began to turn.

"Nile?"

Sometimes you've got to put your head in the lion's mouth: the same voice. "It's time."

"Time to do what? Report them? Call the cops? Tell them that they trespassed on land that doesn't belong to us? That they killed a cat?"

"Time to put my head in the lion's mouth."

Céleste pushed her glasses a little higher on her nose. "You all right?"

"Hunters, like water, seek the line of least resistance. Animals are easy to brutalize."

Céleste pondered this to the count of three, her eyes half-closing. "You want to run that by me again?"

"It's the end of the line."

"You already said that."

"It's time."

"You already said that too. Time to do what?"

"Hunt the hunters."

"Track them down, you mean? Kill them? We don't have to track them down. They'll come to us. And soon."

I waited for the room to stop turning, waited for the words to register. "I ... I told Gervais if he came anywhere near this place again, I'd kill him. Literally. In the undertaking sense, in the Sixth Commandment sense. And I meant it."

Céleste squinted at me, sizing me up, as if I were a suspect stamp she was examining through a magnifying glass. "He'll be back. Except next time he won't be giving the orders."

"No? Who will?"

"Alcide Bazinet."

I wondered why I even asked the question. I was about to ask another but was distracted by lines on Céleste's brow. Thinking was a visible process for her—ideas chased across her face like wind across a pond.

"I have a plan," she said.

"I thought you might."

☙ ☙ ☙

Alcide Bazinet, it's no secret, was a rabid psychopath on the loose. But neither the QPP nor the RCMP seemed overly concerned. Why? Because his violent psychosis was taken out on animals, not humans. At least until recently. Was I going to gather up evidence, submit it to the Quebec and Canadian police, try to get him charged with attempted murder? No. I was going to murder the man as soon as he got out of the pen. Céleste's plan, however, was subtler and safer—and when my mind was clearer I agreed to it.

By now the entire community assumed I was a wildlife officer, so I wore the uniform everywhere. On patrol in my painted wagon, trolling the streets and forests in quest of the elusive bear truck. At the post office looking for extinct animal stamps and letters from Brooklyn. At Earl's looking for new shipments of micro-greens. At Walmart looking for the witch who beat the dog with her broom. At the vet's looking for ... the vet.

Céleste promised to stay put in the attic while I was gone, to keep watch with her telescope and mayday me at the first sign of danger. But I was having none of that. I was not going to leave her alone again, ever. She would be traveling with me, I instructed her, from now on.

"Uh-unh," she replied, shaking her head. "Veto. First of all, I'm not well enough to bounce around in that rattletrap van of yours. Second, I don't want anyone to see me, 'cause I don't want to go back to the foster home where everybody's a 'tard. Third, no one will be coming back here before Baz gets out."

I looked at her as if she needed my help and protection. She looked at me as if I needed her help and protection.

"Trust me," she said.

I had learned to trust her eyes, the light in them, emeraldine and topazine and shades there were no names for. "When he gets out, where'll he go first?"

"To his cousin's. Here, take this. Can you get these things for me?"

She handed me a piece of paper ripped from her scrapbook, a list of items required for "The Plan":

- *clay (5 one-pound boxes)*
- *flour (2 bags)*
- *gesso (1 bottle)*
- *acrylic paint (one tube of white, ivory, red, blue & green)*
- *clear mat acrylic (one bottle)*
- *ski poles (1 pair)*
- *hockey skates (girl's size 36 or 6-1/2)*
- *new tires for the van (studded)*

"Do you mind?" she said. "I know it's a lot of money but I'll pay you back. Do you know where to get the art supplies?"

"Walmart?"

"No."

"Earl's?"

"Yes."

"And Canadian Tire for the tires?"

"No, for the skates. And poles."

"And the tires?"

"I'll draw you a map."

Her detailed map, no doubt to scale, led me to the northern fringe of Ste-Madeleine and a tumbledown Centre du Pneu Express, where I could get "the best illegal mud/snow studded tires money can buy—ask for Ray." In the same neck of the woods, coincidentally, Gervais and his clan resided, in a purple house she had marked with an X.

"He's got a family?" I asked.

"Three boys."

"Good Christ." What kind of future, I wondered, could his sons expect? Which would come first—prison or coffin?

"And a doormat wife. Last time I saw her she had a couple of black eyes so bad she looked like a panda."

"And what about Bazinet?"

"What about him?"

"Does he have a family?"

"Sort of. He hates women, especially if they're in law enforcement, but somehow he's got a daughter. Around my age. Who lives with her mom north of Tremblant."

"You know her?"

"Never laid eyes on her."

Ray, a gentle tattooed mountain of a man, wore a size of blue jeans that I didn't know existed, and a belt with a silver buckle as big as a pie tin. He installed the new tires and said if I put four hundred pounds of sandbags in the back I'd stay on the road. "Or you could ride with me," I didn't say. The streets were all avian. With the sandbags in the back I made a solid left on Rossignol, right on Hirondelle, left on Alouette. On sharp turns the right front tire rubbed against the fender and sang like a screech owl. At the end of Alouette, a short cul-de-sac, I spotted a black pickup parked some distance from the curb. I went for a closer look, pulling up beside it. It had a raised chassis and rack of lights, but no grille, no platform, no busted headlight.

On the driveway closest to it was a car that looked familiar: a silver Saab. It had backed in, so I couldn't see the license plate. Did it end with RND, I wondered, like the one I saw in the Walmart parking lot?

I was about to get out and check when I heard some

laughter. I looked left and right but couldn't see where it was coming from. What I did see was a young dog, not far from the Saab, a golden retriever. He had a short rope around his neck, right under his jaw. The other end was tied to an aluminum fence post. He was gasping and choking for breath. The more he tugged the worse he made it.

Two boys, sitting on the steps of the porch, were laughing like jackals. I reached into the glovebox for a pen knife.

« Having a good time? » I yelled to the boys, in French, from the sidewalk.

"What's it to you?" one of them yelled back in English.

I cut the twine and the dog breathed easy again. The grateful beast wandered off toward the van, shaking his head about.

"What do you think you're doing, buttwipe?" said the same boy.

I closed the blade, pocketed the knife.

"Why don't you mind your own business, limpdick?" said his friend.

"And get the hell off our property!" said the other.

I was innocent of what happened next. I arranged my mouth into the most beguiling smile and sauntered unmenacingly toward them. "What are you guys up to?" I asked with a kindly, avuncular tone.

"Bakin' a fuckin' cake. What does it look like?"

As I passed the Saab I glanced back at its license plate. Within a couple yards of the taller boy, who had just spoken and was now spitting in my direction, I pointed back toward the dog. When he turned to look I lunged like a fencer and delivered a head-ringing slap. He was one mighty surprised boy. "Mommy!" he cried. The stockier one scrambled to get away but I grabbed him by the ankle and pulled his writhing body toward me. I slapped his face too, backhand and forehand, movie style. Hard, but not as hard as I would've liked.

Both remained silent, in frozen recoil, their cheeks flushed and mouths an "o" of shock. "Next time I catch you doing something like that, you won't get off so easy. Next time I'll throw you in a jail cell." I pulled out my wallet. "And if you're too young for jail, I'll slap your asses into next week. Is that clear? I said *is that clear?*"

The two nodded quickly, triple-speed.

"Here, take my card. Give it to your mother, tell her I videoed her beating that dog with a brush. Posted it on YouTube. I said *take it.*"

I got back in the van, which I'd left running. Not a good time to have ignition problems. The dog watched me from the sidewalk. The boys had skedaddled, but I saw the drapery move in the front window. Should I take the dog with me? Poor little guy, what a lousy roll of the dice he got with this family. I opened the door, called him, but he ran back toward the house.

🕊 🕊 🕊

Back to Hirondelle, then Héron, where I saw an elderly woman throwing handfuls of rock salt from a child's wagon. As I approached I thought she was waving at me in a friendly way, so I waved back. But she stepped out onto the road, holding her hand up like a traffic cop. I stopped and rolled down my window.

« Officer, I was wondering if you could help me. »

« How'd you know I was an officer? »

« That's your showcar, right? »

I paused. « I can't comment on that. How can I help you, ma'am? »

« I lost my dog. »

« A golden retriever? »

« No, she's a little terrier pup. Well, a mongrel actually. Almost all black with a little white on the muzzle. »

« I haven't seen her, but I'll be on the lookout. I'm on my rounds now. Where do you live? »

She pointed to a white wedding cake of a house behind her. A mini Santa's Village was still on display in the front yard and driveway, incorporating a large Oldfolksmobile. « Thank you, Inspector. Or is it Sergeant? »

« I ... it's Detective Inspector, actually. »

« Thank you so much, Detective Inspector. »

« Any time. Oh, by the way, I'm looking for a black pickup with a big grille and broken headlight. You haven't seen one like that by any chance? »

« A souped-up monster for hunters? With a mean bulldog face? »

« That's the one. »

« I don't know if it has a broken headlight, but I've seen one like that two blocks down. On Rossignol. Turn left. A dilapidated purple house on the right, you can't miss it. »

Purple? « On Rossignol? It doesn't belong to a man named Gervais, does it? Tall man, scruffy black beard? »

« Gervais Cude, that's his stinking place all right. »

« Much obliged, ma'am. Here, take my card. »

The swaybacked house of leprous lavender was more of a barn, with a roof built partly of canvas and odd-shaped boards. An automotive boneyard lay out front, a Quonset hut out back. There was a fence around the property, a sagging wire affair, and a sign, DÉFENSE D'ENTRER, on the makeshift gate. But no vehicle in sight. Or any member of the Cude clan. Where were they? In the barn, eating baked beans out of a can, sharing the fork? In the hut, playing their fiddles or stabbing one another to death with ice-fishing implements?

Back on Héron a black pickup came at me, in my lane. In a game of chicken? No. Its monster tires made a squealing right on Hirondelle, which led straight to the highway.

From beneath the passenger seat I pulled out the portable beacon. Put the magnetic cherry out the window and clapped it onto the roof, its power wire strung across my lap. Hit the siren and light switch on the console. Then pressed on the accelerator.

I followed the truck into the parking lot of a two-story eyesore with a red neon sign. Through falling snow I watched it stutter with two burned-out *e*'s: BAR CAV. The driver pointed his electric key at the truck from twenty feet away and its doors obediently locked themselves. He didn't even turn to look at me.

I pulled in beside the pickup and could see right away this was not what I was after. It was a 4 x 4 double cab with a gun rack and spotlights. But no reinforced bumper, no steel platform. I yanked off the cherry, killed the engine. Took off my parka and tossed it in the back. If anyone knew about a one-eyed bear truck, this would be the place to find him.

The Bare Cave might have had charm when it was first built—back when stamps cost 2 cents—but its original wood and stone had been covered with aluminum siding and its large windows painted over like a mortuary. The padded front door, which further sealed the place from all natural light, was covered with Day-Glo stickers and Magic-Marker scrawls, among which:

SAVE A HUNTER—ROADKILL AN ACTIVIST

DO YOU WORK FOR A LIVING—
OR ARE YOU AN ENVIRONMENTALIST?

SAVE THE POLAR BEARS—FOR DINNER

REGISTER HOMOS, NOT FIREARMS

There were only two dissenting voices on the entire door,

one at the top and one at the bottom, both obscured by hand-drawn penises:

HUNTER: THE VEGETABLE IN QUEST OF THE ANIMAL
IF YOU KILL FOR MONEY YOU'RE A MERCENARY.
IF YOU KILL FOR PLEASURE YOU'RE A SADIST.
IF YOU DO BOTH YOU'RE A HUNTING GUIDE.

I pulled on the caribou antler that served as door handle and entered a fluorescent foyer that smelled like an Amsterdam café. A black bear greeted me, standing on three legs in an attack stance. I drew closer. Its menacing paw was extended, but its claws seem to have been lacquered, manicured. Its chipped tongue was made of red plastic, and one of its marble eyes was blue. A brass plate at its feet read: "Shot by Didier Cude, Mont Rolland, 1979."

On the wall beside it was a plaque outlining the history of the Bare Cave, originally spelt Bear Cave. It was built as a hunting lodge by a nineteenth-century industrialist from Philadelphia named Harold K. Beechum, who wanted to host large hunting parties and wild-game banquets for celebrities and politicians. When it opened on November 22, 1906 (the same year as the church), it was remote and hard to get to; it was now on a highway.

Next to the plaque was a framed photocopy of the lodge's inaugural Thanksgiving Dinner Menu:

Procession of Game

SOUP
Venison (Hunter Style)
Game Broth

FISH
Broiled Mullet, Shrimp Sauce
Baked Black Bass, Claret Sauce

BOILED
Leg of Mountain Lion, Ham of Black Bear,
Venison Tongue, Buffalo Tongue

ROAST
Canvasback Duck, Black Duck, Northern Pintail Drake
Blacktail Deer, Ruffled Grouse, Snowshoe Hare
Loin of Bison, Ham of Grizzly, Leg of Elk
Opossum, Wild Turkey, Sandhill Crane

BROILED
Labrador Duck (when available), Passenger Pigeon (when available)
Jacksnipe, Eskimo Curlew, Bufflehead
Plover, Woodcock, Northern Flying Squirrel

ENTREES
Marsh Rabbit Braise, Cream Sauce
Fillet of Grouse with Truffles
Ragout of Bear, Hunter Style

ORNAMENTAL DISHES
Pyramid of Game Quebecois Style, Prairie Chicken en Socle
Pyramid of Wild-Goose Liver in Jelly,
Red-Wing Starling on Tree
Boned Quail in Plumage, The Coon Out at Night

I pulled on another antler and walked into a bank of
bluish-gray smoke. Beer signs, glowing like beacons in a fog,

guided me to the bar, where a half-dozen men in faded camo jackets and ball caps sat on high-back stools, barely moving. In front of them was an ashtray big enough to serve an entire cancer ward.

« Only thing I heard was *pow-WHOP, pow-WHOP,* » said one of them.

« What'd it weigh out at? »

« I heard two-forty, dressed out, so live weight must have been close to three C's. Déry said it could be the biggest ever bagged in this province, a sixteen-pointer too. »

Seven men, seven guts. The one with the largest, peering over tinted glasses, turned to eyeball me. Beer froth made gold foam on his black mustache. « Help you? » he asked in a tone that made it clear it was the last thing he intended to do.

I moved on, toward two pool tables at the back, where Québécois country music was blaring from torn black speakers as big as children's coffins. The room, whose blue lights made it look like it was underseas, contained a collection of mounted fish, including muskie and northern pike with lures dangling from their mouths.

A larger, adjoining room, which might have once been a small ballroom, contained dart boards, video poker machines, a tabletop Ms. PacMan, big-screen TVs and a variety of dead animals. Two giggling senior delinquents, well lit up, were tossing darts at a stuffed moose.

"Hey, what the *hell* are you guys doing?" I said, to my surprise. To my greater surprise, the pair apologized as they reeled out of the room, rubbery-legged, arms linked.

I examined the perforated moosehead and then a row of decoy ducks on a shelf next to it. The expression "a sitting duck," I reflected, comes from the unsporting act of shooting a duck sitting on the water. No skill is required to hit a sitting duck, and no hunter would admit to shooting one. Which made me wonder why so many of these decoys had bullet holes in them.

I looked around. The room contained taxidermal ornaments by the hundreds, many of them quite old. Stuffed rabbits and baby foxes stuffed into the mouths of stuffed wolves. A baby moose sporting a ranger hat and a Ministère des Ressources Naturelles badge. A deer head with a cigarette stuck in its mouth. A moth-eaten cougar named Kitty, sprawled flat like a rug. And birds. They were everywhere, perched on ledges, tables, sills and shelves, or suspended from the ceiling by guy wires. I was thinking that if all the eagles, falcons, hawks, harriers, ospreys, cormorants, kingfishers, owls and woodpeckers suddenly sprang back to life, they could team up for some interesting revenge.

I moved on, toward a roped-off room at the very back, its door padlocked and covered in green baize. A small sign said PRIVATE MEMBERS ONLY. There's always an inner circle, I thought, always a velvet rope, even in hell-holes like this. By the door was a man dressed like an astronaut. Not a real man, but a mannequin, and not in an astronaut's suit but a bear-proof suit made of layers of steel, titanium, chain-mail and rubber. On the floor, under his foot, a piece of red paper caught my eye, which protruded about an inch.

« They got some heavy-duty stuff in there, » said a voice behind my back. A familiar voice. « Triple-X ultrahorror. »

I turned. Looked up. It was the ropy young doper from the real estate office. Wearing a billed hunting cap of eye-hurting orange and the battle dress uniform of the U.S.S.R. In a lower leg pocket was a bulge about the size of an eight-ball of coke.

"'S up?" I said, trying to be young. Or black. He offered his fist to me. I looked at it. « You selling this place? » I asked.

He laughed hard, although I hadn't said anything funny. « That's just a sideline, eh. It's not my real job. » He looked at his fist, put it back down.

« What's your real job? » Selling dope?

« Memorabilist. You know, like vintage hunting and fishing stuff? »

I paused to think about this. « You mean like elephant-tusk ivory billiard balls from the nineteenth century? Or Amazon necklaces made of jaguar teeth? That kind of stuff? »

« Well ... yeah. Got any? »

« No. »

He reached into his breast pocket. « Want a hit of X? »

« No thanks. »

« It's tripindicular. »

« I believe you. »

He unsnapped a leg pocket. « How about some Z? »

A new one on me. « What's that? »

« Zieline. It's killer shit. »

« It's a horse tranquilizer. »

« It is? »

« Yes. »

« Shall we boot some up? »

« No. »

« Want me to show you around? »

I nodded toward the roped-off room. « What's in there? What's triple-X ultrahorror? »

« Members-only stuff. » He put his finger to his lips.

I nodded. I'm not sure I wanted to know anyway.

« Want me to show you around? » he repeated.

Sure you're old enough to be in here? « Okay. »

« This place is famous, eh? People have been shot in here. Cut to ribbons. Knocked unconscious. Girls have been dragged in right off the street, forced to get up on stage and peel. Plus it's the last place in Quebec you can smoke in. »

I asked the obvious.

« 'Cause the cops don't enforce the laws, that's why. The last guy who tried got a pool cue rammed into his mouth. You know, like a cigar? What kind of stuff you into ... Mr. Nightingale, right? Can I call you Neil? »

« If you really want to. Though my name's Nile. »

Another laugh, overloud and overlong, like sit-com laughter. The kind you get after smoking your way through a large bag of hay. « Come, » he said when recovered. « The best stuff's upstairs. »

As he walked toward a staircase, I ducked under the rope and pulled out the sheet of red paper protruding from the bearman's foot. Crumpled it into my back pocket.

We climbed a wooden staircase to the second floor. Oxblood double doors swung open and I stared into the mist and gloom, waiting for my eyes to adjust, slowly taking in the décor. The ceiling was low, as if to serve the stunted, requiring all but children or the bank manager to stoop, and the pall of smoke beneath it could not have been thicker if someone had thrown tear gas into the room. I'm hardly an expert in interior design, but I'm pretty sure the combination of smoke, blackness and red lava lamps would go down really well in Hades.

Patrons here had two entertainment options: watch animal-kill or bestiality videos in curtained stalls, not unlike masturbatory chambers at fertility clinics; or sit before a stage and watch human females take off their clothes. Chalked on a clip-lit blackboard, as in a restaurant, were the day's specials:

- Les Braconniers au ciel (Poachers in Paradise)
- Phallus in Timberland
- Diane Chasseresse (Diana the Huntress)
- Eva Gobère, Winner of the 2001 Miss Nude Penitentiary Contest

The stage, now empty, was ringed with faint red bulbs, five watts apiece, and a dozen stupefied trackers, skinners and lodge boys sat in front of it, waiting for Diane and Eva. Some of them turned and gaped at me, as if an alien had landed on their soil.

We found an empty table, the agent and I, next to three mountain men whose aggregate hair could have stuffed a sofa. "You shittin' me?" said one of them in English, looking in my direction. His T-shirt pictured a buck with crosshairs strategically placed for a heart-lung shot. "What were you shootin'?"

"Got me a .300 Savage."

"And you bagged *twenty*?"

"By sound alone."

From the fog a figure gradually emerged, a waitress wearing makeup as thick as drywall and a T-shirt as small as an infant's. Her pierced face flashed more silver than the hooked fish downstairs.

The agent, pointlessly talkative, began a monologue that neither I nor the waitress, if her eyes were any indication, could follow. Something to do with drowning and the number three. « When people drown, eh, they come up to the surface exactly three times before they die. And count to three on their fingers as they're drowning ... And a drowned body that sinks and is not recovered will surface after nine days, eh? In other words, three times three ... »

« What can I get you? » asked the waitress, impervious to this sort of stuff.

« What you got? »

The waitress stood with the edge of her tray against her hip, staring at the floor. « I'm trying to make that question work in my head. You want me to list, right now, every goddamn drink we got in the house? »

« Boréale Noire, » the agent replied. « A pitcher, two glasses. So here's my advice, free of charge. »

The waitress paused, thinking she was about to get some free advice.

« I'm talking to my client. » He shooed her away, backhanding the air.

« You do that again, » she said, « I'll pour the beer down your pants. »

« She's a real chunk of change, that one, » said the agent, behind a cupped hand as the waitress walked away. « You see her ring finger? »

I shook my head.

« It's longer than her pointer. »

« Which means ... »

He groaned, as if explaining something to his kid brother. « Which means she's *highly sexed*, » he replied. « A *nympho*. »

I nodded, for brevity's sake.

« She's like a goddamn porcupine, eh? Porcupines have sex every day of their lives. You knew that, right? »

« No, I didn't. »

« Here's something else you may not know. The orgasm of a female ladybug lasts ... you ready? Nine hours. »

I expressed surprise.

« Nine. You know who told me that? »

I shrugged.

« The *waitress*. You see what I'm saying? »

I nodded.

« So here's my advice, Nile. What I suggest you do with the unit you just purchased is this. Take out the clawfooted bathtub, take out the marble basin, take out the two fireplace mantels. Then burn the place for the insurance. »

I was turning these words over when he banged his forehead with the heel of his hand, like a bad actor. « I forgot something downstairs! » Another long and loud laugh. « My girlfriend! »

As he trundled back down the stairs, I looked around. Girlfriend? Who would bring a girlfriend here? There wasn't a woman in the entire place, at least not among the patrons. Not a single one ... Hang on, there was one. The last person I expected to see. Sitting alone by the stage, looking fearlessly attractive, was ... the veterinarian. She seemed in a world of her own, seriously involved with her drink and nothing else.

"The one I'm sellin'?" said one of the lumberjacks at the next table over. He took a hit off a joint camouflaged to look like a stubby cigarette. "A jacked-up eighty-eight Dodge 4 x 4." He coughed, hawked, cleared his throat. "With thirty-eight-inch rubber."

This might be the right man, I thought, to ask about a one-eyed bear truck.

"Where's my brew?" slurred one of his friends, struggling to roll a Drum cigarette on his lap. "What's holding up the delay?"

"You know how many wives I've porked?" said someone else I couldn't see.

"Please assure that gentleman," said the cigarette roller, pointing at me. "Of my sobriety." This set the table aroar.

After much wavering I decided to go the men's room,

which would take me by the veterinarian's table. As I passed it, she turned her head and looked at me with her large doe eyes—or rather through me, as if I were one of the moose heads on the wall.

When I heard close footsteps it became obvious that she was looking not at me, but rather beyond me, at a large black suit with wraparound shades and red bandanna over his head, also headed her way. While pushing in the washroom door I heard a voice. In English. "How's your ... animal?"

I stopped, turned. Was this question for me? She seemed to be looking at me, straight in the eye. I stepped back and let the door reclose. "I'm sorry? Were you ..."

"Your pet. Everything all right?"

"Yes, fine ... better."

"I can't hear you."

I approached her table and she pointed to a chair. A chair very close to hers. "It's a kind offer, but I'm already spoken for," I didn't say. With counterfeit calm I pulled back the chair, my heart banging in its cage. The sunglassed man, after seeing me sit down, made an about-turn.

"Canine?" she asked.

"Feline."

"What happened to her ... or him?"

"Her. Young female. Some ... depraved soul sliced her up, threw her in a swamp."

"Are you serious? Do you know who?"

"I'm trying to find out."

She glanced quickly, from side to side, then over her shoulder. "Did you report it? Why didn't you bring her to the clinic?"

"I ... was afraid she'd die if I moved her. I ended up stitching the wounds myself."

She looked at my face, my clothes. "Are you a doctor?"

"No."

She lifted her glass, which had a metal frame and handle. It had been sitting on a red napkin, whose shade and texture looked familiar. "Do you always look away when talking to people?"

I had been talking to her with my head in profile. I was afraid I wouldn't be able to talk sensibly if I looked into her eyes. Helen of Troy couldn't have been more striking. So striking I felt like giving her a congratulatory shake of the hand. I turned, looked into her eyes: deep, liquid, knowing. They had done something to me at the clinic, under fluorescent lighting, but in this roseate near-darkness I couldn't see them as clearly, especially without my glasses. "So are you ... from the area?"

"Montreal. Or just east. St-Hyacinthe."

What was a *veterinarian* doing at a strip joint? Moonlighting? Was she on next? No, probably something to do with the animal snuff films.

She ran one hand through her bountiful hair. "My daughter was hanging out with the wrong crowd, as they say, so I took a job up here. Hoping she'd finish high school."

"High school? You must have had her young. When you were ... what, ten?"

Her smile was slow-growing. "A bit older than that. But thank you."

"Eighteen?"

She looked at me warily. "Bingo. You should work at a carnival."

Which would make her around thirty-six. An age that Balzac thought was a woman's zenith. Cleopatra's age when Marc Antony gave up the Roman Empire to be with her.

The T-shirted waitress interrupted us, giving me a nasty what-the-hell-do-you-think-you're-doing-changing-tables look. « Your asshole friend back there, in case you're looking for him, is curled up under the table. » She shook her head, earrings jingling, before banging down two glasses and a *pichet* of frothy stout.

"Can I offer you a drink?" I asked the vet, while reaching for a roll of twenties in my back pocket. She declined.

"Snorin' like a goddamn lawnmower," the waitress added. Her scowl turned magically into a smile when I handed her my customary tip. She took the bill from my fingers and gave them a squeeze at the same time.

The vet put her hand to her mouth, muffling a cough or laugh. I filled up both glasses in the event she changed her mind, then halved one of them as a long silence unspun that neither of us seemed able to stop. It was her turn to ask a question, I decided, but no question came. Instead, she picked up a pencil lying by her *café allongé* and performed a kind of baton-twirl with it. I was on the verge of mentioning the photo I had seen of her, the one in Céleste's locked drawer, but wisely stopped myself.

For complete strangers, we were sitting very close to each other, a hair's breadth from touching. Close enough to know that she wore no perfume or eau de cologne. If a woman wants to attract a man, that's the way to go about it.

"Is this where we tell each other highly edited versions of our life stories?" she asked.

"I ... well, we could."

"Ask me a question."

A clicking sound, like that of a shutter release button, came from her direction. Or perhaps just beyond her. I looked over her shoulder at the next table, but there was no one facing me, no one holding a camera. The bouncer was now standing by the wall, but his back was turned and his hands were in his pockets. I paused, gathered my thoughts.

"Why did you give me the drugs I asked for? At the clinic."

"The cephalexin?"

"The pethidine."

"What's that?"

What's that? "It's an analgesic. Like morphine."

"Ask me another question."

Why don't you know what pethidine is? Does it go by another name up here? "Does it go ... did things work out for you up here? For your daughter?"

"Hardly. Her new friends are just as bad as the old ones. Worse."

"Is she a student or ..."

"She's a stripper." She pushed back her chair and stood up, displaying a patch of sweat under her arm. "She's on next."

Watching the daughter take her clothes off, I had a feeling, would do little to ingratiate me with the mother. Besides, I was dead. All this noise, all these people was a six-month allotment for me in one night. Worries about my ward, my sad-eyed lady of the highlands, were draining me as well. If I hadn't left the two-way in the van, I'd page her right now ... The clock-hands on the sandwich board by the stage said I had five minutes till showtime. I looked around at the faces— grinning, morose, laughing, blank. Then stared, for some reason, at the red napkin beneath the vet's glass coffee mug. Except it wasn't a napkin, it was a folded piece of paper. Like the one I had in my pocket ...

I was reaching for it when the vet came into my peripheral vision, on her way back from the ladies' room. There was pride—more, majesty—in her stride and bearing; all heads turned toward her like heliotropes toward the sun. Put another way, they drooled.

As I stood to hold her chair I entertained the idea of putting my hand lightly on her back, or long tress of hair, but entertaining it was as far as I got. She sat down as the music started and the lights dimmed.

"I really should go," I said. "And care for my patient."

Another slow smile. "If there's anything I can do for her, let me know."

"You wouldn't ... no, never mind."

"I wouldn't what?"

You wouldn't want to live in a church would you, you and your daughter, and becomes Céleste's stepmother? "I'm looking for a black truck, a bear truck. Big tires and broken headlight. Does that ... ring any bells?"

She shook her head. But with a faint look of surprise?

"A shot in the dark," I shrugged.

She offered her hand, which I thought of brushing with a kiss, but shook instead. It was unflinching, her handshake, as firm as marble, perhaps reserved for clients whose pets she could not save. "You know how to reach me," she said. "But take this anyway."

I took what was offered, a green business card. "You know I'll try." The words came streaming out and made my heart somersault, somersault like a teenager's heart.

"I know."

I told her my name, which I should've done earlier, but she didn't tell me hers. She turned to look at the brick-built bouncer, now lurking by the bathroom door, and then at the stage as Diana the Huntress, with pink bow and arrow, made her entrance.

☙ ☙ ☙

He kissed the veterinarian, whose name he still did not know, on the mouth. Without premeditation or hesitancy or overhaste. They were haunch to haunch, heart to heart! He could not imagine what had taken possession of him ...

I was trying to rewrite that last scene while descending the stairs, but was distracted by a figure on the bottom step. The real estate agent. He was leaning against the banister, minus hunting cap, minus girlfriend. He looked rather drowsy. And didn't return my greeting or appear to know who I was.

Outside the snow was still falling, but the neon sign no longer blinked; it buzzed and fizzed instead, like a beehive. I cleared snow off the Westy with my forearm, then climbed inside. Fired her up first try. Turned on the heater, then the wipers. While watching them, thinking about the vet, I flashed to the green business card and red slip of paper. I plucked each from my back pocket, put on my glasses, turned on the dome light. The card had a poaching hotline but no other number:

SOLANGE LACOURSIÈRE, M.Sc., Ph.D.
Morphologiste légiste
Centre québécois sur la santé des animaux sauvages
St-Hyacinthe (Québec)
SOS BRACONNAGE 1-800-463-2191

I turned it over. Her cell number was written in pencil, double-underlined.

The red sheet was next:

XXXMAS ULTRA-HORROR—BY INVITATION ONLY

1. *Casuistry* (Canada, 2002, 88 min.) In May 2001, three young
artists from Toronto torture a cat to death and videotape
themselves doing it. *Casuistry* takes its title from a word
for specious reasoning that rationalizes dubious behavior.
The leader of the group says he discovered the word in a
dictionary directly above "cat." Two local gallery owners and
a government grant officer defend the action on the grounds
of artistic freedom.

2. *Bleu blanc et rouge IV* (Canada, no dial., 26 min.). In this
continuing series, a Laurentian hunter-artist once again dips
an animal—this time a wolf cub—into a vat of blue enamel,
slices off its paws, and the animal slips and slides across the
canvas until he has breathed his last and another red-white-
and-blue masterpiece is born.

3. *Black Macaques* (Indonesia, subtitles, 45 min.). A Taiwanese
captain of a tuna trawler orders a dozen crested black
macaques delivered to his boat, alive. Trappers are sent to the
jungle, to the Tangkoko Nature Reserve in Indonesia, to bag
the rare monkeys. To take the babies alive, the mothers are
shot. Aboard the trawler, galley hands bind the animals' hands
and feet. Using sharp bamboo sticks, the crew then punctures
the babies' soft skulls. As the convulsions ebb, the brains are
served raw.

Good Christ. This may explain why they built a psychiatric
institution nearby. And why the vet was here tonight. What

are the laws regarding animal-kill videos? If the outdoorsmen shows on TV are any guide, I would assume there aren't any.

I blew out onto the highway with tires spinning, thoughts spinning, stomach churning, unaware that I was speeding dangerously, with no pedal left to go. That's all I need, more disturbing images running around my perma-fried brain, banging at the walls. More things to impair me when I think of them and madden me when I dream of them.

I never tailgate, but I did so on this occasion. My bicameral mind was in a state of entropic frenzy, with billiarding thoughts about cats and cubs and black macaques and mausolean strip clubs. I was driving one-handed, white-knuckled, buzzing Céleste while passing the car in front, recklessly on a blind curve, when it registered. That the car in front was a squad car.

XXVIII

Every time I write in this book I ask myself, "Will this be the last time?" Bazinet will be out soon, any day now, and I don't know what's going to happen. I'm working on a defensive plan that will save Nile & an offensive plan that will probably get me killed.

So I'm going to assume this will be my last entry & talk not about humans but animals, really interesting ones that no longer exist.

Around 10,000 years ago, 3/4 of the large mammals in the Americas were wiped out. Like the Mastodon, Woolly Mammoth, Sabre-Toothed Cat, Woolly Rhinoceros, Cynodesmus (a giant dog), Cave Lion, Cave Bear, Giant Ground Sloth, Mountain Deer, Four-Pronged Antelope, Dire Wolf, Castoroide (a beaver bigger than a bear), Peccarie (a pig bigger than a tiger) & our own native Horses, Lions & Camels.

What caused the great dying? It wasn't a meteor or anything like that. It was something scientists call the Pleistocene Overkill. When the first tribes came across the Bering Strait (which was land at the time) & down through the Canadian Rockies, they entered a hunter's paradise: forests with around 100 million large mammals. The animals hadn't a clue about humans & their ways, so the hunters' spears & arrows caught them by surprise. Totally. And killed them by the hundreds of thousands. The human population exploded. And whenever you satisfy the basic needs of life, anthropologists say, people use their free time for sport. The early tribes killed these great beasts not only for food & clothing but for fun, for trophies. Hunting was seen as an act to test & prove your manhood.

Modern man has done as much damage as the Clovis hunters of the Pleistocene era. From the 18th century on, North American hunters have wiped out many more species, including the Sea Cow, Great Auk, Labrador Duck, Eskimo Curlew & Eastern Cougar. Not to mention the Passenger Pigeon, whose flocks could number up to 50 million birds, who could blot out the sun as they passed. And whose last member was shot in Canada.

I would like to talk briefly about 4 of these animals, ones that don't get a lot of ink.

Sea Cow

On land the only bigger mammal was the Elephant. So "Sea Elephant" might be a better name than "Sea Cow." The largest specimens, females, could reach 10 metres (32 feet) & weigh over 6,000 kilos (7 tons). It was a common species in the North Pacific, but ancient hunters practically exterminated them. They survived only around the Commander Islands in the Bering Sea, where nobody lived. The first European to see these creatures was a German naturalist named Georg Steller. In 1741 he described the way they were hunted:

> Their capture was effected by a large iron hook, with the other end being fastened by means of an iron ring to a very long & stout rope, held by 30 men on shore.... After an animal was harpooned in the back, the men on shore, grasping the other end of the rope, pulled the desperately resisting animal laboriously towards them. Those in the boat made the animal fast by means of another rope & wore it out with continual blows, until tired & completely motionless, it was attacked with bayonets, knives & other weapons & pulled up on land. Immense slices were cut from the still living animal, but all it did was shake its tail furiously & make such resistance with its forelimbs that big strips of its skin was torn off. In addition it breathed heavily, as if sighing. From the wounds in the back the blood spurted upward like a fountain....
>
> They have an extraordinary love for one another, which extends so far that when one of them was cut into, all the others were intent on rescuing it & keeping it from being pulled ashore by closing a circle around it. Others tried to overturn the yawl. Some placed themselves on the rope or tried to remove the hook from the wound in the back by blows of their tail, in which they actually succeeded several times....
>
> It is most remarkable proof of their conjugal affection that a male, after having tried with all his might, although in vain, to free a female caught by the hook, and in spite of the beating we gave him, nevertheless followed her to the shore, and that several times, even after she was dead, he shot unexpectedly up to her like a speeding arrow. Early next morning, when we came to cut up the meat & bring it to the dugout, we found the male again standing by the female, and the same I observed on the third day....

After modern man first saw it, the Sea Cow survived for only 27 more years. Which makes it the all-time record-holder for the quickest extermination of any species.

★ ★ ★

Great Auk

The 10th-century Vikings were probably the first Europeans to see these fabulous flightless birds, these "penguins of the North." They were quick in water but slow on land. So they were totally helpless when nesting.

When Jacques Cartier visited Funk Island off the coast of Newfoundland in 1535, his crew captured hundreds of the birds & crammed them into barrels. And robbed the nests of as many eggs as his crew could carry. The Great Auks nested not only around Newfoundland, but also on the Magdalen Islands in the Gulf of St. Lawrence, and in the Gulf of Maine & Massachusetts Bay. In the eastern Atlantic, they nested on various islands, especially St. Kilda (off the west coast of Scotland), and several tiny islands off Iceland. Everywhere they nested, they were slaughtered.

Here's how the Auks were greeted on Funk Island off Newfoundland circa 1800. Thousands of the birds were herded into huge pens, crammed so tight the poor things could barely move. Gangs of men then waded through the birds swinging spiked clubs, either killing them or stunning them. Other men followed the strikers & threw the birds over the walls of the pen into piles by the fire pits. To loosen their plumage, they were boiled dead or alive in giant cauldrons with the oil of the birds killed before them. Another gang stripped the feathers off them, which would be sold to make pillows & powder puffs. The naked bodies were then thrown into the fire.

By 1830 there were almost no Great Auks left in the world. Their last stronghold was Geirfulasker, a volcanic island off the coast of Iceland, which erupted that year & sank. The few birds that were left had just one place to go — the island of Eldey. On June 3, 1844, some sailors landed there, sent by a collector to see if any Great Auks could be found. They spotted a pair standing high above the smaller seabirds. The female was sitting on an egg — a last hope for the future of the birds. The two Great Auks frantically tried to reach the water, but one was trapped between some rocks, and the other was caught at the very edge of the sea. Both were clubbed to death. And the egg was crushed under a sailor's boot.

★ ★ ★

Eskimo Curlew

This AMAZING bird had the most complicated & dangerous migration cycle ever. It started in the north, in the Canadian sub-arctic, then followed a huge clockwise circle: east through Labrador, down through the Atlantic & across the southern Caribbean, then on & on until reaching the Argentinean Campos south of Buenos Aires! In the spring it completed the cycle, crossing Texas & making its way through Kansas, Missouri, Iowa & Nebraska back to Canada. It seems to have travelled with every single one of its species, in one gigantic flock. Some people compared their singing to the "jingle of sleigh bells."

When they landed the sight must have been awesome: a flock covering nearly 50 acres was once seen in Nebraska. But you have to realize that this might've been the entire world population of Curlews.

When the birds reached Newfoundland they were stalked along the beaches. Men would come after them in the darkness, blinding them with lanterns & hitting them with sticks. When the Curlews got blown into New England by gales, every gunner got to work.

On their northern route over the great plains, the "prairie pigeons" flew into gigantic ambushes, annual massacres. Hunters would fill wagonload after wagonload of dead birds. Sometimes they'd leave huge piles of them to rot & then go back & shoot some more.

In the late '50s there were some sightings (and even one photograph) of single migrating birds in Texas, and in 1964 a Curlew was shot in Barbados. People still report seeing them from time to time. But assuming they're not seeing ghosts, there's no hope for these single survivors. Their instinct is to migrate the length of two continents — but in the safety of large numbers. So if there are any Eskimo Curlews still out there, they're doomed.

★ ★ ★

Eastern Cougar

This big cat goes by many names — Cougar, Catamount, Mountain Lion, Panther, Puma concolor — and once roamed over all of the Laurentians, all over this continent, by the tens of thousands, in the old-growth Boreal forests. They were wiped out — hunted, poisoned, trapped — a half-century ago. Up near Mont Tremblant, a guy named Jimmy Doucette turned in over 200 cougar scalps for the bounty between 1896 and 1906. Today, the only mountain lion remaining in the Laurentians is Kitty, a stuffed & moth-eaten specimen on display at The Cave on Hwy 117, killed on Christmas Day in 1958. Officially, the animal is extinct.

But people up here keep claiming they see cougars or their tracks up & down the Laurentians. And scientists say there may be a small number of them living in the wild. In the 1990s DNA evidence from droppings confirmed that they hung out in Quebec, Vermont & Massachusetts. And an apparently healthy male cougar was killed by a bus near St-Jovite in the summer of 2006.

Nile says he's seen a big cat in the cemetery, once in December, once in January. And I believe him even if he doesn't believe it himself. It's the only hope I've got left, it's all I cling to — that the woods out there are still big & deep enough for the last of their lines to live.

✐ XXIX ✐

The squad car, its gumball turning, did not pull me over. Its driver was speeding too, obviously out for bigger fish than a two-beer joyrider like me. I eased my foot onto the brake, pulled back into my lane. Spared for a future time.

At the rectory all the lights were on, including the one in the attic, which I had instructed Céleste never to leave on. Its shutter rattled as tangled strings of cold black wind wound the house.

On the kitchen table was a note, whose handwriting I recognized. I had a dreadful feeling about it, and was almost afraid to read it. The letters went in and out of view, as if written in disappearing and reappearing ink. A ransom demand? Suicide note?

"Céleste!" I called. "I'm home!" No answer. With banging heart I stared at the note until the letters stopped squirming. *Lawyer Volpe called.*

I ran up the stairs and down the hall to the attic door. Flung it open, took two steps up. "Céleste? You all right?" No answer. I ran back to her bedroom, whose door was open the merest chink. I pushed it all the way.

My heathen angel was spread-eagled on the bed, writing or drawing in her sketchbook. "Hello, Nile," she said huskily, without looking up. "I must be going deaf. I didn't hear you knock."

"What are you doing?"

"Drawing," she said, drawing. "But I refuse to say another word until you greet me decently."

"I buzzed and buzzed. Why the *hell* didn't you answer? Did it ever occur to you I might be *worried*? That I almost had a *stroke* when you didn't answer? And I don't mean that figuratively. I am borderlining as we speak."

"Hey, chill. The machine's busted."

"How can it be busted? What'd you do to it?"

"Nothing."

"And did we or did we not agree that whenever I was away you would stay *locked in the attic*? With only your *booklight on*? With the two *guns* by your side?"

"Don't have kittens over it, okay? It's cold in there."

"But that's what the space heater's for."

"It's busted too. See for yourself. And I can't find the guns."

"You can't *find the guns*? Can't find the Taser, can't find the Sig Sauer? What the *hell* did you do with them?"

"Nothing. You're the one who took them downstairs, took them outside, remember? To practice?"

This was true. I'd left them in the kitchen, I think. "Why didn't you *look* for them, for Christ's sake?"

"Easy, guy. Mellow out. You have a rough day at the office?"

I wiped the sweat off my brow, rubbed the back of my neck. My head throbbed with what felt like a post-speed hangover and my eyes burned. A preview of hell can do that to you. "You could say that, yes."

"You got that coffee-isn't-working-yet look you get every morning. Lawyer Volpe called. I got to it on the hundredth ring."

"What'd he want?"

"You."

"You talk to him?"

"There was music in the background, like from the forties or something. So I could barely hear him. But I know one thing—he's got good news for you."

"Which is ...?"

"Phone him and see."

In the kitchen I searched everywhere for the two weapons. Closed my eyes, rubbed my eyes. To goad my memory I microwaved some laceratingly strong coffee and drank it down black. The grandmother's bowl was abnormally deep and wide—I could have washed my hands in that basin. As the machine beeped three times on a refill, a knock came from the front door, three times in unison. I peered down the hallway with mad, caffeinated eyes. Through the narrow rectangle of glass, I saw the revolving red and blue lights of a police car.

Let's see, to what do I owe this visit? Speeding, driving a stolen vehicle, assaulting two minors, impersonating an officer, or child abduction? Take your pick, officer, it's your lucky day. Three more knocks, this time louder.

"Who's that?" Céleste yelled from the top of the stairs. "The cops?"

"Get in the attic, I'll deal with it." Breaking with tradition, she didn't argue. I heard her scurry away like a mouse, down the hall and up the attic stairs.

I walked slowly, leadenly, to the door, as though climbing the steps of a gallows. The floorboards emitted a sharp crack underfoot, like a trapdoor unlatching. My mind was sprinting, my vision speckled with black dots. They got my name from the bank. Or real estate office. Ran it through the computer, radioed the New Jersey State Police. Two more knocks.

« *Oui?* » I called approaching the entryway, and again after opening the door.

« Monsieur Nightingale? » said a policeman with the standard-issue mustache. His partner didn't have one, being a policewoman.

I nodded dumbly.

« I'm Sergeant Larose and this is Sergeant Viau. Sorry to bother you at this time of night, but we'd, uh, like to ask you a few questions if you don't mind. »

« Not at all, » I said with a stiff smile. « Come in, come in. » I could feel my legs softening, melting like cheap candlewax.

« Thanks, this'll just take a few seconds. It relates to the ... the unfortunate occurrence that ... well, occurred the other night. Involving the snowmobiles? »

« Right. »

« We know who you are, » said the female, a half-smile hovering on her lips and one eye out of true. She stamped her boots on the mat. « Just so we're on the same page. »

Was she about to cuff me, read me my Miranda Rights? Or do they do that in Canada? « I see. »

« We know you're with the Department of the Interior, » said the male, closing the door behind him.

I nodded, exhaled through tight teeth. « I was trying to keep that quiet. Who blew my cover? »

« We, uh ... came across one of your cards while investigating a complaint. »

« I'd appreciate it if you kept it— »

« Don't worry about that, » said the female. « We understand you're after Alcide Bazinet. Is that correct? »

« Well, yes, but it's, you know, hush hush. How'd you manage— »

« We're on your side, » said the male. « We want Bazinet out of here, the sooner the better. The guy's killed more animals than a hundred winters. Got a sheet it takes a day to read, more charges than a power plant. You and your partner want him for crimes in the U.S., I understand? Wildlife violations? »

My partner? Who's my partner? My ghost neighbor? « That's correct. He and his cousin. Up in ... down in Vermont. »

« We thought it was New Hampshire. »

« Both. »

« Alcide makes his cousin look like an altar boy. Hope they both burn in the chair. You Yanks still got the chair, right? »

« Oh yeah. »

« Wish to hell we did. »

The policewoman smiled at me. « There's another reason for our visit. I mean, besides wanting to assure you there will be no more ... home invasions. There's a young girl who's gone missing. By the name of Céleste Jonquères. She ran away from a youth care center in Ste-Madeleine a few weeks back, and we thought she might've come here. You haven't seen a girl of fifteen, by any chance, black hair, green eyes, glasses, part Aboriginal? Tats on both shoulders, bit of a tomboy? »

« No, I ... haven't. But I'll keep an eye out for her. »

« She's a ... well, practically a celebrity up here. A whiz kid, total brainiac. There was an article about in her in *L'Information du Nord*. »

« Why would she come here? » I asked.

« She used to live here, with her grandmother. Who died not too long ago, back in ... when was it, René, October? »

René nodded.

Did Céleste kill her? is the question I wanted to ask. « Really? In this house? How'd she die? »

« It was ruled suicide. It was assumed the girl assisted her. »

« And did she? »

« Hard to say. No charges laid, in any case. »

A faint squawking on the police-band radio made the officer nod goodnight. When she opened the door I was able to make out some of the words, something to do with a *10-23* and request for back-up. Then the crackle and whine of another car responding. At the same time the phone in the kitchen began to ring.

« Looks like another fender-bender, » said Larose, putting his gloves back on. « So I'll be on my way. Let you answer your phone. »

« Before you go, » I said, « can I ask you a quick question? »

« Shoot. »

« Why'd you arrive with your flasher on? »

He winked at me. « You should know the answer to that one. »

I nodded woodenly, not knowing. But took a stab at it anyway. « You ... wanted to make it look like you didn't know who I was. Like I'm a suspect in the girl's disappearance. »

« Bingo, » he said.

« Very clever, » I said. « And, uh, about my partner. Just so I know how you managed to ... »

« We have our ways. We're not as backward up here as you may think. We're the ones who set her up, in fact. »

« Set her up? »

« At the clinic. »

I stared thoughtfully at the floor. The veterinary clinic? The vet was working undercover? Of course ...

☙ ☙ ☙

I watched the patrol car pull away as the phone continued to ring. In the kitchen I watched the rings fluttering upwards, like moths, into air that was dark and spangled with dots like buffed chrome, like fireflies. I picked up.

"I've got good news and bad news," said a faint voice into a crackly line that had been crystal clear until now.

"Just get to the punch line."

"Your ex," said Volpe, "has dropped all charges."

I felt only mild relief, and no surprise. I was still thinking about the vet. "You told her I squandered away my inheritance?"

"You better not have, for the love of Christ. It took your old man a lifetime to double the fortune he inherited. With my advice, of course. Well, maybe not quite doubled, after the market crash and—"

"He told me he was leaving everything to charity."

"He left half."

"So why'd she drop the charges?"

"Brooklyn won't cooperate, won't testify."

I paused to think about this. "What's the bad news?"

"She's run away. I got a call from her from ... you ready for this? Atlantic City. From a motel and I'm sure you can guess which one. Where she'll probably end up hooking to pay the bill. She wants your number, address. Wants to go and live with you in Canada."

Was this my destiny? To raise two teenage girls? "That's not bad news."

"She's on the warpath with her mother. Claims she took her cell away, erased all your messages. I think you should come back. You still have to face the other charges, remember. DUI, mischief. I'll get you off with a thousand-buck fine. License suspended for a year. But you've got to come back, put in an appearance. I can't do it alone, guy."

I gazed up, out the window, at a purple-black sky sown

with uncountable stars and nearly full moon, then down at the tilting tombstone shadows. East to west is how they sleep you in your grave. "I'll try." I had a brewing suspicion that the Garden State had seen the last of the Nightingales, that the House of Nightingale would be winding down here in this northern graveyard.

"Soon, right?" said Volpe. "Like a plane out of Montreal first thing tomorrow?"

A lozenge of moonlight, almost peacock-blue, lay on the floor. "Give Brook what she asked for."

"Roger. Oh, and Nile ..."

"Yeah?"

"Try to avoid more felonies."

I stared at the phone, my mind a blizzard, for what seemed like an hour but was probably a minute. *After killing the cousins you will carbonize the Cave, blow it sky-high ...* When the phone's black Bakelite began to melt and steam I snapped out of my trance. Took out the vet's business card, punched in her cell number: "The customer you have dialed is currently unavailable. Please try again later." No point calling the St-Hyacinthe number, because she's not in St-Hyacinthe.

I walked to the foot of the stairs. "Céleste?"

"Yes?" She was sitting at the top of them.

"What are you doing there?"

"Nothing."

"Did you go to the attic like I told you?"

"*As* I told you."

"Just answer the question."

"No, I didn't."

"Where were you? What were you doing?"

"I was on the floor of my bedroom, listening through the vent. You did well."

I sighed. It was no time for a lecture. "Do you have a phone book?"

"A what?"

"A phone book!"

"On top of the fridge!"

Yellow pages. Into the *V*'s once more: *Véhicules, Vêtements ... Vétérinaires.* Looked at the clock, which was hard on ten. There'd be no one there, I'd leave a message, she'd get it tomorrow.

I picked up the phone and began dialing, but there was someone shouting into the line. With music in the background.

"I hate that fucking sound," said Volpe, "when somebody dials into your ear."

"I'm trying to make a call—an important one."

"This is more important, something I forgot to mention. About your father's car. It was found in a farmer's field in upstate New York. With the keys still in the ignition."

"Can I call you back?"

"You know anything about that?"

My mind was restless, zigzagging to other things. Sometimes it's just not possible to shut things down.

"Nile?"

"What was the question?"

"Your father's car—you know anything about it?"

"Can I take the Fifth on that?"

"What do you want me to do with it?"

"You want it? As payment for your services?"

"Partial payment, you mean?"

"Right."

"There's no charge for my services, you idiot. I'll have it put back in your garage."

"You've got a key?"

"No, I'm going to leave instructions to have it driven through the garage door. Of course I've got a key. What are you going to do about the house, anyway? Who's going to look after it?"

"I left the heat on."

"And what about Paris?"

He was referring to a top-floor apartment in a building on the avenue Wagram.

"You want me to sell it?" he said.

No, there's a girl here who might need it one day. "No, I might need it one day."

"When are you going to sort through your father's affairs? Hold on a second, got another call."

He put me on hold not for seconds but minutes. For almost all of Eddie Cochran's "Three Steps to Heaven."

"Nile? That was your ex. Brooklyn's back, safe and sound. And now she's got your number. So what I want ..."

"Perfect. Can you set up ..."

"... you to do now is—"

"... some sort of trust fund for her, education fund or whatever it's called?"

"Nile, we're talking at the same time."

"Can you set up a trust fund for Brook?"

"Of course I can, but first what I want you to—"

"And leave everything else to Céleste Jonquères? Write it up and send me the papers?"

Silence. "Am I getting this? Leave everything else to *who*? That smart-ass kid I talked to on the phone? What are you talking about, Nile? A *will*?"

"And sort through Dad's private stuff and take whatever you want?"

"Nile, think about this, think about this long and hard, I don't advise this, I've seen this kind of thing before, these wild impulses, a thousand times and—"

"Are you the Nightingale family lawyer?"

"What?"

"Are you, or are you not, the Nightingale family lawyer?"

"Well, yes, I suppose I am but—"

"Then shut up and do as you're told."

One two three four five. "Spell out the girl's name. And address."

I spelled them out. "If for any reason I'm not around to sign, I want you to forge my signature. And the witness's. Can you do that?" From what I'd heard, it wouldn't be the first time.

"It wouldn't be the first time."

"You promise you'll do it? On my father's grave?"

"Of course, if you put it that way."

"Say it."

"I promise on your father's grave."

"Thanks, Leon. You're a good man."

For the second time that evening I stood half-tranced, staring at the telephone. Then punched in a number I now knew by heart, the veterinary clinic's, and left a meandering message.

XXX

Skating on Ravenwood Pond was common in the olden days. My grandmother has a stack of black & white photographs to prove it. Lots of people, hundreds at a time, used to figure skate or play hockey or circle the pond in the moonlight. Kids would hurry out after school, rush home for a quick dinner, then go back to skate under the stars. One time back in the fifties, according to Grand-maman, the Wildlife Ministry built a bonfire, right on the Pond, for skaters to warm up.

Not anymore. The current policy is no skating allowed. Ever. Even if the ice is a foot deep & can support a fleet of ten-ton trucks. They don't measure ice thickness like they used to, and certainly won't be building any more bonfires. And not just because the ice isn't as thick as it used to be.

There have been three fatal fall-ins in the Pond — in 1906, 1972 & 2002. On December 29, 1906, 11-year-old Wallace Ward fell through the ice while skating with two friends. On February 14, 1972, 7 teenagers aged 14 to 18 were playing hockey on the Pond despite "No Skating" signs. When one boy fell through the ice, the other 6 boys formed a human chain to reach him. More ice collapsed & all of them plunged into the water. Their bodies were never found.

On January 1, 2002, another person died, but not while skating. A 27-year-old woman was walking across the snow-covered pond barefoot, according to the last person to see her alive. She was under the influence of drugs. Her body was never found either. That woman was my mother.

It was after she drowned that my grandmother's obsession with ice began. She seemed to forget about her sermons altogether, and focused on her first love, mathematics. And in particular cryoscopy, the study of freezing points. I became her assistant, which was part of my home-schooling.

She wanted to find a numerical model to simulate the variables of lake ice growth & decay. In particular, she wanted to be able to predict future thicknesses of the ice on the Pond. To estimate how many days the temperature had to be at a certain minimum level to cause formation of a 5 cm thickness of ice, a 7 cm thickness & so on.

Once a week we measured the Pond's snow depth & density, ice thickness & temperature. With an ice augur we bored holes into the ice. Ice at the edges is thicker than in the middle, so we needed to test a lot of spots. We fastened a 30 cm brass rod with a nylon string attached to one end to a 10 m tape measure & lowered it through the newly drilled holes. Once it was through the ice, we slowly pulled the tape measure upward, allowing the brass rod to catch on the bottom of the ice cover. We then recorded the distances from the bottom of the ice cover to the water level, and to the top of the ice cover. The difference between these two measurements ("freebore") gave us an idea of the topographical features of the ice cover, and the density of the ice. We would finish our ice coring around Easter & measure the melt rates throughout the spring.

During her third winter with me at the rectory, Grand-maman began to work part-time for Parks & Wildlife as a volunteer, measuring the thickness of ice on the surrounding ponds & lakes. And posting warning signs if necessary. No Skating, No Snowmobiling, things like that.

She began to discover that Ravenwood Pond is not typical of the bodies of water in the area. Not at all. It has some very strange properties. It's almost perfectly round for starters, and though not huge, it's VERY deep, much deeper than any lake or pond for miles around. It's easy to estimate the thickness of the ice on the others, easy to determine when they're safe for skating or snowmobiling or ice-fishing. Often by colour alone. But not the Pond.

Here is our "colour code":

• Black ice — this is new ice, very common early in the season.
• Clear blue, black or green ice — this is the strongest for its thickness.
• White ice/opaque — this ice is usually found midwinter, after the temperature has been below freezing for many days. It must be twice the thickness of clear blue, black or green ice to support the same weight.
• Mottled ("rotten") ice — this ice fools you because it may seem thick at the top, but it's rotting away at the centre & base. It's most common in the spring & often has browns from plant tannins, dirt & other natural materials that are resurfacing from thawing. Not suitable for even one footstep!

Here are our safety guidelines:

- 7 cm (3") (new ice) — KEEP OFF
- 10 cm (4") — will hold approx. 200 lbs.
- 12 cm (5") — suitable for one snowmobile or ATV
- 20-30 cm (8"-12") — suitable for one car, or group of people
- 30-38 cm (12"-15") — suitable for a light pickup truck or a van
- 60 cm (25") — suitable for 13-ton aircraft

On Ravenwood Pond, there's really no such thing as "safe ice." It can be rock hard in one spot & open up like a trapdoor in another. Mostly because of its natural springs & currents, which are warmer and weaken the ice from below. They're dangerous because they're not easily noticed. Or predictable. Especially near a rocky patch at the northern end. There's no rhyme or reason to them.

But there are other reasons that the Pond is hit & miss. First of all, it has dark patches of vegetation sticking out, or floating beneath the surface (like the hair of suicides?), which absorb heat & transmit it into the ice. Decay also generates heat. So areas where there are sedges and weed beds are much weaker than areas where there are none.

Second, the Pond is brackish, briny. Salty ice is weaker & needs to be thicker to support the same weight as fresh water.

Third, ice forms more quickly over shallow water than over deep water. At the northern part, near some "submarine crags" or black outcrops of rock, the Pond is unbelievably deep — maybe as deep as Loch Ness, who knows? There are Algonquin legends & 19th-century tales about the bottom of Ravenwood Pond, but they're mostly forgotten. Only my grandmother & the village librarian (& me) seem to have read them. In one tale a man falls in and his body is found years later, floating in a lake in China. In another, at the Last Judgment, the Pond becomes the Lake of Eternal Fire, which all sinners are thrown into. God pours them out like "a bag of nails."

No one's ever measured the depth near the outcrops, and no one has ever been able to figure out the springs & currents around them. They move in mysterious ways. But after spending the last few days skating around there with Nile, drilling & measuring & pounding, I think I've got at least a few things figured out.

❧ XXXI ❧

They came not in snowmobiles but in trucks. An old snowplow with a barrel sticking out of its Plexiglas turret, and a black pickup with raised chassis and bulldog grille, its empty headlight socket staring back at me. This time there weren't as many of them, only two—the forest king and his fool—and this time it was in broad daylight.

Céleste spotted them first, through the lens of her telescope. She sent me a mayday—not on the walkie-talkie, which was broken, but with a two-finger whistle: one short and one long, one short and a long repeated, an owl's warning cry that set our plan in motion. Her plan, I should say.

We met in the kitchen, each of us unaccountably calm, as if all this were a shared dream that would soon end. There was a beatified radiance of resignation about Céleste as she laced up her snowboots. I held out the Kevlar vest for her, trying to keep my hands steady.

"I've changed my mind," she said. "I'm not wearing it."

"Put it on," I said.

"It's too big for me and it's too heavy."

"Put the damn thing on or the plan is off. Stop trying to be Wonder Woman."

She sighed as she held up one arm and then the other. I strapped up the front. She put on her parka but left it open.

"Zipper it," I said, and she did. "You sure you don't know where the gun is?"

"The Taser or the Sig?"

"Either."

"No. And I don't need them anyway."

I looked her in the eye and whispered two departure clichés. "Take care. Good luck."

To my surprise she responded with a hug, short and sweet. "See you later, alligator," she whispered in my ear.

As she walked out the back door, her skates slung over her shoulder, I walked toward the front door, my rifle slung over mine. But after leaning against a wall by the entrance, feeling close to blacking out, I retraced my steps, back to the kitchen for a slug of *la fée verte*. Through the window I glimpsed Céleste coming out of the church with a big burlap sack. Like the one that enwrapped her in the bog ...

I was about to run after her, to ask what the hell she was doing, when two shots rang out, seconds apart. One hit the church bell, the other thudded against the front door of the rectory. Would there be a third, aimed at Céleste? I watched her as she scrambled down to the Pond, dragging the burlap sack, beyond their field of vision.

Two forces pulled at me in opposite directions. The stronger one pushed me down the hallway. I didn't want to go, didn't want to see what was on the other side of that door. I wanted to be with Céleste. But there was no resisting that force.

Standing to one side, I peered through the small rectangular door pane. No one there. At least no one on the porch. In the front yard, blade up, was the plow, its turreted gun trained on me. It rumbled closer and closer, and for the second time I wondered if it was going to stop. It did.

For the occasion Gervais was wearing a kind of green sash over his parka, like that of an Eagle Scout or South American president. With a demented grin he saluted me military-style with gloveless hands, first the right, then the left. Square and hairy hands that reminded me of joke-shop gorilla paws.

Bazinet—who else could it be?—was sitting on the shotgun side. He climbed down and walked toward the door, his lips in an "o" as if whistling. I drew a long slow breath of air to fill my lungs for what lay ahead, to help me seem as calm as he was. *Anger chases fear, anger chases fear*, I repeated mantrically. It would not be in their best interest to kill me now, I reasoned as they do in the movies, but in real life you never really know. Another deep breath and I seemed to be fine: a bit of stage fright, little more. I flung the door wide open—and was astounded by what I saw.

The great villain I had pictured as a shadowy figure with scorching, Satan-tilted eyes. Mishealed, animal-inflicted scars on his face. A dark cloud over his head, like a reverse halo. Instead, he was a man of preposterous ordinariness: average height and build, forgettable face, corporate hair of some elusive shade between brown and black. A nondescript par excellence. The only peculiar thing about him was that he was not wearing winter clothes, only a gray blazer over a gray turtleneck, black doeskin gloves and gray dress pants, pressed and pleated with military precision. Conservatively dressed, running a bit to fat, he looked like a golfer. Or bowler. Or some ready-to-ship facsimile from the taxidermy shop. I say this because he carried death with him in some odd way, because his eyes were like inert gray stones, his hair and face like a wig and mask.

« *Monsieur Bazinet, je présume,* » I managed to blurt out.

« *À votre service, Monsieur Nightingale.* »

« We were expecting you on Saint Valentine's Day. Or at least a card. »

A plastic smile. « I thought today, Ash Wednesday, would be more ... fitting, shall we say. » His voice was plastic too: colorless, inflectionless, without his cousin's Franglais or argot or nasality. « But let's dispense with the pleasantries, shall we? I have some private business to discuss with the girl. She has some items that belong to me. Bring her to me now and you won't get hurt. »

I let a few seconds go by, playing for time, time for Céleste. « Do you mean like poaching videos and bear-farming photos? Do you want Gervais' army boots and rubber gloves as well? »

He directed a long stare, glassine-like, not at me but at a point just above me. Perhaps at the bullet hole in the door. « I've told you what I want. » His lips were set in a straight line, and even when speaking he scarcely opened them, like a ventriloquist.

I began to smell something pungent. Not the smell of a backwoods moonshiner like his cousin, but of cologne, something outmoded like Brut or Hai Karate, which seemed to have been applied with a fire hose. Unusual for a hunter. Was it to mask his natural odor, because animals could smell the vileness in him, the bentness, and stayed away? Sensed that those who didn't would have very short futures?

« Fair enough, » I said. « You're welcome to her. But in return you have to do something for me. »

A tiny stretched smile. « And what would that be? » His voice now had a strange lilt to it, as charming as elevator music.

« I just want a few things cleared up. For my file. »

He darted a glance back at Gervais, then gave another pursed smile. « I'm going to humor you, Nightingale, not for long, but I'm going to humor you. » Like a cyborg he avoided eye contact, and the cold seemed not to affect him. « It'll be like a last cigarette for you. »

« Okay, but I decline a blindfold. »

« If we're going to chat, exchange quips, should we not do it inside? Perhaps I could measure for drapes while we're at it. The place is really mine, after all. Or will be soon. We could discuss the art of hunting. Or choose some final prayers for you from a prayer book, assuming Madame Jonquères had one. Over a glass of wine perhaps, like gentlemen. What do you say? »

You're madder than I thought. « We're out of wine. But I might be able to whip you up a vodka hemlock. »

His face remained immobile. « Excellent, I admire a man who can make jokes as time winds down on him. »

« So tell me what happened to Céleste, speaking of time winding down. Was it you who tried to kill her? »

« I was in prison. A fair alibi, no? »

A leathern thong over his turtleneck caught my eye; at the end of it, according to Céleste, was a piece of dried bear heart, for courage. « But it was you who gave the orders? To bleed her to death like an animal? »

« Bleed her ... Of course not. She's like a daughter to me. »

I could feel the needle of my cranial pressure gauge creeping clockwise. "You're a liar," I said in a whisper. For the second time, I had this mad urge to start swinging my rifle like a bat. « A goddamn liar, » I said in a shout.

« Watch the Lord's name there ... And get your hand off that barrel or my cousin will remove your face. »

I clenched and unclenched my fingers. The door of the snowplow slammed shut and its driver was clambering down. With an assault rifle.

« Gervais, » said Bazinet, barely turning his head or even raising his voice. « Get back in the truck. »

« But I *told* you, Alcide. What he did to Jean-Marc. He went *batshit*. With that same Win Mag. »

« Get back in the truck. »

« I wouldn't trust him farther than I can piss. »

« In ... the ... »

« He's crazy as a shit-house rat. »

« Truck. »

A dumb-ass pawn, Gervais still knew better than to cross the bishop. He turned on his heels, spitting out a string of religious oaths, including *hostie, câlisse* and *tabarnac*.

Bazinet turned, raised his voice. « I've told you before— don't use those terms around me. »

« And her grandmother? » I said, watching Gervais climb back into the cab with his big furry mukluks. « Dr. Jonquères? What happened to her? »

« From what I heard, she committed suicide. Assisted by her granddaughter. Mortal sins, both. »

« But you were happy to have her out of the way, am I right? »

He shrugged. « She was a hunt sab, like you and the girl. And the vet. »

« Hunt sab? »

« Saboteur. »

« So that's why Gervais killed her? »

Bazinet laughed without smiling, then raised his hand to his mouth as if embarrassed. On his little finger, deeply embedded in the flesh, was the plain gold ring of a nightclub singer. « The whale that spouts gets harpooned, as they say. »

Gervais, I couldn't help noticing, was now bobbing up and down on his seat as if listening to music. Or needing to pee.

I wanted to kill the pair on the spot, or die trying, and forget about the plan. But it wasn't the right time to die.

« And the forest ranger, the American one? You kill him too? »

He shook his head. « I don't do humans. Oh, I'd like to, I'd like to cull them, harvest them like animals. Especially women, who've plagued mankind since Adam. Do you realize there are more women in this world than anything else, except insects? And Indians would be second on my list. They've gone from a hundred thousand a century ago to over a million today. But I'm not stupid. Animals don't call 911. Animals don't lock you up in jail. Animals don't come after you with a gun, looking for revenge. You know what I mean? »

Did I know what he meant? Oh yeah, I was hip deep in what he meant. « I do. But it's not what I asked. »

He tugged on the heel of each glove, pulling them snug over his knuckles. « The ranger was found by Inspecteur Déry. In his SUV, stiff as an icicle, buried in a snow ditch. »

This didn't make any sense. If the ranger went missing— weeks ago—why didn't Fish & Wildlife send someone looking for him? « But that doesn't make any sense. If the ranger— »

« He was acting on his own. Retired. Bounty-hunting for yours truly. »

I nodded, trying to digest all this. « So his death was an accident. »

« Looks like it. But you'll be charged with his murder. »

« For burying him in a ditch? »

« Déry swears he found his body on the floor of your cabin—with a bullet hole in his back. From a Sig Sauer with your prints on it. It doesn't look good for you. A man on the run, considered armed and dangerous, wanted in the state of New York. »

« New Jersey. »

Another wax-museum smile. « I stand corrected. The Garden State. » His cloudy gray eyes were hard, with a polished inorganic quality, like marbles. « Give me the girl. »

« She's not here. Search the place. » I stepped aside.

His eyes darted about in their sockets, resting on the Winchester slung over my shoulder. He was as wary as a crow. With his gloved hand he pulled his blazer to one side, perhaps for my benefit. I looked down. On his hip was a black leather sheath, showing the grooved twin handles of a butterfly knife, like ones I'd seen in China. « And where is she, may I ask? »

« Out for a skate. »

« On the pond? » He shot another glance back at Gervais, then at a spot above my head. « I'll be back. If you are toying with me, Mr. Nightingale, you will be used as bear bait. Dipped in maple syrup and tied to a tree. »

🕊 🕊 🕊

In my role as watcher of the tower, keeper of the treasures, I hauled myself up the stairs to the attic. Everything was still behind the wall, including Céleste's sketchbook, locked inside my father's Halliburton. My hands were now trembling, but I don't think from fear. It was more like ... horror. Not the same thing. There was something about Bazinet, something that went light-years beyond bad vibes. After positioning and adjusting Céleste's telescope, I sat on her wicker chair, fingers drumming, kneecaps pumping, waiting for her plan to unfold.

I felt minor-parted and miscast, and while glaring at the sweep hand of my watch I wondered why I ever accepted my role. I had told Céleste that her scenario was flawed, that I wanted to be on the Pond with her, that she wasn't well enough to be there on her own. But she mulishly stood her ground, insisting I was needed here. "Besides, where I'm going it'll be too much weight for the two of us. And if you're there with me, Baz will stay away."

Now with a long fur coat on, Bazinet made his way down to the Pond at a trot, displaying no athleticism, no agility of leg. There he inspected the ice, wiping the frozen surface with his boot and pounding it two or three times. It was rock-solid, I knew, from the drills and measurements we had taken that very morning. And there was much to suggest this: the trails of ice fishermen and the charred stubble of their fires; snowmobile and animal tracks—deer and rabbit and what looked like some large breed of dog.

Céleste skated along one of the snowmobile lanes then veered off toward a rocky islet at the northernmost end. I could see her, and so could Bazinet. It was hard not to: she was motioning vigorously, sirenically, with her right arm. She skated a few feet before turning sharply and stopping in a knight's L. Which signaled "so far so good."

In his cloud of cologne Bazinet walked slowly back to the snowplow, as if pondering his next move. I prayed he wouldn't spot the van, which was now parked by the Pond and camouflaged with snow and downed branches. He stopped right in front of it, but instead of turning his head a few degrees to the side, he looked up, as if directions for what to do next were printed in the sky. He pulled his gloves tight, caressed the knife handle on his belt. Then continued on his way, whistling, back to Gervais' plow.

He climbed into the cab and waited there for the duration of a cigarette, then got out and walked toward his pickup. His cousin followed in lockstep. From the bed of the truck they lowered two metal ramps, like ladders, and wheeled a shiny black snowmobile down them. With Gervais at the wheel and Alcide riding shotgun behind, they roared off toward the Pond.

Céleste, by this time, was skating back to shore. I was screaming at her through the window, senselessly, when I saw it ...

Here we reach the undependable part of the story: my visual memory stubbornly insists that what I saw was a mountain cat. Like the vision I'd had twice before. It's obviously a protruding rock, I told myself. Or perhaps Kitty, the stuffed cougar from the Cave. Except it seems to be moving, creeping to within a few feet of Céleste. But how can that be? She's now at least fifty yards away. Are there two Célestes?

I pulled back from the telescope, wiped my eyes with my fists. Shook my head then looked through the lens again. Everything was out of focus, the glass as wavery and distorting as tears. I moved the scope, adjusted the lens, until the two men came into view. Glued one eye shut and the image sharpened, but its colors seemed to be off, too gray, as if from another era.

They had come to a complete stop, on the south shoreline. Bazinet was standing by the sled, staring straight ahead, his body frozen like a hunting dog. He then made a flurry of hand gestures, pointing excitedly at something. He jumped back on and the sled lurched forward. I moved the scope to see what they were after. Céleste, obviously ...

But I couldn't find her. I scanned madly from one side to the other, then back again, slowly. Stopped at that rock again. A light brown boulder ... with a tail. It sprung forward and broke into a run, toward the spot—the outcrops of gray and black rock—where I'd just seen Céleste! I moved the scope and saw her, standing by these very rocks—stiff as a statue, as if frozen in fear.

Two shots rang out. After the first the lion continued to run, at full gallop. With the second his knees buckled and he went down. But he got up, his hip a crimson smudge on my canvas, and loped on. With a third shot he was dragging his hind legs along the ice. He stumbled and fell, quivering, trying to push his insides back in with his paw. He wobbled to his feet and staggered on, but soon tripped over his bowels, which were trailing out behind him like tangled red ribbon.

The cousins followed, without firing, until the exhausted animal, puffing and blowing, collapsed by the submarine crags. They circled him twice before stopping. Bazinet aimed the rifle and paused, lips moving, perhaps muttering some mantra, some drum-song of murder, before blasting more shot into the lion's face. Gervais was hooting and fist-pumping and Bazinet climbing off the snowmobile to inspect his trophy when they went down.

No buckling, no heaving, no warning. The ice opened up like a trapdoor and they went through. Only a few seconds of thrashing, flailing and screaming before they went down, came up, went down, and didn't come back up. An electric stillness followed, of such force that it seemed to stop time in its tracks.

I blew down the stairs and out the kitchen door, a dizzying parade inside my head, a retinal circus of chessmen and stamps and animals. Along with questions twirling like juggler's pins afire: *What if none of this is real? What if you're MUCH madder than you thought? Irreclaimably mad. Or wait, maybe you're not mad at all, maybe, drum roll, you're DEAD. You died in the bog trying to save a stranger and all this is after-death experience, your voyage through the afterlife. God having a lark with you. Or Lucifer. Or you've hallucinated this from beginning to end—your crowning delusion—from your sickbed, deathbed, in Neptune. You've never even been to Canada ...*

I set these questions aside, dropping them at the edge of the Pond, and screamed out Céleste's name. The voice seemed real. I kicked at the ice, felt my face. I seemed to be in the here and now. My thoughts turned to the reason I was here, now: the plan, and how things had not gone according to said plan. Céleste was to have been the lure, not a providential lion, and her savior mathematics, cryoscopy, not a *leo ex machina*. After waving at Bazinet, she was to have hidden behind one of the crags, in a crevice that only a child could fit into. Which is why she'd been starving herself for the last few days. Was she there now? Or had she gone down too? Or was that her gut-shot body lying out on the ice?

I was ten yards from shore when I saw what looked like her shape and colors—standing upright!—in the distance. Yet at the same time I heard her voice, behind me, from the direction of the cemetery. "Céleste?" Stone silence. I turned. Was she calling from the spirit world?

The voice was shallow and thin, as if it had been worn down by screaming, by torture. I headed toward it, feeling the sweat in both armpits dribbling down my sides. An aura of royal blue came from under the skirt of a big bushy cedar. In a panic I parted its branches and saw a body half-entombed in snow. Dead?

I called out her name. More silence. As I approached I saw movement: her body was shaking. And her eyes were teary, rimmed with red. With her mitten she wiped the fog from her glasses.

I knelt down, threw my arms around her. "Céleste! Thank God. Are you all right, are you—"

She said something strange, in what could have been an ancient tongue—Laurentian?—as she pushed me away. She sat up and began to unlace her skates. They were old and battered, not the new ones I had bought her ... Was this really her? Had someone exchanged Célestes on me?

I had a thousand and one questions about what had happened, or not happened, but my mind and mouth were filled with contending sounds and images. "*¿Cómo habría podido sucede ... Εἴδατε ... 美洲狮... Penso che stia perdendo ... Est-ce que c'était vraiment ... Ich brauche einen Arzt ...*"

She looked at me as if I were delirious, feverish, speaking in tongues. Which I was. Words that only I could hear were vibrating my eardrums, photons carrying images that only I could see were striking the rods and cones of my eyes.

She tilted her head, looked over the top of her glasses. "You all right?"

Killing deer and moose, I now saw, were diminishing pleasures for the likes of Alcide Bazinet—animals like these were a dime a dozen. What they now wanted was the rare specimen, and the rapture that came with taking down the last of its kind ...

"Nile, are you in there?" She waved her hand by my face.

I wanted to make sense of all this but the neuroacrobatics would not stop, the ghosts would not line up. I tried to speak but my jaw went tight, the words jammed. I closed my eyes, breathed deep, and with an imaginary windshield wiper tried to wipe my mind clear. Back and forth, back and forth. An old trick of mine that worked but seldom. I half-raised my arm. "Present."

"No you're not. You're in that state of yours—when you look like you're dead and alive at the same time."

I had trouble hearing her words, as though the air were molasses. What was going on? Nitrogen narcosis, delirium tremens, alcoholic hallucinosis? I took another deep breath, trying to reoxygenize. "What ... what were you doing in ..."

"Hiding. Now let's get out of here." She slipped into her boots, dumped her skates in a mound of snow. "As soon as I get this damn thing off." She unzippered her parka.

It took me a few seconds to understand what she meant. "No," I said, stopping her. "Don't. Leave the vest—"

The sound of engines barged in. We turned, each of us, toward the cemetery. Black snowmobiles, four of them, gunning their engines. And behind them, with gumball spinning, a police cruiser I'd seen before.

A pop inside my brain brought some clarity, the visual equivalent of waterlogged ears unblocking. Sergeants Larose and Viau ... "The cavalry's arrived!"

"It's no rescue mission. Let's go." She led.

"But I know them. And besides, they've blocked off—"

"We're going the other way."

I shook my head and my neck cracked. "Across the Pond? You know how much the van weighs, with us inside it?"

"To the half-kilo. Go where I tell you and we'll be fine."

We cleared off the snow and branches from the van— Céleste slowly and I frenetically—then climbed in. I hit the ignition, which ground and ground but would not catch.

« You are under arrest! » said Sergeant Viau's magnified voice. « Get out of the vehicle and put your hands in the air! »

As the van fired up, the snowmobiles and their vizored Darth Vaders raced toward us. They caught up to us in seconds, a few feet from the shore, but didn't fire. They rode patrol style: two outriders a few yards up front, two as a rear guard directly behind, trading paint, playing bumper car.

Céleste pointed the way, which she had marked with small blue fleur-de-lys flags. "Nice and slow," she said. I didn't have to ask why since she'd already told me. The weight of the vehicle presses the ice down—as you advance you create a wave motion that can bounce off the shore or islands you're approaching or leaving, and can cause even thick ice to fail. So the slower the better.

We rode not along the smooth tracks left by snowmobiles, but along rough patches of snow. "We're ... getting near the hole," I reminded Céleste. Was a double suicide part of the plan?

"Keep going," she croaked, teeth chattering.

I took off my parka, steering with my knees, and despite her protests wrapped it around her. It covered her from head to toe, but didn't stop her from shaking. Was she shaking from the fall-ins? Or from the killing of the *Puma concolor*, the fracturing of its fearful symmetry?

Two of the snowmobiles, the ones riding my bumper, stopped as we neared the killing field. Blood was splattered over the ice and welling out of the cat's flank and snout. It was a young animal, not yet full grown. Were its parents nearby? A single track of blood ran down its cheek, as if it were weeping even in death.

I was chilled down to the bones of my hands, nearly crippled from a swat of cold nerves. "Don't look," I said, turning to Céleste. But it was too late—she was already following my gaze.

"Don't look at what?"

I looked at her face—it registered no surprise, no shock, no horror—then back over my shoulder, at the cougar. There was nothing there, no body, no tracks, nothing but a black-and-tan rock protruding from the water, a craggy rectangle the size and rough shape of a lion in winter ... Had the cat gone through the ice too? I could not unsee what I saw.

The other sleds continued on to the far side of the Pond, circling so as not to telegraph their intention, which was likely to set up a roadblock. But they too stopped, then reversed directions when they saw their comrades shouting and waving at them and pointing at the edge of the hole, at something snagged on a shard of ice: Gervais' red-white-and-blue cap.

Seconds later, possibly minutes, they congregated in a four-sled powwow, then peeled off, one by one, back toward the police duo standing on the shore. We lumbered on, to the one place no one would follow us: the watery grave. It was Bible black, as dark as outer space, the ice around it "rotten," mushy, pockmarked with browns, bronzes, rusts. We came to within ten yards of it, five yards of it, onto a magic carpet of clear blue-green, and the ice held.

Near the hole, tied to a stake in the ice, was ... Céleste. Or rather, her twin. Standing like a scarecrow but a fuller version, a high-definition version, like one of those *trompe l'oeil* mannequins found in art installations. Wearing a Joan of Arc wig and wire-frame glasses and Céleste's blue ski jacket and pants. And skates, brand-new ones that looked familiar. Size 6-1/2. I looked to my right, at the real Céleste, then back at the clay-faced decoy.

The real Céleste threw open her door and climbed out onto the ice. She was walking straight toward the hole! Onto the water, like Christ!

"Céleste! Don't! Get away from there! Please. Don't ... jump!"

On the chapped lip of the crater, which somehow held her weight, she pulled down her double from its stake. Then tossed it, head-first, into the black void. It floated, semi-submerged, for several seconds before being dragged down by its ski-pole skeleton and steel-bladed feet.

🐦 🐦 🐦

The next thing I remember is the solid ground of a clearing on the far shore. Remnants of an unused road, said Céleste, which someone had tried to clear with a bulldozer until someone else told him to stop. It was snow-covered but had wide ridges and furrows that the van's tires were able to grip. A mile or so on, the trees closing in, we passed a crumbling cinder-block foundation for a house that was never built.

"Where does this lead?" I asked. To a freeway? The interstate?"

"We don't call them freeways in Canada. Or interstates either. It goes to Lac St-Nicolas. We should be there in twenty minutes."

"Twenty minutes Canadian?"

She looked at the dash clock and speedometer. "Or longer. You should have a calendar in here, speed you're going."

I couldn't go any faster. It was murderous terrain, up and down gullies, over fallen logs and branches. Twice the van sunk to the back bumpers in black mudholes that lay under the deceptive snow. The studded tires spun as though in oil. A Caterpillar, I was sure, couldn't have pulled us out, von Guericke's vacuum principle being what it is, but each time we prised the truck out with logs as levers and branches as mats, I lunging, Céleste rocking the wallowing vehicle as the wheels spun out gouts of cold mud. Much of it onto me.

"What are we going to do on Lac St-Nicolas?" I asked, back behind the wheel, wiping my face with slimy, peat-scented gloves.

"My grandmother's plane is there. I hope."

"And we're going to do ... what with it?"

She dug into her side pocket and held up a ring of gold keys. "What do you think? If it's not there, we'll drive across the lake."

I paused to think about this. *Is madness contagious?* "Are you ... all right, Céleste? How do you feel about ... you know ..."

"About what?"

"About what happened." I didn't dare spell anything out. The cousins, I was pretty sure, had vanished into a dark hole, as utterly and completely as if the devil had snatched them down to hell by the heels. But had there been a cougar?

"You mean what happened to Baz and Cude? The fall-ins?"

Okay, at least that happened. "Yeah."

Céleste paused to think about this as we bounced along. A long pause, at least for her. "I feel like ... like a fish released into a stream." She put her hand to her mouth, as if about to throw up. "Or a duck trapped under the ice who's been set free." She coughed into her mittens, a barking, brassy cough. Bronchitis? Croup?

"You okay?"

"Or ... like I've been strapped to a bomb and the last wire's been cut and the ticking stops."

An unexpected wind howled through the trees, seemed to push us forward, deeper into the forest. The path grew smoother but narrower, twisting and turning randomly. We wove in and around large boulders and towering pine, spruce, fir. Finally the path disappeared altogether in veins of scrawny saplings—either burned or drowned—and a copse of elderly crippled maples, trunks knotted and knurled from surviving disease. The old van, snorting and twitching, plodded on.

In the early twilight, everything seemed to have a supernatural clarity: I marvelled at the way every mound of snow, every branch and boulder seemed distinct as if framed in black, as if the entire landscape were a series of paintings executed with superhuman skill. I looked at Céleste and saw, as though in time-lapse photography, the same degree of detail, all the lines present and future in her young and old face ...

With a patch of the lake in view, its surface blindingly white, the Vanagon stalled. I ground and pumped, but her heart was dead. If only I'd taken her in for repairs. This will cost us our lives.

"Forget it," said Céleste, pointing. I squinted, sheltering my eyes from the setting sun. Out on the lake, or perhaps on the shore, was a small blue-and-white craft. A boat, I thought, which would be of no use to us. Beyond that was a small red-and-white cottage, candy-striped.

"Do you have the rifle?" she asked.

I'd forgotten it. A stupendously stupid thing to do. I waited for some words from my father, but no words came. I opened the glovebox, pulled out the plastic .38.

"Does the battery still work?" she asked.

I switched on my left blinker. "Yeah, why?"

"Can you put the flasher and siren on?"

"Yes, but—"

"I know the guy down there. We've got to try to ... well, distract him, confuse him, throw up some smoke."

From underneath Céleste's seat I once again grabbed the

portable beacon light. I plugged the wire into the cigarette lighter and set the cherry onto the roof. Then flicked two switches.

"Who is it?"

"Take your coat," she said as the siren sounded and the red light revolved.

"Keep it, I'm fine." Adrenalin had numbed me from the cold.

"Take it," she repeated, her body shaking, her words leaving a vapor trail.

We climbed out of the van and highstepped downhill through thigh-deep snow that was crusted on top. Just punching through it took a lot of strength, so I took small steps so that Céleste could follow in the holes I had left. As we reached the frozen lake I could see a long, snow-free lane bisecting it. At the near end of it was the blue-and-white craft. A headless man in black stood beside it, his top half lost under the opened engine cowling.

It was not a boat, but a plane. With short "skis" under the wheels like flat metal shoes. When the pilot saw us he slammed the cowling shut, tossed a cigarette onto the ice. From under his reaper's hood he looked toward the blinking van, hesitated a few seconds, then climbed into the cockpit.

"Run!" Céleste rasped. "Don't let him get away!"

I ran hard, into the teeth of the wind, slip-sliding across the ice, waving the pistol and screaming out battle cries like a backward Indian. My face, I'd almost forgotten, was warpainted with mud. The pilot put his hands in the air.

« Can you give us a lift? » I shouted. I was panting, gasping, like a fish breathing poisonous oxygen.

The man shook his hooded head, made sounds I couldn't make out. Spit-filled, Donald Duck sounds. He was looking not at me, but beyond me. I turned around and saw Céleste running pegleggedly toward us, clutching the collar of her coat around her throat with one hand, looking like she was about to drop.

The dull sound of distant motors. A mile or two away, red and black snowmobiles swarmed on the shoreline like red and black ants.

« We need a ride, Inspecteur Déry! » said Céleste in a hoarse high yelp. «Now! Otherwise we'll have to blow your head off! »

Inspecteur Déry, obviously off-duty, wore a black leather jacket over his hoodie, all zippers and snaps, with "Aigles Noirs" written on the back. He turned to face Céleste and stood up. He was a big man my age with a slightly houndish sag to his face. His big sloppy body looked like it was about to fall over.

« Do you know why your grandmother sold me this plane? » he said, his words squishing saliva. He put his hands back down to his side. « Dirt cheap? »

« Put your hands back up, » Céleste shouted.

« So that I wouldn't go near you again. Or my sons either. So that I'd keep an eye out for you. » He smiled. « But since she's dead now, and since your friend's holding a water pistol ... »

A revolver was coming out of his pocket as I aimed and futilely fired. A thunderous shot rang out, but from another direction, from the cottage. My eyes darted to Céleste. She was fine, it seemed, unhit, but her eyes bulged as she gaped at Déry. I turned. The blast had scalped him and shattered his teeth and all but severed his neck. A clot of hairy gray matter hung from his upper lip and smoke poured out of a hole where his nose used to be. He stumbled out of the cockpit, arms in front like a blindman, still holding the gun. His legs folded like marionette limbs as he fell into the snow face down. Or half face down. The white around him turned to red, like drippings from a child's Popsicle.

"Get down!" I jumped in front of Céleste, arms raised. Grabbed her by the shoulders and pulled her to the ground as a second blast rent the air, louder than the first. It came not from the cottage but the opposite direction, from the van, and the spray of lead found its target.

After a splinter of time, too small to register on the brain, too soon to feel pain, a third and final blast came from the cottage, one to help not harm us.

∽ XXXII ∾

*I've had visions before but nothing quite like this. Nothing
on this scale. It begins with a fade, like theater lights
coming down, but goes more to gray than to black. A pain
inside my rib cage jolts me, fills me with light and heat—
balls of fire, showers of sparks, flame-wheels of blue and
red. And then night—my mind fills with night. No stars,
nothing. I have no thoughts, nothing rational at least, only
the power to feel, like an animal. The chemicals of thought,
what's left of them, kick in and I realize we've fallen, into
black winter water. From a plane? I open my eyes and see
a blue light shining high above me with an almost churchly
cast, as if, impossibly, it were slanting down from a stained-
glass window. My senses are sharpened, and everything
they record is clear, magic-realistically vivid. Something
in the commotion of my parts has turned my eyes into
telescopes and ears into stethoscopes. In the forest on all
sides I can see each tree, the texture of its bark: the rugged
fissured coats of maples; the patchy gray-browns of pines;
the peeling white paper of birches; the dark gray ridges
of elms (or their ghosts because elms are all dead). I see
the prismatic colors of icicles hanging from their highest
branches, the hexagonal crystals of their snowflakes. But
all is contained within frames as small as postage stamps,
jagged squares that embrace the beginning and the end
of things. A white-throated sparrow flies overhead and I
hear its song as if it's perched on my shoulder, singing*

into my ear. The discordant calls of other birds—blue jays, chickadees, ravens—merge in a soft melody inside me. A glossy-coated mink (or muskrat or otter) swims beneath my eyes and I hear the swish of its dark chocolate body—the sound, I am sure, the animal itself hears! The world begins to whirl, and I see a candy-cane cottage of red and white, an airplane of turquoise and cream, a lion of butterscotch and black. I am astride the animal as in a merry-go-round and hear its heart-breaking moans. Black vortices of water, bloodied swords of ice, armies of hunters hunting me— all is blended and blurred, caught in this gyrating mass. When it stops I see that same blue light, scattering jewels onto the snow. A distant bell tolls the hour. I fade again, but reawaken to find myself back home, standing before the cemetery gate.

"We made it! We escaped!" I cry to my partner in crime, my precocious little murderess. But I do not see her, and she does not hear me.

So here I lie beneath a canopy of trees and fix my eyes on the darkening heaven. And I will hear the stroke of six but not the stroke of seven.

🕊 🕊 🕊

Céleste is bleeding, I am bleeding, our blood joins in a pool at our feet. The distant engines are louder, the rival snipers silent. I smile at Céleste and she gives me a laughing, full-toothed grin, like the one she wore in the photo with her grandmother.

"Are you hurt?" I ask, but there is little voice in it. "Can I take a look at your wounds?"

She doesn't seem to hear. "Where to?" she says, looking

heavenward. "Neptune?"

"You know how to fly this thing?"

She remains silent, studying the instrument panel. Fiddles with the floor-mounted stick, moving it in all directions. Pushes on a small black button on the right, then gets out onto the ice and pulls the prop through twice by hand. She climbs back in, grimacing, and turns a switch to "Both." Eases the throttle all the way forward. Nothing happens. "Oil pressure, oil temp, RPMs," she tells herself. Tries again and the prop begins to turn. Slowly, dream slowly, we begin to wobble along the lake as if wounded.

The black and red snowmobiles are now upon us, within firing range. Bullets whip the surface of the ice like hailstones. A tire explodes. A mirror shatters. There is a rich tang of gunpowder, like the smell of fireworks. Céleste rights the plane and we pick up speed, faster and faster, a fifty-yard dash along a snow-free lane. At the finish line she pushes the stick forward and the plane's tail lifts up. Then back on the stick and we begin to rise.

Gazing down, we see muzzleflashes as hunters continue to shoot at us from the shoreline. We hear a sharp metallic ping and dip suddenly over a small island, brushing the crown of its sole tree. One of our wings begins to leak.

But we rise up again, like endangered birds, like birds seen only if believed in, over treetops and streams, mountains and marshes, higher and higher, into the setting sun and animal-shaped clouds ("White Whale, White Lion, Polar Bear!" I cry), following the path of winged predecessors ("Eskimo Curlew, Labrador Duck, Passenger Pigeon!" she cries), and it comes to me, like something resurfacing from memory, that I will never see anything more, ever, but what lies in this heavenly mist.

XXXIII

I would've flown that plane to the end of the Earth, through all eternity — but it wouldn't start, I couldn't get it off the ground, I couldn't remember how!!

I tried & tried with hands that wouldn't stop shaking, pumping the primer, pulling the prop through again & again, pushing the throttle all the way forward ... I stopped when I saw something flying overhead — a blaze-orange & blue helicopter, like a giant candy-coloured dragonfly. And then two police sleds, one red, one black.

When I looked at Nile in the rear cockpit he was slumped in his seat & blood was trickling out his mouth & down his throat. "We made it, we escaped," he said softly. But nothing more. I screamed his name over & over but he wouldn't answer. He'd bled to death. A bullet had entered his rib cage. I'm sorry, Nile, for not knowing how to save you.

★ ★ ★

A service was held at the Church of St. Davnet & I thought no one would come. But I was wrong. Lawyer Volpe came & sat in the front pew & the sweet old man cried his eyes out. In a gentle voice he said it was such a shame because Nile was just starting to "turn things around." He also said he didn't like the idea of Nile being buried in this Quebec mud, far from the family vault in New Jersey where his father lay. I told him that he wanted to be buried here with the other rovers & renegades, next to Moon, and that it was a question of respecting a person's final wishes. Lawyer Volpe believed me & I'm glad because I was telling the truth (except for the bit about Moon). He asked me if I knew who killed Nile & I said no, but that it was either the cops or Jacques Déry, Jr. "The police say the son killed his father as well, accidentally?" "I guess so," I replied, though I later found out this was impossible. Déry Sr. was killed with a Nitro .500 & so was Déry Jr. But Nile wasn't. Lawyer Volpe put his hand on my shoulder & asked if he could speak to me later about a "private matter."

Beautiful Brooklyn, with legs as skinny as a praying mantis, was sitting next to him & she cried & cried too. I haven't talked to her yet, but I will. The peewee banker & his beanpole son came, as did the entire village of St. Davnet, or almost. People talked to me, including two guys my age who'd never talked to me before.

I didn't read anything during the ceremony, like a Psalm or something, because I don't believe in God, but I slipped a card inside Nile's coffin:

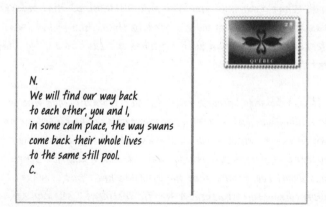

N.
We will find our way back
to each other, you and I,
in some calm place, the way swans
come back their whole lives
to the same still pool.
C.

The two Weskarini Indians, the anarchist & artist, told me they were very sorry about what happened to Nile. It was the first time I'd heard the artist speak. The anarchist said that the Cave was "a pyre awaiting the torch, waiting to be roasted to ash & fed into the sky." And that they were "all over it." I made them promise on the bones of their ancestors.

Earl came too & he gave me a big hug & a bag of black licorice & offered me a job at the store. I thanked him & said I would certainly think about it. He pointed at my shoulder & I said it was just a scratch, that a Kevlar vest got most of it. An old man with a white beard & duct tape on his shoes & bicycle clips on both ankles & red long johns peeping out of both pant legs was standing beside him & it took me a while to figure out it was Mr. Llewellyn! He kissed me on the forehead & pressed something into my hand: an American twenty-dollar bill folded into a tiny hard square. He told me he'd been "released" & that Nile had promised him a job at the church & I said I would keep that promise. I asked him if he needed a place to stay & he said no, he was living in a "candy-cane cottage" on Lac St-Nicolas. With a "Nitro for protection." He winked at me & I understood in a flash. What a dummy I am! Why didn't I think of that before? I was about to ask him more — and to thank him — but I was interrupted by a woman with crutches & a cast on one leg that went from hip to toe.

It was Solange Lacoursière — the vet from St. Mad who's not really a vet but a forensic mammalogist. She kissed me on both cheeks & said how sorry she was about everything that happened — almost everything, that is — & I said how sorry I was about everything that happened to her. "But ... what happened exactly?" I asked. A traffic "accident," she replied,

making quotation marks with her fingers. It happened in the
parking lot of the Cave after she met "Mr. Nightingale." Which
is why she never replied to his phone message — she was in the
hospital. "Were you in love with him?" I blurted out stupidly,
wishing I could've taken it back. She didn't answer. Just gave
me a slow smile & asked if I wanted to study wildlife detection
when I "grew up." I said that I didn't know & that I was already
grown up. She asked if I still wanted to set up a sanctuary in
the church & I said I didn't know that either. How? According
to Gran, it would cost five thousand a month. What I didn't say
is that I was going to be so spectacularly screwed up starting
like, tonight, that I wouldn't be able to do anything except maybe
collect stamps. That I wouldn't be able to live with the guilt of
getting Nile killed, or my anger over his leaving the world while I
still had to stay. Solange asked if I'd heard about the new cougar
sightings & I said no. I was interested in what she was saying,
I really was, but I kept looking around for Mr. Llewellyn, who
seemed to have vanished into thin air. I was also on the lookout
for Baz's thugs & triggers, who I was sure would come & spoil
things. But they stayed away. All but one, that is.

You may wonder how a ceremony could be held at a church
that was so badly wrecked & robbed. Because in the days
before the funeral a small forest of people arrived out of
nowhere — including two look-alike brothers with bib overalls in a
flat-bed truck, and two look-alike sisters with paint-splattered
tools — & repaired everything, or almost (not the stained
glass, not the pine floor) & while they worked they listened to
Mr. Llewellyn's cassettes.

And some of the stolen stuff began to come unstolen, like
pressing rewind. I don't know who pressed it & no one seems to

know. Everyone was super-nice, super-neighbourly. They said that the arrival of my friend "Inspecteur Nightingale" was a godsend, a "bénédiction du ciel."

I know I said that I couldn't go on, that I was going to leave in an Exit Bag after we ridded this planet of a certain black heart. Or two. Or three. But I changed my mind. Not because I feel better about myself or the world or human beings — it'll take more than a few repairs & tears to do that — or because I love grouchy old ladies like Gran & hope to live long enough to be one. No. It's because a spent-wing angel saved me, and I don't want it to be all for nothing.

And yet ... it might all well be. A girl my age, dressed in a grey blazer & turtleneck that matched her smoky grey eyes, kept staring at me, glaring at me, from the back of the church. She hung around to the end, the last one to leave, and I knew she was waiting for me. "You're dead meat — you're going to get cut open like a fish, bled like a deer," she said in a flat voice, like a voice underwater.

AUTHOR'S NOTE

The Laurentians, of course, is a real place and well worth a visit. But the characters and almost all other places mentioned in this story are fictional. I would like to thank Céleste Jonquères, head of the Quebec Wildlife Detective Agency, for her assistance in researching this novel. I would like to, but she doesn't exist, nor does the agency. But maybe one day, with any luck, something like them will. For information on the (nonfictional) bear bile business and poaching trade, I am indebted to the World Society for the Protection of Animals and Quebec's Natural Resources & Wildlife Ministry. Despite their lukewarmth toward my original titles (*The Extinction Carol* and *The Extinction Choir*), I would like to thank Marlène, Laura and Nicole for their counsel and complicity.

NOTES

8   **CHEMIN SAISONNIER**   seasonal road; also on page 24

8   **UTILISEZ À VOS RISQUES ET PÉRILS**   Use at Your Own Risk

23   *« As-tu mal? »*   "Does it hurt?"

23   *« Est-ce que tu souffres? »*   "Are you in pain?"

30   **BIENVENUE ... BELGIQUE**   Welcome to Sainte-Madeleine, Population 4,200, Elevation 810 meters (Sister City to Geel, Belgium)

34   *« Je ... je pense que oui. »*   "I ... I think so."

34   *« Bonne fin de journée. »*   "Have a good day."

35   *« Pareillement. »*   "Likewise."

39   **Maison d'Hébergement de Jeunesse** Youth Shelter

59   **Wehmut ... Weltschmerz** (German) melancholy ... sentimenal pessimism; sadness over the evils of the world

69   *« Il y a quelqu'un? »*   "Anybody here? "

69   *« Jusqu'au bout, à gauche. »*   "Last door on the left."

75   *« Farme ton crisse de téléphone! »*   "Turn off your goddamn phone!"

78   **L'Étang des Noyés**   Lake of the Drowned

78   *« Allons donc »*   "Oh, come on!"

188 « *Non, mais t'es fou ... ce chemin-là.* » "Are you nuts? In this hole? But ... you might find something at the end of that road over there. "

192 *Je me souviens* I remember

208 **la fée verte** the green fairy (absinthe); also on page 340

233 **Sauberkeit!** (German) Cleanliness!

237 « *À* **la limite** » "In a pinch"

241 **Nunc et in hora mortis nostrae** (Latin) Now and at the hour of our death

292 **Rossignol ... Hirondelle ... Alouette** Nightingale ... Swallow ... Lark

295 **DÉFENSE D'ENTRER** DO NOT ENTER

312 **Morphologiste légiste ... SOS BRACONNAGE** Forensic Morphologist, Wild Animal Health Centre of Quebec, POACHING SOS